BENT OUTTA SHAPE

THE HYBRID OF HIGH MOON - 2

RICK GUALTIERI

COPYRIGHT © 2019 RICK GUALTIERI

Edited by Megan Harris:
www.mharriseditor.com

Cover by Damonza:
www.damonza.com

Published by Freewill Press

DEDICATION

For Russ and Amy. Team TW raises a toast to your happiness. May your love never leave each other ... dare I say it ... bent outta shape.

ACKNOWLEDGEMENTS

Very special thanks to my Bent Beta Crew: Faith, Kristi, Keith, Pete, Kennedy, Eric, Chris, Elinor, Josh, Lynn, Susan, and Jeremy. When I asked for harsh feedback that's exactly what you sent back ... but this story is all the better because of it.

PROLOGUE

BEFORE

The young witch slipped through the trees, each step as carefully chosen as the one before it. The heavy foliage masked her trail as if she were but a phantom in the woods, but she knew that could be undone in a second. Even a single misplaced footfall, no more than a snapped twig, could betray her location.

Though her mother had taught her there was honor to be had in defeat, she refused to accept it. History was written by the victors. Even at the tender age of fourteen Lissa McGillis, future Queen of the Monarchs, understood as much. If she was to be remembered, it would be as a ruler who offered no quarter and ceded no ground.

Despite the silence of her passage, the hairs on the back of her neck stood up. She'd learned to trust her instincts, and right then they screamed for her to move. With no hesitation, she threw herself in a hard dive to the left, changing her trajectory just in time for the sharp *crack* that came from above. The splintered remains of a large tree limb fell to the forest floor just as an invisible hand gouged a chunk from the ground where she'd been standing a moment earlier.

There was no doubt in her mind: her foe was good. She had to be better.

Lissa landed, rolled, and pointed her hands toward the sky, making her best guess as to where her enemy was. *"Adh iongantach!"*

A wave of purplish energy lanced out from her body, cutting a wide swath through the trees above her, angled so that any falling debris was deflected away from where she lay. Honor be damned, it would be the height of embarrassment to lose due to something as stupid as being crushed by the aftermath of her own spell.

Such an outcome was unacceptable both to her teacher and herself.

Sadly, the counterspell undermined all her efforts at stealth, giving away her position – unfortunate, as there came no cry of pain from her foe. She'd miscalculated her shot...

There!

She sensed movement from high above. It was a momentary flash, nothing more, a brief glimpse of a figure flitting through the high branches only a few feet from where she'd aimed.

It didn't win her this battle by any stretch, but it gave her a probable trajectory – more than enough. Lissa was considered gifted among the Draíodóir, the venerable order of mystics from which she was descended. However, she was also adept in several mundane proficiencies, math and physics among them.

Though her peers didn't consider such studies important in the grand scheme of the coven, Lissa knew better. Every advantage, no matter how insignificant, could affect the balance in the grand chess match of life – whether it was fending off rivals from within her own clan or dealing with their ancient enemies the Lycanthropes.

From a young age, she'd been raised to be a leader – a

duty she took seriously – but her opponent was cut from the same cloth, had the same teachers and training. And, though Lissa couldn't discern the thoughts of others, it was quite possible her foe shared the same ambition. If so, she couldn't afford to make any more missteps, because none would be afforded her.

Lissa rolled to her feet and plastered herself against a thick tree trunk, doing her best to mask her presence. The base of the oak was at least four feet in diameter. It would take a spell of considerable strength to pierce it in a single shot. Considering how long this fight had played out, she didn't think her adversary had enough left to do that.

Problem was, she realized, gulping down deep breaths of air, she didn't either.

No. This game was nearly at its end. The next few moves would determine the victor.

Lissa knew she should play it safe, wait for a move and then counter it, but safety wasn't a waypoint on the road to leadership. No, not when everything in her life was a test. There were always eyes upon her, judging her, looking for the slightest weakness in her armor.

She couldn't, *wouldn't*, give them the satisfaction.

At the risk of leaving herself vulnerable from above, she turned her eyes toward the ground, spotting several dead branches no more than a few steps away.

Perfect!

Leaving her cover, she purposely stepped on one – giving away her location even as she gathered power for another spell.

Any second now...

"*Wind blade!*"

Though the voice carried down to her with a trebled echo, she was well-versed enough in the ways of spellcraft to home in on its true source.

Lissa spun in a circle, her hands raised, letting loose

every bit of power left in her lithe frame. *"'BRISEADH UCHD!'"*

The incantation was instantly draining. Her strength ebbed and her vision narrowed to little more than a dark tunnel as unconsciousness threatened to consume her, but she fought tooth and nail to remain upright.

It was worth the effort.

The power erupted from her in an almost three-hundred and sixty degree arc. Her foe's spell was effort-lessly parried as her own shook the very forest around her. The shockwave felled smaller trees, and branches shattered by the dozen. A shower of leaves fell from the sky, blan-keting the forest floor.

Best of all was the grunt of surprise and pain from above, followed a moment later by the stunned form of her opponent.

Lissa tried to raise her hands for another spell, but she was spent.

Before her sister could slam into the ground, though, a gust of wind cut through the trees, catching Carly and slowing her descent so that she touched down upon the forest floor no harder than if she had tripped.

Trying to mask how winded she was, Lissa stumbled over to where her younger sister lay and smiled down at her. "Gotcha, Car."

"I ... almost ... had you," Carly replied, dazed but apparently no worse for the wear.

"Horseshoes and hand grenades."

"A hand grenade is exactly what you used," a stern voice called out from the surrounding trees, "when a scalpel was called for."

A middle-aged woman stepping into view and approached the two girls. Though streaks of white cut through her auburn hair, she was still quite fetching to behold. Unfortunately, that beauty was marred by the unrelenting expression etched onto her face.

"Mother," Lissa quickly replied.

Her sister scrambled unsteadily to her feet and repeated the greeting a moment later.

"Look at you two," Vanessa McGillis said. "That was unacceptably sloppy on *both* your parts."

"But I won," Lissa protested. Of the two siblings, she'd always been the bolder.

"Yes you did, by the skin of your teeth. That was a risky move, expending that much power. If you'd missed, you'd have been at your sister's mercy."

Lissa hadn't missed, though, but she kept that opinion to herself, not wishing to press her luck with the coven's formidable matriarch.

Her mother raised an eyebrow. "And what are you smiling about, young lady?"

Carly tried and failed to hide the grin on her face, no doubt at her sister's scolding. Though they were close, both in age and demeanor – Lissa was only two years older – their mother had instilled a sense of competition in them. Once a duel was called, they both knew there could only be one winner.

"Do I need to remind you that, tactical advantage or not, you still lost?"

"No, ma'am," Carly replied, averting her eyes.

Lissa glanced sidelong at her sister. Carly was an aerokineticist, gifted with the ability to control the very air itself. Conjurers like her had given rise to the old wives' tale of witches riding broomsticks. Though Lissa's power was ostensibly stronger, her sister's gift was both rare and difficult to defend against, making their duels a constant challenge.

"And what was that nonsense back there?" Vanessa asked, obviously not done dressing them down.

"What nonsense?"

"You casted in English," Lissa said, knowing this was the sort of detail their mother liked to latch onto.

"Your sister has a point. Don't roll your eyes at me, Carolyn."

"Sorry," Carly quickly blurted. "But I don't see why we need to use the old tongue. My spell worked fine. And besides..."

"Besides what?"

Carly lowered her voice to a bare whisper. "I can barely pronounce any of it."

Lissa expected her mother to explode, but the older witch merely let out a sigh and put a hand on both their shoulders. "True enough. The words are a mere focus, nothing more. Our magic comes from within."

"Good, then..."

"But what lies within us?" She turned and faced the trees. "Is it merely flesh and blood? If so, what separates us from the mundane? From our enemies, for that matter?"

Both girls were silent. They'd done this dance enough times to know their mother was asking a rhetorical question.

"I would argue that our true strength flows from a deeper place," Vanessa continued, "the very soul within us. It is the wellspring from which the divine power of Queen Brigid and her most holy court flows."

"I still don't understand why my language matters," Carly replied.

"It's not us for whom it matters, but our ancestors." Their mother turned back toward them, a smile on her lips. "Death is but a doorway to the eternal. Our blood connects us to those who came before. They sit at our queen's side watching and guiding us." She locked eyes with Carly. "Tell me, why did you lose today? Quickly, what does your heart say?"

Carly shrugged. "Lissa got lucky."

Lissa opened her mouth to protest, but her mother held up a hand.

"Oh? And what is this thing called luck?" She let them stew on the question for a moment before continuing. "Luck is nothing more than a confluence of events converging in such a way to be either for or against our favor. The slightest nudge can change luck against you. Our ancestors not only watch, but they judge us, too. And though their hands don't wield the same might as when they were alive, they can still influence this world. That's why we use the old tongue to empower our spells. It acknowledges and honors them. In doing so, they grant us their favor."

"Or take it away," Lissa added.

"True enough. We should live our lives honoring those who came before. That's what separates us from the dogs of this world. Remember this and remember it well, my daughters. For when you turn your back on that honor, the only path it will lead you down is one of ruin."

1

Sweat poured down my face from the oppressive heat. It was hard enough to breathe in this hell as it was, and that wasn't even taking into account the monstrous reptilian tail coiled around my throat.

I tried to pry the creature off before I passed out, managing to catch a glimpse of my watch in the process.

Shit!

Riva was going to be here soon. I needed to find a way to wrap this up and stay alive in the process. She was going to have a hell of a time explaining it to my parents if I managed to get my dumb ass killed.

But if so, at least I wouldn't be dying alone.

I glanced over at the cocooned bodies of the Junior Crypto-Hunter Society – named after some stupid TV show – a bunch of geeks into Bigfoot and crap like that. Apparently these geniuses had gotten a *hot tip* about a monster on campus, which had led them here, of all places: the basement of the Bailey University historical manor, the oldest building on campus and one of the largest.

It was only dumb luck that a fellow member of the

Bailey U wrestling team had overheard talk of their disappearance, leading me to track them here.

Good thing, too, because campus security sure as hell wasn't equipped to handle something like this. But that's where I come in.

The name's Tamara Bentley, Bent to a few close friends. I'm a sophomore, here on a sports scholarship with a major in environmental science. Sounds simple enough, but that's about where me and normal diverge.

Case in point, I grabbed hold of the lizard-man's tail before he could drag me up the wall with him and uncoiled it from around my neck. Digging the fingers of my free hand into the masonry for purchase, I heaved with everything I had, flinging the scaled monstrosity away from me.

I dropped to one knee long enough to catch my breath and look over at the box lunches waiting to be rescued. Far as I could tell, they were still alive, for now anyway.

The lizard thing rose up off the ground on its hind legs looking like a mix of the velociraptors from *Jurassic Park* and Jack Colmy, the manor's groundskeeper. At the very least he wore Jack's skin, now ripped to shreds to accommodate the much larger frame of his true self, some kind of reptilian throwback with a hard-on for kidnapping nerds.

"I don't know what you are, but you ssshould have ssstayed away," he said with a hissing lisp. "Now you, too, will nourisssh my children."

That definitely didn't sound pleasant. As we began to circle one another, preparing for another go, I glanced past him toward the crypto-geeks. It was like a scene from that old movie *Aliens*. They were cocooned in a viscous ... excretion, for lack of a less gross term. All around them lay soccer ball-sized eggs. Maybe Jack was actually a Janet, now that I gave it a moment's thought, but that was fine. I was equal opportunity when it came to kicking ass.

More importantly, I needed to keep this thing's focus strictly on me and away from the fact that it had half a dozen hostages to use as leverage if it so chose.

"Sorry to break it to you," I replied, sweat dripping from every pore, "but I'm not looking to save on my car insurance."

Behind me, a trio of massive furnaces roared, spitting out enough heat so that I didn't even care how lame my comeback was.

Thankfully, this thing didn't require much goading. It spun, lashing out with its whip-like tail. I countered and managed to grab hold of it, but the creature was ready for that. The lizard-man twisted its upper body a hundred and eighty degrees, nimble little minx, and tried to take a bite out of my favorite face.

Its mouth was filled with hundreds of needle-like teeth dripping with some sort of secretion that probably wasn't drool. Yeah, considering the semi-comatose nerd herd in the room, it seemed a safe bet that I didn't want this thing chomping down on me.

I let go of its tail with one hand and grabbed it by the throat, keeping its jaws just barely at bay. Not a good strategy on my part, as that left its arms free to drive an uppercut into my chin, sending me flying.

Oof!

Fortunately for me, the scalding hot grate of the middle furnace was there to stop my flight. I hit it with a steaming *clonk*, thankful – despite the heat – that I was wearing a coat. But even with the protection it offered, I could still feel my backside burning.

The gecko from hell, whatever it was, had turned the basement of Bailey Manor into its own personal terrarium.

Even with an Illinois winter raging outside, this place was about fifty degrees warmer than I was comfortable with.

But hey, if this thing liked the heat, then maybe it was time to turn it up.

I pulled my hands inside my sleeves to afford them a bit of protection, then grabbed hold of the furnace door. The thing was old, heavy, and hot as fuck. Thanks to my unique heritage, though, I was strong enough to make short work of it. I yanked, tearing the door off with a squeal of metal and opening up the flaming inferno beyond.

Then, before the red hot grate could sear through the fabric, I spun and flung it at the approaching monstrosity. It was a sloppy throw, one the creature dodged easily before launching itself at me.

Exactly as I hoped it would.

I bolted forward to meet it. With any luck, I'd timed this right.

Just as it slammed into me, I dropped back onto the coal-littered floor, letting the creature's much greater mass take over. Then I kicked out, sending it flying over me and into the waiting mouth of the furnace. *Oh yeah!*

I scrambled back to my feet as the beast screamed in agony, then turned to slam the door shut ... *Goddamnit!* ... before remembering I'd torn the damned thing off. Okay, maybe not my best plan.

Guess I'd have to do this the old-fashioned way.

I stepped closer to the furnace, the heat nearly unbearable despite my enhanced durability.

Sure enough, the former groundskeeper – its leathery flesh now blackened and burning – tried to pull itself out. Just as its head cleared the opening, though, it met a double axe-handle fist from me, driving it back hard enough to hear the *clang* as it slammed into the other side.

And that was all she wrote for the lizard monster of Bailey Manor.

I stepped back to catch my breath – no easy feat since it was still hot as proverbial balls. Then I turned to the not so wonderful task of shoveling the creature's foul eggs into the furnace, too.

I wasn't sure where this thing had come from or how long it had been here, but it didn't appear that peaceful coexistence was on the menu. Neither was leaving a bunch of evidence for the crypto-buddies to find.

I finished up quick as I could, then started on the disgusting task of peeling this thing's would-be victims out of their mucus cocoons. *Gross!*

Thankfully they were all still alive, merely unconscious. Although not for long, it would seem. They began to stir the moment they were freed. Whatever they'd been sealed in must've also acted as a sedative of sorts, one that was rapidly wearing off.

There was no time to lose.

Quickly tossing any remaining gunk into the fire, I caught sight of my watch again.

Damnit! Riva was going to be here any minute. I needed to get going.

Sadly, I couldn't do that without leaving these guys some sort of plausible explanation as to what had happened. While I doubted anyone would actually listen to them, the last thing I needed was a group of nerds screaming to the administration about monsters on campus. I looked around, hoping I saw something that might...

Ah, that looks promising.

I crossed to the far corner the basement where groundskeeper Jack/Janet had set up some living space. Cabinets lined the walls above its cot, as good a place as any to check for possible alibis.

"Bingo!" Old Jacky might have been a lizard monster, but that hadn't kept it from developing a taste for cheap bourbon.

I grabbed the bottle of Rebel Yell from the cabinet, walked back, and began pouring it out over the still prone Junior Crypto-Hunters. And not a moment too soon either.

One of them, a guy with dark skin and thick glasses, groaned and opened his eyes.

I knelt down, placing the bottle on the floor next to him. "Hey. You okay?"

"Oh, my head," he grunted. "What happened?"

"I don't know," I replied, feigning ignorance, "but you guys picked a hell of a spot to party."

"Party?"

"Yeah." I glanced down at the empty bottle, as if just noticing it. "Good thing I found you before security did. If you want my advice, next time find a less creepy place to pass around the Christmas cheer."

I beat a hasty retreat before too many questions could be asked, leaving the crypto-dorks to sort out their own mess, then raced back to my dorm so as to change out of my singed clothes. With any luck I could grab a shower before...

Crap!

Riva Kale, my best friend in all the world, was already waiting for me at the front door. "I've been buzzing you for the last ten minutes."

"I was ... out."

"No shit."

"Um ... happy holidays!" I stepped in to give her a big hug, which she didn't immediately return.

Instead, she stared back at me with raised eyebrows. "So are we talking werewolves or rough sex?"

"Neither," I replied sheepishly. "Okay, maybe closer to the former."

She rolled her eyes. "You know what, save it for the trip. We have a long ride ahead of us."

I had a feeling she was prepared to grill me for the entirety of the long drive back from Illinois. That was fine. We hadn't talked all that much since the fall semester had begun. I probably owed it to her to get caught up on things, both normal and extranormal.

Either way, it was nice to finally be on winter break.

I only wished I was taking a break from any supernatural weirdness, too, but I knew that was mere folly on my part.

Our destination was High Moon, Pennsylvania ... my home and where it had all started for me.

2

"You need to tell them, Bent."

"I know."

"You've had over four months."

"I'm well aware."

One of the *benefits* of being best friends since childhood was that Riva felt no compunction against pestering me about things I really didn't want to talk about. "You were supposed to."

"I've been busy."

Truth of the matter was, school hadn't been quite as boring as I'd hoped when I returned following this past summer. I'd assumed I could slip back into my normal life, but that hadn't worked out so well. As I was beginning to realize, the moment you stepped foot into the world of the weird, there was apparently no turning back.

I explained as much to Riva, bringing her up to speed on Jack the lizard thing and a few other tidbits. Needless to say, she was irked that I hadn't told her sooner. But it was for her own good.

I had little doubt she'd have abandoned her own studies to come and help me out. But I didn't want that.

As awesome of a friend as she was, not everything was her fight. She deserved a normal life ... one I could never hope for.

See, normal and me had never been the best of friends, but that had gotten dialed up to eleven this past July when I'd learned my parents weren't quite the middle class Millennials I'd assumed them to be. Not by a long shot. Turned out my mother's a witch, a freaky powerful one. Not to be outdone, Dad can turn into an eight foot tall werewolf when the mood suits him.

In retrospect, it seemed like something that would be hard to hide for nearly two decades, yet they managed to pull it off with a bit of magic and some bald-faced lying.

You see, being their daughter entailed having a few genetic quirks of my own, quirks that they'd hidden from me via the pills I'd taken for most of my life – so-called medication that actually suppressed my powers and rendered my scent undetectable from normal humans.

Learning all of that had led to some *stressful* confrontations, culminating in the near destruction of High Moon. But now it was my turn for secrets.

Shortly before returning to college, I'd promised my folks that I'd start taking my *meds* again ... a vow I kept for less than a week before Riva managed to talk me out of it.

Guess deceit ran in the family.

I turned to my friend as she navigated her beaten-up Subaru Outback through holiday traffic and summed it up best I could.

"You know, in a way all of this is your fault."

~

"You want me to come in and help soften the blow?" Riva asked as we crossed the town line into High Moon.

I'd been lucky to finagle a ride home with her, having

given my parents the run-around, claiming to want to spend some quality road trip time with my friend. That much wasn't a lie. It was more knowing that my secret would likely be out the moment they both laid eyes on me. Quite frankly, getting screamed at for the entirety of a ten hour drive didn't particularly appeal to me. However, my reprieve was rapidly coming to an end.

"You can't," I replied. "They think your mind is ... what did they call it?"

"Blanked," she said with a small trace of bitterness.

After the shit that had gone down this summer, in which my father's pack nearly tore High Moon a new asshole, Mom's people had stepped in and magically erased everyone's memory of that night ... everyone except for Riva. She knew the truth but, like me, had been forced to live a lie ever since. The thing was, the worst my parents could do was yell at me. For Riva, however, there was always the threat of making good on wiping her memory. I didn't want that. Not only was she my friend, but I needed someone in my corner back home who I could talk to without dancing around the truth.

"I appreciate the offer, but this is something I have to do myself."

"I understand," she replied.

"Although maybe you can sit in the driveway with the motor running ... just in case it goes badly."

"Wimp."

I stepped through the doorway, bags in hand, trying to look like I was struggling with them more than I actually was. Hopefully I looked convincing. Wrestling was my forte, not acting.

Before closing the door, I spared one last glance back.

It was partially to give Riva a nod goodbye, but also to see if Mom's garden gnomes – standing guard in front of her now defoliated rose bushes – had moved at all.

"I've got my eye on you fuckers," I whispered to myself before finally turning around and facing the music, so to speak.

That would have to wait, though, as the only one in the living room was my skeeve of a little brother.

Chris had changed his hair. When last I'd seen him, he'd been going for skate punk. Now he seemed to be in a douchebag pop singer phase.

"Hey," I said, kicking the door shut behind me. "Nice 'do. Makes you look like a wannabe pedophile."

He opened his mouth, probably to say something rude in return, but then took a sniff of the air and covered his mouth. "Ugh. You smell like a French whore."

Sadly, I couldn't argue. Once I stepped out of Riva's car I might have spritzed on the perfume a little heavier than was called for. It was necessary, though. Werewolves like my dad had a freaky good sense of smell – something I'd inherited, sadly. Hell, even breathing through my mouth, I could barely talk without gagging.

For all my powers, there I was trying to forestall the inevitable by a few more minutes. Riva was right; I could be a wimp when I wanted to be. But I wasn't about to let Chris know that. He was unaware that his adopted family was a bunch of freaks. That, and he was a total dork. "How would you know what a French whore smells like?"

"You're right," he said, grinning the grin of a sibling who knows he's tempting a beating and wants to make sure he deserves it. "I bet French whores smell better."

I dropped my bags and headed toward him, stepping around the Christmas tree already up and decorated. "Time for your annual holiday beating, you little..."

"Tamara, is that you?" Mom's voice floated to us from upstairs.

I lowered my own and whispered at my brother, "Saved by the bell, you little shit."

He flipped me the finger, quickly covering it up as footsteps could be heard coming down the stairs.

I adopted my best innocent smile as our mother descended to join us.

"I'm glad you made it home when you did," she said conversationally. "The weather is supposed to turn nasty tomorrow. I hope you gave Riva my regar..." She trailed off, her nose twitching. "Are you wearing perfume?"

"Yeah ... it's called Aphrodite. I picked up a bottle the other week."

Her eyes narrowed suspiciously. "You do realize you're supposed to spritz it, not bathe in it."

"Riva hit a pothole while I was freshening up. It went all over the place. You should smell the inside of her car."

Her expression relaxed and she nodded. "I'm sure."

That was one hurdle crossed.

"Christopher, would you mind changing the laundry?"

Or maybe not.

Chris looked between us for a moment then grinned. "You gonna yell at her for something?"

"No, but if you bring up those towels without folding them, I might yell at *you*."

My brother gave her a disgruntled look as only a twelve year old could, the one that said the entirety of his life was so unfair, then he got up and did as he was told.

Smart boy ... although not really.

The fact that my mother folded her arms and waited until Chris's footsteps faded in the distance told me that perhaps my perfume ruse wasn't quite as clever as I'd hoped.

So much for happy holidays.

3

"*hó Slabhrai!*"

Without warning, Mom's voice trebled, although she kept the volume low, no doubt to keep Chris from hearing her scream out a Gaelic spell like some sort of banshee.

The words weren't the issue, though, so much as the strands of orange light that flew from her fingertips like some sort of spectral whip. They wrapped around my legs, pinning them together, then moved up my body to ensnare the rest of me.

Too bad I'd seen this trick before. I managed to get one arm free before the strands of laser light could completely entwine me.

Mind you, that didn't help my balance much. I tumbled over and landed on the floor with a thud, hurting my pride more than anything. "Really?" I asked. "You couldn't have just said hello?"

The anger I'd felt toward my parents, for essentially making me a junkie to my meds for all those years, had mostly burned out. But a little ember rekindled to life as I lay there entwined by her spell.

I used that to my advantage and grabbed hold of the strands with my free hand before common sense could tell me such a thing was impossible. Good thing, too, because they turned out to be substantial enough to hold.

Magic – I tried not to question it too much.

I was more concerned with whether or not I could break free. Last time she used this spell, she'd caught me by surprise. This time...

I pulled and there came a sound like a dozen guitar strings snapping. As quickly as the whips of light had appeared, they all dissipated, leaving me free.

As an added show of badassery, to compensate for falling on my ass a few moments earlier, I did a quick kip-up to my feet and then faced my mother's stony glare.

"So," she said, after a moment. "I see you've been lying to us."

"Obviously..." I trailed off as her words sank in. "Wait. You didn't know?"

"I had my suspicions. Salting your dorm room to keep me from scrying on you. Then there were the late night calls asking about oddly specific myths, all for purported study projects."

"They could have been," I replied lamely.

"You're studying environmental science, Tamara, not creative writing." She moved to the love seat and sat down. "But, needless to say, I didn't know for certain until you shattered that construct like it was made of glass. You've gotten stronger, haven't you?"

"You could have ... just asked." The strange calmness in her voice was freaking me out, putting me on the defensive far more than if she'd laid into me. Even if she hadn't known, she certainly wasn't surprised either. "You were expecting this, weren't you?"

She shrugged. "You're my daughter and I remember

how I reacted to authority when I was your age, no matter how rational the advice."

Okay, that dig was more like her. "So ... then why aren't you yelling?"

She locked her gaze on me, and it was as if a bolt of electricity appeared behind her eyes for a moment, her way of trying to be intimidating. "Don't get me wrong, young lady. I'm not happy about it, but you're lucky you caught me on a day when I have ... other issues to deal with." Mom turned and looked over her shoulder toward the hallway. "Besides, I know how your brother folds towels. I don't expect that to keep him busy for long."

Almost as if on cue, Chris reappeared, laundry basket in hand piled high with linens that appeared to have been folded by an armless blind man. "Here you go."

Mom merely stared him down. "I believe you know the way to the closet." As he stomped off, obviously put out by the great labors foisted upon him, she added, "And I want them stacked neatly."

Despite knowing that she was probably waiting to explode, I allowed myself a smile. With me away at college, Chris had inherited at least some of my chores.

But then Mom's words about other issues hit me and I felt guilty. There I was, making it all about me, forgetting that my parents had a life, issues, all that stuff. And that wasn't even taking into account them both being ranking members of two warring races that were supposed to hate each other. "So, is everything okay?"

The corner of her mouth raised in a grin. "Finally remembered you're not the center of the universe?"

"Not every universe can be as awesome as mine."

"I see this semester hasn't contributed much to your humility."

"I am my mother's daughter."

This time when she smiled, it was real. I still had a

feeling I was going to get a serious talking to once Chris was out of earshot, but the fact that she wasn't completely losing her shit gave me hope. Mind you, no amount of screaming was going to force me to become a slave to my pills again. Maybe she finally realized that and was coming to grips with it.

That, or she was already plotting some way to zap some sense into me. Guess I'd have to be mindful of any glowing Christmas presents under the tree this year.

Still, it was a bit odd. And even though a part of me wanted to change the subject to anything that didn't involve me in the hot seat, I still lowered my voice and said, "What's going on? I kinda expected this to be a bigger deal for you."

She nodded then replied, "Business and family stuff."

"Oh? How bad?"

I expected her to tell me about an internal power struggle – perhaps rival warlocks plotting against each other. Instead she said, "I was working on the quarterly taxes when you pulled in."

"Really?" I asked, deadpan.

"Your father needs to start holding onto his receipts better. He's making it a nightmare to calculate our deductions correctly."

"Not exactly what I meant."

Mom pursed her lips, but kept her voice equally as low. "I don't know what movies you've been watching, Tamara, but in the real world, magic only solves so much. Even the most aggressive wealth charm can't make up for poor accounting."

I held up my hands, not wanting an economics lesson. "I get it. But you said family, too. Is Dad...?"

"Your father will be home soon. He was over in Morganberg today dealing with some preparations. Apparently he has a get-together with his ... *people* tonight to celebrate the Winter Solstice and there were some details to hash out. Nothing that concerns me.

"Oh."

"When I said family, I actually meant your poor Aunt Carly."

"What's wrong?"

"She called me this morning to let me know her fiancé had broken up with her."

"Oh no!"

"Yeah, she's a mess."

Of all my extended family, Aunt Carly was probably my favorite. She'd always been super cool to me. Of course, she also thought I was adopted and not a were-wolf/witch hybrid – something that could change her demeanor if she found out, as it had with my late unlamented uncle.

But, for now anyway, she was still Aunt Carly, a quirky free spirit who baked really good blueberry muffins. She was a sweetheart, so when I'd heard she'd gotten engaged, I'd been super happy for her.

"This is also going to have political ramifications," Mom added.

"Political...?"

She leaned over and patted my knee. "Nothing you need to worry about, dear."

"Hold on." Again, I lowered my voice. God, this would be so much easier if we simply told Chris and didn't have to tiptoe around the issues this way. "Is Roger a..."

Mom nodded. "That's not what he actually calls himself, but yes. He's a reputed psychomancer."

"A psychomancer?" I asked, visions of a spellcasting Norman Bates running through my head.

"A specialist. Some of us are born with a proclivity toward specific schools of magic."

"Oh? And how many schools are there? I mean, besides Hogw...?"

"Don't say it." Mom rolled her eyes. "Eleven, if you must know, but again, it's nothing you need concern yourself with."

"But..."

My but would need to be left hanging, though, because just then there came the sound of our garage door opening.

"Your father will be happy to see you." She glanced over her shoulder, again at the hallway. "Let's go out and say *hi* to him."

Her meaning was clear. If there was a reckoning to be had, it was going to be now, with both of them in the room.

So much for winter break starting off on the right foot.

4

We stepped into the garage just as Dad was climbing out of the minivan. Say what you will about monsters in general, but it was seriously hard for me to get past the image of an alpha werewolf driving a Dodge Caravan.

"Hey, Tam Tam!" he cried happily as he laid eyes on me.

For a moment, the love I had for him swelled in my chest but, then I watched as his nostrils flared.

Here it comes.

In that same instant, my mother pulled the door shut behind us and cried out, "*Sàmhach!*" in that weird echoey voice of hers. A strange translucent light appeared around us, like being trapped in a giant soap bubble.

Though I wasn't even remotely versed in the finer points of magic, I ventured a guess that this was some sort of privacy spell designed to keep my brother's prying ears from overhearing.

As for my father, his grin turned serious. "Oh, Tam Tam. What have you done?"

"I'm gonna venture a guess that the perfume didn't fool you."

"Please tell me you didn't actually think that would work."

I held up my thumb and forefinger. "For maybe a second."

"When we're done here," he said with a sigh, "do us all a favor and take a long shower."

Gladly. Though he wasn't aware of it yet, the smell was driving me nuts, too. The original manifestation of my powers some months back had included enhanced speed, strength, and durability. Since then, things had continued to evolve for me. Both my hearing and sense of smell were now far stronger than I had ever thought possible, which wasn't always a godsend, mind you. It's amazing the things people said when they thought you couldn't hear them. Equally disturbing was how many thought they could get away without bathing in the morning. *Ugh!*

Mom stepped to my father's side, no doubt to present a unified parental front against their wayward daughter.

"You're disappointed, aren't you?" I figured I might as well start things off. It had taken me some time, but little by little, I was coming to grips with being an adult. Cowering before them like some kid who'd broken a window was a mindset I'd been working to overcome.

Still, nearly twenty years of conditioning was hard to shake off, especially with them both staring me down.

"Yes," my mother said.

"No," Dad replied simultaneously.

So much for a unified front. "Do either of you want to change your vote?"

"Don't be a smart mouth, Tamara," Mom chided. "This is serious."

"We're hiding in the garage so Chris doesn't hear us.

You'll forgive me if I don't find the *atmosphere* exactly conducive to an interrogation."

Mom looked like she wanted to say something to that, but Dad quickly spoke up. "This isn't an interrogation, honey. But we talked about this. You remember what happened last summer."

"Kinda hard to forget."

Mom jumped in. "Then you know the risks. I told you what my people will do if they find out."

"How do we know they don't already?" I countered. "Dad's pack already knows what ... I mean *who* I am."

"That's different, they don't..."

"Fraternize with the enemy?" I was definitely sailing into choppy waters with that one but needed to put it out there. This wasn't the nineteen-hundreds anymore. We lived in an age where it was really fucking hard to keep a secret once someone found out. "Don't look at me like that. You two did it. What's to stop someone else?"

"Your father controls..."

"Oh please," I interrupted, on a roll. "Does he keep an eye on them every single minute of the day? Even if there isn't another illicit romance going on, what's to stop them from being friends, acquaintances, or running into each other at the supermarket and chatting? And that's not even talking about fucking Facebook. Let's be realistic here. Counting on werewolf pinky swears isn't a reliable strategy."

"I think you underestimate the power of tradition, young lady. Oh, and I'll remind you to curb your language while you're in my house. If you can't talk like an adult, then..."

"You've gotta be kidding me." I could feel my temper starting to fray, but I pushed it down and took a deep breath, not wishing to be sidetracked. "Fine, but even if every other werewolf out there hates every single other ...

Draío-whatever, what if one of them thinks the same way Uncle Craig did?"

Dad winced at the mention of his late brother. It was low of me to bring him up, as he was likely still hurting, but I didn't see another way around it. "What if one of them comes looking for me one day? What then? I won't be able to protect myself or anyone else if I'm powerless. Will a treaty or promise keep them from hurting me if they're dead set on it? Will it keep them from hurting anyone who gets in their way?"

That was my ace in this argument and I knew it. I'd witnessed the attack on High Moon by my uncle first-hand. I'd seen how many had blindly followed him. But I'd also been aware that a few had gone out of their way to cause minimal harm. Hell, my own father had been chief among them. It told me all I needed to know: a werewolf alpha's authority was strong but it wasn't absolute. And if some had balked at Craig's orders, then the same thing could happen to Dad now that he was in charge.

"Like it or not," I continued, the floor still mine, "I will not be responsible for anyone getting hurt when I could have done something to stop it."

"Tell me, Tamara," Mom replied, deadpan. "Did you rehearse that speech in front of the mirror until it sounded convincing? If so, bravo. But have you considered how selfish your circular logic is? You feel the need to protect people if they're attacked, but the only reason they might be attacked is because of you. It's a slippery slope to use the nuclear deterrent argument when you're the first to bear arms."

"Are you saying it couldn't happen?"

"I'm saying you know very little about either of our people. Have a little faith in us. This isn't our first rodeo. We kept you safe for almost twenty years, through sacrifice and..."

"Lies?" I offered.

"Selective truth," she corrected. "True, one side now knows. But I trust your father to keep the..."

"Tamara might be right about her pills."

I'd been so busy sparring with my mother that I hadn't realized Dad had fallen silent. I assumed he'd just stepped aside to let Mom have at it, as she was more the bulldog when it came to arguments. But the look on his face said otherwise.

Mom noticed it, too. "What do you mean, Curtis?"

Dad continued to hesitate, prompting me to say, "Okay, spill. What, cat got your tongue?"

Mom actually chuckled, causing me to raise a curious eyebrow.

"Sorry, honey," Dad said after another second or two. "It's just that your mother and I have kind of a standing agreement to not discuss *business* with each other." Before I could say anything, he added, "Emergencies notwithstanding of course. Keeps the bickering to a minimum."

Okay, I could understand that. My parents loved each other. That much I couldn't deny. But it was also obvious there was no love lost as far as the rest of their respective people went. Hell, when it came to werewolf business, I had a feeling any advice my mother gave would involve burning down the hollows – the woods east of High Moon that Dad's pack called home.

"So ... is this an emergency?" I asked.

Dad shrugged. "Not yet, but it could be. There's a small contingent in the pack, guys who were close with Craig, that have been a bit ... vocal as of late. They didn't say anything after I first took over, but I guess the shock's worn off. I've become aware that they're still irate with regards to the subject of..."

"Of?"

"Of you," he finished.

"And they're still breathing?" Mom asked, her eyes narrowed.

"Contrary to popular belief, we don't settle every disagreement with a fight to the death. We do occasionally talk through our problems."

"Kinder, gentler werewolves," I muttered. "Social media would love that."

"If they're threatening my daughter..." Mom continued, ignoring me.

"*Our* daughter," Dad countered, a bit of heat in his voice. Suddenly it became clear why these two had an agreement to avoid talking shop. "And they haven't threatened her yet. They're simply concerned."

"Yet?" Mom asked, the air around her crackling with power.

It was time for me to step in before this could devolve into a marital spat between two ridiculously powerful beings. "What are they concerned about?"

Both my parents turned toward me as if just noticing I was there. Pity. I should have slipped away and grabbed a sandwich while I could, but now I was committed.

"They're accusing me of favoritism," Dad replied. Before Mom could say anything, he held up a hand. "Which isn't entirely untrue, although I can't tell them that. Remember when we fought, Tam Tam, and how afterwards I told the others you were a part of the pack now?"

"Don't remind me." I was tempted to point out that our battle hadn't exactly been fair, but now was not the time to be petty. Besides, I doubted I could actually fight him without holding back at least a little.

"Well," he continued, "I know you're not exactly familiar with the nuances of pack society, but there are certain obligations and expectations."

"What your father is saying is you're behind on your quota for burying bones and chasing rabbits."

Score one for Mom in the snark department.

Dad glared at her for a moment, but then apparently decided against commenting. "It's not a requirement that the full pack show up for every occasion. Despite our instinctive nature and the pull of the moon, we live in modern times. People have jobs and other commitments."

I tried my damnedest not to laugh, but it was hard to not envision a werewolf apologizing for a missed hunt because he had to go to his mother-in-law's birthday party.

"Including college," he continued. "But you're kind of a special case. The fact that you haven't been there at all and I've been doing my best to move the pack in a different direction has caused certain elements to become ... vocal."

"As alpha it's your job to..."

"Don't tell me my job, Lissa. I don't tell you how to be queen of your monarchs."

Whoa. It was rare to see Dad snipe back. Growing up, he'd been more of the "yes, dear" type.

Something he'd told me over the summer popped into my head. My father had once been the alpha-in-training, for lack of a better phrase. But then, once he and my mother got together, he'd been forced to step down, accept being the beta to his brother's alpha. He'd told me that meant adopting a beta mindset. But that was over and done with. He was in charge now. Had that required a similar attitude change on his behalf?

If so, I had to wonder whether that was having an effect on my parents' relationship. Having two A-type personalities in the house, especially leaders of warring clans, struck me as a potential cause for concern.

But that could wait. For now, I was curious what was going on in the hollows that had my dad rethinking his stance on my pills. "Go on," I prompted before this could devolve into a full-blown argument.

He turned, giving Mom the side eye for a moment before focusing on me. "It's because you're unique."

"A hybrid?"

"Exactly. Though they won't admit it, a lot of them are still scared of you. I thought keeping you away from the pack would be a good thing, but I was wrong. Not all of them made it back to Morganberg the night of the attack. Some of them lost friends, loved ones."

"Not everyone made it out of High Moon either," I snapped, gritting my teeth at the memory.

I must've sounded even angrier than I realized, because my father held up his hands in a placating manner. "I know, honey, and believe me, I'm sorry about that. But I have to deal with both sides. There's people in the pack, folks like my cousin Mitch, that haven't been able to move on. With you away, there hasn't been any closure for them. I thought those wounds would heal on their own, but they've festered. Not in everyone, but in enough. Don't get me wrong, nobody is threatening me or my position, but it's becoming worrisome." There was a pleading quality in my father's voice that I didn't like.

"What do you need me to do?"

Mom stepped in front of me. "You don't need to do anything."

"Your mother's right. You don't *need* to do anything."

"Fine. How can I help?" Fucking word games. "Voluntarily and of my own free will."

Mom started to say something, but Dad cut her off. "It would ... help if they could get to know you. See that you're not the monster – sorry – they've come to think of you as. And yes, I know a lot of them already know you, but it's all changed since that night. They need to relearn that you're a good person with feelings and empathy. They need to know that you're still Tamara."

I nodded, but then remembered the start of our conversation. "Okay. But if so, then why did you agree with me about my pills?"

Dad looked away, and for a moment I thought he wasn't going to say anything. But then he turned back and locked eyes with me. "Because if that fails, then you might need to remind them exactly why they *should* be afraid of you."

5

M om wasn't pleased with our plan of action, but she really didn't have much say in it.

This was pack business, and Dad was right. Technically I'd been a part of it since that night. Personally, I didn't give a single shit about any of that. If their leader had been anyone other than my father, I'd have told them to take a flying fuck off the Philly Phanatic's nose.

But he had a point about family. Much as we'd managed to piss each other off — some of us more than others — we'd always been closely knit. Anger didn't mean I was about to let any of them, even Chris, hang out to dry — not if I could do something about it.

So much for me settling in and discussing holiday plans. Christmas was less than a week away but — go figure — there was a gathering in the hollows this very evening and daylight was already burning. A part of me wondered if it was merely a coincidence, this all happening on the day I arrived home. Seemed a bit too convenient, but I'd probably pushed my luck enough. Calling out my parents again could wait. I mean, heck, I didn't need to be back at school until after the New Year. Might as well space out the drama a bit.

Chris came looking for us not long after the plan was set, forcing Mom to drop her spell and for us to go back to pretending we weren't a family of freaks, ironic since my brother was pretty much one twenty-four seven.

Sometimes life is funny like that.

Mind you, going back to the hollows – aka werewolf central – was more funny crazy than funny hah-hah.

There wasn't much time to prepare. I had a feeling Dad wanted us to leave early so as to keep Mom from trying to talk me out of it. A part of me wouldn't have minded that, but if my father needed me, then I'd be there.

Nevertheless, as I took some time to unpack in my room, I gave Riva a call.

"*Still alive, I see,*" she answered.

"And with no new assholes chewed into my backside."

"*TMI, Bent.*"

"Deal with it."

"*So, spill. Did you fess up or wimp out?*"

"They know. Oh, and the perfume didn't work. Told you it was a stupid idea."

"*It was better than anything you came up with. So what...*"

"I'm supposed to go with my dad to the hollows for a werewolf jamboree."

"*Whoa. Hold on. Back up a bit there.*"

"You heard me."

"*Shit! Is he pissed or something?*"

"No. It's more like I've been absent too long. He wants to parade me in front of the pack to show I'm still a whipped puppy." Before she could comment, I added, "Relax. It's all political. A dog and pony show."

"*I hope you don't end up engaged again.*"

"You and me both. But I think we're safe on that front. Dad probably has to put on a good show, but he's not Craig."

"*Believe me, I'm happy about that. But I'm not really sure safe is the word I'd use.*"

"Safer than if I was still on my pills."

"*Touché.*"

"I just wanted to let you know in case you tried to reach me later."

"*Fuck! You mean it's tonight?*"

"Yep. Winter Solstice and all."

"*I thought that was a witch thing.*"

"It might be. Mom didn't really elaborate on her plans."

"*Whatever. I'll be over in just a few...*"

"No, Riva. Sorry. Members only."

"*Yeah, but it's ... the hollows.*"

She had a point. Ever since that night back in July, the hollows had weighed heavily on my thoughts. Even knowing what I could do, I was still afraid of the place. That first night had scared me badly enough. But ... what happened a month later with Jerry Sandwich, my short-lived fiancé, well, I was still processing that. Weird didn't even begin to explain it. It had haunted my dreams ever since, and not just because I'd been forced to kill him.

No. There'd been more. Much more.

I hadn't even told Riva the full extent of it. The rest of that night, the attack on High Moon, that had been enough. She'd managed to escape having her memories erased, but that didn't mean I wanted to burden her with even worse ones than she'd already lived through. Some burdens we had to carry ourselves.

Besides, I wasn't sure I could explain it without sounding like a loon, and this coming from someone who knew that witches, werewolves, and more existed.

"Believe me, I know," I replied. "But my dad will be there. He'll keep me safe. And if he doesn't..." I let the statement hang. We both knew what I could do. And the thing was, I was more capable now than before, but I kept that to myself. Call it a secret weapon, if you will. If things went south, I figured a little something extra in my back pocket couldn't hurt.

But that was a worst case scenario. For now, I chose to trust my dad, and I needed him to know he could trust me.

"*Are you sure?*"

I wasn't by a long shot, but knowing she was in my corner meant a lot. "Not really, but how hard can one little werewolf shindig be?"

~

"I am not getting naked."

"I didn't say you had to, Tam Tam. I'm just explaining what you should expect."

"But why? Are you guys allergic to pants or something?"

"It's symbolic. A true servant of Valdemar relies upon his own strength, nothing more."

"I prefer to rely on my coat. It's fucking freezing out."

"A wolf pelt is quite warm, even in the snow. You'd be surprised."

I gave Dad some side eye from the passenger seat of the minivan. "Last I checked, I didn't grow fur. Unless there's something I should know that you're not telling me."

He shrugged. "Not really. Although I'll admit I was kind of curious whether you would or not. Hey, did you ever see that movie *Underworld*? There's this hybrid monster in it ... not that you're a monster, honey, but anyway he turned into a..."

I held up a hand. "Didn't see it, but I heard Chris talking about how tight Kate Beckinsale's ass was in leather pants. Y'know, just in case you two haven't discussed the birds and the bees yet."

"Oh. Well, then I guess that reference is kind of lost."

"Just a bit. But regardless, I've been paying attention to these things. Haven't had to shave my legs any more than usual ... thank goodness."

He turned to me and smiled. "It's not just fur. Claws are useful, too. And not just for the messy stuff. They're super handy when you can't find a bottle opener."

"I bet you were a hit in high school."

"I did attend my fair share of keggers. Oh, don't look at me like that. You may find this hard to believe but once upon a time, I was considered cool. Hell, I'd practically snap my fingers and the ladies would..." He trailed off, as if remembering who he was talking to.

"You were saying? Or would you prefer to opt for plausible deniability in case Mom ever asks?"

"Think I'll take the Fifth on that one. But that *does* bring up a good point about tonight."

"If you think you're going to snap your fingers..."

"Nothing like that, sweetie. But I do need you to be on your best behavior. Werewolf packs aren't quite like actual wolf packs. We're not entirely dictated by instinct, but there's a good deal of influence. Standing and appearance mean a lot. We'll joke around just like any other get-together, but there are lines to be mindful of."

"I think I get it. As the alpha you need to look like you're in charge."

"Not look like. I need to *be* in charge. It's a whole different mindset. When you're a beta, your job is to make the alpha look good – agree with them in public, enforce their rules, that sort of stuff. But when you're an alpha you need to believe in everything you do. There's no Congress or parliament. The buck stops with you ... err, me. Once upon a time that was second nature, but you have to understand I was the beta to your uncle's alpha for twenty years. Also, I kind of like letting your Mom take charge at home."

"Gross."

He glanced at me and sighed. "I meant in the day to day stuff. Budgeting, decorating ... house things."

"Oh. Sorry."

"Now ... it's been a bit weird. Before, home life and pack life were the same mindset. But now that I'm in charge, it truly is like living in two different worlds. It's ... hard to explain."

He didn't need to. I'd already sensed it and didn't envy him. Mom was a force to be reckoned with, even without her powers.

"But that's neither here nor there," he continued. "What matters right now is tonight. I know you're still learning to appreciate doing your own thing and I respect that, but I need you to fall in line. Don't worry, I'm not going to ask you to do anything crazy. No standing on your head or..."

"Or marrying someone I don't want to?"

"Not going to let me forget that anytime soon, are you?"

"I wouldn't count on it."

Dad took his eyes off the road for a long second to stare at me. I had a feeling he had questions he wanted to ask, like about what had happened to Jerry that evening. From what I'd heard, his body had never been found. If so, I wasn't sure how to answer.

Thankfully, he decided to let the dead stay buried, so to speak.

"Anyway, try to be respectful. You won't understand everything that goes on, but I think most of it will be fairly easy to follow along with."

Dad was right to be concerned. I wasn't known for falling in line in my day to day life. Nevertheless, I'd managed to be a team player in wrestling for over a decade, with few blips to mar my record. This wasn't necessarily any different. You didn't give your coach lip. Not in public anyway, and especially not if you wanted to stay on the team. I just had to think of it that way. This was an away wrestling match. Sure, the opposing team was bigger, hairier, and infinitely more terrifying, but that wasn't any reason to lose my cool ... mostly.

"I can do that."

"Great, sweetie. Now that that's settled, back to what I was saying. The participants will be sky-clad for the most part."

"I already said..."

"I know and I heard you. But you might need to compromise a little bit. The pack does have their traditions, after all."

6

Even with my dad, and knowing that he was the one calling the shots, it was still an effort to keep my knees from shaking as we stepped into the hollows. The darkening skies and lengthening shadows made it seem as if the forest was closing in around us.

It was probably just my imagination, but it felt as if this place was alive.

Well, duh, it kinda was. I could hear and smell all sorts of things – chittering in the trees, scampering among the bushes, the fact that something had recently taken a crap not too far from where we walked ... ugh!

Sadly, though my hearing and sense of smell had greatly increased since last I'd been here, my eyes hadn't gotten the memo. No night vision for me, which seriously sucked.

Fortunately, Dad kept an emergency flashlight in the minivan. I was using it to keep up although, once things got under way, it would need to be set aside, along with some other stuff I was trying really hard not to think about.

I didn't look forward to that. It was late December and

pretty fucking cold out, if I did say so myself. Yeah, my body was a lot tougher than a normal person's, so hopefully frostbite was not in my future. However, that didn't mean I had to like it.

Thankfully, we didn't have as far to walk as I'd feared. Dad had taken a small turn off of Crossed Pine Road, the main throughway that connected High Moon to Morganberg, its neighbor to the east. I'd passed by it several times, thinking it an old abandoned game trail, but it turned out I was wrong. Though narrow and hard to see where it met the main road – no doubt to keep folks from actually using it – it widened once we were a ways in. It was a rough stretch, pretty uncomfortable in a minivan, but nothing that required a four by four with monster tires to navigate.

Of course, once we parked and started walking, it simply stood as a reminder that I was much deeper in the hollows than I was comfortable with. Sadly, there wasn't much I could do about that. I needed to suck it up for my dad's sake. And, even if not, I needed to remember the things I could do.

Yes, there were predators in the woods this night, but there was also at least one thing those predators feared.

Mind you, that would have been a lot more convincing had I not let slip a quick yip of panic once I heard the sound of multiple feet tramping through the underbrush ... still distant, but definitely there.

"You okay, honey?" Dad asked, his tone easy. He probably knew these woods like the back of his hand.

"We're not alone," I whispered before realizing I was about to let slip the new tricks up my sleeve. "I mean, they're out there, aren't they?"

"Oh, yeah. We're definitely not the first. But that's okay." He chuckled. "Being the alpha means you can arrive fashionably late."

"I just hope they're not serving raw squirrel as an hors d'oeuvre."

Just like that, I caught murmuring from somewhere ahead of us. Someone was bitching in a low voice about the joke I'd just made. I needed to remember that my ears were supercharged now, but so were theirs. If I could hear the pack, they could hear me.

Almost as if reading my thoughts, Dad said, "You might want to keep it down, Tamara. We're almost there."

I couldn't help but notice his use of my proper name. He was the alpha here. The leader of the pack, its master. Referring to me by his cutesy nickname probably wasn't becoming to one of his station. It likely also belied the fact that I was here to prove I was standing in line like a good puppy.

Call me snippy, but I had a feeling it was going to take everything I had to keep from losing my mind, especially since I didn't doubt some of the participants were probably hoping to test my *allegiance*.

Speaking of which, we stepped out into a large open area. It wasn't a full clearing, but here the trees were spaced out and the grass beneath our feet was matted down as if it had seen a lot of foot, or paw, traffic.

I expected to see a small army of snarling werewolves waiting for us, but it was apparently too early for that. There were plenty of people milling about, but they looked as human as we did – the irony of that not lost to me.

Not helping to cement my belief that I was in Danger Central were several picnic tables at the far end of the clearing. They were piled high with coolers and Tupperware containers. On one sat a keg, a pyramid of plastic cups stacked next to it.

I half-turned toward my dad and whispered, "Is this a sacred ceremony or a barbecue?"

He smiled down at me. "A little from column A..."

"Curtis!"

I turned toward the voice and narrowed my eyes. It was my father's cousin Mitch. He'd been there the day my uncle found out about me, had been pretty much all for having me executed right then and there. I'd been wondering if he'd been among the wolves I'd killed when they'd invaded High Moon. At the time, he was one of the few who knew I was a hybrid. Guess that meant he was smart enough to steer clear of me that night.

Point in his favor, I guess. But if he was hoping to start shit with me, he was going to end up regretting...

"May Valdemar smile upon you on this darkest of nights," he said to my father, clapping him on the arm.

Dad returned the smile. "And may your enemies cower in the shadows at your approach."

Guess this was their version of a secret handshake. Kind of dopey, if you asked me. And people wondered why I hadn't bothered to join a sorority.

The pleasantries finished, Mitch turned to me, his expression souring. "Hello, Tamara." He pronounced my name as if it tasted bad. Call me crazy, but I had a feeling he was one of the assholes who'd been talking behind my back.

"Mitch," I replied curtly. "Haven't seen you since I almost kicked your..."

"Tamara," Dad said, cutting me off. "Mitch is my beta."

Him?! The look on my father's face was the only thing that kept me from saying that out loud. I'd promised him I'd be good and being good meant fitting in, not pummeling the very first werewolf I met ... tempting as it was. Instead, I somehow managed to shove all that down and reply, "Oh? Congratulations on the ... promotion."

"A promotion that was only necessary because..."

My dad put a hand on his shoulder. Though I didn't consider my father a particularly intimidating man, in that instant my view of him changed. I mean, yeah, I'd seen him as a werewolf. He was scary as all hell, but before now it was easy for me to separate the two. He'd mentioned his attitude change upon taking charge, but here, with that simple gesture, I understood. Menace, authority, certainty, all of it was conveyed in that one small gesture and, judging from the look in Mitch's eyes, I wasn't alone in seeing it.

It was weird, almost frightening, to see such a transformation and he hadn't even grown so much as five o'clock shadow yet. I won't lie, it was kind of badass, too. Growing up, we all want to think our dad can beat up the other kid's dad. Much as I loved mine, though, I never quite fully believed it ... until now.

Holy crap, my father was actually cool.

What was this world coming to?

Dad had some stuff to take care of before howling at the moon, so he tasked his beta with making sure I got properly settled.

As we walked away, Mitch lowered his voice to a volume that was meant for my ears only. "Don't think I've forgotten what you've done."

I kept my mouth shut despite the effort it took. This wasn't the first time I'd been goaded. Being a woman in a man's sport meant hearing trash-talk from every asshole with a pair of lips. Most were just trying to get beneath my skin, hoping I'd make a mistake – basic competition shit. But some had been downright cruel, from the type of people who didn't want to see me step out of what they considered my pre-assigned place in life.

I'd survived both in my day. I would survive this.

"I know Curtis is still bewitched by that whore mother of yours."

Mind you, some of it was harder to swallow than others.

"Your uncle was right. You don't deserve to exist. You belong in a shallow grave, rotting and forgotten."

I turned and locked eyes with him. I'd promised my father I'd be good and meant to keep my word, but I'd be damned if I was going to let this asshole treat me like his personal bitch. I held his gaze for a second too long, then hooked a thumb at the picnic table. "So, what kind of sandwiches do you guys have?"

Now it was his turn to glare at me. Too bad I refused to blink.

Then, just as I felt the tension reach the point where punches would be thrown, promise or not, Mitch smiled. Pity that it was the smile of a creep who'd just lured a kid into his pedovan. "I'd say you look settled enough. The gathering begins in an hour. Prepare yourself."

Prepare myself? Yeah, that was only slightly threatening.

Before I could properly retort, he turned and stalked off, leaving me standing alone with no clue what to do. As far as tour guides went, he kinda sucked.

I looked around and realized there were *a lot* of eyes staring at me. Some appeared curious, a few cautious, but far too many were hostile. I was beginning to see what Dad had meant.

Worse, there were a lot of familiar faces among them. I'd grown up with many of these people. Some were extended family, others folks I'd seen whenever I hung out in Morganberg. Now they were all staring at me like I was the poor kid in an exclusive country club.

Hoping to find a friendly face among them, someone who hadn't completely drunken my uncle's Kool Aid, I spotted Melissa Haynes, a girl I used to babysit, standing in a group of teens her age. She looked my way and I smiled at her. For a second, I thought she might return it – tell me that things were okay between us – but then she turned away and refused to acknowledge me.

It was heartbreaking but not entirely unexpected. She was the first werewolf I'd encountered, albeit I didn't know it was her at the time. Sadly, she'd also been the first werewolf I'd beaten the snot out of. Worst of all, it had happened twice. She'd attacked me during the assault on High Moon, wounding me badly. In retaliation, I'd pretty much knocked her block off.

Still, it hurt. More importantly, it told me that – my father's position be damned – it was unlikely that I'd ever fit in with...

"Hey. Are you just going to stand there holding down the ground?"

"Huh?" I turned to find a blonde girl, roughly my age, looking down at me ... mostly because she was tall, at least five-eight. "Excuse me?"

"You heard me," she said, her blue eyes sparkling like ice. "Because if so, you're going to miss out on Mrs. Brokinsky's potato salad. It's to die for."

7

S he was right, it was good potato salad.

Now I was weirded out. The hostility was painful, but not unexpected. It was familiar territory with this bunch. But sitting there at a picnic table, eating food off a paper plate with a girl who was surely a werewolf, was a whole new level of strange.

"See, I told you," she said after I'd swallowed a few bites.

Mitch could have taken a few lessons from her. She'd thrown me off my game much better than he had. I was half tempted to tell my father that she'd make a better beta on that point alone.

She held her hand out after I put my fork down. "I'm Ester, but you can call me Cass."

I wasn't entirely certain how one got that nickname from Ester, but whatever. I reached out and took her hand.

"I'm named after my grandmother," she explained. "She's cool and all, but Ester sounds like I should be chain smoking menthols in a bingo hall."

I laughed despite myself. Her tone was easy, relaxed. There was no way someone could fake that so naturally. It was dumb of me to lower my defenses, and I had no intention of doing so, but I figured it wouldn't hurt to lighten up a bit. "I'm Tamara, but my friends call me Bent."

"Bent?"

"Short for Bentley."

"I get it. That's cool."

"It is, except for the guys at school who keep telling me I have a future in porn."

"How have you not kicked their asses?"

"Through extreme self-discipline ... and reminding myself I don't want to be expelled and end up waiting tables for a living."

She laughed, and it sounded genuine enough that I felt a smile forming on my lips. But then I realized what I'd said, and quickly added, "Not that there's anything wrong with waiting tables ... in case that's what you do?"

Cass held up a hand, the fingers long and slender – probably a cheerleader once upon a time. She had the look, albeit not the attitude I remembered. Comparatively, I was short and muscular, a direct contrast to her. "It's cool. I flipped fries at McDonald's for two summers back in high school, but that's about it."

"You went to Morganberg?"

She shook her head. "No. My parents sent me to Saint Edgar's over in Hazelton."

"Ah, that explains why you don't look familiar. St. Ed's didn't have a wrestling program, if I recall."

"No idea," she replied. "I was more on the debate team side of things. Didn't pay much attention to sports."

Not a cheerleader. Poor assumption on my part. "So, I'm guessing you know who I am."

RICK GUALTIERI

She gave me a solid *duh* look then said, "Yeah. Hard to miss. One, I haven't seen you here before, and two..." She lowered her voice. "The pack gossips like a bunch of old ladies. Oh, by the way, nobody else here is going to say it, but I heard what went down over the summer. I'm sorry it happened."

"Heard?"

"Yeah. I was busy counseling at a summer camp when the call went out."

"You weren't there?" The question came out more accusatory than I'd meant. If anything, I found myself glad I hadn't had the chance to kick her ass.

"Nope. Missed it, blood moon and all."

"Hold on. That was an option?" I asked, genuinely curious. "I thought when the alpha said jump you all, you know."

She shrugged, looking a bit uncomfortable. "Usually. But we're not animals. I mean, I was on shift. I would have gotten fired if I'd just up and left. So I kinda just hoped nobody noticed I wasn't there, and by nobody, I mean Craig."

"Not an issue anymore," I replied, perhaps more blithely than warranted. Remembering my promise to Dad, I quickly added, "Sorry. That was cold."

She actually threw me a wink. "It's cool. Believe me, despite what he wanted to think, he wasn't universally loved, at least by those of us he would've deemed the fairer sex."

"Not barefoot and pregnant enough for him?"

She inclined her head. "It was never that bad. But he did have a few opinions about pack bloodlines that were a bit ... antiquated." She stopped and looked around before smiling sheepishly. "But maybe this isn't the best place to talk about it."

That was an excellent point. Of all the places to

52

exclaim *ding dong the witch is dead* – figuratively speaking, of course – this was potentially the worst one. I was here to smooth things over with Dad's ... *my* pack. The goal was to show everyone that my father had me on a short leash, so we could all go back to being one big, happy, flea-bitten family. The current conversation, if overheard – which it surely would be if we kept at it – would pretty much do the opposite.

I respected my dad too much for that. It was time to change the subject. "So ... come to these things often?"

"Don't you mean, what's a nice girl like you doing in a place like this?"

"Not quite what I was getting at."

She let out a laugh. "I usually only come to the big functions. I don't know about the rest, but I don't have time to drive out here whenever someone wants to howl at the moon. But tonight's the solstice. My mother wouldn't let me hear the end of it if I ditched. Besides, I heard through the grapevine last week that we'd be having a special guest." She pointed a finger my way. "Although I'm not sure everyone here is happy about it."

"Wait, last week?"

"Yeah."

I glanced toward where last I'd seen my father. He was nowhere in sight. Call me cynical, but I had a feeling my presence here was not quite the surprise he made it out to be. Guess that was a conversation for the ride home.

"Everything cool?"

I turned back toward Cass. "Yeah. Just wondering where our exalted leader has gotten off to."

"Probably business. There's always something going on."

"Let me guess. Stuff about their war with the Draío ... the other side?"

She giggled. "Don't feel bad. I can barely pronounce it myself. But no. It's usually less important."

"Like?"

She thought about it for a moment. "Like, for instance, last time I was here, the alphas were having an argument about respecting the state's bag limit during deer season. I mean, seriously, it's not like any of us carry around our hunting license after we change."

I chuckled. Yeah, pockets didn't seem to be a big deal among the werewolf ... hold on. "Wait, did you say *alphas*? As in plural?"

She nodded. "Uh huh. The alpha male and female."

"There's an alpha female?"

"Of course. Every pack has one," she replied as if this was common knowledge.

"Really?" Oh, we were definitely having a discussion about this on the trip home.

"Yeah. It's kind of sexist, if you ask me. The male is typically the face of the leadership while the female is usually behind the scenes putting out all the fires, stuff like that. Not like anyone here ever asks my opinion about it." She looked at me and must have seen the questioning expression on my face. "You really are new to this, aren't you?"

"My first playdate," I said, trying to staunch the growing concern in my gut. I couldn't help but wonder who this alpha female was and what her relationship to my father amounted to. If they were anything other than coworkers, then there was going to be hell to pay...

"How about I be your pack buddy tonight?"

That drew my attention back from a mental image of my mother fricasseeing Dad for being a louse. "Excuse me?"

"You're new and, no offense, but it's pretty obvious you don't know what's going on. I wasn't trying to eavesdrop, but it sort of looked like Uncle Mitch ghosted you pretty hard back there."

"Uncle Mitch?"

"Yeah. Second uncle, anyway. Don't sound so surprised. Most everyone here is related in some form or another."

Huh. I guess that made Cass my second cousin or something like that. Cool, I suppose.

"I mean, some of the bloodlines are more distant than others, and there are a few recruits..."

Now *that* was potentially interesting. I remembered my uncle mentioning something like that over the summer, that sometimes outsiders were allowed in. It was how I ended up in an ill-fated engagement. It made me realize that, for all the time I spent punching werewolves last summer, I still knew very little about them. "How's that work?"

She shrugged as if it wasn't a big deal. "Depends on the person. Sometimes it's by marriage and they're brought into the know. I don't think anyone like that is out here tonight, though. Amazing how few normals show up when it's freezing cold."

I considered my own discomfort. "Yeah, amazing."

"Others get turned and brought in that way."

"Turned?"

"Oh, yeah. Not everyone here was born a lycanthrope. Some are recruited after the fact – late bloomers if you will."

"So, they get bitten during a full moon or something like that?"

Cass pursed her lips as if thinking about it. "I'm not entirely sure. I know it's more complicated than the movies let on. You don't just bite someone and they grow fur. Otherwise half the state would probably be overrun every time the Flyers won the playoffs. No. There's a whole ritual involved. Supposedly they have to invoke the old gods ... if you believe that stuff."

Half a year ago I would've laughed at that suggestion, but then I remembered what happened in the glade with Jerry. His death had been the epitome of weird and terrifying, all rolled into one. Since then, I'd been trying to convince myself that it was all a trick of the light, that I hadn't seen or heard what I thought I had.

But it was a stretch. I kept coming back to the same thing: if werewolves and magic were real, then why couldn't other *things* be, too? Hell, I'd seen some of those other things back at school – not exactly old gods, whatever they looked like, but enough to tell me the world most of us lived in was only the tip of some horrific iceberg.

We weren't kept waiting much longer, although that wasn't exactly a fortunate turn of events. I was just about to see if maybe I could sneak a beer without anyone objecting when there came a low-pitched howl from somewhere close by, deep enough to be felt in my bones.

"It's starting," Cass said conversationally. "Time to get ready."

She'd told me that all the pups – her word, not mine – got a pack buddy for their first few times. It wasn't much different than being a chaperone at a dance ... aside from the fur and claws. She actually seemed surprised that Mitch hadn't assigned me one, but I kept my opinions on that to myself.

Even if I didn't outright slug someone, not knowing what to do would inevitably lead to some faux pas or another, maybe one that would give them all an excuse to tear me limb from limb.

Cass assured me, however, that all I had to do was stick close to her, follow her lead, and it would all be good. Even if I made a mistake, it wouldn't be an issue, as she was designating me an official "pup" for the evening.

Had anyone else said that, they might have ended the night several teeth short of a winning smile, but I found myself liking my new pack buddy. Possibly naïve of me to drop my guard in current company, but I figured I could always pummel her later if it turned out she was setting me up for failure.

Although, just for the record, I really hoped that wasn't the case.

Besides, at that moment, I had more pressing matters to be ticked off about. Cass led me over to a series of benches where she proceeded to remove her coat and set it down. Despite the freezing temperatures, her shirt was next, and her bra followed closely thereafter. Within moments, she was naked as the day she was born.

Glancing around, I saw the rest of the assembled wolves doing the same ... which meant it was my turn. *Oh, joy.*

After some back and forth with my father, we'd come to a compromise of sorts ... more of an impasse, really. We'd reached a place where neither of us was willing to budge, so that ended up being what we agreed upon.

Thinking back on it now, I realized I'd probably gotten the short end of that stick. The spot where I'd planted my flag was actually a lot closer to his side of the argument. Grrr. Score one for the parents.

Still, I'd made a promise, one I intended to keep until such time as I was forced to do otherwise.

I followed Cass's lead, first removing my coat. I tensed as the cold air bit through my blouse and realized it was only going to get worse from there. Might as well do what one does in the summer when faced with a cold swimming hole – dive in and get it over with.

My shirt joined the coat. Next came my boots, and that's where I hesitated – just when my bare feet touched the ground. "Oooh, that's cold!"

"It's okay," Cass said with a chuckle. "It'll be a lot better once you change. Believe me."

"Um, you know I don't do that, right?"

"You don't?" She sounded genuinely surprised to hear it, reinforcing my opinion that she was on the up and up. "Not even a little peach fuzz?"

"Nope."

"Then sorry. It actually won't get better."

I rolled my eyes and removed my pants, leaving me standing there in the middle of the fucking hollows in nothing but my bra and panties. Oh well, at least I'd had the foresight to not wear anything sheer.

"The rest?" Cass prodded.

"Not gonna happen."

"But the..."

"I talked it over with the alpha on the way over," I explained. "He's cool."

That seemed to satisfy her concerns. "Just for the record," she whispered with a conspiratorial smile. "You don't have anything to be ashamed of."

I smiled back. Truth of the matter was she didn't either, which wasn't something I could say for the majority of this crowd. Yikes.

When I think of nude beaches, I typically imagine endless six pack abs wandering pristine shores, but I've heard from some of my college friends that the reality is more ... well, what you see in everyday life. The basic fact of the matter is most people don't look like Instagram models. I saw beer bellies on display, hunched shoulders, and enough liver spots to play connect the dots. Continuing to look around, I spotted one sour-faced old lady staring my way, her pasty skin a sharp contrast to the darkening woods behind her.

I was about to turn away, but then did a double take.

Son of a...

I couldn't be certain, but I could have sworn I'd seen her before – this past summer when I'd gone to talk to Jerry, prior to accidentally murdering him. At his place of work, I'd let slip to one old prune that I was there with Craig's blessing. In return, she'd given me shit about being on drugs.

Hard to tell, but if that was her, then what a bitch.

Oh well. She was the least of my worries. I made the mistake of making eye contact with a couple of the men loitering around and ended up getting some salacious glares back. Great. So they not only wanted to kill me, but some were apparently fine with fucking me first. I hadn't thought I could be more uncomfortable. Guess I was wrong.

"I feel like a piece of meat," I whispered to Cass.

"Yeah, this is the part I like least." She nodded ruefully, then leaned down close to me.

For a moment, I thought she might be trying to go for a kiss. She was cute and all, but that was more Riva's cup of tea. Mind you, college was usually considered the time to experiment, and I could definitely do worse...

Instead, however, she lowered her voice even further and said, "But it's not *all* bad, if you catch my drift."

Cass lifted a finger and subtly pointed off to my left. I turned my head to follow and ... ooh, now there was something to take away the evening chill. Washboard stomach, muscled arms and ... off came his pants, revealing the rest of him.

After a second or two of silent gawking, I looked at his

face and realized I recognized him. "Isn't that David Hood?"

Cass turned to face me. "You know him?"

"Yeah. He went to Morganberg High. We wrestled a few times."

A scandalous smile creased her lips. "I have got to hear about this."

"On the mat," I clarified, feeling a blush rise to my cheeks despite the cold. "He was on their team. Decent wrestler, but I didn't know him too well otherwise. Although I'm kind of wishing we'd gotten better acquainted."

"He could pin me anytime."

It was crazy. There we were, standing naked – or nearly naked, in my case – in the middle of the frozen woods of Pennsylvania, surrounded by people who would soon be dropping the people act, and giggling like two school girls.

"His wolf isn't bad either," Cass whispered, "although that might be more an acquired taste."

"I don't mind a hairy chest, but I have limits."

She laughed, then peeled her eyes away from David, albeit with some effort. Couldn't quite blame her. He was an oasis of hotness in a desert of flab.

"It's almost time," she said, turning serious. "Everyone will change on the way, including me. Just stay close by. I don't know if you can scent me or not, but I'll try my best not to get too carried away and run off."

"Try your best? I thought you guys … um … had it all under control."

"We do, for the most part. But the change can be a bit heady. Our senses ratchet up to eleven and our bodies become more attuned to hunting than hanging out at Starbucks. It can be a bit … overwhelming at times, especially when you're with the pack. Pheromones or something like that, but the more of us who are around, the easier it is to lose yourself and run off chasing rabbits."

I considered her statement and the overall attitude toward me here.

If everyone kept a level head and played by the rules, I should be fine. But, if they lost their minds even a little bit, I had a feeling I could very well become the rabbit in this equation.

8

I think the only thing worse than being half frozen and scared to death is being half frozen and bored out of my fucking skull.

I'd expected ... well, I don't exactly know. I kind of envisioned an orgy of fur and blood, something primal and animalistic that would send me running like a victim in a horror film.

Instead, it was more like a high school pep rally,

There were two of those mega-wolves up front directing everything. While all the werewolves I'd seen to date had been large, a few seemed to come in extra-extra terrifying. It was as if everything about them was exaggerated to nightmare levels – taller, more muscular, darker fur, bigger fangs, the works. Imagine if a Hollywood effects guy took your typical Howling-style monster and decided they were missing a heavy steroid addiction.

Anyway, I was fairly certain the larger of the two was my father. He seemed to be calling the shots. As for the other, I wasn't sure if it was Mitch or that mysterious alpha female Cass had told me about. I mean, it seemed to be all business between the two leaders – no groping or any of the aforementioned orgy stuff. So that was a plus.

But, aside from the general terror of being in the hollows and surrounded by supernatural creatures, it wasn't much to write home about.

I imagined it was kind of like that in any secret society. Hell, I had friends in the sororities back at school. According to them, things were played off as mysterious and creepy, until you actually got in and realized it was more of the same shit found anywhere else. Looking in from the outside could be a crazy experience, but it was all pomp and circumstance.

There was a lot of howling, growling, and what may have been a bit of dancing beneath the moon ... it was hard to tell. There was structure to it all, but far less menace than I'd expected – even knowing the majority of the wolves there probably hated my guts.

Rather than focus on the fact that my feet were numb and my breasts felt like they were going to snap off, I remembered what Cass had told me about scenting her. So I practiced that, trying to hone my nose first on her, then on some of the others nearby, and seeing if my sense of smell was keen enough to distinguish between them.

Go figure, it was easier than I would've thought. I'd probably still need to practice but, even when I closed my eyes, I still seemed able to tell her apart. She had an earthy scent to her, as all the wolves did ... probably a testament to them being naked and covered in fur. But beneath it were multiple layers: skin, deodorant, body wash, a light perfume that smelled of apples.

I made a note to ask her about that. It smelled a lot better than the crap I'd hosed myself down with before arriving home.

Every wolf seemed to have their own distinct under-odors – some more pleasant than others. I smelled cookie dough, motor oil, manure, grass, marinara sauce, all sorts of things I'd never thought to consider before. But it made sense in a way that people would retain traces of not only what they wore, but what they did throughout the day.

I'd always heard that dogs smelled in a kaleidoscope of sorts, to the degree that scents were almost colors to them. I had never appreciated that before. Hell, even when I'd first noticed my senses heightening – shortly after returning to school at summer's end – I'd focused on the macro level: things either smelled good or bad. But now, sensing those layers, I realized it was all – much like the famous smut novel – just different shades of grey.

I considered this once it was over and we were heading back to the clearing. If I could master this new sense, then maybe I didn't need to see in the dark to find my way around...

Goddamn it!

It figured. The second that thought passed through my head, I tripped and stubbed my toe. Karma could be a real bitch sometimes.

Cass stopped next to me and inclined her head. She made a slight whining sound, then her features shifted ever so slightly. Her muzzle retracted about halfway, leaving her head in a place somewhere between werewolf and human. "*You okay?*"

"I'm fine," I replied. "Well, maybe not my pride."

She let out a chuckle, then her features shifted back to her wolf form again. That halfway point seemed to make speech easier for her kind, but the fact that I hadn't seen any wolves stay in it for long told me that maybe it wasn't the most comfortable setting on their dial-a-mattress.

I glanced around, hearing twigs snap and smelling the scents of other wolves, but I couldn't see any of them. And it wasn't just because it was dark. Once the main meeting broke up, werewolves wandered every which way. Maybe some of them had gotten caught up in things, like Cass warned, and were even now heading off to hunt.

Thankfully that didn't seem to be the case with her. She probably realized I was pretty damned cold and wanted to get dressed again ASAP. Credit to my father, though. He was right. I didn't feel like I was in any danger from the elements. Guess my body was tough enough to take it. But it was uncomfortable as all hell, especially stepping on sharp rocks every thirty seconds or so.

Was this what a parent felt like walking through a playroom full of Legos?

Cass inclined her head toward me again, a gesture more curious than worried.

"Let me guess, you want to know what I thought of it all?"

She nodded, a guttural sound escaping her jaws that might have been a yes.

I proceeded to tell her, perhaps sugarcoating it a little, but not too much. Even as a werewolf she was a bit disarming to be around.

Cass chuckled and I continued, speaking more freely about werewolf pep rallies.

It was weird. I loved my dad. Once upon a time I'd loved my Uncle Craig, too, and thought he loved me back, but that had quickly changed when he found out what I was. The siege on High Moon had followed shortly thereafter, a bloody affair no matter how you looked at it. Since then, immediate family aside, my opinion of werewolves hadn't been particularly high. They'd mostly acted like rabid dogs around me, so that's how I'd treated them.

But now, having met another who actually seemed able to look beyond the tip of her nose and not automatically assume I was some kind of abomination, it was ... humanizing.

In the movies, things were always so easy. You were

either the hero or the monster. If you were the monster, the audience cheered your death. The problem with real life, though, was when it began to desensitize you. I'd always been a tomboy growing up, acting tough and living up to the part. But I never considered myself a bully, or worse.

Going into this night, I didn't have high hopes. Now, however, I saw that meeting Cass was a good thing, because it potentially pulled me back from some unforeseen line in the sand, beyond which I became a remorseless monster hunter – not caring if there was an actual person beneath the teeth and claws.

I didn't want that. All I wanted was to live my...

A branch broke somewhere close by, maybe too close. Almost immediately, my nose filled with the scent of another werewolf. I'd been lost in my thoughts and had allowed it to approach with my guard down.

From the look on Cass's face, she'd done the same.

A low growl escaped her lips just as a massive figure stepped from the bushes ahead.

Cass's wolf form was large, over six and a half feet tall, possibly inching toward seven. But the creature that appeared before us was even larger.

In the time it took me to adopt a defensive stance, its face shimmered, pulling back in on itself so it could speak – leaving it somewhere between man and monster.

"*I have a bone to pick with you.*"

There was no time to think or remember my promise. Instinctively, I prepared to knock this thing into next week.

Before I could let my fist fly, though, the rest of its body began to shift. There came the disturbing sound of bones and skin re-arranging itself as the wolf transformed.

Tanned skin, visible even in the moonlight, replaced fur, and with it I caught a glimpse of tight muscle.

Aw no. Not him. I didn't want to kick David Hood's ass. Why couldn't it have been one of those paunchy wolves?

"I don't know if you remember or not," he said, once he was fully changed, "but you pinned me in the county finals two years ago."

Forcing my eyes above his neck and trying real hard to forget that I was almost as naked as him, I tried my best to act tough. "I pinned a lot of guys."

Okay, that wasn't nearly as smooth as I'd hoped.

I might have gotten away with it but Cass, still in her wolf form, let out a guttural chuckle. I gave her a quick elbow to the ribs, then turned back toward David. "What I meant is, I won a lot of matches."

He smirked and folded his arms across his chest. Did I mention how naked he was? "Fine, then I have a question, and I want you to be honest."

I really hoped he wasn't going to ask the same question I'd asked on more than one first date: whether they were aware my eyes were up here.

"Did you cheat?"

"Excuse me?"

"I lost, but I was able to accept that you were simply that good. I mean, hell, you were in all the papers."

"At least until the state finals," I muttered under my breath.

"But now we all know what you can do," he continued. "You're strong like us, but without changing."

"So you want to know if I unfairly kicked everyone's ass by virtue of being a freak?" The question came out sharper than intended, but sue me. Competing in a sport that was traditionally dominated by men had made me a bit defensive.

"Pretty much."

"Kind of a loaded question coming from someone who can turn into a seven foot wolf monster."

Cass turned and stared at me but I kept my focus on David, and not just because he was a hottie. If this was going to turn bad – probably not helped by me being a smart-ass – then it would be now.

But if my accusation bothered him, he didn't show it. "True. When we shift we're strong, but like this..." He gestured at himself, which was only majorly distracting. "I'm not much different than anyone else. To access our powers we need to initiate at least part of the change."

"And you never did that on the mat?"

He laughed. "Would be hard to miss. In case you forgot, those unitards don't leave a lot to the imagination."

More than your current outfit is leaving. But instead of pointing that out, I replied, "Fair enough. Truth of the matter is, I didn't know I had powers until earlier this year."

"How did you not..."

I opened my mouth to answer, but then realized I was potentially giving away a secret that my parents, Mom in particular, as her uncle had devised the formula, would likely not want known by the general werewolf populace. Hell, I probably didn't want that either. Knowing there was a concoction that could take away my powers, even temporarily, was probably an invitation for a roofied drink – followed by me being torn limb from limb. "One day I was powerless, the next I was..." I mimicked his gesture but at my own body, realizing a moment too late that I was pretty much inviting him to stare at my underwear.

The snicker that came from Cass told me it hadn't

gone unnoticed. I turned to her. "Don't you have a bone to bury or something?"

Almost immediately her body shrank in on itself. That disturbing sound of flesh re-arranging filled the night air for several seconds and then she was as I'd first met her, albeit less clothed.

She smiled coyly at me and said, "I wish." Then she turned to her fellow werewolf. "Hey, David."

"How's it going, Cass?" he replied in the easygoing tone of someone greeting a friend or first cousin, which for all I knew they were.

A faint grimace of disappointment shone on her face for a moment, but then she covered it up by turning toward me. "So what you're saying is you're a late bloomer."

"I guess so."

She nodded. "That's not unheard of. My cousin Paul couldn't fully change until he was almost twenty-one. Used to get all sorts of crap for it."

Whether or not that was true, it appeared to satisfy David. All of the tension seemed to leave his body and he smiled. "Okay. If you say so, I believe it. I just wanted to know. I mean, it's silly. It happened two years ago, but..."

"It's a pride thing," I finished for him. "I understand."

"Good. Hope I didn't insult you too badly."

"Me?" I said with a flirtatious laugh. "You're the one who got pinned."

He squared his shoulders, adopting a neutral position as if we were about to start a match. With a grin, he replied, "Well, if you ever want a rematch, let me know."

I tried to say something, but no words came out. It wasn't what he was doing – well, partially because of what he was doing – as much as knowing that the first move he'd make was known as a *penetration step*. Considering his current state of undress, I doubt anyone could blame me for assuming a double entendre.

As I stood there dumbstruck, Cass stepped behind me and not-so-subtly nudged me forward. "Go on, you can take him."

Distracted as I was, I stumbled forward into David's arms.

He caught me easily enough, and I had just enough time to register how tight his chest was when an unearthly roar rose up from the forest around us.

9

One minute I was clutching a seriously cute naked guy and the next I was airborne as something large and dark erupted from the bushes and hit me with the force of a small locomotive.

I slammed into a sapling, snapped it in two, and landed hard on the cold, unforgiving ground. The blow dazed me but seemed more intent on surprise than precision. The attack had been brutal but sloppy.

Thank goodness, too. God, how stupid was I? There I'd been, gawking like a preteen on her first date, completely forgetting that I was, in essence, standing at ground zero of enemy territory.

Not wishing to give my assailant a chance for seconds, I rolled to my feet, simultaneously adjusting a bra strap that had slipped off my shoulder. It was a subconscious move, one I was barely aware making, but it apparently gave the impression I'd shrugged off the hit like nothing because the enormous black werewolf, one of those megawolves, stopped short in its approach.

"You get that one for free." I forced my voice to

remain steady despite tasting blood in the back of my mouth.

Before either of us could do much more than posture, Cass stepped in front of the monster wolf. "What are you doing, Mitch?"

I should've known. I'd guessed it might have been him helping my dad run the show earlier. Mind you, that knowledge didn't make me feel better. Normal werewolves were dangerous as all hell, but these ... they were a step above. My father was one and my uncle had been one, too. I'd faced both and just barely lived to tell the tale, and that was only because Dad had been holding back.

Mitch's face transformed to that halfway state ... just enough for me to recognize his asshole features. "*Out of the way, Ester. She attacked our brother here.*"

"But..."

"*That's an order, girl.*"

Cass glanced over her shoulder at me and I saw fear in her eyes as well as regret. This wasn't her doing, but she couldn't do much to stop it. Disobeying the beta was a challenge to his authority and Mitch was a superior foe, one she had little chance of besting.

"It's okay," I told her.

Mind you, I wasn't entirely sure of my chances either, but I also wasn't so easily goaded. Forcing down every instinct that demanded I feed him his own teeth, I broke eye contact. "I'm sorry. It was an accident."

The look on Mitch's face was one of absolute outrage, but he hesitated to charge me. The ball was in my court and I wasn't volleying back.

As we faced each other – my mind racing to figure out how to end this in a way that saved him face and likewise saved *my* face – my ears picked up others heading our way. Mitch's battle cry had summoned an audience. He was probably hoping I'd take a swing, giving him plenty of witnesses that the hybrid had turned hostile and thus was fair game for murderizing. But instead, they were going to be my witnesses that I wasn't going to play his game.

"*What?*" he growled.

"Like I said, it was an accident. I apologize."

For a moment, I thought my gambit was going to pay off. Score one for diplomacy. But then David stepped in.

"She's right," he said. "It was my fault. She didn't ... Ugh!"

Mitch backhanded him away, knocking him to the ground like a ton of bricks. "*Nobody asked you, whelp.*"

Cass took a step toward David's prone form and Mitch raised his hand menacingly at her. That was all I needed to crumble diplomacy up and toss it into my mental trash can.

I balled my fists. "Like I said, that was an accident. But what comes next won't be."

Even as I raced forward, a part of me questioned the sanity of what I was doing. I didn't know what made mega-wolves like Mitch different from the rest, only that they were. They were like a boss battle in a Final Fantasy game, except I doubted I'd get the chance to restart the level if I failed.

Mitch took a swing at me, his enormous paw looking like a frying pan with knives glued to it, but his advantage in height was offset by the fact that I was barely five three. I ducked his attack easily enough, stepped in, and drove a fist into his gut.

Physics was never my best class but, despite having plenty of evidence to the contrary, I still expected the outcome of me punching the living equivalent of a brick wall to be a shattered hand. After all, that's how things worked in the normal world.

Pity for him that normalcy ended where the hollows began. My fist sank in and he doubled over as all the air in his lungs was forcibly expelled.

I spun, reached up to wrap an arm around his throat, and flipped him over my shoulder like a bag of trash.

He landed hard on his back, panting like ... well, a dog.

As frightened as I was to face him, I remembered two little factoids. He was big and terrifying, but I'd always considered him a bit of a dim bulb, even next to Craig. Second, and perhaps more important, when I'd faced my uncle, I'd been injured and near exhaustion.

But I was fresh now and just getting warmed up, in a manner of speaking anyway. Suddenly Mitch didn't seem as big or bad as I'd thought.

Mind you, just because he was an idiot didn't mean I wasn't one, too. I allowed myself an ill-advised moment of self-satisfaction, noting all the wolves who'd appeared from out of the shadows to watch, when I should have been pummeling the snot out of my opponent.

Somedays I could be a real amateur.

Still on his back, Mitch reached out – his arms more than long enough for the job – grabbed hold of my ankles, and yanked my feet out from under me. The back of my head impacted against a tree root, making me see stars, and then I was flung like a ragdoll again as Mitch rolled to his feet and tossed me away like a bad habit.

This time the tree I slammed into was the real deal, a big, old oak with a trunk at least four feet across. I felt something shift uncomfortably inside me and realized I'd probably cracked a rib. Still, I was lucky. A normal person would have been splattered like a bug on a windshield.

Of course, a normal person would have run away

screaming their head off, not pulled themselves to their feet for round two.

I winced while trying to stand up straight. Yeah, that collision had definitely taken something out of me. Good thing the light wasn't better, otherwise I'd have been able to look down and see all the bruises covering my body.

Instead, I turned my head skyward. My ears told me Mitch was on the move again. I didn't have time to worry about bruises when he was intent on making me a corpse.

There! A sturdy branch hung about six feet out of my reach – impossible for most, but barely a game of hopscotch for me.

I leapt as Mitch closed the distance between us, grabbed hold of the branch, and then kicked out with both legs.

The dumb fuck made the mistake of looking up at the wrong moment, allowing me to connect right beneath his chin. His jaws slammed shut with an audible click of teeth meeting teeth. It wasn't my best shot, but it was enough to back him up several steps and give me some breathing room.

The only question now was whether to go up or down.

Down was more familiar territory, being a wrestler and all. Problem was, any advantages I had in this fight were negated by the fact that he was so freaking big. He could easily shred me in the time it took to get within arm's reach, and I didn't even have the meager protection of a t-shirt covering my body.

No. Up made more sense. Gravity was the big equal-izer. Well, that and the fact that growing up a tomboy in rural Pennsylvania had afforded me plenty of practice climbing trees.

My poor mom. She'd wanted a little princess and had gotten me instead.

The upside, though, was that it was pretty awesome to be me somedays.

I easily pulled myself up onto the branch, then started to scramble higher, making sure to get out of reach of Mitch's vertical game.

If he wanted me, he'd have to come and get me.

10

What I lacked in practice, and proper climbing attire, I made up for by being super strong.

Where there wasn't easy purchase, I made some, digging my fingers into the bark and pulling myself higher.

I'd ascended to what I guessed to be about twenty feet up, when the *crack* of wood from below caught my attention. I glanced back, the bare branches allowing just enough moonlight to filter down for me to see, and caught sight of Mitch scrambling up after me.

That right there was my advantage. I could use the branches to move about. At a hundred and thirty-five pounds – most of it muscle, thank you very much – I had a lot of options for footing. Mitch, on the other hand, had to be pushing four hundred if he was an ounce. Far as I could see, he had a choice: either stick to the trunk or figure out how to fly.

I was betting on the former.

Sadly, he wasn't quite as dumb as I'd given him credit for. As he climbed, he swung his heavy paws at any branches within reach, splintering them off and sending them crashing to the ground below. He knew I could play hit and run up here and was doing his best to not only negate that advantage, but try to ensure that if I wanted to come back down I'd need to get past him.

Pity for the dipshit that we were in the middle of the fucking forest. There was no shortage of other trees nearby, which I proved by leaping from one branch over to its next door neighbor.

"This is fun!" I called back. "Might build a treehouse up here. Of course, I'll need a rug. Care to volunteer, asshole?"

Petty, I know. But at this point I was way past my promise to be good. In for a penny, in for a pound.

I heard Mitch snarl from somewhere below, then almost lost my grip as he launched himself at the tree I was currently in, hitting it hard enough to make the whole thing shudder from the impact.

Okay, so much for playing the taunting game. There was no prize for best one-liners in this match. It was either win or lose, and I aimed to win.

Mitch started climbing again, shattering more branches as he went. He was smart to be consistent but dumb in that he gave me an idea.

I headed up once again, wanting to get a bit more height for this to work. Truth of the matter was, I was getting a little nervous. I was far more durable than a regular person, but there was still the question of exactly *how* durable. There was definitely a chance that doing what I had planned might break my legs, or worse. If so, and I didn't take Mitch out, then it would be game over for me.

Wind whipped through the bare branches, biting cold against my naked skin. This was really not my idea of a good time, no matter which way I looked at it. I had to face facts. All of my options sucked, so I might as well go big or go home.

I had to be over thirty feet off the ground by then, maybe more. I dared a glance down and saw Mitch within ten feet of overtaking me. It was now or never.

Come on...

He clubbed a good-sized limb, sending bark and splintered wood flying. I waited for him to be distracted by the debris then did the same thing – he wasn't the only living wood chipper in these trees. I grabbed hold of a branch parallel to the one I stood on, broke it off with a solid *crack*, and flung it toward his ugly mug.

In that same moment, a chorus of howls rose up in the night. I doubted they were rooting for me down below, but that was fine. In any sport you eventually learned to ignore everything but your opponent and the referees. This was no different, minus the ref.

As expected, Mitch swung a club-sized fist and batted the projectile effortlessly aside, again sending a small shower of splinters raining down upon him.

He closed his eyes for the barest of seconds until it passed, but when he opened them again he no doubt realized a second object was hurtling toward him ... me!

I slammed feet first into the mega-wolf, my heels driving into Mitch's shoulders while my back was against the trunk. Despite his size and strength, it wasn't any contest to overcome his grip in the relatively fragile bark and send us both hurtling to the ground below.

Thankfully, I'd timed our collision right, meaning I was on top.

Mitch slammed into the ground with a hearty thud. I

landed on him barely a moment later, my legs – and his stomach – taking the brunt of the impact.

My aching abdomen didn't like that at all and, again, I tasted blood in the back of my mouth. It should have worried me, given me cause to be cautious, but all I could think about was finishing this.

Besides, this wasn't the time to gawk. The fall had knocked the wind out of Mitch, but he wasn't down for the count yet.

I aimed to change that.

Letting loose a snarl of my own, I straddled his chest and nailed him with a right cross that snapped his mammoth head to the side.

Yeah, that was more like it.

I followed up with a left, then another right – each blow connecting on the side of his jaw with a solid *crunch*.

How do you like this, asshole?

Finally, Mitch's eyes rolled into the back of his head, stunned. By then, I was breathing hard from the effort, with bruised knuckles and at least one cracked rib, but at least I wasn't freezing my ass off anymore.

Screw it. I healed quickly. Before the sun rose I'd be good as new. Problem was wolves were fast healers, too. It wouldn't be long before Mitch shook off my attack and tried his luck again.

Despite knowing I'd won this fight, I decided to make sure he got the message loud and clear.

Grabbing the fur beneath his chin with my left hand, I pulled back with my right, fully intent on making sure he ate his kibble through a straw for the next week – assuming I didn't knock his head clean off.

Fuck it. The asshole had it coming.

I gritted my teeth, seeing red, and started to let fly.

Just as my arm began its lethal downward arc, a gravelly voice cried out from behind me.

"*ENUFF!*"

In the same moment, something dragged me off my fallen foe. Lost in the rush of battle, I spun, wanting to see who else needed a lesson. "You want a piece, too...?"

Just as quickly as the words left my mouth, they dried up as I beheld the massive wolf standing over me ... over eight feet tall with salt-and-pepper flecks coloring its black fur.

"Dad?"

~

For a moment, I wasn't sure what to think or say. My brain was still fuzzy from the battle. It was like someone had dipped my head in glue. A part of me wanted to leap back onto Mitch, tear his jaw off and beat him to death with it, but my father held my gaze.

It was only then that I realized we were completely surrounded. Some of the pack was in their human forms, but most weren't. Realization slowly sunk in. I'd just kicked the crap out of their beta. From a sports stand-point, this was the equivalent of pantsing the opposing team's assistant coach in front of his home crowd.

Riots had been started for less.

Undressed as I was, I suddenly felt far more naked than my underwear accounted for.

Problem was, rational thought was slow to seep into my brain. Even had it not been, I didn't know what the proper werewolf etiquette for a situation like this was. Did I apologize, act tough, or stand there and let them tear me to shreds? Either way, I'd lost my head and committed far more than a minor faux pas.

After a few long minutes of this, in which the forest became deathly quiet even to my super keen ears, Dad's face changed, shrinking in on itself to that half-wolf state.

"*Get dressed and wait for me in the car,*" he said, as if I were a child who'd thrown a temper tantrum at the toy store. "*I'll deal with you later.*"

"But..."

In an instant, his face transformed back into that of a monster wolf. "*Now!*"

Go figure. My dad, even in his werewolf form, could still use his parent voice. What a world we lived in.

Needless to say, I scrambled, turning and heading back into the woods, heedless of the direction. It didn't matter. Any wolves standing in my way stepped to the side, parting like the Red Sea before Moses.

Within seconds, I was cloaked in darkness, heading blindly away from the scene of the crime until...

A hand closed upon my arm, almost causing me to cry out.

I turned and found Cass standing there in her human guise.

For a moment, I wasn't sure what she'd say – whether she'd curse me out for what I'd done, or proclaim me a freak that shouldn't exist.

Instead, she hooked a thumb over her shoulder. "You're going the wrong way, silly."

11

I doubt I'll ever enjoy getting dressed again like I did at that moment. I was still cold, don't get me wrong, but having socks and shoes on again ... pure heaven!

Cass likewise got dressed next to me. As she was zipping up her boots, which were seriously cute, by the way – strange the things we focus on when we're stressed – she glanced over at me. "Listen. I didn't want to say anything back there, but thanks for standing up for me."

"Do you think he would've actually hit you?" I asked.

"Probably." But then, just as quickly, she added, "but it's different when we're out here. There's a lot of snarling, biting, and slashing going on. You have to understand, when we're changed, a part of us stays us, but there's a lot of instinct screaming in our heads, too."

"You were human at the time," I replied, letting some bitterness into my voice. "David was, too."

"Don't worry, he'll be okay. We may not be as strong in this form, but we can take a hit. We still heal fast, too. I know it might've looked brutal to an outsider, but it wasn't really all that far out of the ordinary. It's just the way things work in a pack. Authority needs to be constantly reinforced, especially with the young jocks."

"Then why are you thanking me?"

She let out a laugh. "Just because I accept that's the way things are doesn't mean I actually like getting slugged in the mouth. I'm not a masochist."

"I might be. Don't know if you noticed or not, but I kind of lost it there at the end. Didn't mean to. I don't know what came over me."

That was bullshit. It was this place – the hollows – that had come over me, but I wasn't sure this was the right time or company to discuss that with.

"You sure as hell kicked his ass. If I hadn't seen it with my own two eyes, a beta laid out like that..."

"So what happens now?"

She stood up straight and put her coat on. "Let's go. I'll walk you to your car. We can talk on the way."

We started heading back, the woods thinning out as we reached the trail my father and I had taken in. Though I couldn't see much further than the beam of the flashlight I'd retrieved after getting dressed, I kept my ears open and made it a point to breathe through my nose. They were still out there somewhere, although it seemed that, other than the normal woodland creatures scurrying about, they were keeping their distance for the time being.

"Curtis seemed ... pretty angry," Cass said after we'd walked for a bit. "That's not normal."

"He's usually happy when someone kicks the shit out of his lieutenant?"

"No, it's not like that. A pack beta isn't a nepotism thing. It's supposed to be reserved for whoever earns it as the second strongest or most cunning. At least that's how it is on paper."

"Oh?"

"Yeah. I mean, back when Curtis was the beta, we all kinda knew it was because of special circumstances."

"The treaty with the Draío... witches?"

"Exactly. It's a bit before my time, but some of the older wolves like to gossip. He was supposedly a shoe-in for being the next alpha. Most of the pack were all for it. He was the next big thing – one of those once-in-a-generation leaders. But then he stepped aside, and people were confused for the longest time."

"Why?" I asked, realizing this was the story of my parents' marriage, except from the perspective of a third party. I was curious what she had to say on the matter.

"They thought the Draíodóir did it on purpose. According to rumor, they were afraid of Curtis, so they set things up in a way where he couldn't actively be the alpha."

I considered this. "So what's changed now?"

"What do you mean?"

"He still lives in High Moon. The treaty's still in place. Why is he alpha now but he couldn't be back then?"

"That's getting deeper into pack politics than I usually like to, but," she lowered her voice, "and this is just my theory, I think it's you."

"Me?"

"Yeah. No offense, but he defeated you in fair combat. Who in their right mind is going to stand up to that and tell him no?"

I guess she had a point. But I still found it a bit strange. From what I'd heard, before Mom and Dad hooked up, the situation between their people had been near explosive. I might have bought the excuse that things were different now, had the Morganberg pack not tried to gut High Moon earlier this year.

"But anyway, that's neither here nor there," Cass continued. "We were talking about Mitch. Normally, when a ranking pack member is beaten, the higher-ups take a businesslike approach to it. The victor is promoted and the loser gets knocked down a peg on the ladder. If the change is at the top, alpha or beta, there's more to it. The winner is brought before the..."

"Hold on," I interrupted. "So does this mean I'm the new..."

"Don't say it," she said. "I honestly don't know and it's not really a good idea to talk about it here, more so for me than you. The thing is, you're in the pack, but you're..."

"Not one of you?"

She hemmed and hawed on the answer for several seconds before finally admitting, "Yeah. We're in new territory here. Alphas and betas have been beaten by outsiders before, but that's an enemy thing. I don't think I've ever heard it happening for someone who was brought into the pack but never formally turned."

I let out a bitter laugh. "So, in short, nobody knows what to do with me. Story of my life."

We were approaching the minivan. I couldn't see it yet in the darkness, but I caught a whiff of metal and stale exhaust, something I'd never thought to *look* for before. I'd really need to take stock of this scenting thing Cass had told me about. Maybe I could attach a scratch and sniff sticker to the TV remote for the next time Chris lost it, which was pretty often...

That thought trailed off as the sound of footsteps caught my ears – still distant but closing fast, as if in pursuit. Just my luck.

I gingerly touched my side – still tender, but not debilitating. If someone else was looking to even the score, they were liable to get a field goal right between the eyes.

We reached the clearing where the minivan waited unattended. A part of me expected to find it sitting on four flats, making escape impossible, but apparently that was just my paranoia acting up.

What wasn't paranoia, though, were the footsteps now rapidly approaching. They were muffled, not the thud of boots, leaving me to believe that whoever was coming was barefoot, or bare pawed.

Odd that Cass hadn't let on that she'd noticed anything.

Whoever it was, they'd be on us in seconds. I quickly debated my options. Tearing off one of the doors and flinging it at them? Effective, but likely to put me in even worse hot water than I was, especially since that would be a bitch and a half to explain to the insurance adjustor. I pointed my flashlight down and scanned the surrounding area.

There!

A stone, just over a foot in diameter, jutted from the ground a few feet away. I bent down, grabbed it, and yanked it free from the frozen Earth.

Hmm, thirty pounds, maybe forty. Definitely heavy enough to ruin someone's day.

As the crunch of foliage sounded from just outside the clearing, I reared back ready to send it flying.

"Wait!"

Cass stepped in front of me, her arms held out as, behind her, a large shape stepped from the woods.

"Calm down," she said, "it's just..."

The werewolf picked that moment to change.

"David?"

And, of course, he was still bare-ass nude.

No wonder Cass hadn't reacted. She must've recognized his scent from a ways off.

Mind you, that didn't preclude this from being an attack. For all I knew, this was some stupid male honor thing, him being pissed that a girl had saved him.

Cass moved to the side and David approached. As he stepped within range of my light, I saw that the right side of his face was discolored and bruised — no doubt a souvenir from Mitch.

"Um, I hope that's not for me," he said, noticing the big ass rock in my hand.

I was still on guard, but a part of me relaxed a little, especially when I realized the flashlight beam was making his nakedness a lot more obvious. I quickly lowered the light and tossed the rock away. "Sorry. I wasn't sure who was following us. Figured if anyone was looking for trouble then it was a nice night to go bowling for assholes."

He held up his hands. "No trouble here."

"Glad to hear it. Also, glad to see you're okay."

He smiled awkwardly. "Yeah, I heard what you did ... or about five different versions of it. Sorry about that."

"Why are you sorry?"

"I was just joking around. Didn't realize Mitch would take it so seriously."

"I don't think any of us did," Cass replied.

David shook his head. "I should've known better. There's still a lot of bad blood after last summer."

I was tempted to reply that it was on both sides, but that seemed like pouring gasoline onto a lit match. Instead, I replied, "So is that why you're here, to say you're sorry? Or did you come all this way just to see me off?"

I did not just say that. Gah! What a loser I am.

As much as I was hoping for a positive answer to my lame question, he said, "Curtis sent me."

"Oh." I glanced sidelong at Cass, and the look she gave me wasn't exactly reassuring. "Well, hit me with it. What's it going to be? Torture, beatings, a cold flea bath?"

Cass snickered before trying to cover it up as a cough.

David, for his part, didn't appear insulted. Not a bad

thing, all in all. "Nothing like that. He said to tell you to drive home on your own. Keys are in the ignition. He's got some stuff to take care of. Said he'll grab a ride later."

That didn't sound promising. "Did he elaborate on *stuff* at all?"

"Nope." He reached up and touched his bruised cheek. "And I wasn't about to ask, if you get my drift."

"Oh, he would never..." But I let that sentence trail off. Truth of the matter was, I didn't know what my dad would or wouldn't do out here.

Regardless, I'd been given an out. And though I still had questions of my own, it spared me from what was sure to be an unpleasant drive back. My side was still sore, so I'd gladly take a reprieve from any brow beating to add to it. "Okay. Thanks for letting me know."

"Cool." He stood there for an awkward moment, still naked as naked can be. "Well, good seeing you, Tamara."

"You, too." *Especially all the extra bits.*

He turned and started walking away, but then Cass called after him. "Wait up. I'll walk back with you."

David nodded and paused at the edge of the clearing while Cass faced me. "Are you going to be okay?"

"Yeah. I'm a bit weirded out, but nothing I haven't been through before."

"Okay. You good getting out of here?"

"I'll figure it out. And if I get stuck in a ditch, I can always just drag the van out myself."

"Good point." She held out a hand for a moment, but then stepped in and gave me a hug. I found myself returning it, surprised to realize it meant so much coming from someone who was supposed to be an enemy but was perhaps instead a friend in the making.

She stepped away. "Oh, hey. Look me up on Snapchat. I'm Casswolf97."

I smiled. "Subtle."

"More so than sixty-nine," she replied in a low whisper, almost causing me to crack up.

Cass walked to where David waited for her. Once she reached him, he turned and started heading back into the forest. She spared one last glance toward me, pointed at him, and mouthed, "Check out that ass," right before disappearing into the tree line.

～

I gave the minivan a quick circuit before climbing in, making sure nothing was hiding in the back rows. Call me paranoid, but even with all my power, that was one horror movie ambush I didn't ever want to fall prey to. Not sure my heart could stand it.

The keys were, as instructed, still in the ignition. Kind of dumb, but I guess there was a point to be made that nobody was likely to steal a minivan way out here in Werewolf Woods during the longest night of the year.

I glanced at the display as I locked the doors and started the engine. It was late, but not obscenely so.

Riva wasn't exactly a night owl, but I had a feeling she'd be waiting up to see if I checked in or not. I reached into the center console where Dad had forced me to stow my phone before heading into the woods.

As I pulled onto the narrow trail leading out of this place, the hands-free finished connecting and I dialed her number.

She answered on the second ring.

"You're getting slow in your old age," I scolded.

"*Sorry, I was in the bathroom.*"

"TMI."

"*No, TMI would be giving you a play by play.*"

"True enough."

"*So...*" she said cautiously, "*how was your night?*"

"You can relax. It's just me. Dad stayed behind."

"*All right then. Let me have it. How many werewolf asses did you kick and how badly?*"

I gave Riva a rundown of the night's events, switching to the high beams as I navigated the narrow dirt path. It was slow going, but more out of a sense of unfamiliarity and how close the forest was on either side of me.

"*That's it?*" she said a few minutes later. "*No virgin sacrifices or anything fun like that?*"

"Sorry, but you wouldn't have qualified anyway."

"*Not as far as my parents are concerned. They think I'm pure as the driven snow.*"

"Well, since neither of them was there, you're still out of luck."

"*Get back to the part where you kicked that guy's ass while butt-naked.*"

"I wasn't naked. I had my underwear on."

"*Whatever. Probably gave the hairy pervert a thrill.*"

"Yuck."

"*I bet he had a giant wolf stiffy.*"

Gross! Good luck trying to get that image out of my head. "Sorry. I didn't bother to check if he was sporting wood while I was rearranging his ... OHMYGOD!"

I'd looked up from the display just in time to see something dart across the trail right in front of the van.

"*What is it? What's wrong?*"

I ignored her to slam on the brakes. Though I was barely going twenty miles an hour, it seemed to take a small eternity for the minivan to coast to a halt on the loosely packed dirt. "What the hell was that?"

"*What was what?*"

Riva continued to ask what was going on until finally I told her, "Hold on. I almost hit something. I'm gonna get out and check."

To her protests, questioning whether I'd lost my mind,

I put the van in park and climbed out. The trail ahead of me was well-lit by the high beams, but the bushes, mostly evergreens, on either side of the path were thick enough to prevent the light from reaching too far.

Nevertheless, there was nothing to be seen and, I realized a second later, aside from the hum of the idling motor, there were no sounds to be heard either.

I took a deep breath through my nostrils, noting nothing more than the minivan's exhaust mixed with the general scents of the forest. That shouldn't have surprised me. My nose wasn't exactly Animal Planet. It's not like I could tell what something was by smell alone. Even if so, the thing I'd seen had been ... *weird.*

The hairs on the back of my neck stood up so, rather than do something dumb, I got back into the van and locked the door.

Riva's voice was waiting for me. "*Bent? Are you there?*"

"Yeah, I'm back."

"*What happened? Come on, you're killing me here.*"

"Something ran out in front of the van."

"*What was it?*"

"I'm not sure."

"*A werewolf?*"

I shook my head despite nobody being there to see it. "No. Those are kind of hard to miss. This was small, knee high."

"*A rabbit?*"

"No. Not a rabbit either." I let out a sigh, and began scanning the side windows. Suddenly, I wasn't so sure there was nothing around to see me gesturing in the driver's seat. It was probably my nerves acting up, but I had that weird vibe of being watched. "Not unless rabbits walk on two legs."

"*Two legs?*" she asked. "*What did it look like?*"

"I'm not sure. I only saw it for a second. It was small, grey, and then it was gone."

"*So ... a were-rabbit maybe?*"

Yuck! What a creepy concept. "You think you're funny, but you're not."

"*Sorry.*" Riva was silent for a moment, as if thinking. "*It was probably just a raccoon.*"

She was, in all likelihood, right. There was a good chance that spending a night in the hollows, surrounded by monsters, had unnerved me more than I'd realized. At this point I'd be liable to hear a squirrel chittering and mistake it for the gates of Hell opening. What can I say? The hollows had that sort of effect on me. "A raccoon. Yeah. I can buy that."

"*Works for me,*" she replied. "*Now how about you stop talking about it and get the fuck out of there?*"

She didn't have to tell me twice. I put the van into drive and made it a point to nudge it a *bit* higher than twenty.

12

I stopped by Riva's place once I got back into High Moon to find her already outside waiting for me.

I'd started feeling better the second I pulled out of the hollows and onto Crossed Pine Road, and that feeling trebled once I crossed into my home town.

Nevertheless, I wasn't even close to tired. I wanted to talk, and Riva definitely wanted to listen, so I figured it made sense to pop by and grab her for an impromptu sleepover. I wasn't sure what time my father was planning on getting home, but I really wasn't in the mood for a lecture about werewolf etiquette. Considering both my parents thought Riva's memories of all the strange shit going on around our town had been erased, they'd likely tiptoe around the issue until they could get me alone.

By then, with the sun up and maybe half a pot of coffee in me, I would hopefully be in a mood to be yelled at.

I wasn't sure if my mother was either home or awake by this point, so I took the scenic route, as it allowed Riva and I to chat freely ... assuming, of course, Mom wasn't scrying on us. But there wasn't much I could do about that. Hopefully she had enough of a life that spying on me wasn't on her docket twenty-four seven. If not, well, that was just plain sad.

There was another reason for my long circuit around the edge of town. The last time I'd been in the hollows I hadn't returned alone. Hell, an entire freaking army of werewolves had been on my tail.

I sincerely doubted that was the case now, but it made me feel better to indulge that bit of craziness. Besides, it was late and close to Christmas. The traffic at this hour was nearly nonexistent, but the drive was made more pleasant due to the fact that nearly every street was lit up by at least one house that had gone overboard decorating.

"So you actually made friends with a werewolf?" Riva asked, looking out the side window so all I got was a view of her long, black hair when I turned to answer.

"Maybe two."

She glanced back at me, a sly grin on her face. "You mean that guy you saw naked?"

"Technically I saw them both naked."

"Really? Which one would I have liked better?"

I giggled, thinking back to Cass and her perky blonde cheerleader looks. "I think you would've been happy either way."

"Maybe being the meat in a wolf sandwich isn't such a bad thing."

"At least until they get hungry."

"I like to think I could satisfy their cravings."

My chuckle turned into a full-on laugh. "Down, girl."

"Seriously, though, that's cool. Definitely a lot better than all of them wanting to kill you."

"Not all," I said. "Just most. And I think that's still the case for the majority. But they were on their best behavior tonight."

"Sheep in wolves' clothing?"

I nodded. "More like no clothing, but yeah."

"Sounds kinky."

"It might've been if it wasn't so cold."

"That's what body heat is for," she replied.

"You are way too oversexed, sister."

She pushed her seat back and put her feet up onto the dashboard. "I wish. Talk about a dry semester."

"I hear you."

"What about that Justin guy you were telling me about?"

Justin Helferman was a lot of things: my friend back at college, teammate, and a closet nerd who was enamored with the fact that I had super powers. I couldn't claim I hadn't thought about it. Even so... "We're just friends."

"I've heard it said that a guy friend is nothing more than dick under glass ... break in case of emergency."

"Yeah, well, the team has a no fraternization rule, and even though my dating life has been nonexistent, we haven't reached emergency yet."

"Fine. But when you finally do, you need to call and give me all the details."

I turned and looked at her, taking my eyes off the road for a moment. "As if I wouldn't."

"That's my girl!" She held up a hand and I high-fived her. Then she went back to looking out the window. "Ooh, that one's nice."

I dared a glance. One of the houses on this block had outlined all of the trees and bushes in their front yard with Christmas lights. "How the hell do they do that?"

"No idea. Looks like work to me. I barely want to help trimming the tree in our living room."

That always brought a smile to my face. Riva's family was Hindi, but for as long as I could remember, she'd always had a Christmas tree around the holidays. Growing up, I'd thought maybe it was to fit in. High Moon was fairly progressive for rural Pennsylvania, but we had our fair share of assholes ... not that I expected her family to invite anyone like that into their home.

I'd finally gotten bold enough to ask a few years back and it turned out her parents – her dad in particular – just liked it. Diwali, the festival of lights, was only a few weeks earlier, and it gave him a chance to extend some of the bright cheeriness of that holiday into another. Her father was just that kind of guy. All in all, I could think of worse attitudes to have. Speaking of which... "Don't be a Scrooge."

"Bah humbug," Riva replied as I turned the corner.

"Huh," I muttered as we passed by a house I recognized, a For Sale sign on the front lawn. "Did the Crendels move out?"

"More like bugged out," she said. "They just packed up and left. Didn't I tell you?"

"No."

"Yeah, it wasn't long after..."

"Wolfageddon?"

She nodded.

That was strange. Of all the people affected by the attack on High Moon, the Crendels had been pretty much left untouched. I knew because Riva and her parents had sought refuge with their family. The Crendels had been preppers, complete with a bomb shelter out back. Though their son could be a bit of a creep, it had been a small price to pay for having a nearly impenetrable fortress to stash my best friend in while I dealt with the murderous wolves rampaging through town.

I turned to her. "Want to go check out their shelter for old time's sake?"

Riva rolled her eyes at me. "No thanks. You might've had your hands full with monsters, but at least you didn't have Bobby Crendel trying to put the moves on you all night."

I burst out laughing again. "I'm so sorry to hear of your suffering."

"Next time that happens, I'm staying by your side."

Next time. That wasn't a thought I really wanted to entertain. But it was always a possibility, especially now that my parents knew my pills were off the table going forward.

However, it was also a concern for another day, as it seemed all was quiet in High Moon this evening.

It was time to head back home and see what else fate had in store for me.

Turns out fate was in the mood to take the rest of the night off. The house was empty when we got back. Dad must've still been out playing werewolf. But neither my mother nor Chris was around either. I guess that wasn't too surprising. I didn't know much about Mom's culture, but she'd mentioned something about being busy tonight, too. Besides, according to the movies, the winter solstice was a good time to cavort in the woods, conjure demons, and do other witchy stuff.

As for Chris, he was technically old enough to leave home by himself, but he was also a dipshit teenager. I doubted my parents were keen on the concept of letting him watch over the house. Hell, I was sixteen before they trusted me enough and I was a good kid ... depending on who you asked, anyway.

Nevertheless, nobody was waiting for us when we got to my place outside of maybe Mom's army of creepy garden gnomes – made infinitely creepier thanks to the bushes they normally guarded being dead from the winter frost. In a sense they were more like graveyard gnomes right now, which was an even less appealing concept.

I really need to smash those fucking things one of these days.

Thankfully they kept a silent, unmoving – thank God – vigil on the front lawn as we went in and made ourselves comfortable.

The next morning I awoke to find Riva gone and voices coming from downstairs. I eventually pulled myself out of bed to find her and my mother in the kitchen. As far as I could tell they were talking about inane holiday plans and other overly cheery stuff.

Fucking morning people.

Mom looked up as I stepped over to the Keurig seeking caffeinated sustenance. "Good morning, sunshine. I was just telling Riva of our plans for Christmas. I didn't realize she was staying over last night."

I shrugged. "Dad had some stuff to take care of when our ... shopping trip was finished. I was bored and she was free."

Riva stifled a grin at my awkward cover story but played along. "I'm so glad I exist solely to amuse you."

"You should be honored. You're in the presence of royalty."

Mom narrowed her eyes, no doubt at my not so subtle dig toward her stupid witch title, but said nothing. It was kind of surreal. Secrets all around the table, if you will. It made for a decisively awkward moment.

Hell, if I wasn't certain Mom wouldn't immediately try to melt Riva's brain, I'd have been tempted to just tell her that last summer's memory wipe hadn't taken hold so we could all stop beating around the bush.

Instead, we chatted about mostly nothing for a few minutes, which at least allowed me time to properly wake up. "Is Dad back yet?"

"No. He must've gotten called in early to work."

Yeah, right. "What about you and Chris? What time did you guys roll in?"

I was trolling Mom and she knew it based on the look on her face. Boo fucking hoo. After twenty years of lying about who I was, the least she could do was tolerate some forced improv.

"Early. We spent the night at Carly's."

I was tempted to ask if my brother had slept in a bed or had spent the evening locked in a closet under a spell-induced trance, but figured that might be pushing my luck.

Mom got up to rinse out her cup. "Riva, dear, do you need a ride home?"

My friend used the opportunity to lip sync, asking if I was going to be okay. Or at least I assumed that was the case. Lip reading wasn't my specialty. I nodded in the affirmative. In the daylight, things seemed a lot less intimidating. I was also fresh and healed up. Whatever injuries I'd sustained during my fight with Mitch appeared to be gone with nary a bruise to show for it.

"That's okay, Mrs. Bentley. My dad has some errands to run this morning. I'll give him a call and he can pick me up."

"If you're sure," Mom replied before turning back to the sink.

Riva glanced my way as if to double check and I nodded again.

With Dad still out, I wasn't sure if there was even much to discuss, but either way, it was time to get my day started.

Fifteen minutes later, I said my goodbyes to Riva, telling her I'd call her if anything *interesting* happened.

We really needed to do something about the status quo between her and my parents, but I'd already dropped one bombshell on them and hadn't even been home twenty-four hours yet. Maybe this next one could wait until at least Christmas had passed. Hopefully by then everyone would be in a jolly enough mood to not lose their shit.

"I assume your father had pack business to attend to," Mom said once we were alone again.

Rather than answer, I glanced toward the stairs leading down to Chris's room. "Are you sure it's..."

"It's fine. I doubt we'll see your brother any time before ten. He had a long night."

"Where were you guys?"

"Over in Crescentwood at your aunt's, just like I said ... for a while anyway. She's a mess. But I also had a ceremony to preside over, as well as some items of interest to take care of."

"Items of interest? So, witch stuff?"

"*Witch stuff* is both a gross oversimplification as well as somewhat insulting, Tamara."

"Uh huh. Like I said, witch stuff." I sat on the couch. "Anything good?"

"Nothing you need to worry about."

"Ooh, that means it *is* good."

Mom sighed, obviously coming to the conclusion that she needed to throw me a bone if she wanted to get on with her day. "I received a couple reports of dark rituals in the woods."

"Dark rituals?"

"Summoning circles, that sort of thing."

I leaned forward. "Sounds kinda serious."

She actually laughed in return. "Quite the opposite, really."

"So ... conjuring Satan isn't a big deal?"

"I'm not talking Ouija boards or any of that nonsense. These are complex incantations meant to commune with creatures from outside our world."

"Still sounds like a pretty big deal."

"It might be," she said, "if it didn't happen all the time. I'm serious. It's always the same thing. Some teenager thinks they know more than they do. They decide to impress their girlfriend or boyfriend and then botch it up because they're too busy trying to look cool."

"But..."

"Even if that's not the case, I meant it when I said these things are complex. We're talking advanced magic. It's not like assembling an IKEA bookshelf."

"You're sure?"

"Trust me, I get at least a handful of reports like this on every solstice and equinox."

I shrugged. She probably had a point. For someone

like me, this was all new. But for anyone in the know, it probably wasn't even a blip on their radar.

Changing the subject, I asked, "So where was Chris while you were off combing the woods for wannabe Slytherins? Did you melt his brain into an even bigger puddle of goo than it usually is?"

Mom glared at me. "Contrary to what you might believe, we don't use magic to solve every problem and I don't relish using it on my own family. He stayed at Gavin's."

"You just left him there?"

She waved off my concern. "He turned his basement into a man cave last year, with pretty much every video game console ever made. Believe me, your brother didn't even notice I was gone."

She probably had a point there. Slap a big screen TV and an Xbox in front of my brother and you could burn the house down around him.

"Oh, about what Riva and I were discussing..."

"Have you heard from Dad?" I interrupted. If he was pissed at me, she would be the first person he told.

"No. I try not to bother him on nights when he's with the pack."

Or maybe she wouldn't be.

"Okay. So aren't you going to ask me what happened?"

"No," she replied. "I neither want to know, nor think it would be wise to ask."

"But..."

"I trust your father to take care of you and likewise trust him to make the right choices. But the simple fact remains that, outside of this house, we have divided loyalties. It would be unwise for him to let me know too much, as it would be unwise for me to let your father know the detailed goings-on in my coven. More importantly, doing so would violate the treaty we both signed."

"You mean the treaty you guys came up with so you could have a fake marriage to cover up the real marriage you have going on?"

"Don't be a snot. Your father and I did what was needed to be together. But just because we took a few liberties doesn't mean we don't respect the overall terms of the treaty."

Wow. I'm pretty sure a poli-sci class would have a field day with that logic. "Okay, but I'm not a part of..."

"Yes you are. At least you are now. Sort of, anyway."

"Way to be clear about things, Mom."

She narrowed her eyes at me, obviously not pleased that I was exercising my adult right to mouth off. But rather than take me to task for having an attitude, she instead took a deep breath as if to collect her thoughts. "I doubt this will come as any surprise to you after everything that's happened, but you're an unknown, Tamara. The treaty didn't take you into account because we never intended for you to be a part of this world. So, you see, while technically becoming a member of your father's pack does include you..."

"I'm not one of them."

"Not entirely. And the treaty was specifically worded to give gravitas to each races' ... personal conceits. Mentions are made of the summer court, Queen Brigid, the children of Valdemar, all of that. It's meant to establish and acknowledge both our peoples' unique heritage, as well as draw clear distinctions between them."

I began to see what she was talking about. "But I straddle those lines."

She nodded, a small smile on her lips. "From a purely modern viewpoint, one can argue that your abilities are a result of the mixing of our genetics. But, though I doubt either race would wish to acknowledge it, from a classical stance you are a marvel ... descended from not one, but two higher powers. If it weren't for our peoples' mutual dislike and distrust of one another, you would likely be revered. But instead..."

"They want me dead because each side thinks I pollute their precious bloodline."

"To put it mildly. Or would want you dead if they knew, which my people do not. That's a status quo I intend to maintain, which brings me to my next point."

I leaned forward, not sure what to expect.

"There's been a change of plans for the holidays."

Talk about changing the subject. "There has?"

"Yes. We – and by *we* I mean *all* of us, your father included – will be spending Christmas in Crescentwood with my family."

$$\sim$$

I tried to remember back to past holidays. Now that I actually thought it through, a lot of them had been spent here at home. Sure, we'd visit relatives over in Morganberg or Crescentwood, but I realized it had been rare for either Mom or Dad to cross into respective enemy territory. And when it did happen, it was usually short and somewhere public.

Whenever we'd spent time at a relative's home, one of my parents would almost always be conveniently sick or busy. Headaches, emergency business meetings, all sorts of bullshit that me and my brother never thought to question. And why would we have? It was simply a part of our life. There was nothing strange about it ... until you stepped back and really looked at the situation.

Talk about hiding in plain sight. I mean, sure, there were the occasional digs. My father's family was pretty blatant in their dislike of Mom. As for her side, Dad was basically *persona non grata* to them. The less said the better.

I, and later on Chris, just always assumed it was normal family squabbling – never once suspecting that if we'd ever tried to arrange a big Thanksgiving get-together that it would have likely turned into a bloodbath.

Strange how much perspective a little insight could give. A part of me envied Chris's ignorance, even if he was spared the bullshit pills I'd been forced to take for the better part of two decades.

Yeah, I was still a wee bit bitter about that. A part of me probably always would be. But right at that moment my pills were far from being a concern, or so I assumed.

"Wait. All of us in Crescentwood? Dad, too?"

"That's what I just said, Tamara," Mom replied. "I swear, for a descendent of your father's line, sometimes I worry about your hearing."

It's a good thing I wasn't drinking anything, because I'd have likely choked at that moment. Heh. My parents weren't the only ones who could keep secrets. And with Mom constantly trying to scry me, or whatever she called it, I'd become a little protective about my privacy. "But how, or why? Isn't that ... a bit unwise?"

"The hows are somewhat complex."

"Oh? What about the whys?"

Mom looked away for a moment, a sheepish smile on her face ... rare for her. Usually she was the composed one. "Fine. I'm worried about Carly. She's really depressed about the breakup and I didn't want her to be alone for the holidays."

That ... was actually a nice answer. I'd figured there was something darker at play but – despite my mother's grandiose talk – she was just a woman worried about her little sister. It was kind of sweet.

That still didn't explain Dad, though.

She apparently sensed my unspoken question, because she continued. "Your father doesn't know yet, but I'll talk to him. In my role as Queen of the Monarchs I have been, little by little, putting forth the idea that, with Craig out of the picture, a new dawn is on the horizon. You see, your uncle had a rather ... tempestuous relationship with me and the rest of the Draíodóir court."

"You don't say."

"Preaching to the choir, I know," she replied with a grin. "But ever since you were born, your father has made it a point to be diplomatic wherever possible. Oh, don't get me wrong, there have been spats here and there. Your father isn't one to roll over and play dead."

I chuckled despite myself.

"But," she continued, "his relationship with my family has been sedate enough that I put forth the idea that perhaps it might be a step in the right direction were we to offer an olive branch to the new Morganberg Alpha."

That was actually kind of cool to hear. The way they'd explained it to me last time I was home, it sounded like – aside from them – the chances of witches and werewolves playing nice together was pretty much nil. Perhaps they'd had a change of heart since then.

There was just one catch I could see. "Awesome as that sounds, it's not like you can discuss politics with me and Chris there ... or Chris anyway. Unless, that is, you're planning on giving him a big box of the truth for Christmas."

"Not likely," Mom said with a shake of her head. "Chris is a mundane and we'd prefer for his life to remain normal. There's also the fact that I'm not entirely confident in his ability to remain coy about our existence."

That was a potential understatement right there. "So then how..."

"Christmas itself will be at your aunt's place. It's my family's ancestral home, where she and I were both raised. However, it'll merely be a neutral family affair – presents, mistletoe, a roaring fire, that sort of thing."

"Just a normal holiday celebration? Nothing more?"

She flashed me a conspiratorial grin. "Maybe you got a bit more from my side than I suspected. Very well. It will also be to test the waters. With you and Chris there, neither side will be able to bring up our true grievances with each other. You two will be the buffer. It'll be a chance to explore if our two people can act cordially in an extended setting. If all goes well, then formal peace talks will happen in subsequent days."

"Oh, then maybe I can sit in and..."

"During which you'll be home babysitting your brother while we conduct business."

Fuck!

Oh well, that wasn't exactly a fate worse than death. Chris would most likely be sequestered in his personal dungeon, jerking off to whatever new games my parents got for him. And if it would help dull the Sword of Damocles hanging over High Moon's head, it would be more than worth it to be cooped up for a few days. "Okay. I can live with that. I'll help however I can."

"I'm glad to hear that, Tamara, because I do have one important ask of you for Christmas day itself."

"What do you want me to do?"

"I need you to be back on your pills."

What?!

14

What followed was the end of our civil discussion and the beginning of a slow burn of anger from my end.

How dare she? After everything that had happened. After what I'd told them. After deciding to take control of my own life, she was asking me to go back to living a lie?

Needless to say, my off-the-cuff reaction wasn't particularly positive.

"Keep your voice down, please," Mom said. "If you wake your brother..."

That's what she was worried about? Goddamn. She'd mentioned conceit before, but she really had no clue. "Don't tell me to calm down. This is not a subject where you get to do that."

"I understand your ... reluctance, but this needs to happen. The Draíodóir are still not aware of your existence. Nothing has changed about that, which means their likely response hasn't changed. That's not even taking the Morganberg pack into consideration. If my people learn you've aligned yourself with them, it could be disastrous."

"I haven't aligned myself with anyone."

"Semantics," Mom replied. "You're a member of the pack. Willingly or not, that's all that matters."

"I don't see how they'll even know. Unless you're telling me they'll be able to sniff me out like the were-wolves can."

Mom shook her head. "No. Our senses are within human tolerances, unless we magically enhance them."

"Okay, then we just need to make sure nobody..."

"It's not that simple, Tamara. Despite my assurances, the Draíodóir will not open their territory to the lycan-thropes without safeguards. Thresholds will be warded against any weaponry, and I guarantee the magic used will be serious."

"I won't be carrying any weapons."

"You *are* a weapon."

She sorta had a point there. "So are the wolves. And besides, I thought I was resistant to any zappy magic you guys could conjure."

"That's exactly the problem. Even if you don't set anything off, you could very well appear as a magical null when you cross those wards. If anyone notices, there will be no explaining your way out of it."

"Then I'll stay home."

"I already told you, we need you and Chris as a buffer. Your presence will ensure that everyone plays nice. No one will risk exposing themselves in front of you. It would be ... bad form."

"Bad form?"

"You may not realize it, but appearance and decorum mean a lot to both our races. Breaking covenant for nothing more than petty quibbling would mean a loss of face for the offending side. And before you say it, since you and your brother are connected to both of us, neither side will risk our wrath by harming you."

"Oh yeah, us poor adopted waifs," I replied, throwing another of my parents' lies back in her face.

"You're being selfish and unreasonable, Tamara."

"*I'm* being selfish? You're the one asking me to pretend to be someone I'm not."

"Yes," she replied adamantly. "If it means a tentative peace for both sides, a chance for us to relax our guard after centuries of tension, then that's exactly what I'm doing. I'm asking for one day out of your life to help make that happen."

I dropped my gaze and looked away. Though I hated to admit it, she was right. It was just one day. Worst case was it didn't work out. But if it did ... maybe, just maybe, it could allow my parents to stop living a lie and acknowledge that they loved each other.

Wasn't that worth it?

I remembered back to the previous night, Cass telling me about the alpha female. My parents had both seemed resolute on not wanting to know the other's business when it came to their respective clans, but this seemed like something that should be discussed. Dad's new attitude as the pack alpha already had me a bit worried, yet I had a feeling Mom would stuff her fingers in her ears and make la la la noises if I tried to bring it up.

But that might not be the case if these peace talks were successful.

The thing was, if I went with my first reaction and told Mom to cram it, then this whole plan could potentially collapse. We'd be right back to the secrets. I wasn't sure I wanted to risk pushing my parents apart, all because I couldn't suck up being normal Tamara Bentley for a few hours.

Mom must've seen the crack in my resolve because she picked that moment to shove a wedge into it. "Did I mention that your aunt is really down in the dumps? This isn't just some cold war summit. It's also Christmas and she specifically asked about you."

"She did?"

"Yes. She said how much she was looking forward to seeing you."

That cemented it. I'd always gotten along with Carly. She was the cool aunt. Whereas Mom could be cold and stuffy at times, her sister was always chill. She was the type to hand me a beer back when I was in high school and tell me it was our secret.

Did I really want to turn my back on her now, when she was in pain from her breakup? And all because I didn't want to play pretend for one measly day.

When I finally looked up again, triumph gleamed in my mother's eyes. She knew she'd won, but I had to say it to make it official. "Fine. But one day only."

"One day," she repeated.

"I'm serious. If you want to go back there for New Years, you're on your own. You're not dragging me along as some distraction."

"For who?" my brother called from the hallway. "Guys who like trashy women? Don't worry. I think Mom's safe."

"You little shit...'

"Language, Tamara."

And just like that, the real conversation was over and I found my fate for the holidays sealed.

Snow started to fall a bit later that morning and, in typical Pennsylvania style, it wasn't long before it began to stick and turn everything white. Cold as I'd been the night before, at least the weather had been clear. Getting my ass kicked while half naked was bad enough. Snow would have only added an extra touch of "fuck you" to it all.

But that was in the past, at least until a big ole four-by-four pickup pulled into the driveway. My father hopped out, thanked the driver, and walked up to the porch.

I was there to greet him at the door, curious as to what had gone on after I'd messed things up. I can't say I was looking forward to being yelled at, but at the same time the anticipation was eating at me. Better to rip that bandage off quickly.

However, before Dad was able to get much more than a "Hi, sweetie," out of his mouth, Mom stepped in.

"Tamara, your brother wants to go sledding with his friends over at Swallowtail Park."

"So?"

"So, I want you to go with him."

"He's twelve. He and his loser friends can take care of themselves. We need to talk about Christmas at..."

Mom's eyes narrowed. "It's coming down pretty heavy and I would prefer an adult be there to supervise."

"What about Christmas?" Dad asked, sounding confused.

"We'll talk about that in a moment," Mom replied sweetly, no doubt trying to butter him up a bit first. "I'll meet you upstairs."

Upstairs? "Oh, gross! You two aren't going to..."

"We have things to discuss," she said, her voice and eyes both filled with steel. "And you, young lady, have a brother to look after."

~

"Can I ask you a question?"

I couldn't say I looked down at my younger brother to answer. He was getting too tall for that. But, seeing him there in his ski coat and goggles, carrying his snowboard and trying to look far cooler than he was, I replied, "Yes. You will likely die a virgin."

"Better than giving out discount blowjobs at truck stops," he replied, making sure to stay out of my reach. "What I meant was, did Mom and Dad just kick us out to have a quickie?"

"Ugh! Shouldn't you be asking me about Pokémon or something lame like that?"

He brayed that annoying guffaw of his. "Jealous that someone in the house is actually getting some?"

I turned and gave the not-so-little jerk a shove, knocking him into a pile of the rapidly accumulating snow. "It sure as shit ain't you. Unless we're talking about your right hand."

He got up, dusted himself off, and actually laughed. Odd. Usually he'd keep sniping until I was forced to put the hurt on him. "Just for the record, I hope they are."

"Gross!"

"Seriously," he replied, looking like some sort of giant, dorky insect with his reflective ski goggles staring back at me. "I think they need it."

"Why do you say that?"

"While you've been off skanking up college, they've been acting a bit strange. Remember what we talked about before..."

"Yes, I remember, and no, I don't think they're getting a divorce. They love each other. Things have just been weird."

"How so?"

Hmm, yeah, I'd kind of backed myself into a corner with that one. I guess I could have grabbed the nearest mailbox and folded it into origami to show him what I really meant, but I had a feeling that would've gotten me another talking to. "Things are ... y'know ... changing. It's scary for them. I'm away at college. They're getting older. And everyone is worried that no zoo will take you after they're gone."

In response, he grabbed a handful of snow and prepared to chuck it at my face. Too bad for him I'd seen that trick before. I stepped in to block his arm before he could...

What the?

I spied movement in the reflection from his goggles ... something near the bushes behind me, small and quick moving.

Curious to see what it was, I spun around. *There!* I caught the briefest glimpse of something disappearing into the...

Whap!

Cold wetness hit the back of my head and a small bit of icy slush slipped down my coat and onto my neck.

"You fucking little dweeb," I cried, turning and glaring at the asshole grin plastered on Chris's face.

"Never turn your back on the enemy."

"Dickhead." I glanced back over my shoulder. There was, of course, nothing to see there now. "Damnit, where'd it go?"

"What?"

"There was something over there in those bushes."

"Probably one of your former boyfriends hiding from you."

"I'm serious."

"Jeez, chill, Tamara. It was probably just a squirrel or..."

"Raccoon?"

"Yeah."

He was probably right. Maybe my imagination was still working overtime from the night before. Coupled with the knowledge that I'd be saying hi to the old me again in a few days, it was probably stressing me out more than I wanted to admit.

Maybe it was time to let off some steam.

I bent down, scooped up some snow, and packed it tightly in my gloves. My ears didn't need to be supersensitive to hear the sound of my brother running away as I straightened up.

"Get back here!" I yelled with a grin. "I have an early Christmas present for you."

We were both soaked by the time we got home. We met up with some of Chris's friends at Swallowtail Park, who proceeded to join his side in our snowball war. Pity for them I had better aim and a much stronger arm.

After pelting the snot out of each other for about fifteen minutes, they got bored and decided to embarrass themselves on their snowboards. It gave me a chance to stand there and shiver while I waited for the geek squad to tire themselves out.

Still, I was forced to admit I was in a much better mood by the time we got back.

Mom and Dad were waiting for us in the living room. I couldn't help but notice they were wearing different clothes than when we'd left ... which of course gave my brain additional horrors to process.

However, that was apparently the only issue on my radar for the rest of the day.

According to Mom, our Christmas plans were set. And then later, when I managed to get Dad alone for a few minutes, he told me not to worry about the previous night. That we'd discuss it another time.

I was tempted to press the matter, but realized I was most likely being let off easy.

Rather than tempt fate, I decided to accept it for what it was – a Christmas miracle – and try to make the most of the next few days before I was forced to once again become someone I wasn't.

15

"Merry Christmas to me," I muttered, looking down at the yellow pills in my hand.

"Is everything all right?" Mom stepped into the kitchen and saw me standing by the sink. "I hope we didn't disappoint."

I turned and smiled. "The iPad is great, thanks."

"Just remember, it's for school, not messing around."

"But the camera app has all sorts of cool filters for nude selfies." Seeing the look on her face, I grinned. "Relax. I'm kidding."

"I figured, but it's good to hear you say it anyway."

Looking down again, I lowered my voice and became serious. "Promise me I'll never have to see these things again."

Mom stepped up and put a hand on my shoulder. "I wish I could. But I can't foresee the future."

"Some witch you are."

She chuckled. "I'm good, but not that good. All I can offer you is my thanks. I know you're not ... entirely happy doing this."

I opened my mouth to say something, but instead

popped the pills in and swallowed before I could think better of it. After washing them down with some water, I turned back toward her. "If you can make the peace work, maybe reach a point where you and Dad can show how you really feel about each other, then it'll be worth it."

Mom smiled. "I'll do my best, but one step at a time. Sometimes a single stone can change the course of a raging river. Speaking of which. Here." She pulled a small gift-wrapped box from behind her back and handed it to me. "A little extra thank you from your mother."

"What is it?"

"Typically there's one way to find out," she said with an exaggerated eye roll.

"Oh, yeah." I proceeded to rip open the packaging, then opened the velvet box it contained. Inside sat a stunning bejeweled pendant in the shape of a monarch butterfly. I stared at it for several seconds, taking in its exquisite details. "It's gorgeous."

"I thought you'd like it. Those orange stones are amber and the black is obsidian."

"Does this mean I'm officially the princess of monarchs?"

"Like I said, baby steps," she replied with a shrug. "But that doesn't mean it isn't special. Think of it as a little something extra for when you're back at school."

"Back at school?"

"Or are you going to try telling me that all those calls asking about monsters were for actual term papers?"

I laughed. "You wouldn't believe the craziness I've had to deal with."

She held up a hand. "I would believe it, but I don't want to know. Ignorance is perhaps bliss in this case. Knowing too much is potentially risky. Not to mention, you're my little girl and I'd be porting myself over there far too often if I knew more. This is my way of helping without crossing that line."

I lifted the pendant from the box to take a better look, noting that the chain felt warm to the touch.

"Platinum," Mom explained. "Mostly."

"Mostly?"

She grinned, leading me to think I was holding something likely to blow a metallurgist's mind.

Wow. I wasn't sure whether it was the Christmas spirit invading her personal space or if she'd simply come to terms with the fact that I had my own life. But either way, it was a far cry from how she'd treated me this past summer.

I leaned in and gave her a big hug before the moment could pass. "So, care to show me how it works?"

"We can go over that another time. There's still plenty of winter break left. Go put it away in your room for now."

"Away? I figured I'd wear it today."

Mom's eyes opened wide for a moment. "Absolutely not. Not where we're going. Trust me, you don't want to walk in and be accused of radiating magic, especially since you're not even supposed to know it's real."

That sucked. It really was pretty, but I guess it was more for fall colors than what I was wearing.

I brought the pendant upstairs and put it away in the top drawer of my bureau where I stored knickknacks like that. The closest I'd ever come to owning a jewelry box had been an old Tupperware bin filled with ring pops I used to keep hidden under my bed.

Peering into the drawer, I gave it one last glance. I couldn't wait to show it off to Riva, although perhaps it might be best to wait until Mom told me what it actually did. Accidentally disintegrating my best friend would be a real holiday downer.

The first wave of nausea hit me just as I stepped away from the dresser – a side effect of my pills, always remembered but never missed.

Here it comes.

I lay down on my bed as my stomach clenched and a heaviness began to set into my muscles.

A part of me had hoped to never again have to go through this, but I understood the reasons why I had to. This time it really was for a good cause.

Although maybe I should ask them to try developing a new pill that doesn't make me want to hurl.

That would have to be a discussion for later, though. For now, I waited for my strength to drain away, all while doing my best to not puke my guts out.

When I finally came back downstairs, Chris and Dad were packing presents into the minivan, as if our destination was nothing more than a regular holiday get-together.

The thing was, so far as I was supposed to know, it *was* just a mundane party with eggnog, gifts, and lots of banal small talk. I smirked at the back of my brother's head. Poor dweeb. He was the only one not in the know. If he had any clue what he was getting into he'd probably piss himself ... which made it all the more tempting to tell him.

Sadly, at the moment I was a little short on party tricks to convince him with.

"Hey, honey," Dad said, stepping in for another bundle of gifts. "How are you feeling?"

"Disturbingly normal," I replied.

"Normal?" Chris asked with a guffaw. "That's a first. But if it helps, you look just as bad as you usually do."

Before I could rearrange his face, just like a *normal* big

sister would, Dad stepped in. "If you have time to talk, champ, then that means you're not carrying stuff to the car fast enough."

Once Chris stepped out the door again, I turned to my father. "How about you?"

"A bit ... tense," he replied. "But cautiously optimistic. This is new ground. But if it works, it'll be worth an uncomfortable afternoon."

"And if it doesn't?" I really hadn't meant to put it out there as bluntly as I had. The truth was, my father was essentially crossing enemy lines. Big and bad as he was, he would be surrounded by the Draío ... gah! I really needed to see if they offered Gaelic as an elective at school. Anyway, Dad was going to be vastly outnumbered. If things went south, well, I'd seen what my mother had once done to a roomful of werewolves. She was terrifying by herself. I could only imagine a house full of people like her.

Dad looked down at the floor for a moment before locking eyes with me, resolve on his face. "I trust your mother."

"And she trusts you," I said, suddenly remembering that alpha female again. Though I'd kept it to myself, in light of everything going on, it still bugged me. But now was not the time to bring it up. Tensions were already high due to this preemptive peace party. Any questions – or accusations – could wait until things had once again died down to a dull roar.

"I know," he replied just as my brother stepped in the door again. "All set, champ?"

"That's it," Chris said. "The only thing left to stuff in the back is Tamara's fat..."

"Can we please be nice for one day out of the year?" Mom asked, her voice floating down the stairs to us.

I looked up and saw she'd changed her clothes. She

was wearing what would, in other households, be called her Sunday best, a stark contrast to the ugly Christmas sweater my father wore. However, the illusion was somewhat dispelled by the Santa hat perched crookedly on her head. They really were going all in with the illusion that this was nothing more than Christmas dinner.

Still, much as I was looking forward to seeing Aunt Carly and some of my other relatives, knowing what was actually happening put a slight damper on my enjoyment. Besides, the sooner this party ended, the sooner my pills would wear off so I could get back to being me. Twelve hours and counting.

Perhaps it was selfish, but I'd only recently begun to feel truly whole. There'd been a part of me that had been locked away – one that I hadn't even been aware I was missing until I'd discovered the truth less than half a year ago. Regardless, the me standing in my living room right at that moment was an illusion, a ghost ... a half-finished puzzle.

As normal as I felt physically, deep in my mind I knew this would never feel normal again. It was like wearing a full-body straight jacket, one that I couldn't wait to take off.

But a promise was a promise. I'd already disappointed Dad once by letting Mitch goad me. I didn't intend on doing it again, especially in a situation that was potentially far more explosive. I could suck it up for one day. "All right, are we ready to head out?"

"Not yet," Mom replied. "We're still waiting for our company."

"Company?' Chris and I simultaneously blurted.

"I thought we were the company," I said.

"We are," she explained. "But..."

"It's been a rough year at the old homestead," Dad said, "what with Craig's passing. Your mother's family was good enough to open their doors, so I extended the invitation."

He did?

Dad's expression was neutral and, with Chris in the room, there was no way to ask him what was really up. Nevertheless, I couldn't help but think this had little to do with my not-so-dearly departed uncle.

"Speak of the devil," Mom replied, her choice of words likely deliberate. "Looks like they're here."

A pickup pulled up beside the minivan in the driveway.

Though I was both surprised and a bit disturbed to see others from Dad's pack in High Moon again, I probably shouldn't have been. Asking him to go in there alone with no allies was kind of unfair. This way he at least had his own mini-delegation to...

That train of thought derailed almost instantly as I saw the driver's side door of the pickup open and Mitch step out.

For God's sake! Why him?

Mind you, logically it made perfect sense. If the high-muckety mucks of magic were going to be present, shouldn't one of Dad's higher-ups also be there? Of course, that made his cover story sound a bit less likely since I couldn't recall his cousin ever being super tight with us. But whatever. It wasn't like they needed to fool anyone except...

Mitch wasn't alone, however. A slim, blonde figure stepped around the side of the truck and joined him.

Cass?

She didn't look at all happy to be here.

That made two of us.

16

This made no sense at all. Mitch was the beta of the pack. He had a say in the hierarchy of things. But Cass?

She was just a normal werewolf. So far as she'd told me, she neither had a place of power in the pack, nor wanted one. Had she lied about that?

I glanced at my father who was standing by the door. One of his eyebrows was raised slightly, his only tell, but it was enough to let me in on the fact that he found this odd as well.

However, that was the extent of the surprise he showed. Once Mitch reached the front door, Dad extended a hand to him. "Merry Christmas, man."

"Merry Christmas, Curtis." Mitch turned and gestured to Cass. "You remember my niece Ester, right? She's visiting, so I asked if she'd like to come along. I hope I didn't overstep."

"Not at all," Dad replied, moving aside to let them in. "You're welcome to join us, Ester. Merry Christmas."

We all knew Mitch from previous gatherings ... including ones well before I'd been forced to punch his stupid lights out. Cass was new to the rest of my family, however. Dad began introducing her to everyone, albeit using her given name.

Before I could say anything, Chris muscled past me and held his hand out to her. From the goofy look on his pimpled face, it was safe to assume he'd noticed she was a pretty girl and was swooping in like a lame-o moth to a flame. "I'm Christopher."

"Hi," she replied in a friendly, but not *that* friendly, way. "I'm Ester, but my friends call me Cass."

I stepped between them. "That means you can call her Ester." I turned to her and smiled. "Don't mind him. He's pure as the driven snow and three times as desperate."

"Tamara!" Mom snapped.

By then, however, I'd stepped in and given Cass a hug, which Mom thankfully didn't question. That was good, because I didn't feel like making up some bullshit story. Fortunately, High Moon and Morganberg were both close and small enough that it wasn't considered odd for folks in one to be tight with people in the other.

When Cass stepped back, though, I saw a confused look on her face. Then I noticed her nose working over-time. *Shit!* I'd forgotten that the pills changed my scent in addition to depowering me.

From the look on Mitch's face, he'd noticed it, too. Just what I needed – a pissed off beta wolf with a grudge and me with no way to defend myself.

Merry fucking Christmas indeed.

I gave Cass a subtle shake of my head before turning to my father. "Hey, Dad. Can you help me with something upstairs?"

"Now? We're getting ready to leave."

"It'll just take a second."

Fortunately, he seemed to notice the concern etched onto my face.

"It's okay, dear," Mom said. "I'll entertain our guests while you take care of it."

A part of me rued Chris's presence, because otherwise I had a feeling Mom's *entertainment* would consist of telling Mitch just how badly she could flash fry him if she wanted to. Oh well, I'd just have to imagine it.

I headed upstairs to my room with my father in tow and shut the door behind us.

"I know what you're thinking, honey," he said in a low voice. "But he's under oath to not say a word about you. And believe me, he won't break that."

"A heads up might've been nice."

He shrugged. Part of it was apologetic, but – if I was reading him right – the rest was a mix of telling me that he was both my parent and the alpha. In short, he was under no obligation to tell me jack shit. Fine. I could deal with Mitch for the day, so long as he didn't try to finish what he'd started.

"Okay, so why is Cass here then?"

Dad's face went blank and I knew the answer a second before he said it. "I don't know. I could understand if it was one of the hopefuls, but Ester has shown no interest in pack politics."

"Hopefuls?"

"Potential Alphas. Young males who might one day challenge me. Oh, relax. Every pack has them. It's all about grooming the future."

"So what's Cass being groomed for?"

"Like I said, I don't know. So far as I'm aware, she's happy attending the occasional event then going back to her life when it's done. She's always been a bit of an outsider."

Guess that explained why I'd taken an instant liking to her. She was the proverbial black sheep of the herd.

"It doesn't matter, though," Dad continued. "She's

here now. Maybe this is Mitch's way of getting her to show some initiative."

"Or maybe..."

"Is it going to be a problem?"

"Her?"

"Either of them," he replied.

I was tempted to tell him that hell yeah it was a problem. It was bad enough I was powerless and spending the day with a bunch of people who'd nuke me from orbit if they found out what I really was. But now there was going to be an asshole present who had both the knowledge and cause to rat me out.

On the upside, at least I had a friend coming along now ... or someone I hoped was a friend. And, she was likely to be even more uncomfortable than me, considering the circumstances. Besides, having someone to talk to was bound to make the day go a little faster. "No. I'm fine. If he ... they ... can behave, then so can I."

Now to see if that was a promise I could keep.

Going to be a long day. Can't elaborate now. Hopefully talk to you later. I hit send on the message and heard the soft beep of my phone acknowledging it.

I wasn't the only one, though.

"Who are you texting, Tamara?" Mom asked from the driver's seat. She and Dad usually traded off the driving duties, but I couldn't help but think there was something deliberate about the fact that she was behind the wheel today.

"Just wishing Riva and her family a Merry Christmas."

"Tell them we said the same."

"Already did."

Despite the fact that all of us were crammed into the

minivan, conversation was sparse. Mom and Dad were up front, doing little more than occasionally asking if everyone was comfortable and other banal shit.

Chris and Mitch took up the center row. My clueless brother was busy trying to show the werewolf beta some stupid game on his phone. Mitch, for his part, appeared to be doing his best to feign interest.

At least that part was amusing.

That left Cass and me in the back. Problem was, we couldn't even whisper to each other without half the ears in the car overhearing us.

But maybe we didn't need to.

I nudged her in the arm to get her attention. Then, once I had it, I showed her my phone, muting the sound and turning off the vibration settings. After a moment, she nodded and did the same, both of us keeping them low in case any prying eyeballs decided to turn around.

Once that was done, we both typed our respective numbers on our screens for the other to see. Just like that, we were in business.

What are you doing here?

Mitch, came the reply.

Was he telling the truth?

All bullshit. He called me up, told me I had to join him today.

So he lied?

Can't tell Curtis.

Why not?

Please don't.

I glanced sidelong at her and saw the fear in her eyes. Turning my attention to the asshole in the center row, I found myself boring a hole into his head with my gaze. He was damned lucky my powers were currently neutered, because otherwise I'd be tempted to jam my fist through the seat and rip out his spine, even if it meant getting yelled at for messing up the upholstery.

"What are you girls up to back there?" Dad asked all of a sudden. "You're awfully quiet."

Too noisy or too quiet – both situations that caused parents to grow instantly suspicious.

"I'm checking out Facebook."

"Words with Friends," Cass added.

Mom glanced at us in the rearview mirror. "Tamara, please try to be social with our guests. This is not a holiday to spend with your nose buried in your phone."

Fortunately, it was an idle comment. She quickly turned her attention back toward the road. We'd gotten a decent amount of snow a few days earlier, and though the streets had been plowed, it was still cold enough to prevent much melting.

Mitch turned and glared in my direction for a moment, but I gave him my sweetest, most innocent smile in return. *Oh yeah. If I had my powers...*

Cass gently nudged me with her elbow and I glanced down at my phone again to find, *So what's up with you?*

Huh?

You smell different ... human.

I had a feeling that one was coming. Though my secret was out as far as the Morganberg pack was concerned, they didn't know the whole story. If Craig had ever questioned my father as to how he'd kept my scent under wraps for nearly twenty years, they hadn't told me. I liked Cass, but that seemed a dangerous truth to admit to. I wasn't quite the comic book nerd that my brother was, but I knew enough to understand that Superman didn't go around handing Kryptonite to every bad guy who came along. *It's hard to explain.*

OMG. Is that actually something you can do?

There was my out. I didn't care to lie to someone I

liked, but it seemed safer to fudge the truth a bit. *Sorta. It's a long story.*

Oh well, I never claimed to be a master at spinning yarns. Hopefully she got the hint that this wasn't something I cared to talk about over text.

Mitch said we're supposed to act like this is a normal dinner. Why?

Good. She wasn't going to press. At least this next part I could discuss. *Because of the little turd muncher sitting in front of us. FYI, he doesn't know. So this is supposed to be a normal Christmas ... a test run to see if peace talks are viable.*

LOL. What peace talks?

Huh. *They didn't tell you?*

AAMOF, no.

I glanced toward her with raised eyebrows, to which she gave a single shake of her head. That was weird. If she wasn't a part of the peace talks, then why was she here?

Suddenly, the answer became clear. I wasn't a part of these talks either. I was a buffer for today, someone whose presence would force both sides to pretend this was nothing more than a holiday get-together between estranged family who didn't get along. *You're here because of me, aren't you?*

IDK. Maybe.

I debated pressing the matter, but instead chose to take her at face value. Going the other way was a slippery slope. A part of me was giddy at the prospect of having a friend among the werewolves. I really didn't want to fuck it up, and there was no easier way to do that than by being paranoid. But even so... *Is he planning on doing anything to me?*

There was a pause before I saw Cass's fingers start moving again. But eventually she typed out an answer.

Not that I know of. Please don't tell him I said this, but I think I might be here because he's afraid you might do something to him.

17

I mostly sat there silent, contemplating Cass's last text for the remainder of the ride to Crescentwood, just west of where High Moon lay.

Of all the things I could imagine Mitch doing, I hadn't considered that he might simply be too afraid to act. Guess I was used to that do or die macho mindset that seemed to be so pervasive.

All at once, Cass's presence made sense. Yeah, it was possible it was so she could cause me to drop my guard long enough for him to strike. But what would that win him? In the long run, he'd still have my father to deal with. And I had to think the twin faux pas of the peace talks being ruined and the murder of his only daughter would probably not leave Dad in a forgiving mood toward his beta. He'd be dooming himself for nothing more than petty revenge.

But what if Cass was instead brought to act as a buffer between us? I had no intention of picking a fight with Mitch today, but he didn't know that. If anything, showing up to find me smelling like a normal human had probably thrown him for a loop. He'd been expecting a badass hybrid, hoping that the friend I'd made would be enough to keep me from stepping over the line. I technically wasn't a member of either race. Who was to say I maybe didn't give a shit about some stupid peace treaty?

Well, my parents, for one, but Mitch likely didn't take that into account.

Okay, so maybe I didn't need to rip his spine out after all. Good, because it wasn't like I could anyway.

However, it would probably behoove me to not let slip that my powers were gone for the day. Yeah, my scent was telling, but Cass seemed to think it was some natural camouflage ability I had. Personally, I saw no reason to correct that oversight. Even if Mitch was afraid of me, knowing I was helpless might be too much of a temptation to pass up. If so, then...

I was pulled out of my introspection by the sensation of the van slowing down. Glancing out the window, I realized we were almost there.

We turned right onto Misteria Lane — a pun so bad that I was surprised I never noticed it before despite having been here several times. A few seconds later, the large Victorian where my mother grew up loomed before us.

Growing up, I'd always thought this place had an Addams Family vibe to it, at least on the outside. Now I realized perhaps that was intentional, some bit of Mom's family that lived up to the stereotype of witches and monsters. I guess Hollywood had to have gotten it from somewhere.

Of course, the comparison to the creepy mansion from that old TV show was superficial at best. Aunt Carly's home was well maintained, not a hint of disrepair on either the light grey exterior or the maroon highlights.

Dual turrets rose from the main structure, and several rows of cheerful Christmas lights blinked outside, made no less festive by the daylight hours.

Also, I knew for a fact she didn't have a seven foot tall zombie butler, or at least she hadn't last time I'd visited.

There were already several cars in the driveway. We weren't the first to arrive, which probably made sense. Considering what was at stake below the surface, I doubted there was any chance of them wanting my father to be the first guest to waltz through the front door.

"Hey, Dad," Chris called out. "I have a question."

"Huh?" he replied, as if his mind was a thousand miles away. He didn't show it, but I had to imagine he was nervous as all hell.

"Have you ever been here before?"

"What?"

"I don't remember you ever coming to visit Aunt Carly with us."

Mom finished parking the van and glanced back, throwing me a quick warning look in the process. The little turd didn't realize how close he was skirting to the truth. It was a rare bit of insight for a kid who usually had to be reminded to shower every day.

"Of course your father's been here," she said.

"You're almost right, champ," Dad chimed in, not missing a beat. "It's been a while."

"Okay," Chris replied, none the wiser and apparently not caring to pry further.

Regardless, I figured I'd do my part, so I leaned forward and flicked him in the ear. "You may find this hard to believe, dork, but they actually had a life before you came along."

My brother clapped a hand over the side of his head as he turned toward me, a look of mock horror on his face. "Great. Now I've got the syph."

Cass chuckled while my mother cried, "Christopher!"

Despite her scolding, she threw a look my way which held the barest hint of gratitude.

That's me. Always happy to help.

~

With Mitch and Cass helping out, we managed to unload the minivan in one trip. That was probably a good thing. It spared me and my brother from pulling pack mule duty as well as giving Dad a chance to rethink things and drive off without us.

Wouldn't that have made for some interesting Christmas gossip?

The six of us, now laden with presents, walked up onto the front porch as Mom pressed the doorbell.

A cheery Christmas tune played in response. If I had to guess, Aunt Carly was over-compensating a bit for her breakup. Still, it wasn't my place to judge. Just because my love life sucked didn't mean others hadn't experienced true heartache. Besides, I liked my aunt. I'd maybe become a bit jaded, but that didn't mean I should take it out on her.

"You ready for this?" I asked quietly.

Cass gave me a thumbs up from behind the small mountain of gifts she was hefting.

I glanced over and saw Mitch flash me a dangerous look, but fuck him. My question was innocent enough, nothing I wouldn't ask any friend being dragged along to someone else's house.

"Just a minute!" came a cheery reply from somewhere inside.

A few moments later my aunt opened the front door. It was show time.

~

Carly was maybe an inch taller than my mother and had jet black hair to her auburn. You could easily see the family resemblance even though my aunt's face was a bit more rounded and she smiled a lot more – giving her a down-to-earth feel my mother usually lacked. She was in her late thirties but still a knockout. I could only hope I looked half as good at her age. Roger, in my opinion, was quite obviously a raging idiot to dump her.

She stood in the doorway beaming at us with a look of what appeared to be pure joy on her face. It was hard to tell if she was putting on a brave face for the holidays, but her expression certainly fit her outfit. She was dressed like one of Santa's elves, if Santa had been fashion conscious. She wore a bright green dress with red accents, complete with matching leggings and an adorable elf hat.

She might have been a powerful witch, but it was hard to look at her and not be swayed by the smile on her face.

"You made it!" she squealed.

Despite the gifts in my mother's arms, she stepped forward and gave her sister as big a hug as she could.

Aunt Carly then gestured for us to enter. "Come in, come in, all of you. No need to stand out there freezing your tuchuses off."

Mom walked in, followed by Chris. Carly gave his cheeks a pinch, doting on how big the little jack-off had gotten since last she'd seen him ... which actually was only a few days ago. But whatever. That's the sort of thing family did.

Dad and Mitch were next in line. Both hesitated ever so slightly before Carly said, "Curtis! I'm so glad you could make it! Come on in here and give me a hug."

Dad stepped past the threshold and she was right there to throw her arms around him in what looked to be a genuine expression of affection. For a second or two I almost forgot that they were, in actuality, part of two warring races, but then I saw my aunt's eyes flick ever so slightly up toward the top of the door frame.

Mitch came next. Dad introduced him and Carly gave him a welcoming handshake – a bit less touchy feely, but no less warm. Again, I watched as her eyes glanced upward for a moment, even as the smile remained plastered on her face.

Odd.

Not seeing any mistletoe hanging over the doorway and knowing what this party really was for, I couldn't help but wonder if she was checking some sort of magical metal detector or something. I couldn't exactly ask, but it seemed logical, especially considering the anti-werewolf wards I'd discovered on my house over the summer.

I guess she was checking to make sure they weren't carrying any, I dunno, wolf weaponry, whatever that might be. Either way, they apparently passed inspection. That left me and Cass.

Carly immediately embraced me, hard enough that I almost dropped the presents in my hands. "Look at you, the big college girl!"

"Merry Christmas," I replied cheerfully. Then I lowered my voice a bit. "I heard what happened. I'm really sorry."

An unreadable expression crossed her face for a moment, then she smiled again. "Thank you, sweetie. But let's not worry about that right now. Today is for friends and family. Speaking of which, you want to introduce me to yours?"

"Cass, this is my Aunt Carly. Carly, this is Cass."

Cass stepped inside next to me, and again I saw my aunt's eyes flit upwards. Yeah, cheerful family event or not, there were definitely some tells as to what was really going on here ... if one knew what to look for. Or maybe I was just being paranoid. There was that, too. Mitch's presence still had me on edge.

Regardless, we all made it inside without activating any killing curses or their Gaelic equivalent.

"Happy holidays," Cass said, by way of greeting.

"Merry Christmas to you, too. And might I add, you have a lovely name."

"Thank you."

"Come on in. Put those things under the tree and go make yourselves comfortable. There's plenty of room."

She wasn't kidding. The sitting room had a ten foot high ceiling and off in one corner stood a tree tall enough to stoop against the plaster. It dwarfed the fake Douglas fir we had in our living room and was decorated in a way that could only be described as regal. It was adorned with ornaments that looked older than me. Tinsel, candy canes, and lights were used sparingly, giving it the impression of something you might see in a castle back in the nineteenth century.

Classical Christmas music played in the background.

As expected, we weren't the first guests to arrive. Once we put down our gifts and handed our coats to our hostess, the rest of us stepped into the living room – minus Chris, troll that he was, who immediately took off in search of things to keep his limited attention span occupied.

Milling about were several faces I recognized – relatives – as well as some I didn't. All were conversing, drinking eggnog, or doing other things one might do at a holiday get-together. And likewise, every single one of them paused for the briefest of moments as we stepped in, as if time skipped a beat, before returning to whatever they'd been doing.

Call me crazy, but despite the holiday cheer, I had a feeling this Christmas was going to be far more interesting than I'd have ever guessed when I left school a few days ago.

18

"I can't believe you're still wrestling."

"Yeah, it's totally gross."

"You think everything is gross."

"Are you telling me you'd want sweaty man crotch in your face all day long?"

"Depends on the man."

Cass and I both giggled. We were talking to the twins, my second cousins Mindy and Melody. They were both a year older than me, which meant their eggnogs were spiked, something they made a point of bragging about when I walked over to introduce Cass to them.

Mindy was a former gymnast whereas Melody was studying to be a veterinarian last I'd checked. Considering the side of the family they were on, that likely meant they were both witches, too, although that wasn't exactly something I could ask.

Nevertheless, despite a minor rivalry with Mindy growing up, due to our close age and affinity for sports, they'd always been my go-to group for hangouts like these.

After making the rounds, I'd gravitated their way with Cass in tow. However, as we chatted, mostly about mundane subjects, I found myself occasionally checking to see how Dad was doing.

Carly had spirited my mother off to the kitchen shortly after our arrival, leaving Dad and his cousin adrift in a sea of ancestral enemies. I didn't give a crap about Mitch, but I wanted to stay close in case Dad needed a save, even if it was just a conversational one.

I tried not to eavesdrop, made all the more easy by my hearing being back to normal levels, as well as Mindy and Melody's bickering over just about every point imaginable. However, I did manage to catch some interesting snippets.

"Do you think the Eagles would be willing to make that trade?"

"Maybe," my father replied to the couple he was talking to – Jeremy and his wife Carlotta, distant cousins from my mother's side. "But the Steelers would need to be open to ceding some of their home field advantage."

I couldn't help but grin. Dad didn't follow football, yet he was speaking with authority. I had a sneaking suspicion they were conducting *business,* using poorly disguised metaphors for the sake of looking like they weren't. If so, it didn't appear to be going too badly. The discussion was civil and the tension appeared to be minimal.

Mitch himself didn't look particularly comfortable. I had no idea where his sports allegiances lay, but in a conversation such as this, there was little he could do except agree with my father. Tell me that wouldn't get old quickly. Hah! Too bad, so sad.

"Are you listening, Tamara?"

"Huh?"

I turned back to the conversation at hand to find all three girls looking expectantly at me.

"Earth to Bent," Cass said with a grin.

"Sorry," I replied. "Got caught up in the memories of this place."

Melody let out a huff of breath. "Don't tell me you still go by that vulgar nickname."

"I kind of like it," Mindy countered, taking a sip from her mug. "I bet Kevin did, too."

I rolled my eyes. "He used to, at least until I dumped his ass."

"You didn't?"

"Yeah, last year." I lowered my voice. "I dropped him faster than he could squirt a load ... and believe me, that was fast."

That set all of us to laughing, even Melody, until her sister turned to our guest. "How about you, Cass? Seeing anyone?"

She shook her head. "No. The boys at Saint Edgar's weren't worth it. Half of them were studying to be priests. The other half averaged three kids with three different girlfriends by the time they graduated."

"Tell me about it," Mindy replied. "My friend Daisy went out with a guy from there once. The loser was trying to convince her they were soul mates right before she ditched him."

"Sounds about right," Cass said, causing us all to laugh again.

The best part was there was nothing forced about any of it.

So far, so good.

~

"Take these out to the table, will you?"

Mom had pulled me aside to help with setting up for dinner. She'd originally gone looking for Chris, but he was nowhere to be found. The little nimrod had disappeared, probably to jerk off in a closet somewhere. Either way, it was easier to help than try and find him. This place was massive. Even with the few boarders who rented rooms here – all relatives – it was still probably too much for my aunt. But I could understand her keeping such a big house. Even before I'd been made aware of the true happenings around High Moon, I'd known this had been my mother's ancestral home dating back to even before the Civil War.

Besides, who knew what magical secrets lay inside its walls? I mean, it wasn't exactly Hogwarts, but I had to assume there was more than meets the eye in this old place.

This wasn't a day to go exploring, though. And even if it was, I couldn't exactly take Cass with me without arousing suspicions.

Speaking of which, she asked, "Do you need a hand?" as I passed by her and the twins carrying a tray of deviled eggs.

"Nah. I've got this. Hang tight. I'll be back to you guys in a few."

I would have taken her offer had she seemed the slightest bit out of place. But fortunately, the twins were busy plying her with gossip from their lives. All in all, it was about as normal as it could be for two species doing their damnedest to pretend they were human for a day.

A trio of my great aunts were already seated at the table as I approached, talking among themselves. A haze of smoke hung around them despite the smokeless ashtray sitting between them – none of it out of the ordinary. They were all of that age where they figured anything that hadn't killed them yet wasn't likely to.

That was okay. I had a feeling my constitution could handle a little secondhand smoke, especially once my damned pills finally wore off. For now, I could deal.

"I'm glad the bastard is gone. She was too good for

him," the oldest, Aunt Theresa, said as I laid the tray down as far from their cigarette ashes as I could.

A chorus of agreement erupted from the trio. Looking at them now, it wasn't hard to imagine them standing around a cauldron chanting "Double double, toil and trouble," all while chain smoking Virginia Slims.

"I only wish Vanessa was still alive. She'd have set that son of a bitch straight," opined Fiona, the *baby* of the bunch, eliciting more angry agreement.

She was talking about my grandmother who'd passed away shortly after my parents adopted Chris. While I supposed it was possible she'd peered through the mists of time, seen what a dork he'd grow into, and subsequently died of shame, the reality of it, sadly, was cancer.

Although, now that I had a moment to think about it, I had to wonder if that was actually true or simply a case of what I'd been told. I remember it had been quick. There'd been no time for treatments or visits in the hospital. Six year old me hadn't thought to question that, but now I had to wonder.

Unfortunately, this was neither the time nor place to ask.

"Don't count Lissa out. She still might," Theresa offered before finally noticing I was there and quickly changing the subject.

I had to assume the focus of their ire was Roger, the louse who'd broken my aunt's heart. According to Mom there'd been a diplomatic aspect to their courtship, but I'd spoken to Carly during their engagement and she'd seemed genuinely happy.

I had a feeling today was nothing more than a façade for my aunt in more ways than one. Yes, there was the treaty everyone was busy testing the waters on, but there was the human aspect, too – one poor woman, hurt and alone, putting on a brave face so as to not ruin the holiday.

"Hand me one of those, will ya, sweetie?" Theresa asked.

I obliged, passing her a deviled egg before turning away.

It was time to go talk to my aunt and make sure she knew I was here for her.

∾

"Have you seen Aunt Carly, Mom?"

My mother appeared to have been fully conscripted. She was working to put the finishing touches on various side dishes, grabbing ingredients from the spice rack as if she had their locations memorized.

In a way, it was kind of funny. She was the so-called Queen of Monarchs, a title so stupid I could barely think it without laughing. All of this, Crescentwood and every spell caster contained within, were supposedly beholden to her. Yet here she was busting her butt in the kitchen on Christmas day.

It might be good to be the king, but perhaps the same couldn't be said of being queen.

If she was bothered by any of this, though, she didn't show it, seemingly laser-focused on what she was doing. "Your aunt had to step out for a second," she replied, seasoning the green bean casserole. "I'm pretty sure she went upstairs."

"Do you think she'd mind if I checked on her?"

Mom stopped what she was doing and turned toward me, a smile on her face. "Quite the contrary. I think she would appreciate that."

I smiled back, then left to make sure Cass would be okay on her own. All seemed good in the living room, so I made my way up the old, but meticulously maintained, main staircase and headed toward the second floor.

∽

It was almost like stepping into another dimension. A brief memory of Jerry and me in the hollows popped into my head, but I quickly shoved it away. The transition wasn't *that* dramatic. Nevertheless, a flight of stairs was apparently all it took to mute the sounds of revelry below. Made me wish my own home had such good sound-proofing.

The momentary reprieve was actually kinda nice. Between the ongoing banter downstairs and nonstop loop of Christmas music playing in the background, there was a chaotic element to it all. I couldn't even imagine what it would be like had my powers not been dulled, but then I realized that's exactly what Dad and Cass were likely experiencing. I'd have to make it a point to check on them when I got back downstairs.

Mitch could still go fuck himself, though.

It wasn't exactly the Christmas spirit, but last I checked, I wasn't applying for sainthood.

I made my way toward the master bedroom. Seemed the likeliest place to check. I know some people preferred to have their breakdowns in the bathroom, but it wasn't really my thing. Of course, sharing a toilet with my brother made every pee break a bit of a heartbreaker, so there was that.

Fortunately, I was right. I stepped to the doorway of my aunt's bedroom and found her looking through her nightstand for something. I knocked softly on the door to announce my presence.

Carly spun around, her face immediately softening

upon seeing me. "Oh, Tamara. What can I do for you, hun?"

Taking that as my cue, I stepped in. "I wanted to make sure you were okay."

"I was just looking for my phone. I accidentally left it up here while I was getting ready this morning." She held it up as if to confirm this.

"I meant in general. I tried calling a few times since I got home but kept getting your voicemail."

She sat on the bed and patted a spot next to her. "I know, honey, and I'm sorry. It's just been crazy busy and the truth is, everyone has been walking on eggshells around me like I died or something. I really haven't been in the mood to talk to anyone."

I sat next to her. "It's okay. But I wanted to let you know there's a lot of us who care about you and will listen when you're ready."

Carly let out a laugh, but it didn't hold much humor. "It's funny. I've been learning a lot lately about the people who care about me. It's been eye opening. You think you know someone and then poof, it turns out it was all a lie."

I thought back to my aborted romance with Gary last summer. It wasn't quite the same as what she'd gone through, but it would be a fib to say I didn't understand the concept of betrayal. "Men suck."

"Oh, they're not the only ones," she said. "I don't even think they're the best at it."

I considered my parents and nodded. "But seriously, are you okay?"

"I'll get through this," she said, looking me in the eye. "And you know what? I'll come out stronger than ever. Your aunt is a survivor. Trust me on that. I pride myself in learning from the mistakes of the past."

"Still, it's gotta hurt."

"Betrayal always does, sweetie. But in this case, one door closed and another opened."

"You met someone already?"

She shook her head. "Not quite what I meant. I mean, it gave me a chance to step back, take a look at the bigger picture, and realize what's really important."

"Family?"

"Amongst other things."

"Speaking of which, I'm glad you're hosting Christmas. It's nice to see everyone in one place."

"Oh believe me, there's no one more excited than I am. And I'm so glad your father could make it."

Here was the part where we both had to go back to pretending. It really was a shame. I knew my mother had misgivings about her family, even her baby sister, knowing about me, but I had a feeling my aunt would understand. She was cool that way. Nevertheless, it was probably smart to play it coy. Christmas was a day for surprises, but it was maybe best to save some for a later time. "You know Dad. He's a busy guy."

Carly patted my knee. "I think we're both a bit too smart to believe that, dear."

We are?

I couldn't stop my eyebrows from raising in response. She no doubt noticed, because she continued. "I don't think it's any secret that my family hasn't exactly gotten along with your father."

"Yeah, I guess it has been kind of hard to miss," I replied. *Especially these last couple of months.* "But if it helps, I've never heard him say a bad word about you."

That was the truth. Though he hadn't been around Carly much, there had been times over the years and I seemed to recall those mostly being cordial.

"I'm happy to hear it." She leaned toward me and lowered her voice. "Truth be told, most of us weren't happy when your mother married Curtis. It was so sudden. We didn't know what to make of it. And then you were born soon after and we should've realized at that point it was real, but I think a lot of us didn't want to accept the truth. Oh, the arguments that were fought. I wanted to give my sister the benefit of the doubt, but our mother wasn't nearly so understanding."

I turned away for a moment. Something about what she'd just said was nagging me in the back of my head, a question that wasn't quite fully formed, but she continued before I could coax it out.

"But now I'm hoping we can finally change all of that. It's been going on for far too long. We need to bury the past once and for all, right all of those wrongs. That's the only way to move on, learn from our mistakes and fix them."

"I think that's a healthy attitude."

"Me too," she replied. "Not only healthy, but the *only* attitude." Carly looked away for a moment, then said, "I really am sorry, Tamara. I want you to know that."

"For not calling me back? Don't worry about it."

She stared at me hard for several seconds, as if she wanted to say more, but then finally she clapped me on the leg again. "Enough about that for now. What say we get downstairs and put dinner on the table? We've left your mother alone long enough that I'm sure she'll start thinking I'm an absolute witch."

"Both of us, probably."

Carly laughed. "Maybe. But let's get back down there anyway before she decides to poison the eggnog."

19

Surprise, surprise. Once dinner was announced, my brother decided to slink out from whatever rock he'd been hiding under.

From the sound of things, he'd been hanging out with Gavin – an old friend of my mom's and he of the awesome mancave – probably geeking out over video games or something equally unimportant.

Sadly, we both ended up stuck at the kiddie table. On the upside so, too, were Cass and the twins. Truth be told, it wasn't much of a kiddie table anymore since Chris was the youngest person present. Nowadays it was merely a spillover spot for those of us too young to rate a seat at the main table.

Whatever. The food smelled good, even if Chris kept making eyes at Cass as the dishes were passed around. Guess he had a future as an Internet stalker. It was good to have goals.

I glanced over at the main table and saw Dad seated next to my mother with Mitch on his other side playing the third wheel. However, my misgivings of him aside, it seemed that most of the people there were far more interested in the meal being served than in sniping at each other.

To say that was heartening was an understatement. Breaking bread together was the simplest of acts, yet it was symbolic of so much more. If we could get through dinner without any incidents, it would be a step in the right direction. It didn't necessarily predict how the upcoming talks would go, but every journey had to start somewhere.

So far as I was aware, neither side of the family had a penchant for saying grace before eating. Growing up, I thought it was because we were mostly secular. But now I realized it was because both sides had beliefs that were kinda out there. Dad and his pack worshipped some Germanic god who apparently got his rocks off hunting his minions for sport. As for Mom, her beliefs revolved around tree-hugging fairy courts and shit like that. I could only imagine the blessings for either.

Despite this, Carly stood up before everyone could dig in and dinged her spoon against her glass to get our attention. "Friends and family, both old and new, I wanted to take a moment to reflect upon just how lucky we are on this most precious of days."

Over the course of the next week, my parents would likely take the lead, as heads of their respective clans, but today my aunt was the host so she was taking advantage of it while she could.

"I think we can all agree," she continued, holding up her wine glass, "that the past hasn't always been kind. Hard feelings, compounded by lies and deceit, it's left our spirits fractured and unwhole. But today we celebrate new beginnings."

"Hear hear," my father said, raising his own glass. After a few moments, most of the rest at the table followed suit, even one of my great aunts.

"Let us right the wrongs that have been inflicted upon

us, erase the mistakes that have come before," Carly continued. "To that end, I have one final gift for you all before we dig in to this..."

Cheery Christmas music filled the air, interrupting her.

For a moment, I sat there wondering whether her plan was to break into song in the hopes of getting everyone to join along, but then I realized it was just the doorbell.

Everyone looked confused for a few seconds until my mother started to stand.

"It's okay, Lissa," Carly said, stepping away from the table. "I've got it. Just a minute, everyone. It's probably some carolers."

While she headed toward the door, Cass leaned in and whispered, "Does that mean we can eat? Because this ham smells really good."

It was apparently no question for my brother, who'd already started shoveling spoonfuls of mashed potatoes into his face. *Such a dork.*

I was about to dig in myself, but then I looked up and saw Carly standing at the door. She was talking – no, more like arguing – with someone standing outside, but I could neither see them nor hear what they were saying. Damned repressed powers.

"That's odd," Cass said a moment later.

"What is?" I asked

She lowered her voice, going so far as to lean in and whisper to me ... oh yeah, she still had to pretend. "Who's Belzar?"

"Belzar? Isn't that the guy from *Law & Order*?"

"Why would an actor be standing at the front door?"

That was a really good question. So far as I was aware, I didn't have any celebrity cousins. Although witchcraft could definitely explain some of the careers in Hollywood these...

"Fine. You can come in," Carly snapped, causing all eyes — save my brother's — to turn her way. "But make it quick."

She stepped aside and a man walked in. He appeared to be in his mid-thirties with well-coifed dark hair, striking blue eyes, and a neatly trimmed goatee. By all means, he looked like he should've been serving lattes at an upscale coffee shop. I recognized him, though. I'd seen enough pictures on Facebook of my aunt's former fiancé to know him by sight.

"Roger?" my mother asked, standing up again.

A chorus of voices rose up around the table.

"What is *he* doing here?"

"He's got a lot of nerve."

"Who the hell is that?"

Okay, that last one was from Mitch. Everyone else seemed more shocked than surprised.

"Folks," Roger said, holding up a hand in greeting as he stepped into the living room. "Merry Christmas, happy Chanukah, and a joyous Kwanzaa, too, if anyone's a believer."

His attempt at humor fell flat based on the angry stares that met him, including from Carly who continued standing at the open door.

"I know most of you probably aren't happy to see me, but I couldn't let this day pass with things as they currently are."

"Carly?" Mom asked, ignoring him. "Do you want me to show our *guest* out?"

"Far be it for me to interrupt, your highness," Roger replied with a grin. "But please allow me to say my piece."

Anger turned into wide-eyed disbelief from those at the *adult* table. Hell, even Chris looked up from stuffing his face. This wasn't good.

Roger had just come dangerously close to spilling the

beans. If that happened, I wasn't sure what the result would be, but I had to think it would entail them trying to ... what had Mom called it ... *blank* both me and Chris. In his case it would work, but for me, even with my meds I wasn't sure what the result would be.

"Oh crap," Roger added after a few seconds, raising his hands to his mouth in an exaggerated oops gesture. "Didn't realize there were unremarkables in the room. Sorry. Just ignore the guy who's had too much Christmas cheer today. I might not be in my right mind."

"I should say not," Mom growled, her voice growing dangerous.

"But I am in my right mind with regards to one thing," he quickly added before anyone could get up and throw him out on his ass.

He turned toward Carly. "Carolyn, I want to be with you. Only when we're together am I whole, and I think the same is true for you. We were meant to be. Forget everything that's been said. It's all bullshit, baby. I wasn't thinking straight."

As far as apologies went, his sucked balls. I had a feeling I'd be helping toss this loser to the curb before he could say...

However, rather than tell him to get the fuck out, as she probably should have, Carly approached him, her eyes glassy.

No way. She couldn't possibly be falling for this crap. Hell, I'd been smooth-talked by drunks far cooler than this clown. This was the lame-ass pick-up attempt of a guy at two a.m. who realizes he's about to go home alone and is making one final effort before last call.

"That's it, baby." Roger held out a hand, which she took, then he dropped to one knee.

"Is he going to do what I think he is?" Cass asked.

"I have no idea."

"Carolyn McGillis, will you make me the happiest man on Earth?"

After a beat, my aunt replied, "Yes."

Stunned silence enveloped the room as he rose to his feet and pulled her in for a long kiss.

Done right, this would have been the moment applause erupted in the room, but there was something so surreal that none of us, magical or not, seemed to be able to make heads or tails of it.

Finally, Roger pulled away and looked down at my aunt. "Aces, babe. So what say we sit down to eat?"

I had a feeling dinner was about to go from hopeful to tense, but then Roger paused before she could lead him to the table.

"But first, how about we have some fun and kill all of these treacherous fucks already?"

It was a good thing I hadn't started eating yet, because all of a sudden, I had no appetite.

20

There came a moment of stunned silence as everyone waited to see if there was a punchline to this bad joke. But then, just as I tensed myself to act, albeit I wasn't sure how, Roger started to laugh.

"Just messing with you all!"

A few chuckles were heard as well as several sighs of relief. If this asshole thought he was funny, though...

"Got ya!" he added with another laugh. "Merry Christmas, motherfuckers."

He pulled Carly in for another kiss as half a dozen men raced in through the still open door, all of them inexplicably dressed as Christmas characters.

I realized a moment too late this was deliberate, a way to cause confusion instead of action on our part. This was confirmed as the first of them, a guy dressed like Santa Claus of all people, cried out in a trebled voice, "Ho ho ho ... *A 'briseadh làmhan!*"

Screams erupted from the adult table and there came the sickening crunch of bone. I turned to see great aunt Theresa's body collapse in on itself as if her own personal gravity had been increased a hundredfold. Within the space of a few horrifying seconds, she was reduced to nothing more than a pile of compressed meat.

My first inclination was to launch myself at these assholes and let fly with my fists, but then I remembered I was in no condition to do anything except die an even worse death.

My second, and likely far more sane, course of action was to dive at Chris and throw us both to the floor and out of the line of fire. Cass was apparently thinking the same thing, because she landed next to me a moment later.

Just in time, too, because three of Santa's little helpers cried out in unison, "*Mhéara ar tintreach!*"

Bolts of magical lightning danced across the tops of both tables, electrocuting the majority of those still seated. Most appeared to be merely stunned by the attack, but a few were far less lucky.

From my vantage point, I could only watch helplessly as my cousin Melody's skin charred and blackened. Steam began to rise from her eyes, and then she slumped over onto the table.

No!

I tried to get up, but strong hands grabbed hold of my arms and held me down.

"Get off me, I have to help her."

"*It's too late*," Cass growled, quite literally. I turned to find her growing larger and hairier, her clothes beginning to rip from the strain.

Chris noticed, too, and began to scream. "What the fuck is that?!"

Wimp.

Okay, maybe that wasn't fair. I'd be lying if I said I wasn't freaked the fuck out, too, just for different reasons.

Perhaps the worst part, though, was my aunt. I couldn't see much from my vantage point, but she still appeared to be locked in an embrace with her on again, off again fiancé. I had no idea what was up with her, but hopefully whatever church they booked was okay with swapping a wedding for a funeral, because I fully intended to make sure Roger got fitted for a casket instead of a tux.

Of course, I wasn't exactly sure how I'd do that.

Fortunately, Cass seemed to have a head up on that. She leapt to her feet, fully transformed, her clothes in tatters around her.

Santa was ready for her, though. He stepped past the *happy couple*, still blissfully smooching, and cried out a spell which sent Cass hurtling back as if she'd been struck by a bus.

Damnit!

She slammed into the china cabinet behind us, shattering it and the contents to pieces before slumping to the floor.

For a moment, I feared the worst, but then I saw her take a breath. She was only dazed, thank goodness. Sadly, that wasn't going to mean much if our attackers were allowed to pick us off with ease.

We needed to...

"Tamara! Get your brother out of here!"

It was Mom. She'd either recovered quickly from that electrical attack or was just that much better than the rest. Either way, she was back on her feet. Better yet, Dad was by her side.

"*lann a mharbhadh!*" Mom cried and what could best be described as a scythe of black energy lanced out from her. It flew over the heads of those still stunned at the table before lancing downward and ... yuck ... sheering Santa in half at the waist.

He had a shocked look on his face and a bisected belly, then his guts all spilled out like a bowl full of jelly.

Hard to believe I'd never gotten an A in poetry.

Not content with basking in her gruesome victory, my mother screamed out the same attack again, no doubt intent on cutting our foes down to size.

The words were barely out of her mouth, however, when Carly – still teary eyed – disengaged from Roger and shouted, "*Mists of might!*"

I wasn't sure what it did, but my mother's energy scythe was instantly diverted from its course and up into the ceiling, slashing a nasty hole through the wood and plaster.

Roger let out a laugh. "For shame, your highness. Killing magic? Where's your Christmas spirit?"

Oh yeah, this creep needed someone to erase that smirk off his face. But what about my aunt? What was up with her? Why the hell was she helping this murdering asshole?

Sadly, that question would have to wait because Mom screamed at me, "Move it, Tamara!"

I didn't need to be told twice.

～

"No questions for now, you little turd sandwich," I hissed. "Just do as you're told, okay?"

My brother's eyes were wide with confusion and fear, but my insult seemed to get through to him. As one of my coaches used to say, a boot to the ego is sometimes just as good as a smack to the face.

Chris focused on me long enough to give me a quick nod.

"Good. Now start crawling toward the kitchen."

Once he started moving, I dared a look up. Some of the others at the big table appeared to have recovered. A few muttered something incomprehensible to me, but the meaning became clear a moment later as a screen of pris-

159

matic light appeared between the tables and our attackers.

Please let that be some kind of trippy force field.

Dad had taken the time to transform and stood there growling protectively, a living wall of fur and teeth by my mother's side. Next to him, Mitch was likewise beginning to shake off the effects of the stun spell. I still didn't like the guy, but right then I wished him all the luck in the world.

"Three furballs for the price of one," Roger called out with a chuckle. "It really must be Christmas."

"What's the meaning of this, Belzar?" Mom replied, her body alit with power. Her hair rose up around her as if a breeze was blowing, making it look as if she were surrounded by a mane of fire.

"Can the light show, Queenie," Roger ... or Belzar said. Christ, talk about pretentious. It sounded like a bad username from a Harry Potter forum. "Surrender and maybe we can cut a deal."

"A deal?" my mother spat. "What the hell do you even think you're doing here?"

"Isn't it obvious? Me and my woman are taking over. Sorry, your highness, but consider this a royal coup."

"Over my dead body."

"If it comes to that, so be it," my aunt replied. She sounded out of breath and there was a strange look in her eyes, but she wrapped an arm around ... ugh ... Belzar. "And it might not even be at my hands, dear sister, especially once everyone learns that your so-called marriage of convenience to that *thing* is more real than you're letting on."

Uh oh. How the hell did she know that?

"Tamara!" Mom barked again, rousing me from my inaction.

The time for gawking was over. Much as I wanted to

know what was going on, keeping my brother alive had to take priority.

I spared one last look back at the table. Melody was beyond help. However, her sister, along with the rest, merely appeared stunned. Problem was, I was in no capacity to do anything about it.

But that didn't mean I was leaving emptyhanded. "Come on!" I grabbed hold of one of Cass's arms, much larger than mine in her wolf form, and gave her a shake. Fortunately, werewolf constitutions were off the charts. She blinked a few times and then shook her head to clear the cobwebs. Her first inclination was to bare her teeth. No doubt she wanted back in this fight, but that tactic had already failed once.

"Come with me. You can't win this." After a moment, I added, "Please!"

I couldn't force her to follow, not depowered as I was. All I could do was pray that the one friend I had among the wolves wasn't hell-bent on getting herself killed.

Gritting my teeth, I began to crawl after my brother. It saddened me to have to run from this fight, especially with my parents still in danger, but Mom was right. I needed to protect Chris.

Those goddamned pills. I wasn't even at the halfway point for them to wear off. I was useless here, for now anyway.

Pushing open the kitchen door, I crawled through it.

Before I could call out Chris's name, though, a butcher knife slammed into the floor in front of me, just inches from my face.

21

"Oh shit! Sorry. I thought you were one of them."

I glanced up to see my brother standing there, a doe-eyed look on his face. "What the hell? I said I was right behind you."

"I k-know," he stammered, "but I thought … maybe they got you."

I pulled myself to my feet. "Do me a favor. Don't think. Just do as you're told, okay?"

Enough adolescent rebellion remained in his terrified form to push itself to the surface. "You're not the boss of … oh my God!"

He grabbed a knife from the counter in hands shaking so badly I was surprised he could even pick it up. Fortunately, I saw just enough fur in my periphery to guess that Cass had followed us after all. Thank goodness.

Before my brother could do anything stupid, I caught him by the wrist. I might've only been at a fraction of my strength, but I was still an athlete. "Give me that!"

"B-but, but that's a…"

"It's Cass."

"It's a…"

"*It's me.*" I turned to see Cass shrink down into her human form. "See?"

My brother's eyes opened even wider and I realized he *saw,* all right. Her clothes were shredded to the point where she could only barely be described as dressed. Under less murderous circumstances, she would have been a preteen boy's wet dream come true.

"Her eyes are up there, Romeo."

"Um, sorry," he said after a second, his voice still shaking. "But did you see her? She's a…"

"Werewolf? I know."

"They're real?"

"Obviously."

"But…"

We so didn't have time for this. "You need to relax. Think of all the werewolf movies you and your nerd buddies have watched. Haven't you ever talked about what you'd do if they were real?"

"T-that was mostly zombies."

"Oh." I turned to Cass. "Are zombies…?"

"I don't know. And right now, I *really* don't care."

She kinda had a point there. We didn't have time to play horror movie Q&A. "Same general principle," I told Chris. "Besides, she's a good werewolf."

"A good werewolf?"

There came what sounded like a muffled explosion from the other room, which caused us all to jump. I hoped it was from the good guys. Otherwise, our time was running short. "Yes, now either pull yourself together or I'm leaving your ass here."

"No! Please don't."

"It's okay," Cass said, stepping in and reaching a hand

toward my brother's shoulder. He flinched, but held his ground. "There, see? I'm just a person like you. We okay here?"

That seemed to get through his terror. Either that, or he realized a gorgeous half-naked girl was actually touching him. "Y-yeah. I guess so."

"Good," I replied. "Because we don't have time for Monster Introduction 101. Come on, the back door's over there."

"What about Mom and...?"

"They can take care of themselves. All we're going to do is distract them."

"But we can help," Cass protested.

This really wasn't the time for confessions, but I had a feeling she needed to know the truth. "No. You can help. I can't."

"But..."

"I'm not joking. It's not that I don't want to. I actually *can't*."

Cass raised an eyebrow, then said, "Your scent. You're really...'

"Human? Yeah. This isn't some trick."

"What else is she supposed to be?" Chris asked, missing a prime opportunity to throw me some shade. Guess he really was frightened out of his gourd.

"But how ... oh no."

"What?" I spun, following her gaze, and saw exactly what she meant. The back door was only a few yards away, but we'd stupidly eaten up our lead by talking instead of running. A man wearing plush reindeer antlers, of all things – what the fuck was up with these assholes – was walking up the back-porch stairs. I had a feeling he wasn't there to play reindeer games, especially with Cass around. "Crap! We need to hide."

"The basement," Chris said, grabbing my arm. "The back stairs are in the pantry."

"How do you..."

"That's where I was hanging out all afternoon."

Huh. I'd actually never been down there. When I was little, both Grammy Nessa and my aunt had forbidden it, telling me it was full of dust and spiders. That had been enough to curb my interest.

A part of me was miffed that Chris had just wandered down there of his own volition, but the rest was glad as hell he knew about it.

"Come on," he said. It's huge. There's all sorts of places to hide."

I glanced at Cass, shrugged, then turned back toward him, "Lead the way."

∼

I didn't think Rudolph back there had seen us, but the assholes in the living room had. There wasn't much I could do to help my parents, but I also wasn't keen on letting some creep flank them. So, as a parting gift, I knocked a bottle of vegetable oil over onto the floor before we headed to the pantry.

The cellar door didn't have a lock on the inside, but there was one of those rubber wedges sitting on the top step. Chris and I walked down a few stairs to give Cass room. She picked it up and put a little extra werewolf oomph into it as she shoved the stopper into the tiny recess beneath the door.

It wouldn't hold if someone decided to blast their way through, but it would hopefully slow down anyone looking to investigate.

Just as Cass finished wedging the door shut, I heard a

faint thud from the direction of the kitchen. *Heh. I hope that hurt, asshole.*

Chris reached up toward an overhead pull switch, but I grabbed his arm. "Nuh uh. No lights."

'But it's dark down there."

"That's the point." To emphasize the matter, I grabbed hold of the string and gave it a hard enough yank to snap it. "If it's gonna be dark for us, it can be dark for them, too."

"And if we break our necks before we get to the bottom of the stairs?"

"I'm on it," Cass said, stepping past us. "Hold on to me."

"How?"

"Werewolf," she told him. "I can see in the dark."

"Oh. That's kinda cool."

"You have no idea."

~

I made it about four steps, stumbling around in the dark behind Cass and my brother, before I finally fished my phone out of my pocket and turned on the flash.

"What about no lights?" Chris complained.

"Do as I say, not as I do. Besides, I'm keeping it low so we can move faster. But the second I hear anyone else down here, it's off."

"Fair enough," Cass said from up ahead.

"You can use yours, too, if you want," I told Chris after a moment of his sulking silence.

"Um..."

"You didn't lose it again, did you, dumbass?"

"No ... the battery's dead."

"What?"

"I got bored, so I was playing some games."

"You are such a..."

"*Guys, focus,*" Cass hissed, turning back toward us. Her face had elongated, displaying canine features, and her eyes were now yellow. "*I can't hold this form for long.*"

"Holy..."

Before Chris could cry out, I slapped a hand over his mouth. "Relax. Yes, she can do that, too, and no, we won't live long if you scream every time she does."

After a couple of seconds, he pulled away. "I wasn't going to scream. I was just ... surprised."

"You were going to scream like a bitch."

"Takes one to know one," he shot back.

"*I'm serious,*" Cass growled. "*These halfway forms aren't particularly comfortable.*"

"Sorry."

Sadly, I saw it was likely a necessary evil. Werewolves tended to come in two sizes: extra-large and enormous. Cass wasn't as big as my dad, but her wolf form was still large enough to make navigating the narrow walk spaces down here difficult.

She turned back toward the row of bookshelves we were walking between and continued leading the way. "*How the hell does anyone find anything or even do the laundry down here? This place is a rat maze.*"

"Domestic trolls?" I offered.

She let out a quick laugh even though I wasn't entirely joking. Cass was right about this being a maze, though. Most basements I'd seen were either finished living areas or open space used for storage. This, however, was like the world's craziest librarian had gotten together with a hoarder and decided to play house.

Grammy Nessa hadn't been lying. I saw tons of dusty books and even more cobwebs. Remembering my Harry

Potter, I said a silent prayer that my aunt wasn't breeding her own version of acromantulas down here. Because if so, I was taking my chances with the psychos upstairs.

"You were hanging out down here?" I asked, my voice barely a whisper.

"Just on the stairs," Chris replied. "I only glanced down a few rows to see if maybe she had a TV, but that was about it."

Great. I'd assumed my brother had known what he was talking about. Mistake number one.

"*What the hell is most of this shit?*" Cass asked, passing by a shelf littered with jars full of what looked to be desiccated mice.

"I'm gonna go out on a limb and assume this side of the family is overdue for a yard sale."

"*It all smells old and most of it reeks of gald.*"

"Magic," I explained to Chris.

"Why would you know that?" he asked, turning toward me, his eyes once again wide. "What are you, their pet gremlin?"

"No. I'm the boogeyman. I eat the flesh of dipshit teens that piss me off."

"Aren't you supposed to be hiding in a closet where we can't see your ugly face?"

I was about to pop him one, when Cass said, "*Speaking of flesh, don't touch that book.*" She pointed to one dusty tome in particular.

"Do I really want to ask why?"

"*I'm pretty sure it's bound in human skin.*"

Well, that's certainly gross.

"Cool!" Chris said. "We should see if we can summon Bruce Campbell with it."

"*Who?*" Cass asked.

I could only imagine the look on my brother's face as

he slowly came to the realization that his dream girl was neither human nor a dork.

Soon enough, the only thing they'd have in common was that they were both living, and I had a feeling there were people after us who'd be happy to change that status quo.

22

More booms and blasts sounded from upstairs, shaking the rafters above us, as we finally reached the far end of the room we were in, only to step through another doorway and find ... more labyrinthine corridors. Chris was right on one aspect – this place was huge. It might've just been my skewed perception, especially since I was worried out of my mind, but I would have bet money that the basement stretched further than the foundation of the house above us.

A part of me wondered if this was some crazy magic thing, creating a space that was bigger on the inside than the outside. However, I realized it was just as likely that it could be a case of the house being old and having been home to many generations ... some of whom were apparently fond of digging.

The latter seemed the more sane choice, especially since cluttered among the weird knickknacks we'd seen was plenty of regular junk – an old VCR, a stack of baby strollers, boxes upon boxes of vinyl records. It gave me cause to hope that the chances of running into any dragons down here was slim.

Even so, on and on it went. It might not have been some hellish maze of torment, but it was definitely weird. I mean, hell, who has this much space in their basement and doesn't set up at least a rec room or maybe a spot for some exercise equipment?

Eventually Cass had to revert back to her human form. Sweat stood out on her face, emphasizing the effort it must've taken to maintain that halfway state. Sadly, her night vision wasn't quite as good like this. That, and she'd lost her phone at some point, probably around the time she'd shredded her clothes.

I still had forty eight percent left on my battery – not great but doable – so I took point. Chris was behind me, allowing Cass to protect our flank while keeping my brother from gawking at her nearly uncovered ass.

I swear, there was a fetish video just waiting to be made of this shit.

"Where are we?" Chris asked after a few more minutes.

"Still in the basement, duh."

"I know that, *Ham*ara."

I turned, looking to see if there was anything in reach that I could rub his face in, when there came a loud bang from somewhere behind us. It sounded more distant than it should have, but was unmistakable nevertheless.

"The door!" Cass whispered.

I nodded, then mimed for them to zip their lips.

Cass in return bared her teeth, her canines already elongating.

"Not now," I hissed. "Save it for if we get cornered."

She nodded and her face became fully human again. It was probably for the best. Her advantage lay in speed, raw savagery, and the space to use it. Down here, though, her extra size would just make her a bigger target in the narrow aisle we were walking down.

"Anyone down here?" a male voice cried out from somewhere behind us. "Come on out and we can talk."

Yeah right. Talk, as in recite whatever spell they'd use to fry our asses. Chris and I might've stood a chance of being dismissed as inconsequential, but not Cass. There was no way these assholes were letting a werewolf walk out of here.

I was tempted to send Chris back to them, wagering that as a human they might let him go, but it was a gamble pure and simple. Dweeb though he was, I wasn't about to bet on his life.

No. We were either all walking out of here or...

I turned away, not wanting to consider the alternative. Instead, I adjusted the flash on my phone down to its lowest setting and focused it on the floor in front of me. Hopefully, between all the stuff down here and our bodies blocking the light from anyone chasing us, it would be enough to keep us hidden.

"Or we can simply burn this fucking place to the ground around you!" the voice cried out again. "Everyone upstairs is dead. It won't matter if we turn this shithole into a barbecue pit."

Behind me, I heard Chris draw in a panicked huff of breath. Before I could turn to face him, though, Cass stepped in.

"They're bluffing."

"But..."

"I know your dad and I saw your mom in action," she whispered. "They're not going down that easily. Trust me, they're just trying to flush us out."

"Are you sure?"

Cass hesitated for the barest of seconds. "Yeah, I'm sure."

That seemed to calm him down. Now if I could only convince myself to believe her.

~

More sounds from behind us told me that whoever else was down here had decided to do things the hard way and search the basement.

I didn't find that entirely surprising. I still wasn't sure if Aunt Carly was under some spell or had truly gone to the dark side – praying for the former – but either way, I was hoping she wouldn't be keen on burning her family home to the ground simply to make sure a few stragglers didn't escape. That would have been a serious case of overkill, even in a shitty housing market.

It was up to us to remain one step ahead. I started to vary our route, turning once I reached the end of one set of shelves and then continuing down another, making sure we didn't double back.

The very fact that we were able to bespoke of how huge this place really was. It was crazy. Did my aunt have the fucking Batcave beneath her house? I felt like we'd walked for blocks down in this...

What the?!

I stopped dead in my tracks at the sight of movement from ahead of me. Something had run across the path at the far edge of my light. There was no intersection there, but that didn't matter. Whatever it had been was small enough to run from one bookshelf to another.

My rational mind told me it had to be a rat ... gross enough. But I didn't think so. I'd gotten just the barest of glimpses, but it was enough for my subconscious to be screaming that whatever I'd just seen, it had been bipedal.

If someone tells me that was a raccoon, I'm going to lose it.

Sadly, before I could focus my beam on the spot, Chris bumped into my backside. Without my powers, it was enough to knock me off balance and send me staggering two steps forward.

"Sorry," he whispered.

I put a hand on a bookshelf to steady myself and felt what had to be at least a century's worth of grime beneath my fingers. *Eww!* Wiping my hand off on my sweater as quickly as I could, I spun around.

My brother, no doubt thinking I was pissed, backpedaled a step, but I ignored him. "Cass, do you smell anything?"

Keeping the light low as I was, I couldn't quite make out her face, but I could hear the confusion in her voice as she whispered back, "Dust, more dust, and maybe some mouse droppings covered in dust."

"Anything else?"

"No. It's too thick in the air. I can't even tell how many people are behind us."

"What about ahead of us?"

"You think there are..."

"Just take a sniff and let me know if you sense anything ... strange."

I really had a gift for understatement. We were in the basement of a witch's house and I was asking a werewolf if she smelled anything weird. The concept was so ridiculous that I should've laughed, but right then, I didn't find it particularly funny.

Cass hesitated for a moment, probably thinking the same thing, then I heard her inhale. When we finally got out of this mess, I was definitely introducing her to Riva as "My friend Cass, who occasionally does what I ask of her."

Or maybe not. Knowing Riva, she'd try and talk her out of being cooperative.

That thought, however, was comforting. It meant I was already looking ahead to this being over. Of course, we still had to make that a reality.

After a second or two more, Cass said, "There's something up ahead."

Uh oh. "I knew I saw..."

"Not living. It smells like chemicals, but again with a heavy undertone of gald."

Chemicals?

Sadly, any questions I had were rendered moot as the corridor next to ours lit up like the Fourth of July, thanks to what appeared to be a freaking lightning bolt flaring through it.

Guess I'd been smart to vary our course a bit.

Unfortunately, any chance of us hoping it was nothing more than our pursuers trying to flush us out was lost as my brother cried, "Holy shit!"

"Whoever's down here, you'd better march your ass out now. That was your only warning."

The voices still sounded distant, but they were much closer than the last time. Guess they hadn't taken our silence at face value. Now they knew for certain at least one person was down here.

But maybe we could use that.

"Come on," I whispered, "and be quiet!"

I led us forward as quickly as I dared. Chris had already given us away, but his had hopefully been the only voice they'd heard. So far as our pursuers were concerned, there might have been nothing more than one scared kid down here ... assuming they hadn't had time to compare notes with Belzar.

I couldn't count on that, though. There were too many variables, and I wasn't exactly a statistician. What I was, however, was a wrestler. For most of my career I'd been a constant underdog in a male dominated sport. It was time to go back to basics, remember those uphill battles. This was no different, other than the fact that my opponents weren't human.

"Over there!" Cass whispered several seconds later.

I didn't need to ask her where. The shelves on our right gave way to a wall of roughly hewn stone even as the path before us appeared to continue onward into the darkness.

I was right. There was no way we were still beneath Carly's house.

"This whole place reminds me of something I read about," Chris whispered. I expected him to blather on about fortresses of solitude or other stupid crap, but he surprised me. "In history class we learned about the Underground Railroad. Think about it. This basement would have been the perfect hiding spot."

I shared a glance with Cass, both of us probably thinking the same thing. It was hard to imagine the Draíodóir being so generous with anyone not their own.

Of far greater interest than history, though, was the alcove in the wall I spotted mere moments later. This was no simple cubbyhole either. It was at least ten feet deep, but the size wasn't what caught my eye.

Tables covered with bowls, beakers, and jars stood within. A good many were full of liquids of varying hues, giving off acrid odors that didn't strike me as particularly friendly.

Faced with Satan's chemistry set, I was suddenly glad my sense of smell wasn't stronger.

"Ugh, what reeks?" Chris asked.

Besides unwashed preteen? I kept the comment to myself, though. I'd been serious about keeping quiet and using that against our pursuers.

I shushed him just as the corridor around us began to light up.

What the?

Candle sconces along the walls began to ignite, one after another, revealing that we'd stepped from the

176

confines of the basement and into the beginning of what appeared to be a long tunnel.

The only question now was: did we trip some magical light sensor, or had we been found?

23

I grabbed Cass by the arm and dragged her into the alcove with me.

Chris made to follow but I held up a hand even as I doused my phone's flash. Fortunately, the candlelight only reached to the main tunnel itself, leaving the junior alchemist's lab bathed in shadows.

"But..."

"Trust me," I said. "Please."

I realized I was taking a risk with my brother's life, and a part of me hated myself for it. If the assholes on our trail took a shoot first, ask questions later approach, I'd have doomed him as surely as if I'd killed him myself. But I didn't think that would be the case.

Whoever was chasing us had a purpose. They could've burned the house down around us if they truly wanted to be certain. But they hadn't. They could have likewise continued firing recklessly in the hopes of hitting us, trashing the place in the process.

"I'm scared," he whispered a moment before a voice cried out from the dark.

"You there! Don't move." There was a slight southern

twang to the man's voice. Definitely not Belzar ... God, what a stupid name. But maybe dealing with a minion wasn't such a bad thing.

Chris threw one more glance our way, then put his hands in the air and turned back toward the cellar.

I looked at Cass and she nodded even as she began to change, hopefully sensing we were about to unleash an ambush of our own. That done, I turned toward the beakers and began picking up random jars.

$\approx$

I peeked out as much as I dared. It didn't afford me a particularly good angle, but it was enough to see what appeared to be a ball of light approaching.

The fuck?

Remembering who we were up against, I half expected it to explode or maybe transmogrify into an army of rats or something.

However, as it drew closer, I saw it was likely no more than a light source. Two figures walked beneath it, both male and both dressed in ridiculous Christmas attire. The ball of light followed their steps, lighting up the path around them – the Draíodóir equivalent of a flashlight.

As they neared the tunnel entrance where my brother stood shaking, still bathed in candlelight, they slowed and the light ball winked out above them.

"Where are the others?" one of them asked. Despite the dim light, I made out felt reindeer antlers on his head and the fact that his clothes appeared stained ... as if maybe he'd slipped in oil and fallen on his ass.

I had to pull back lest I start snickering.

"What others?" Chris dutifully answered, sounding convincingly scared ... most likely because he was.

"Don't pull that shit, kid. I know you came down here with that freak."

I had a feeling Cass wouldn't take too kindly to...

"And that filthy mutt, too," the other replied.

The fuck?!

Either these assholes somehow knew what I was, or they were serious dicks.

"T-that t-thing ran off in the dark without me."

"Thing?"

"T-the werewolf."

"Huh," Rudolph said, his tone suggesting he was humoring my brother. The jig was likely up, but it was still too early to make a move. Even with Cass's speed, I doubted she could close the distance before at least one of them could fry her. "See, that's kinda funny. We have it on good authority that you came down here with two bitches. And while I don't doubt a mutt would run off and leave a little limp-dick like you all by your lonesome, I'm betting your sister didn't."

Fuck! These guys had definitely been briefed. The bigger question was whether that gave any credence to their earlier proclamation that everyone upstairs was dead.

Sadly, that was all the thought I could spare my parents. If I got too caught up thinking about them, I'd hesitate. And it wasn't just my life on the line here.

"Come on, kid, spill," the second one, the guy with the southern twang, said. "You want to be reunited with your mom, right?"

"But you said..."

"We were just trying to scare you," Rudolph replied, adopting a friendly tone.

"Yeah, buddy," Southern Twang added. "She's fine. We can take you right upstairs to her. Hell, you can all go home together and be a big, happy family. But we need to know where the others are first."

Come on, Chris. For once don't be stupid.

My brother, no doubt summoning whatever bravery he had left, instead replied, "I don't believe you assholes."

Ballsy. Probably not bright, but definitely ballsy. I'd have to remember that the next time I gave him grief.

"Fine, kid," Southern Twang replied. "Have it your way. Doesn't take too many brains to figure out they're close by. Probably waiting for their chance to take us down. Hell, they're probably in that alcove you're standing in front of, hoping we're dumb enough to stick our heads in."

Shit!

"Keep an eye on our six," he told Rudolph. "I'm gonna burn out anything that's hiding in there."

I saw panic bloom on Chris's face. He was about to crack. "No, don't..."

"Too late, partner. You've got no one but yourself to blame for the funeral arrangements."

Not good, but maybe I could make some lemonade out of these lemons. I glanced down at the jar in each of my hands. With any luck they were filled with something a bit more lethal than actual lemonade. Because if not...

I sensed movement behind me, and I glanced over my shoulder to find Cass crouched and prepared to race out. I quickly shook my head, hoping she wasn't too lost in her instincts to understand.

There was only one chance and, sadly, I was it.

"*Sèididh...*"

Now!

I'd seen my mother perform enough magic to have a sense of how these things worked. I had to act *before* he could complete his spell ... whatever it was.

"*...teine!*"

Just as Southern Twang spat out that final unintelligible syllable, I stepped from around the corner and let loose with both jars, one high and one low.

There wasn't much strategy to it. I couldn't throw for shit with my left hand, so I figured I'd hedge my bets rather than sending the second jar flying off into the darkness.

Both of my projectiles went sailing toward him even as a ball of red-hot flame appeared in his hands. The low throw shattered on the ground in front of him, the viscous liquid inside splattering onto the ground and ... not doing much else.

Fuck! Strike one.

The second impacted with the fireball just as it began to move away from Southern Twang. The jar exploded, sending a drenching spray of liquid onto the wizard even as the ball of flame continued flying toward me.

Oh crap. Strike two.

I could only stare wide-eyed as my death approached, but then powerful hands grabbed hold of me and dragged me to the ground.

The fireball passed by overhead, hot enough that I was certain my hair was singed, and then it impacted against the far corner of the alcove. There came a muffled thud followed by a small shower of pebbles raining down from the roof.

I glanced over to find Cass by my side. I was happy to see she hadn't done anything suicidal, like throw herself in front of me, but at the same time she was now in full sight of our attackers, meaning there wasn't much chance of us doing anything before they could launch another volley at us.

Rudolph spun back toward us and let out a laugh. "Well, damn. Isn't this a sorry ass..."

Whatever he had to say next, however, was drowned out as Southern Twang began to scream, and this wasn't some good ole' boy victory whoop, either. His hands and clothes were all smoking where the liquid from the second jar had touched him. As I watched, his clothing began to disintegrate as the flesh on his fingers sizzled.

I'd been hoping for some magical boom juice, but I'd settle for some good old fashioned acid.

That was all the distraction Cass needed. She bolted to her feet, nearly seven feet of angry werewolf, and pushed my brother to the side.

Sadly, I still didn't think she was going to make it. Rudolph, rather than help his friend, simply stepped around him and opened his mouth. "*Dorn an...*"

Before he could finish, though, the puddle of goo from that first beaker erupted at his feet. *Holy shit!* One moment it was a stain on the floor and the next it grew exponentially, reaching up, solidifying, and engulfing the wizard in what appeared to be tentacles of living gelatin.

Behind him, Southern Twang continued to scream, his hands now little more than sinewy bone as the disturbingly caustic acid continued to eat away at him.

No wonder Grammy Nessa hadn't wanted me down here.

Cass took a step toward where Rudolph continued to battle Hell's Jell-O, but I grabbed her by the arm. "Don't."

She spared him one last snarl, then turned to me and shrank back to her human form. "Probably a good idea."

"Ya think?"

"Come on," she said, waving Chris over. "Let's... What the hell?"

"What the what?" I asked.

She inclined her head. "Didn't you hear it?"

"I only hear that asshole screaming."

"Below that," she said, as if it made any sense. "I could have sworn I heard ... footsteps retreating, but they were faint ... or small like..."

"A raccoon?" I offered.

She looked at me, shrugged, then turned and began heading down the now lit tunnel.

"You coming, turd muncher?" I asked.

Chris stepped toward me, his eyes still locked on what was going on behind us.

"Come on, we need to hurry."

"Yeah, okay," he said in a small voice.

"Hey." I clapped him on the shoulder. "You did good, bro."

That seemed to get through to him. "Thanks."

"Now let's blow this pop stand."

As we followed Cass down the tunnel to God-knows-where, he again turned toward me. "Quick question. Did you release a blob monster against that guy?"

"Don't know. Don't want to know."

24

I'll admit, my imagination might've gotten the better of me as we ran.

There were more alcoves in the tunnel. Some were empty. A few appeared to be used for storage, and two had iron bars across the entrances as if they'd once been used as prison cells. All in all, it didn't do much to bolster my optimism.

The whole thing was giving off too many horror movie vibes for my own personal edification. Hell, I wouldn't have been surprised to turn back and find Freddy Krueger chasing us.

We caught up to Cass and continued on at a brisk but cautious pace. It didn't seem smart to dawdle, but at the same time the candlelight wasn't quite enough to give me confidence for a full-out panicked run for our lives. Besides, there was something to be said about conserving our strength for when we needed it.

I had a feeling neither of the two yahoos we'd left behind was going to be up for hot pursuit anytime soon. One was gonna be busy being fitted for hooks, while his buddy was currently the world's freakiest Jell-O shot.

There was still the nagging question of what Cass had thought she'd heard. It jibed with the fact that I'd seen *something* down here. It hadn't been the first time either. It seemed like things had been crossing my path ever since I'd gotten home from school.

Yeah, it could be that High Moon had maybe been infested with raccoons in the time I'd been gone, or maybe it was Mom's fucking garden gnomes – although if given the choice, I was definitely hoping for the raccoons.

I tried my best to push that nightmare fuel out of my mind as something up ahead began to take shape in the gloom.

I wasn't sure how far we'd come. Made me wish I'd enabled the fitness app on my phone. Regardless, it appeared we were nearing the end of the road, so to speak. The tunnel ended up ahead of us ... at least the horizontal portion of it.

An old spiral staircase stood at the far end of the passage. Upon reaching it, we realized it went both ways. It descended through an opening in the stone below and did the same above us into the ceiling.

"Which way?" I asked.

It was probably a stupid question, and both my companions seemed to agree with that. Down led to God knows where. Considering we were deep in witch territory, it could have been any of a thousand nightmares. Or it could be a fucking coffee shop for all we knew. That said, I wasn't willing to bet on it.

Up on the other hand, well, that hopefully held some promise.

～

On the surface – pun intended – up seemed the right choice. The stairs led to a small circular chamber. Based on the lockers along one wall and the robes hung on hooks next to them, I took a guess that this was some sort of changing room. That was fine. I could handle that. You usually didn't find monsters, demons, or human sacrifices in places where you could try on a new dress.

Though I didn't know what the people who used this place were meant to change for, that seemed unimportant compared to a short flight of stairs on the far end leading up to a pair of cellar doors beyond.

"This way," I said.

"Hold on a second."

I turned to find Cass rooting through the lockers. "Please tell me they're full of guns."

"No such luck." Not finding much, she grabbed a robe from one of the hooks and wrapped it around herself.

"You look like a first year Gryffindor," I said with a grin.

"Better than a first year porn star."

"On Christmas day, no less."

It was gallows humor, but by then blowing off a little steam was kind of necessary.

"Come on, you guys!" Chris cried. standing near the doors leading out but not quite brave enough to venture forth without us.

"Just like a guy," I said to Cass. "The second you cover up, they lose all interest."

"This isn't a joke, Tamara."

I turned to my brother. "Relax, skeeve. We're just taking a minute to catch our breath."

"Speaking of which," Cass said, "stand back."

"Why?"

"I'm going to see what I can do to dissuade anyone from following."

She stepped forward, changing into that halfway form

again, grabbed the spiral staircase, and gave it an exploratory yank.

"I wish I could help," I said lamely.

"*Me too,*" she replied. "*This is sunk into the rock pretty deep. I don't think I can budge it. But maybe I can budge those.*"

Cass's body enlarged into her full werewolf form. Amusingly enough, the robe had been a smart choice. It was loose enough so that it didn't tear as she changed. Although, while it had fully covered her as a human, now she looked like a werewolf wearing a small bath robe.

There was almost certainly an Internet fetish for that.

I backed up to where Chris waited wide-eyed as Cass stepped over to the row of lockers.

"Relax," I said. "You've seen this already. She's on our side."

"Relax?" he echoed. "Did you see all the shit that's been happening?"

"You know, Mom would really not approve of your language."

"Language?!" he cried, obviously not appreciative of my attempt at levity. "How the fuck aren't you freaking out?"

Cass dragged several of the lockers from where they'd been anchored into the wall. The sound was deafeningly loud, but there wasn't much we could do about it.

"And why did she ask if you were human?" Chris added once I could hear him again.

And there it was. A part of me was tempted to heed my parents and tell him he'd heard wrong but, dork that he was, I gave him credit for not being stupid enough to buy that, especially not now. What could it hurt for him to hear the truth?

He deserved it.

And if he didn't, Mom could always blank his mind. *Assuming Mom isn't...*

I pushed that thought from my head. "All of this ... is pretty new to me. But *not* as new as it is to you."

"How long have you known about...," he gestured around us, "*this*?"

"Since the summer."

"And you didn't tell me?!"

"Mom and Dad didn't want you to know."

"Why the fuck not?!"

"Ramp down the volume," I told him. "Inside voice."

"I'm not five."

"Then don't act like it." I took a deep breath as Cass continued to pile the lockers over the staircase opening. It wouldn't hold long against a persistent wizard, but every second could potentially count. "They wanted you to have a normal life. That's all. Knowing this stuff without being a part of it, well, it's dangerous."

"Like now?"

"Pretty much."

"So, are Mom and Dad ... like those guys?"

Fuck it. There was no point in giving him a half-truth at this juncture. What was to be gained? Besides, they say confession is good for the soul. "No. Dad's a werewolf like Cass, only bigger and a lot tougher."

She glanced at me.

"Well, he is. As for Mom, she's a Draío..." Gah! I could think it, but my tongue still refused to say it."

"You mean a druid?" Chris asked.

"Huh?"

"They're a player class in D&D. You know, Dungeons and Dragons?"

"Um, sure. Go with that. Bottom line is she can cast spells."

"Can she brew love potions, too?"

189

"Really? That's the most important thing you want to ask about? Sorry. She's a witch, not a miracle worker."

Rather than throw back a snarky comeback, a testament to how scared he must've been, he instead asked, "So what does that make you?"

"Um..."

"I mean, I know I'm adopted. And even though I like to joke that they mixed you up at the hospital with some inbred gimp family, I know you're really theirs."

"You're theirs, too, you know."

He actually smiled at that. "You know what I mean."

Before I could answer, though, Cass joined us, shrinking back down to her human form again. Sweat stood out on her forehead, reminding me that she'd been pulling most of the weight since we'd started running. As if I didn't feel guilty enough. "That's as good as I can do for now. Shall we?"

I nodded. "Ready to venture out to the wild blue yonder?"

"More like enemy territory for me."

"All things considered, that might be true for all of us."

25

W e emerged into a clearing in the woods, but it was instantly obvious this wasn't some mere picnic spot.

Well, okay, there was a barbecue pit off to one end, just outside the tree line. But the rest of it seemed to be taken up by a series of concentric circles, each made of different materials.

The outside was merely a dirt mound that ran around the perimeter. Next were common paver stones, followed by marble. The building materials for the circles seemed to get more exotic and expensive as they approached the middle: quartz, iron, agate, jadeite, brass, silver. Hell, it would've been a dream come true for someone with a metal detector.

The final circle in the middle, right inside the silver one, was the only one none of us could identify. It gleamed almost with a light all its own even though there was no direct sunlight. Also, being that I'm too stupid to know better, I bent down to examine it and discovered it was warm to the touch, despite the freezing temperature out. *Just like my pendant chain...*

"Any idea what this place is for?" I asked Cass.

"Honestly? Beats the shit out of me."

"Who cares?" Chris replied, back in irritating little brother mode. "It's fucking freezing out here."

"Nothing in your wolf mythology?" I continued, ignoring my brother

"Sorry. Lycanthropes and Draíodóir don't fraternize ... at least not normally." She stared at me hard as she said it but then turned away.

Cass headed toward the far edge of the clearing, mentioning that way was east, the direction back to High Moon – and Morganberg, for that matter. Not that I didn't trust her, but I double checked using the compass app on my phone.

"Something on your mind?" I asked once I'd caught up to her.

"What that witch, your aunt, said back there. We'd been led to believe that..."

"Come on, Cass," I said, as we set off through the trees, the woods disturbingly quiet all around us. "Now's not the time to be coy."

"Fine. We'd been led to believe, for years now, that Curtis's treaty marriage was just that – a treaty, a way to symbolically bind our people together. But then, after last summer, a rumor started floating around that ... *you know who* had bewitched him and that's how you came about."

"You know who? What? You think Voldemort banged my dad?"

She chuckled. "Sorry. Nobody likes to say her name. No offense, but your mom ... she's a bit of a boogeyman to us. Some mothers tell their kids that if they're bad the Queen of the Monarchs will swoop down and eat them in their sleep."

"No shit?" Chris asked, his arms wrapped around himself.

I couldn't blame him. It *was* cold out, even more so without my powers. I kind of wished I'd thought to grab some more of those robes to wrap around us. For now, at least, walking and talking took my mind off the fact that we'd likely succumb to hypothermia before making it home.

"Cross my heart," Cass replied to my brother. "But back there, what your aunt said. Are they ... really married?"

"Duh," Chris said, ignorant little dipstick that he was. "Of course they're married."

She turned toward me. "*You* know what I mean."

There was no point denying it. "Yeah, it's true. I mean, it's not exactly some storybook romance. According to them, the whole thing started off as kind of an accident."

"You mean them meeting in college?" Chris asked.

"Sorry to break it to you, bro, but that one is total BS."

"Good. I hate that story."

I smiled but decided to spare him the gruesome details – that our parents had started off trying to kill each other but ended up getting their freak on instead, beneath a blood moon no less. As they say, the devil is in the details. "What they have is real," I continued. "And while it wasn't exactly planned, it wasn't a case of one of them being hypnotized."

"Like in this porno me and my friends..."

I narrowed my eyes at him. "Your friends *what*?"

"Um, heard about."

Yuck! There wasn't enough brain bleach in the world to exorcise the image of my brother and his band of loser geeks having a circle jerk. I was half tempted to turn around and head back to our aunt's house. Surely that was the kinder fate.

"The others aren't going to like that," Cass said, getting

back to the subject at hand. "They're going to see it as a betrayal. I hate to say it but ... I can kind of see why Craig lost his shit about it."

"Do you have to tell them?" I asked.

"You don't disobey the alpha," she said, her eyes downcast.

"I doubt my dad is going to put you on the hot seat."

"I didn't mean him."

There it was again, that mysterious alpha female. And now I had to wonder whether she'd be angry out of a sense of pack loyalty or because of something pettier, like jealousy.

If we lived through this mess, it was a question I'd need to get answered, one way or the other.

∽

"S-so let me get this straight," Chris asked through chattering teeth. "You're p-part witch and part werewolf?"

"More or less." The cold wasn't affecting me as badly, but I was definitely feeling it. My toes had gone numb at least ten minutes ago. Sadly, while I'd love to say we'd made good time, the snow on the ground was making our progress pathetically slow.

I tried to convince Cass to go ahead, try to reach someone who could help, not that I had any clue who that might be. But she refused to leave us behind.

The problem was we had no idea who to trust in Crescentwood. I had to assume most of the Draíodóir living here knew of the planned peace talks. Even so, there was no guarantee they wouldn't immediately open fire on a werewolf in their town. And then there was Belzar. What if there were others here who were in on his attempted coup?

She was right. It was too risky. I needed to get my

brother out of this town and somewhere safe. After that, well, then it would be the time to consider doing something stupid.

"Were you born with fur and a tail?" he asked, continuing his line of questioning.

"No, dweeb. Unlike you, I was a cute baby."

"Too bad it didn't stick," he replied between shivers.

Had we not been in danger of freezing to death, I'd have pegged him upside the head with a snowball.

"Can you cast spells?"

"No."

"Um, are you allergic to silver?"

I reached into my sweater and pulled out the necklace I was wearing, a pretty silver charm I'd gotten for my seventeenth birthday. "Nope."

"Okay, s-so w-what can you do ... besides repel boyfriends?"

Before I could throw caution to the wind and clobber the little shit so as to warm myself up a bit, Cass stepped in. "Don't be so sure. I think David was checking your sister out the other night."

He was?

"Who's David?" Chris asked, cupping his hands in front of his mouth and breathing into them.

"Another werewolf," I said.

"A cute one," Cass added.

"So, did you guys do it doggy..."

I punched him in the arm. "Finishing that sentence would be detrimental to your health."

"Ow! Fine. So then what..."

"I'm strong, okay?"

"That's an understatement," Cass replied. "You kicked the crap out of Mitch."

"Mitch?" Chris asked. "Dad's cousin Mitch?"

I nodded. "He's a werewolf, too."

"And you fought him?"

"More than that," Cass said. "I've never seen anything like it."

"So why the hell didn't you do that back there?" my brother asked, an accusing edge to his voice.

I couldn't get angry, though. For starters, it was a question I knew was coming. Also, it was getting way too cold to fly into a blind rage. "It's because I couldn't."

"Why not? Did you suddenly become a pacifist?"

"I'm not, trust me on that one. It's not that I didn't want to. I *couldn't*. Right now I'm ... not as weak as your scrawny ass, but I'm not much stronger either."

"Why? Do you hulk out under the full moon or something like that?"

I kept my eyes from meeting Cass's. At this point it was probably stupid to keep secrets, but I wasn't sure I wanted my personal weakness out there in the open. So instead I lamed out with a quick, "Yeah. Something like that."

"Too bad. That would have been kinda cool to watch."

A rare compliment from my brother. Yeah, it definitely would be cool to be at full strength, I considered, thinking back to my encounter at school right before Riva picked me up.

Wait ... Riva!

God, what an idiot I could be sometimes. I pulled my phone out and checked it. The battery was under thirty percent now, but that was more than enough. Even better, I had two bars, which meant we weren't too far from civilization.

I pulled up my contact list.

"What are you doing?" Cass asked.

"Calling for help."

"Why didn't you do that sooner?" Chris practically screamed at me.

"Because we were underground and I was too busy saving your stupid ass."

"*Bent?*"

Oh crap. I hadn't realized she'd already answered. "Sorry, Riva. I wasn't talking about your stupid ass."

~

I gave Riva the Cliff's Notes version, telling her that things had gone south and we were kind of running for our lives. It was too cold for a long soliloquy and I wanted to save a little bit of battery in case of emergency ... or another emergency anyway.

Fortunately, she already knew I'd taken my pills for the day. She hadn't approved when I'd told her, but it saved me the trouble of bringing her up to speed.

"*How long before they wear off?*"

"Not soon enough. Any chance of getting a pickup?"

"*Are you kidding? I'm already putting my coat on. Like I'd leave you there.*"

"What are you going to tell your parents?"

"*Nothing. Mom and Dad have the Yule log on TV and they've already killed a bottle of eggnog. I doubt they'll even notice I'm gone. Where are you?*"

I glanced around, noticing nothing but trees. "No idea. Somewhere in Crescentwood."

Riva sighed into the receiver, but said, "*Okay fine. Route 154 turns into Gossamer Lane when it hits Crescentwood. It runs all the way through the eastern part of town from north to south. Make your way there and I'll find you.*"

"Thanks, Riva. I owe you one."

"*Just be safe.*"

"I'll try." It was a promise I wasn't sure I'd be able to keep.

I hung up and put the phone back in my pocket, my numb fingers managing to get it right on the third try.

"W-well?" Chris asked.

"Help is on the way. We just need to make it to Gossamer Lane."

Cass turned to me. "Any idea how far that is?"

"Beats me, I was hoping you'd know."

"Are you kidding? I've never stepped foot in this town before."

I considered her, standing there wearing wizarding robes and not much else. "Why don't you switch to your wolf form? No point in all of us getting frostbite." Chris's eyes opened wide at that. "Oh relax. I'm kidding."

"I hope the heat in Riva's car works."

"You and me both, kiddo."

Cass glanced back at me. "Don't think I haven't considered changing. But here in this town, I don't know. You're probably going to think I'm a wimp but..."

"But what?"

"I don't want to die."

I trudged over and put a hand on her shoulder, noting how warm she felt. "That doesn't make you a wimp."

"Any other forest in this country and I'd be wearing a fur coat by now, but Crescentwood... They talk about this place where I'm from. They say it's like a roach motel, but for my kind."

"Werewolves check in..."

"But they don't check out. My people talk like the whole town is haunted. I mean, no offense, but if Mitch hadn't ordered me, there's no way I'd have come."

I couldn't blame her. I'd been nervous enough coming here, but Cass was a known enemy. Whereas my goal today had been to keep a low profile, hers more likely revolved around ducking any potshots headed her way.

"Considering how things turned out," I replied, "I'm

halfway between sorry we dragged you along and glad as all hell you're here."

"Thanks."

"No prob."

"So ... can I ask you a question?"

"Sure, what?"

"What did your friend mean by something wearing off?"

"You heard that?" I held up a hand. "Never mind. Of course you did."

She smiled. "Sorry. Didn't mean to eavesdrop. It's kind of automatic."

I should have guessed. "It's ... some medicine I took."

"It's about your powers, isn't it?" When I didn't immediately answer, she said, "Hey, look, it's cool. You don't need to tell me and I don't want to know. The only part I'm interested in is whether it's something that can help us."

I shrugged. We were past the halfway mark for my pills, hopefully anyway. But that still didn't put me in any position to make a difference. No. Our best bet was for Riva to find us and then haul ass over the town line to...

But what if that didn't stop them from following us?

High Moon existed as a buffer between the two races, a neutral zone. But it was more a metaphorical barrier, as my uncle had shown...

The crunch of something landing in the snow caught my attention, and I turned to find my brother on his hands and knees. *Oh crap!*

"Are you okay?" I asked, leaning down over him.

"I ... just ... need to rest for a minute."

"That's the hypothermia talking. You need to keep moving."

"I can't."

"Yes you can." *Ugh!* He was heavier than he looked. "Come on. Don't make me plant my foot up your ass."

"Hold on," Cass said, walking back to us. "Let me help."

She hesitated for a moment, a worried look on her face, but then she changed. Her whole body expanded, putting on about six inches in height. A thin layer of fur grew on her exposed skin and her face elongated about halfway.

She reached down and easily hauled Chris to his feet. *"Help me get him on my back."*

I did as she told me, shoving my brother into place until he was able to wrap his arms around her neck and his legs around her waist.

"Now stay put," I told him. "And try not to get any nerd boners while you're at it."

He was in worse shape than the rest of us, but still managed to chuckle at my dig.

"How about you?" I asked Cass. "I thought you said..."

"I know. And I'm terrified out of my mind. But we can't just leave him there."

It was weird hearing something so vulnerable said in a voice that sounded like it was tempered by broken glass, but I was glad to have her help. "How long can you hold that form."

"Hopefully long enough."

"Good, because..." I trailed off as movement caught the corner of my eye. Unfortunately, by the time I was able to focus, it was gone, whatever it was. All I got was a momentary glimpse of grey disappearing into the underbrush.

Cass must've noticed because her head whipped in that direction. *"What was that?"*

"Either another raccoon or proof that I'm going bonkers."

"You're not bonkers. I thought I heard a twig snap."

"That's good."

"Don't be so sure. I can't smell anything that way. There's nothing but... Oh, no."

"Nothing but what?" I'll admit, there might have been a slight edge of panic to my voice.

Cass immediately spun back in the direction we'd been heading. *"I don't think we're alone out here."*

Great. Just what I needed to hear.

26

"I don't suppose it's too much to hope it's just a squirrel and some deer."

Cass shook her head. *"Deer don't usually reek of gald."*

"Bambi might."

The look she gave suggested her opinion of me was rapidly dropping. Sue me for trying to maintain an upbeat attitude. "Okay, so what do we do?"

I'm not an idiot. I was powerless in the woods with my half-frozen brother and a werewolf. Between the three of us, I knew who I'd choose to follow.

"This way," Cass said after a few moments. *"I smell wood burning. There's a house up ahead."*

"Think that's a good idea?"

She merely shrugged, then turned from the course we'd been taking. The best I could do was follow her and hope that my waning strength in the unbearable cold held out.

I knew Cass was taking it easy so as to not lose me, so I tried my best to do my part. It was tough going, though.

The snow hadn't melted much from the past few days, but it had compressed enough so that it was like trudging through a swamp.

After several more freezing minutes, I spotted an opening in the trees up ahead. Past it stood a cozy-looking colonial home.

I'd been debating whether it was safe, or even sane, to approach any of the houses in Crescentwood, but it was no longer an academic question. Cass said we weren't alone out here, and I had no reason to doubt her. And if she smelled magic, well, it seemed a safe bet to assume it wasn't simply a group of preteen warlocks outside conjuring magical snowmen.

I knew how acute werewolf senses could be. Hell, I'd spent the last semester listening to my dorm mates getting it on from several floors away. I knew far more nicknames, passwords, and secrets than I really felt comfortable knowing. And that wasn't even counting the myriad of smells. Don't get me started on those.

"Cass!" I hissed just before she was about to hit the tree line.

She came to a halt and turned to me questioningly.

"You might want to shave your legs before we see if anyone's home."

After a moment she nodded and I helped Chris get down off her back. Thankfully, he was able to stand on his own again.

"How you doing, bro?"

"She's ... so warm," he replied.

"And that's quite possibly the creepiest answer anyone could give."

"He's not wrong, though," Cass replied, having shifted back to her human form. "Lycanthropes typically run about ten degrees hotter than humans."

That definitely explained why she was feeling the cold weather a lot less than either of us. I briefly wondered if my own internal temperature had changed when not in the grip of my meds. It wasn't like I'd been sick since discovering my abilities. Still, that was something best stowed away for now. I could play doctor – preferably with a cutie like David Hood – at some other time.

We stepped from the tree line and onto the property. This place looked familiar. I'd seen it before. Not in an, "Oh, that's where Uncle So-and-So lives" sort of way, but from having passed it before on the way to my aunts place. "I think I know where we are."

"That's good," a voice called out to us as we stepped around a Honda hatchback in the driveway. "Because now we know where you are, too."

～

"Don't be scared," Aunt Carly said to me. "Come on out." She was standing further down the driveway, flanked on either side by two men. In the movies they would have all been wearing wizard cloaks stamped with their coven of allegiance, but this was the real world. My aunt was wearing a coat with the hood up while the two guys with her were dressed in ski jackets, as if they were planning on checking out the local black diamond trails after dealing with us.

As I looked closer, though, I realized they weren't Belzar's goons. She was with Gavin and Jeremy, the wizard my father had been chatting with.

I won't lie. I breathed a sigh of relief at seeing two friendly faces and not some assholes dressed like Christmas elves. That had been starting to seriously weird me out.

Still, whether it was instinct or paranoia, I hesitated to run out with my arms open wide.

I decided to play dumb for the moment, as there weren't a lot of options left at my disposal. Behind me, still semi-obscured by the car, I heard Cass let out a low growl. I held out a hand to her, indicating that she stand down.

Our defensive situation was only marginally better than it had been in the tunnel. If things went south – which I desperately hoped they didn't – there was no way Cass would be able to close the distance before someone got off a spell.

The thing was, that assumed the worst and I wasn't quite sure I wanted to do that. Carly had easily been amongst my favorites growing up. Even so, she'd said some pretty damning things back at the house.

But then I remembered the glassy-eyed look she'd worn when she'd first let Belzar in. I'd assumed it had been tears, but now I had to wonder whether something else was at play.

My aunt appeared clear-eyed now, but that didn't mean anything at the distance we stood from one another. At the same time, I didn't want to see her get injured if she was merely a pawn in this.

Realizing I probably only had a second or two before Chris took off running toward Gavin, his favorite gaming buddy, I took a tentative step forward. "I-I don't know what's going on. All those ... things that happened back at the house. And we've been running ever since."

"I know, honey. And I'm really sorry. Look, everything's been taken care of. Why don't you come over here and we can head back?"

"But ... the things those people did. Roger..."

She nodded, her face growing dim. "I understand, sweetie. Believe me, I do. And I can explain it all. I promise. But come on. It's cold out here. Your brother and your friend there have got to be freezing."

I didn't sense any deception in her tone, and she was

being careful not to mention magic. Maybe she'd been bewitched by Belzar earlier and had finally broken free.

"Come on, buddy," Gavin called out to Chris. "After you warm yourself up a bit, we can play some Mario Party."

He might as well have laid out a trail of cocaine to a drug addict.

I could hear Chris coming up behind me, but I held up a hand, hoping he heeded it. I wasn't quite convinced yet that we should...

"Who's out there?"

We spun toward the house to see an older woman, maybe around sixty, standing on the stoop.

Considering the car in the driveway, I probably should've assumed the owners were home and might eventually notice the not-so-quiet conversation going on in their yard.

The woman, presumably the owner, looked around until her eyes settled on Carly and her two companions. "Carolyn?"

"Merry Christmas, Margaret," Carly called back. "Sorry about the intrusion. We were just out looking for..."

The woman's face immediately softened. "What a relief. I thought it might be some hooligans out causing trouble. I've been hearing the most dreadful rumors lately."

"Nope. It's only us, and we were just leaving."

"Oh, don't be a stranger. Come on in." She turned around. "Peter, put some cheese and crackers on the coffee table."

Okay, this was getting more surreal by the moment.

"Really, we can't stay." Carly said.

"Nonsense," the woman – Margaret, I presumed –

replied. She stepped down the stairs and then turned her head, focusing on the rest of us. "Oh my. What are you children doing out here without coats on? You'll catch your..." Suddenly her eyes narrowed as she looked past me at Cass. "What are you doing wearing one of the matriarch's robes?"

"Oh, Margaret," another voice called out. Back in my aunt's direction, Belzar stepped from behind one of the trees dotting the front yard, a grin plastered on his face. "I'm sorry to say, but you really should have gone back inside, you silly goose you. My dear, if you will."

That last part was directed at my aunt. I turned to face her just as she cried out in a trebled voice.

"*Dust of Devils!*"

～

Despite the odd lack of Gaelic, it was obvious my aunt had just called upon her power to cast a spell. But at who?

Sadly, that question was answered a split second later as the snow covering the lawn directly in front of the house began to whip up into a funnel cloud. This was no mere freak storm, though. A screech came from within, as if dozens of bats had been sucked up into it, and then I caught sight of multiple sets of red, glowing eyes staring out from the rapidly growing vortex.

"Oh my God."

My voice was lost to both the howling wind and Margaret's screams as the miniature tornado slammed into her and her home.

Simultaneously, Gavin and Jeremy both screamed out spells, unleashing sizzling orbs of flame at the house. All the while, Belzar stood where he was, looking smug at the carnage he'd orchestrated.

Margaret disappeared from sight as the roof of her home collapsed from the force of the magical funnel cloud. For a moment, I could hear her screams rising in pitch, only to fall silent against the screech of the bedeviled winds.

The other spells collided with the home in that same instant, both of them slamming through the now destroyed front façade of the colonial. As for me, I'd seen enough movies to have an idea of what came next.

I spun and tackled my brother to the ground just as the house exploded from within. Cass hit the dirt next to us, already changed to her wolf form as debris rained around us.

The only upside was that we'd landed with the car between us and the people obviously not here to save us.

When the worst had passed, I dared a glance behind me. The house wasn't completely leveled, but enough damage had been done to leave me doubting anyone had survived.

Almost as if in confirmation, something landed next to us with a *thud*. Before I could turn my head to see what it was, Chris started screaming.

"Fucking hell!"

I pivoted and found the jagged remains of a skull facing us. One bloodshot eyeball remained in its socket, staring out at me almost accusingly – rightfully so. After all, we'd caused this by coming here.

"Are you still with us, kiddies?" Belzar called out, sounding almost cheerful. What the fuck was up with this bastard?

I narrowed my eyes, anger and sorrow warring for the top spot in my emotional conundrum. "Stay down," I hissed at my brother as I pushed myself to my knees.

"Don't," he warned, but I ignored him.

I pulled myself up just enough to peer past the car. Carly and the two others were standing where they'd been, as if they hadn't just annihilated a house and the occupants within. Belzar was now leaning against the tree, looking bored.

"Margaret was right, you know," Carly said, spotting me. That tired cadence was back in her voice. "That thing isn't worthy of wearing one of our robes."

"Apparently not right enough," I shouted back, unable to help myself. "Whatever he did to you, you need to snap out of it!"

"And there it is, my love." She turned toward Belzar. "Listen to her voice. She's not surprised by any of this. I told you she wasn't what we'd all thought."

Shit!

Behind me, I could hear the heavy crunch of snow that told me Cass was likely getting ready to spring into action. Much as I would've loved to see her kick some ass right at that moment, though, it was suicide.

Jeremy and Gavin began to spread out, no doubt sensing an attack was imminent. I tossed Cass a quick shake of my head, hoping she heeded my advice.

"So when are we going to see this so-called hybrid in action?" Belzar asked, picking his nails. God, I so wanted to feed him his teeth.

"I have no idea what you're talking about," I said, despite it likely being far too late to continue the charade. *When the hell did she figure it out?*

"Oh come now, girl," he replied. "Playing stupid doesn't suit you. That furball changed right next to you in the dining room. The fact that you didn't run in terror right then and there speaks volumes."

"Maybe because I was busy running from your asshole buddies."

"I'm getting bored here. Do we have to fry the fuzzball to get a little show and tell going? Or your brother maybe?"

"Why are you doing this?" Chris cried out from his spot still on the ground.

"Sorry, sweetie," Carly replied, her voice tired and stilted sounding, as if she were talking in her sleep. "I really am. This doesn't include you."

Gavin turned to Belzar and spoke, his voice likewise sounding as if he were swimming through mud. "We could always blank him."

Belzar appeared to consider this. "True. I suppose we could always tell the little unremarkable that his family died in a car crash or something. Doesn't matter much to me."

"Poor thing would be an orphan all over again," Carly added, sounding genuinely regretful. "But that's what family is for – to get through the tough times."

The fuck?! Was I actually hearing this?

"Send your brother out, Tamara," Carly said after a few more seconds.

When I didn't answer, Belzar added, "One-time offer. I'm willing to let him walk away from this. You have my word."

"Your word?" I shouted back. "You killed Melody and God knows who else. It's fucking Christmas, you heartless prick!"

"Well, shit. You kiss your mother with that mouth?"

I turned toward my aunt, hoping to reach her. "She's your sister, for God's sake!"

Carly stared at me blankly for several seconds, making me hope I'd gotten through to her. I'd always heard how close she and my mother were as kids. If love could break through whatever was going on in her head, then maybe...

"She's a traitor," Carly said at last. "She brought this on herself with her lies."

Now it was my turn to fall silent. How the hell did she know about my mother, or about me for that matter? I had no idea, but it seemed smarter to not incriminate myself further. "This isn't you, Aunt Carly. I love you. Mom loves you. You know this."

"Did you get that bullshit from a psychology class or something?" Belzar asked with a chuckle. "This grows tiresome. Do something about it, my sweet Carolyn."

"Keep watch for the wolf," Carly said to the others. "Send your brother out, Tamara. He's free to go. Don't waste this opportunity."

I pulled back and turned toward both Chris and Cass. She was on all fours, no doubt waiting for an opening. He was still hunkered behind the car, his eyes wide as dinner plates.

My aunt was right. He wasn't a part of this. For all the times I threatened to beat the snot out of him, he was still my brother and I loved him. "Go."

"But..."

"This isn't your fight. You need to get out of here and find help."

He looked at me like I was crazy. "Fuck no." Before I could threaten to kick his ass, he added, "You need to read more comics. The bad guys never hold up their end of the bargain. They'd probably just use me as bait."

"Come on, Chris, buddy," Gavin called. "We can be back in front of the Xbox within the hour."

"Here's my answer," Chris yelled back, raising one hand over the hood of the car, his middle finger outstretched.

Crazy and stupid as it was, I had to admit my respect for him grew three sizes that day. Maybe not for his intelligence, but he definitely had guts.

"So be it," Belzar said with a wave of his hand.

My aunt nodded at him before facing us again. "I didn't want to do this, but maybe it's for the best. You, your mother, and that goddamned beast she let touch her. You've desecrated all we hold dear and I, for one, will tolerate it no longer."

27

"*W*ind blade!"

The fact that my aunt's spells were in English was a bit strange, but linguistics were low on my priority list at that point. Besides, at the very least, I could tell she wasn't exactly planning on pulling a rabbit out of her hat.

"Move!" I shouted to Cass, even as I grabbed Chris and dragged him toward me. Good timing on my part, too, as something slammed into the car a moment later, bisecting it.

Holy shit!

It was like the world's biggest and most invisible scalpel, except – judging by the hurricane force blowback that hit me a moment later – it had been made of nothing but air.

Double holy shit!

"Only warning shot you're getting."

Warning shot?!

I realized a moment later that, in throwing ourselves wide to avoid the spell, we were all exposed now. What a stupid hiding spot. If an entire house hadn't been safe from this group, then no fucking way would a mid-sized car do the job.

There was no need for me to tell Cass to run. She was already on the move, heading back toward the tree line from which we'd emerged. Smart. From there she could...

"*Mhéara ar tintreach!*" Gavin cried.

Fast as Cass was, even she couldn't outrun the miniature lightning storm that erupted around her. She was mid-stride when she was struck by several electrical discharges, knocking her to the ground and leaving her twitching.

She was stunned, pretty hard from the look of things, but it was better than the alternative. Sadly, Jeremy was already on the move, heading to provide backup to Gavin. I didn't like Cass's odds against one wizard, much less two, and with her already down she'd be easy pickings.

"Mmm-mmm, Kentucky fried wolf, my favorite," Belzar said with a cackle from where he continued to loiter. Arrogant cock.

"Stay put," I growled at my brother, already pushing off in a run.

There was no thought involved, no consideration that I was doing little more than throwing my life away.

Chris called out my name a split second before the two Draíodóir drowned him out.

"*A 'briseadh làmhan!*"

Throwing myself on top of Cass's prone form, I realized with some horror that I recognized that spell. It was the magical equivalent of an implosion, like throwing a human body into a car crusher set to liquefy.

And, lucky me, I'd just thrown myself right into the line of fire.

～

It was as if my own personal gravity tripled or worse. For a moment, there was nothing but crushing pressure all around me, giving me a second to consider just how bad a way to die this was. Then, just as my ribcage was beginning to bend, the pressure let up and I could breathe again.

The hell?

I glanced back, certain that the duo had pulled their punch at the last second. Perhaps the realization that they were about to kill me – someone they'd known for a good chunk of their lives – had finally cut through whatever ethereal ass they had their heads stuffed up.

However, much as I wanted to believe that, a look of confusion stood upon both men's mugs, their faces red from the effort of the spell.

"What the fuck?" Jeremy asked. "Did we miss?"

Beneath me, Cass let out a groan, starting to snap out of being flash-fried. I never thought I'd be so happy for those insane werewolf constitutions.

"*H-how?*" she managed to croak through her wolf muzzle.

Before I could answer – not that I knew what to say – the two chuckle-fucks who'd just tried to pulp me decided to ratchet things up a notch.

"*Dorn an bháis!*"

Shouted together, it sounded as if a small army of wizards was screaming from the pit of Hell. Far worse, though, was the swirling miasma of black energy that came catapulting toward us, as if they'd summoned the infinite void itself.

"Go!" I shouted to Cass, even knowing she likely wasn't recovered enough to get out of the way in time. I didn't possess her speed, sadly, which meant my chances of dodging were even worse.

Guess I'd gotten lucky once more than I was due this day, because my luck was about to run out.

I held onto my friend, shielding her with my body as best I could, as the bolt of energy slammed into me.

The next thing I knew, we were both sent tumbling end over end.

I'd expected to be outright vaporized. The fact that I hadn't been was definitely welcome, but it still felt like I'd been nailed in the gut with a baseball bat.

Mind you, I considered as I skidded to a halt in a pile of slush, hurting was a lot better than being erased from existence. But how in hell had I even survived? Both wizards had just thrown some heavy-duty firepower my way – killing magic, if I wasn't mistaken. Glancing up, I saw both men panting heavily from the effort, a testament to the fact they hadn't been holding back.

I turned toward Cass. She was already recovering from being tossed about, but her face was still a mask of surprise – assuming I was reading her correctly. And why shouldn't it be? Powerless as I was, those spells should have killed us. Unless...

A thought hit me. *What if...?* I lifted my hand and slapped it down onto the frozen ground.

"Ow!" Nope. Still powerless.

But that made no sense, unless maybe I had a small platoon of guardian angels watching over me. Sadly, I wasn't quite ready to believe that.

"Tamara!" Chris shouted from somewhere close by.

Fuck!

The little turdling had decided to grow a set and was rushing toward us, best as he could anyway.

"Get back," I wheezed at him. "We're okay."

"*Um, how are we okay?*" Cass asked, having shifted her face to that halfway state.

I opened my mouth, ready to tell her I had no clue.

My meds hadn't worn off. I was still under their effect. My strength wasn't...

Hold on a second ... strength!

~

I thought back to this summer, when I'd first learned my pills were nothing more than a concoction designed to keep my powers in check.

They were a combination of science and magic. The thing was, I'd since learned that I had a heavy resistance to the latter. The only way for my meds to affect me fully was to swallow them, allowing the alchemy to work internally because my external defenses were too strong.

My parents had been pretty specific as to what my meds did: they muted my strength and rendered my scent normal. I only realized now they hadn't actually said anything about the pills dampening my resistance to spells. I'd only assumed that was the case.

Another memory flashed through my mind at the speed of thought, the end of summer: I'd just gotten my ass handed to me by my own father. As I lay there on the driveway of our home, listening to him lead the were-wolves away, my mother had appeared, along with Carly and several of her coven. She was leading the cleanup crew, there to erase – *blank* – the memory of the attack from the minds of the survivors ... and to feed me my pills again so the Draíodóir wouldn't suspect I was anything but a victim.

It was that point which struck me now. Seeing the look of panic in my eyes, my mother had leaned down and told me not to worry because the blanking spell wouldn't have worked on me anyway.

I hadn't thought much of it at the time. But why tell

me something like that if the pills would have made it all a moot point?

It wasn't a lot to go on. But it was all we had.

~

"Be ready," I said quietly as my brother continued heading our way.

Cass nodded. "*The tree line isn't too far...*"

"Forget the tree line. We're gonna take these fuckers out."

"*How?*"

I smiled. "You're going to think I'm crazy, but I want you to charge straight at them..."

"*But...*"

"...and I need you to hold me out in front of you like a human shield while you do it."

28

M y request was on the far side of batshit, and I think Cass understood that.

But she was also smart enough to realize we were fucked otherwise. She could have saved herself by racing to the tree line, but even then she'd still be stuck alone far behind enemy lines. Regardless of whether they were infected by Belzar's mind-fucking or not, I doubted there wouldn't be at least some along the way who'd be happy to take a pot shot at the werewolf running across their lawn. The Christmas spirit only extended so far.

The only plan we had going for us was a crazy one, and we needed to do it before Belzar and my aunt decided they wanted a piece of the action, too.

"Now!"

Cass leapt to her feet behind me as I pushed myself up. Her powerful hands grabbed hold of me around the waist, lifted me off the ground – giving me a second to consider the fact that I was about to let a werewolf use me as a meat shield – and then we were moving.

I am so going to regret this.

I screamed for Chris, a mix of horror and confusion

etched onto his face, to get behind us and then I had to close my mouth against the rush of cold air. Holy crap! At full strength, I was pretty fast, but remind me to never race a werewolf across open terrain. We closed the distance to the two wizards far faster than I expected.

Their eyes opened wide in surprise and, proving they loved their own asses more than any lingering feelings they had for me, they both opened fire with a litany of spells.

Crap, crap, crap!

It probably wasn't the best these two were capable of, but what came flying at us appeared more than enough to get the job done.

A ball of greenish flame slammed into my gut, while bolts of bright yellow energy hit me square in the chest. I can't say any of it felt good. It was like that time a few years back when Chris and I were both trying to open the front door and he ended up slamming it into my face ... except now it was across my whole body.

OW!

However, despite the multiple bruises I was no doubt racking up, none of it appeared to get through me and affect Cass.

At the last second, just before I became a battering ram, she dropped me to the side and launched herself at both wizards.

I hit the ground and rolled away, hoping I'd been enough of a distraction for her to do her thing. A splattering arc of blood painted the ground where I'd been only a moment earlier, answering that in a far more brutal way than I'd hoped.

Oh no!

It was over quickly, before I could say anything to dissuade the carnage. In close quarters and with both of them still recharging their magic batteries, neither man stood a chance. Cass ripped Jeremy's throat out before I could even try to regain my feet.

Gavin tried to backpedal as she tossed Jeremy's body to the side like it was trash, but it wasn't enough to compensate for Cass's greater reach. One step and she was upon him, slashing with her claws and dropping his steaming guts into the snow.

I'd only meant for her to disable them, forgetting for a moment her species' deep-seated hatred for the Draíodóir. Coupled with the fear and pain of what we'd both experienced, it was a horrifically lethal combo.

It wasn't fair. Neither man had seemed to be in their right mind. Sadly, I'd learned a harsh lesson this past year: the shadowy underworld that existed all around us could be at times wondrous to behold but, more often than not, it was a world of terrible violence.

I neither knew what had been done to them nor whether it could've been undone, but realized with sad finality that anything less than lethal force could potentially doom my family ... and I likewise understood, with sickening clarity, that wasn't a risk I was willing to take.

I didn't have to like it. Truth be told, I hated it. But none of that changed my reality. The talking was over. What was left wasn't nice, but it was the way things were. I couldn't allow myself to be burdened with guilt ... especially since we weren't out of the woods yet.

There came a gust of wind from somewhere behind me, cold enough to chill me to the bone and strong enough to knock me to the ground.

When I finally managed to blink the snow out of my eyes, I looked back and saw that Carly was gone.

Wait. No, not gone. Movement from above caught my eye and I glanced up to find her hovering a good twenty feet above the ground, her clothes buffeted by wind as if she were held aloft by a great gust of air ... which, now that I took a moment to consider things, probably was the case.

I tried to pull myself to my feet and immediately went down to one knee as the taste of copper filled the back of my mouth.

Ugh!

I might have a natural resistance to magic, but that didn't mean I was totally immune. My gambit had been desperate and stupid, emphasis on the stupid part. Normally I was durable enough to brush off hits like that, but as I was now, no dice. With the adrenaline rush of being used as a shield wearing off, I began to realize I'd banged myself up pretty good.

As if the day couldn't get worse.

Oh wait, it already had. Now I had my aunt hovering above us, beyond even Cass's reach, and us out in the open like sitting ducks. And there was Belzar, too. He still stood where he'd been, but at least gone was his casual arrogance. He'd seen what we'd done to two of his thralls and was apparently coming to the conclusion that he should take us a bit more seriously.

Worse, they were both relatively fresh, too.

"You're nothing but an abomination," Carly called down to us, her voice amplified somehow by the swirling air around her. "Who would have thought it possible? But it seems Craig was right after all."

～

Craig?!

What the hell?

That question would have to wait, however. The air around my aunt began to darken and within it, I could see crackles of energy. She was powering up, and there wasn't much I could do about it.

Cass stepped over where I still sat in the snow. Blood dripped freely from the robe she still wore, although I doubted most of it was hers. She looked up to where my aunt hovered, opened her mouth, and...

A roar of pure animalistic rage ripped through the trees, so loud I could feel it in my bones. It hadn't come from her, though. Judging by the tilt of her head, she was just as confused as me.

"No," my aunt muttered, her voice still strangely amplified.

A blinding flash of light appeared from thin air about ten feet in front of me, bright enough to leave afterimages in my eyes. When it cleared, I beheld a sight that almost brought me to tears.

"LEAVE MY FAMILY ALONE!"

It was Mom, but at the same time, she was more goddess than mother. I'd seen her like this before and it had been enough to cement in my mind that I'd need a couple of screws loose to ever want to tangle with her.

As much as I wanted to grab her in a hug and never let go, however, now was probably not the time.

Her hair whipped around her, a strange light infusing it, making it look as if her head were encased in a halo of living flame. The Santa hat she'd been wearing was long gone and it was as if her dress had been rewoven by some god of the loom, alight as if it were made of the sheer unadulterated power of her will alone.

She was badass and she looked seriously pissed.

"Mom?" Chris called out from somewhere off to my left, but I held up a hand toward him. The last thing she needed was him running in and acting as a distraction.

I glanced up to find Cass facing back in the direction we'd come from. A moment later, I heard the thud of heavy footsteps headed our way.

A massive form, almost pitch black against the snow,

launched itself from the tree line. The enormous werewolf stood there growling, its head alternating between my aunt high in the air and her asshole fiancé.

Impressive as my father was to behold, I could see that whatever had happened back at the house hadn't left him unscathed. His coat was slick with blood and the fur on his left arm had been almost entirely scorched away, leaving the skin beneath charred and raw.

Nevertheless, he appeared to have plenty of fight left in him for which I was glad.

"I see you managed to escape," Belzar said. If he was worried, it didn't show in his voice.

Mom put her hands on her hips. "As if a pissant like you could stop me."

Dad started toward us, snuffling something at Cass as he walked. My werewolfese wasn't up to par, but I assumed it was something about Chris since she immediately loped off in his direction.

"Are you all right?" Mom asked me over her shoulder, her eyes still on the foes in front and above her

"I'll live." It was tempting to throw her some shade about my pills, but that seemed petty considering she was in the process of saving our bacon. There would be plenty of time for I told you so's later on.

She nodded, then turned her focus back to the others, her voice taking on that strange triple tone I'd heard her use when casting spells or her dander was up. "*Enough of this. Stand down now. That's not a request.*"

"I'm through taking orders from you," Carly shot back.

Belzar in turn smiled. "You heard my little love dove. No can do, *your highness.*"

"What the hell is wrong with you? Attacking us on Christmas?"

"What's wrong with *him*?" Carly asked, anger in her

voice despite the stilted speech. "Oh, that's rich. Mother always favored you, her little princess. Always telling me how our ancestors smiled upon you, how I should strive to be more like you. What a crock of shit." Her words were no more than that of a squabbling sibling, but both her and my mother's appearance turned it into something beyond strange.

Since discovering my true heritage, I'd done a bit of research in the campus library, looking into the differing mythologies to which my parents laid claim. Most of it hadn't been particularly helpful – stuff better suited to a bad fantasy novel – but at least now I knew how to tell someone to kiss my ass in Gaelic.

That said, the scene playing out before me – Mom, wreathed in fire, standing against her sister, surrounded by swirling air – reminded me of the mythical rivalry between Mab and Titania, two rival fairy queens, one ruling over winter, the other summer – eternally opposed yet equally powerful.

Though I knew it was just my imagination, it made me feel small indeed. And here I'd thought I was hot shit with my powers. I was nothing compared to this.

"You've been lying to us," my aunt cried, "spitting on everything we hold dear for twenty years ... TWENTY YEARS! And you dare question what Belzar has done?"

By then, Dad had reached me. He bent down, hooked a massive paw under my arm, and lifted me to my feet.

"Careful," I grunted. "Oof, I'm definitely going to feel that tomorrow."

He grumbled something that sounded like "Sorry," then continued to hover over me, no doubt meaning to shield me from any errant magic. Glancing over, it seemed as if Cass was doing the same for my brother.

As much as a part of me wanted to point out that I could take a blast better than either of them, I was more than happy to be Daddy's little girl right at that moment.

"Just look at you," Carly continued. "Can you honestly tell me that's the behavior of two enemies forced to tolerate each other? And the stupid thing is, I bought it. For years I accepted the lie. I wanted so much to believe that my sister was our shining beacon that I ignored the obvious." She pointed toward me. "Hell, she even has your nose, for Christ's sake! Yet I never questioned it once when you told me she was just some poor orphan in need of a good home."

Huh. And here I always thought my nose was more rounded.

"Listen," Mom replied. "I don't know what delusions this maniac has been feeding you, but..."

"Such harsh words," Belzar interrupted, "when we've come bearing gifts. Where's your Christmas spirit?"

"Gifts?"

"The gift of the truth," Carly snapped from above. She reached into her coat, causing Mom to tense up for a moment, and then pulled out ... a cell phone. "My dearest wasn't the one who opened my eyes." She fiddled with the screen for a second or two, never losing altitude, then tossed it to my mom who managed to catch it. "No. That revelation came from a different source, one I wouldn't have expected in a hundred years. Go on, play it."

Mom glanced up once more at her sister then looked at the screen. The strange image of her, aglow with unearthly power while looking at a cell phone, was not lost upon me.

I couldn't see over her shoulder from where I was and, truth be told, it sounded downright suicidal to get closer. However, the volume was turned up enough for me to hear, and what I heard chilled me to the bone.

"Hello, Carolyn," a familiar voice said. It was my late

uncle Craig. "I know we don't see eye to eye on much and you have zero reason to trust me. Hell, under most circumstances we'd probably gut each other on sight. So I think you can appreciate that I'm not doing this lightly. Fact of the matter is, if you're watching this, it's because I'm dead, and I wanted you to know the reason why."

29

I'd heard of videotaped last will and testaments, but this was perhaps the first "fuck you" from beyond the grave I'd ever seen, and it was all directed at me.

The video was a dead man's switch. Craig had left it with a friend, with orders that it be mailed, upon news of his death, to Carly McGillis – the person he figured would feel most betrayed by my mother yet still have the mojo to stand up to her.

From what my uncle was saying, he'd recorded it the night of the blood moon, in the hours before all hell had broken loose. The gist was simple enough: despite his bravado, he'd known he was taking a risk. When I'd confronted him, right before our final showdown, I'd accused him of being afraid of me. Turns out I was more right than I ever wanted to be.

It was all there: the truth about my parents, my birth, and what I was.

"I can't risk this knowledge dying with me, and I can't trust the pack to carry out my wishes when another might now be calling the shots. This needs to be out there in case I fail. I don't know what you do to traitors among your kind, witch. Hell, I don't care. But something needs to be done, and I can only pray to Valdemar you have enough honor to understand that. I love my brother, but what's been wrought by him and your sister cannot be allowed to stand unchallenged."

It was his last gambit, a way to ensure – should he fail – that knowledge of my parents' forbidden love didn't die with him. He didn't try to make amends or build any bridges. His disdain for Carly and her people was evident in the few minutes he spoke. Even in the end there was no love lost, just a hope that his twisted ideals regarding racial purity were shared among the Draíodóir.

I had to admit, as far as final fuck you's went, this one was pretty good. They say that all dogs go to heaven. Well, if the same was true for werewolves, then I couldn't help but think he was looking down and laughing his ass off.

For several seconds after it ended, the only sound was the soft crackle of fire from the remnants of Margaret's house. Then a flash of blue flame erupted from my mother's hand, turning the phone into a charred brick of melted glass and metal. "Goddamn it, Craig," she spat.

"Not even going to try denying it, are you?" Carly replied from her perch high above. "You know, I'm glad mother passed away when she did. Because she would have died of shame at hearing this. To think, her oldest and most beloved shacking up with a mongrel."

"Mother loved you just as much as me."

"That's bull and you know it. You were her great hope, her little *aingeal,* as she would say. And to think she used to lecture me about dishonoring our ancestors. What a crock. Oh, if she could only see us now."

The power around Mom began to fizzle out. Her hair dropped down and the glowing gown around her once again became her Christmas dress. I wasn't sure if it was because of the strain or if she was doing it purposely, but I couldn't help but notice she was breathing hard as she looked up at her sister. "What do you want from me, Car? Is this some desperate cry for attention?"

"It's exactly what I said it is," Belzar replied, looking quite pleased with himself. "This is a coup. You're no longer fit to lead your coven, or any of our people."

High above, Carly nodded. "You should have abdicated from the start. That would have been more honorable."

"So you killed innocent people just to get to me?"

"Casualties of war, your highness," Belzar said. "Or, in layman's terms, omelets and eggs. It's time for a change. Out with the old and in with the new. You see, I'm thinking of merging our covens. But if I have to clean house a bit first, so be it."

"It's long overdue," Carly added. "For too long we've stagnated here, sitting on one side while the mongrels chase their tails on the other. You once promised to lead us into a new future. We're simply picking up where you failed. A fresh start. But in order to do that, we have to wipe the slate clean."

Huh. I found it interesting the way they spoke, almost as if my aunt were finishing Belzar's thoughts for him. Much as it hurt to hear her say those things, I couldn't help but wonder how much was really her and how much was being force fed to her.

"So it's a power play, is it?" Mom asked Belzar. "And you call me pathetic?"

However, it was my aunt who answered. "It's more than that. If you'd merely been in love, that might have been forgivable. We could have blanked you and moved on." She pointed a finger my way. How surprising. "But you know what *she* represents. There's a reason the bloodlines have remained pure and you know it."

Uncle Craig had said as much himself back when he

was alive, but he'd been a bit too foaming at the mouth to get his point across. What the hell was with these guys? This went beyond mere elitism. It was almost fanatical.

Carly's face softened as she turned to me. "I don't blame you, Tamara. None of this is your fault. You didn't ask to be born. Please know that whatever comes next, I will pray that the elders who guide us are kinder to you in your next life."

How not-so comforting.

Behind me, Dad began to growl deep in his throat.

"Curtis," Mom said, keeping her eyes focused on her foes. "Take the kids and leave here. I'll deal with these two."

Dad's growl deepened.

"Don't argue with me."

"There isn't anything to argue about," Carly said. "I'll be generous and allow Chris to walk away. He's not a part of this. Shame on you for dragging the poor child into it. But the rest of you, I'm sorry. You're not leaving."

"You think you've got what it takes?"

"Oh please, Lissa. I can tell from up here how exhausted you are."

"Maybe," Mom replied, "but are you brave enough to find out for sure?"

"I have no doubt my darling Carolyn is," Belzar said. "But me, I'm more a lover than a fighter. Also, I like to hedge my bets."

At his nod, Carly raised a hand above her head and a shimmering spark of power lanced out of it, up into the sky.

Before I could begin to wonder what kind of attack this was, the spark erupted in a spray of lights and colors. I watched the supernatural fireworks display for a moment before it hit me.

It wasn't an attack so much as a signal flare.

~

"What's the matter? Can't fight your own battles?"

Belzar laughed. "I always preferred to fight smarter, not harder."

"Me too," Mom replied, " *'BRISEADH UCHD!'*"

That was new. Before I could wonder what it did, though, I was bowled over by an invisible shockwave.

It was like being slapped in the face with a giant pillow – more than enough to knock me on my ass again. But apparently that was a mere taste due to my unique heritage. My father, more than twice my size and probably weighing four times as much, was blown right off his feet by the attack.

Somewhere to my left I heard a whine as Cass, still shielding Chris, took the brunt of it, too.

However, it was all worth it to watch Belzar sent flying ass over teakettle. I heard a grunt from above and looked up to see my aunt come tumbling out of the sky. Mom was right, she did believe in fighting smart. Splitting her magic between her opponents was risky, especially since my aunt could probably dodge most focused attacks. But this spell had been the magical equivalent of a flashbang, hitting everyone at once. It didn't look lethal from what I could tell but seemed to pack enough punch to cause some chaos.

Unfortunately, it appeared the price tag for this particular incantation was a high one as my mother dropped to one knee. But she was still in better shape than Belzar. Although, I saw with somewhat mixed emotions, it appeared to be a wash as far as my aunt was concerned. At the last second, Carly worked up a spell, causing an updraft in the moment before impact. She still hit the ground hard enough to be dazed, but I doubted she'd stay down for long.

The question now was how to take advantage of this momentary reprieve. Even without my powers, I was pretty comfortable popping someone in the face. But then what?

Defending myself against an active foe was one thing, but killing a helpless opponent? And that was just talking about Belzar. Harsh as my aunt's words were, I couldn't bring myself to believe she was in her right mind despite her possession of Craig's video. Fucking asshole. I swear, if I thought it would work, I'd get an Ouija board and call up his ghost just so I could punch him in his stupid face one last time. I made a mental note to ask Mom about that when this was all over.

Problem was, it wasn't done yet, not by a long shot.

Before any of us could make a move to end this, gouts of fire erupted from the ground all over the yard, coalescing into human form in the space of seconds.

The closest to us never made it. Dad – his head in the game far more than mine – was upon them before the light had faded, ripping and tearing. Whoever it was, they didn't even have time to scream.

Sadly, they weren't alone.

More of Belzar's Christmas weirdos materialized, spells at the ready. Far worse, however, was that several of Mom's relatives appeared alongside them – the same who'd stood with us in the first minutes of the attack.

My cousin Mindy appeared by Carly's side, standing protectively over her prone form.

There was no sign of grief about her at the recent loss of her sister.

The only thing I saw upon her face was the same expression each and every one of them now wore – glazed eyes and a look that screamed murderous intent.

30

"Get your brother out of here!"

"But..."

"NOW, TAMARA!"

Mom's parent voice cut through whatever adult thoughts my brain was currently sputtering and I pushed myself to my feet without hesitation. Sadly, it wasn't as fast as I wanted to. My body was still sore from the magical pummeling I'd taken. Immunity or not, if the Draíodóir put their all into it, I had a feeling they'd break me into bite-sized pieces.

Dad let out a snarl and, a moment later, Cass came loping over with my protesting brother held in one arm. Werewolves definitely had their uses.

"Go!" Mom shouted right before her voice trebled. "*Sgiath creideimh!*"

A dome of translucent energy rose up around us as a hail of spells were screamed out by the assorted witches and wizards present.

More magical power than I'd ever seen on display struck the dome simultaneously – a veritable rainbow of rays and blasts, lighting up Mom's force field like this was a battlefield instead of someone's front yard.

"*Now!*" Dad growled while I was half-blinded by the light show on display, afterimages dancing in my vision. He pointed his charred hand in the direction of the street.

I wanted nothing more than to tell him to go to hell, to stay and fight, to give Belzar and his minions everything they had coming to them. But I knew I'd be next to useless in this battle. Worse, I'd be failing in my duty to protect my brother.

Cass, having been given her marching orders, was already standing at the very edge of the protective dome, no doubt waiting for me.

Chris continued to flail in her arms. "No! We can't leave them!"

He was wrong, much as I hated to admit it.

I turned back one last time to see my father adopting a protective stance over my mother. She was down on her knees, her arms trembling with the effort, but she persisted –screaming out the spell over and over again, until her voice began to crack.

It was only a matter of time. The magical dome, now opaque from all the energy hitting it, was starting to smoke. Even Mom, scary powerful as she was, couldn't hold off this much power for long.

"*Come on!*" Cass's face had retracted to that halfway point, enough for her to call out to me, her voice high and desperate.

I'd hesitated long enough – too long, in fact. I headed her way, a limping run on legs I could barely feel thanks to the cold.

We reached the edge of the faltering dome and Cass stepped through with my brother, unimpeded despite his continued protests.

I followed a moment later and emerged in a thin copse of trees between the yard and the empty street beyond.

We began to run as a rising pitch of crackling energy began to build behind us.

The cold receded as the residual heat from the myriad attacks began to rapidly warm up the surrounding air, making it seem like we'd stepped from the freezer into the oven.

We were almost all the way across the street when the dome of magical energy reached its limit and exploded.

∼

A wave of heat washed over us, hitting my backside hard enough to give me a boot in the ass and propel me a bit faster.

The smell of smoke, acrid and foul, hit me as we reached the trees on the other side of the road.

But that wasn't the worst – far from it.

I dared a glance back and saw the trees in front of Margaret's house engulfed in a sea of unnatural flame. A high pitched, triple-voiced scream rose up above it all. It seemed to echo among the burning treetops but then, just as quickly, it faded away.

Please God, no!

There was no way for me to know for certain, but my heart told me it had been my mother's voice.

Almost as if in confirmation, a low mourning howl came from back the way we'd come, rapidly turning into a snarl of pure primal rage.

I couldn't help myself. I stopped and turned, prepared to run back. I had to know they were all right. I had to...

"*No!*"

A hairy hand closed around my arm and began to drag me away.

I fought my damnedest against it, but in the end, my best simply wasn't good enough.

∾

I finally got a hold of myself, forcing my focus into the here and now of our situation. The truth was, it was suicide to do anything but keep running. Cass was the only one who seemed to understand that. Whether it was logic or her heeding the – *final* – orders of her alpha, I wasn't sure. But in the end, she'd likely saved us again.

Chris, sadly, wasn't nearly as forgiving.

"Let me go, you bitch! Mom, Dad, help!"

"That's ... enough," I said after he'd exhausted himself screaming. "There was nothing we could have done."

"You don't know that!"

"Yes I do. So does she."

"But they could be..."

"I know!" I snapped, causing him to flinch. "But there's nothing we could've done to change it. Do you understand me? We couldn't help them."

He glared at me. "You could have. You could have helped them by not being born."

I stopped in my tracks, his words like a kick to the gut.

Even Cass seemed taken aback. She put him down and stared silently at us.

There was an uncomfortable beat as once again the woods became still around us.

Finally, he said, "I'm sorry. I didn't mean that. I'm just so..."

"Afraid?" I finished, stepping up to him. He tried to back away, but I reached out, grabbed hold of his sweater, and dragged him in for a long hug. "I know. I am, too."

Sadly, I wasn't sure he was wrong about what he'd said.

~

As the adrenaline from our flight began to wear off, the cold once again took its toll. I wasn't sure what was worse: my bruised body or the fact that it was beginning to go numb.

Soon enough, Belzar wouldn't have to hunt us down. He'd simply need to wait for the spring thaw to find our corpsicles. I couldn't even open my mouth to say as much because my teeth were otherwise preoccupied with chattering.

Fortunately, I didn't need to. Without warning, Cass's body shimmered and she shrank down into her human guise. She was still wearing that wizarding robe, albeit it had taken a beating in the battle. Much more and Chris would at least get a free show before we all froze to death.

"Do you hear that?" she asked excitedly.

"A-all, I can ... h-hear, is ... my..."

She didn't wait for me to sputter out a lame reply. "I heard a car. There's a road up ahead, a wide one. I think we made it!"

A few minutes later, we stepped from the tree line onto the shoulder at the side of the road. She was right. This wasn't one of the narrow local roads that crisscrossed the area. We'd finally reached Gossamer Lane.

Now to only hope Riva was somewhere close by looking for us.

31

All the anger, fear, and sorrow of the day took a momentary backseat to the glory that was working heat vents.

"Turn it up," Chris said from the back.

I was tempted to comply, but Riva was already sweating. Seemed rude to give our rescuer heat stroke.

We'd played perhaps the tensest game of Frogger ever for about fifteen minutes, popping our heads out whenever we heard a car and then quickly diving back into the relative safety of the trees whenever we saw it wasn't Riva's old Subaru.

Much as Chris pleaded with us to flag down any vehicle for help, we couldn't risk it. We were still in Draíodóir territory, and no matter how human Cass looked, I had a feeling she wasn't likely to fool any witches on their way to Christmas dinner, especially wearing high priestess robes as she was.

Aside from that, though, we were mostly silent as we waited. I don't think either Chris or I wanted to speculate on what might have happened to our parents. What we'd heard had been awful enough to give me nightmares and probably put Chris into therapy for years to come. But until we knew for certain, we were only torturing ourselves.

Thankfully, right about when I was on the verge of losing myself to despair, I'd spotted Riva's car cruising down the road, sparing me from the reality that I had no plan of action whatsoever. My stark reality was simple: I was in way over my head.

Seeing Riva's face in the driver's seat as she pulled onto the shoulder lifted my spirits from the dark dungeon where they'd been chained. She'd been my best friend all throughout elementary and high school. Hell, she'd refused to run last summer when all of this had started, choosing to stay by my side as we were stalked by a were-wolf deep in the hollows. Though I didn't want to expose her to the danger we were in, I was damned glad to see her nevertheless. She gave me hope, and so long as I had hope, I wasn't ready to give up.

"So, anyone want to tell me what the hell happened to you guys?" Riva glanced in the mirror at Cass seated next to my brother in the back. "And why are you wearing that ... and nothing else?"

I brought her up to speed, several times shushing my brother who seemed insistent on offering unhelpful advice like calling the cops ... as if I were an idiot and wouldn't have thought of that.

Finally, I rounded on him. "And tell them *what,* exactly? The truth? That'll get us locked up. We can't help Mom and Dad from the inside of a jail cell, or juvey for you."

"Do you think they're..."

I cut Riva off. "I don't know. And I'm not sure I want to speculate."

She took one hand off the steering wheel and placed it on my arm. "Are you okay?"

I put my hand over hers, taking some comfort from her warmth and presence. "No."

She glanced into the rearview mirror again. I could tell she was a little weirded out that Cass was a werewolf. No surprise there. Aside from my dad, her wolf experiences up until that point hadn't exactly been positive. She gave me a quick warning glance, no doubt wondering how much Cass knew. "How long until you're ... okay again?"

That was a loaded question, but I pushed it aside in favor of checking the time. "Too long."

She nodded and didn't say more on the subject. Riva was a good friend and perhaps the best confidant I could hope for. That said, Cass didn't pry, which said a lot about her. Mind you, her actions had already spoken volumes. It wasn't something I would easily forget.

"Where to?" Riva finally asked.

"Get us the fuck out of Crescentwood," I replied, despite desperately wanting to turn around and go back. But what then? It wasn't like we were the cavalry.

"I meant after that."

"I know," I replied morosely. "I'm not sure. I guess we should..."

"We should go to Morganberg," Cass said from the backseat.

"What's in Morganberg?" Chris asked.

"Werewolves," I replied nonchalantly, "a whole shit-load of them." At this point, there was no reason to pretend.

"What?!"

"Relax," I told him. "Let's head back to High Moon. The treaty is still in place. Hopefully that'll stop..."

"It won't," Cass interrupted, leaning forward. "Or at least I don't think that will stop them. The whole point of High Moon, from what I've been told, is it's a buffer zone between our territories. But with..." She paused, a pained look on her face. Though I doubted her connection to my father was as strong as mine, I couldn't discount the pain she was likely in. A pack's alpha was special. Some, like my uncle, had ruled out of fear, but my dad seemed to be doing things a different way. Even if he wasn't their actual father, he was their patriarch, their guiding light.

And now that light had been ...

No! I refused to go there, to let those thoughts in.

Not until I knew for certain one way or the other.

"With Curtis ... captured," she continued, taking the optimistic route, for which I was grateful, "the pack will be in disarray, unprepared. Also, let's face facts: it's Christmas. Nobody's going to be expecting anything. Despite our pack lore, a good chunk of the membership are churchgoers. And those that aren't will be home with their families."

"The Tet Offensive," Chris said.

I glanced back at him. "Excuse me?"

"We learned about it in history class. It was a surprise attack by the North Vietnamese during their New Year."

"Look at you, the little history nerd."

He grinned, the first smile I'd seen on his face since Riva had picked us up. "Guess I got all the brains *and* the looks."

"He's not wrong," Cass said. "About the Tet Offensive, I mean. This would be the perfect time for an incursion. These Draíodóir could enter High Moon, hunt us down, or do whatever the hell else they wanted and nobody would be the wiser."

Her reasoning was sound, but I couldn't exactly say I agreed with it. Morganberg, and the hollows in particular, weren't exactly friendly territory where I was concerned.

Before I could voice that opinion, though, I was snapped forward, my seatbelt locking, as Riva hit the brakes.

"Oh my God!"

I faced forward, certain I'd end up with whiplash as the car screeched to a halt, fully expecting to see a blockade of angry Draíodóir, spells at the ready, waiting for us.

What I didn't expect to find was a naked man standing in the middle of the road.

∼

"Is that..."

"Mitch!" Cass cried.

How ... wonderful.

"Mitch?" Riva asked. "As in the guy who started shit with you earlier this week?"

"One and the same," I replied, staring out the front window.

Mitch limped toward us. I could see why I hadn't immediately recognized him. For starters, him being buck-ass nude had startled me a bit. Secondly, he looked like he'd been put through the ringer and back. Blood covered him from half a dozen cuts and, much like my dad, he'd also suffered burns and bruises.

"Should I run him over?" Riva asked.

"Debating it."

"Bent!" Cass cried from the backseat.

"Sorry, it's been a long day." I turned to Riva. "Pull over and unlock the doors."

"Are you sure?"

"No, but I'm hoping that whole enemy of my enemy thing holds true. At the very least, I think he's the lesser of evils right now."

"Not exactly inspiring me with confidence."

"I know."

Riva had good reason to distrust him. He'd been part of my uncle's inner circle, the same group that had targeted her and her family as punishment for me not getting in line like a good puppy. I certainly hadn't forgotten, and I was pretty sure she hadn't either.

Recognition dawned on Mitch's face and he hurried his pace toward us. Guess he was assuming the same reasoning as me.

My brother turned to Cass. "Um ... he can get in on your side."

Riva glanced at me. "So much for speeding back to High Moon."

"Oh?"

"No way do I want to get pulled over with that guy in the back."

There was no arguing with that logic.

～

Fortunately, Mitch appeared far too grateful to throw any shade my way.

"Drive!" he said once he'd squeezed in and closed the door. But it wasn't an order so much as the pleading of a man scared for his life. After we got moving, he turned to Cass and threw his arms around her. "I'm so glad you made it."

"Thanks, Uncle Mitch. Me too."

It would have been heartwarming if he'd had pants on. That said, I couldn't help but notice he didn't extend his gratitude toward the rest of us. Oh well, you could take the asshole off the street, but that still left him an asshole.

Neither expecting any quarter from him, nor wanting any, I got straight to business. "What happened?"

"What happened?" he snapped. "Those fucking ... err ... psychos tried to..."

I held up a hand. "It's okay, everyone here knows. This is my friend, Riva."

"Yeah," she added. "The one you guys put a hit on last summer."

"Oh," Mitch replied, no doubt realizing the awkward situation that put him in. "Sorry about that."

"I highly doubt it," I said, turning to face him. "How'd you get away?"

"Curtis and..." He looked almost sick at having to spit out his next words. "...your mother, too. They fought back, encouraged the rest of us to do so." He shook his head. "In such close quarters, all that magic flying around. It's amazing we didn't burn the place down around us."

I was about to agree, but then I remembered the wards my mother had put on our house the summer before. Considering Carly's place had been home to generations of witches before her, it probably stood to reason it had been properly prepped for errant magic usage.

"We started to push back," he continued, "throwing everything we had at them. I thought we had them for sure, especially after they split their forces to send people after you."

"Trust me, we noticed."

"But then it started to get weird."

"Weird?" Riva echoed.

"We got attacked by Christmas elves," I said. "Like that wasn't weird enough?"

"Not that." He shook his head. "Seeing we weren't surrendering, they changed tactics. It was a spell I'd never seen before – all these flashing lights, making it hard to think."

I held my tongue. There was little point to be had in petty insults at that moment.

"Then, when the flashing stopped, half the people on our side suddenly turned on the rest. Fucking Draíodóir, can't trust them for..."

"Belzar," I said.

"Huh?"

"He's the douchebag who started this crap. He must've done something to them." I remembered what mom had called him – a psychomancer. Ignoring the obvious pun of him being a murderous asshole, it suddenly began to make sense. His magical specialty was obviously the mind, which apparently included taking control of other people's.

That explained why Mindy had attacked us. Despite their bickering, her and her sister had been tight. No way would she have willingly switched sides to join the people who'd murdered her twin.

As Mitch continued to relay his story, telling us how it became a case of every man for himself, I considered my aunt.

Much as I'd wanted to initially believe she was under Belzar's spell, I had begun to doubt it upon seeing her in possession of Craig's video. But maybe I was being hasty. I was thinking of mind control in absolutes, but what if it wasn't that simple?

Mom had said Carly was an aerokineticist. I'd gotten a firsthand look today at what that actually meant. She wasn't just able to call up the occasional breeze. Everything she did pointed toward a mastery of her art. If so, then perhaps Belzar was equally as skilled, allowing for more nuance than simply dominating another.

Case in point, my aunt knew where I went to college. If Craig's video had really pissed her off as much as she claimed, she could have hunted me down anytime in the last four months, or acted against my parents while I was away. But she hadn't done anything of the sort, not until today.

And then there was the fact that Belzar had recently broken it off with her, only to show up out of the blue. She'd obviously told him about me. But how long ago? He seemed to know that today was the perfect time to stage a coup. All signs pointed to this being planned in advance. If so, maybe he'd also had the time to subtly influence her mind and turn her against us.

Either way I looked at it, this rabbit hole appeared to be deeper than a mere surprise attack.

"Damnit."

"What's wrong?" Riva asked.

"Nothing. Just thinking about what happened." I glanced up, noticing our surroundings looked familiar. "Are we...?"

"Back in High Moon? Yep, just crossed the town line."

To say I let out a sigh of relief wouldn't be an understatement, albeit it was probably undeserved. High Moon was an illusion. This was no bridge to Sleepy Hollow that a headless horseman couldn't cross. The only thing keeping either side out was tradition, a treaty that currently wasn't worth the paper it was written on, and me. And right then, tradition probably held more sway than any of the rest.

"Keep going," Mitch said. "Get us to Morganberg."

I rankled a bit at the fact that he was trying to take charge when mere minutes earlier he'd slunk into the backseat like a whipped dog.

Turning in my seat to tell him as much, Cass suddenly perked up. "He's right. Remember what I said earlier about the holiday?"

"Yeah, so?"

"It's all the more important now. Mitch is the beta."

Much as I didn't want to acknowledge it, she had a point. Cass was a bit of an outsider to the pack and I was pretty much a piece of shit, as far as they were concerned. But if there was anyone beside my father who could rally the troops, it would be Mitch. However, I hesitated to say as much. There was more to it than that – an uncomfortable truth.

In the absence of my father – or assuming a worst case scenario – he was the new alpha. Problem was, even if I didn't despise him, that still wouldn't have made me feel better. Mitch was definitely a downgrade, and that wasn't just me being biased. He was a follower, not a leader.

Based on the fact that he was sitting in the backseat, naked as a jay and looking like a kicked puppy, I probably should've cut him some slack. But the truth was, I was a bit lacking in the Christmas spirit right then. "Fine. So, Mitch, how are we going to deal with this?"

"We?" he asked.

"Yeah, we. Cass isn't the only pack member here with you."

Chris looked at me and smirked. No doubt I was going to be on the receiving end of a lot of dog jokes in the coming days. So be it. It was better than crushing despair.

"Don't start," I warned him anyway before turning back to Mitch. "They attacked our alpha and broke the truce. Surely that warrants some kind of response other than hiding in the woods."

Rather than reply with belligerence and authority, as he should have, he broke eye contact and looked away. Just fucking wonderful.

"Okay, so what now?" Riva asked, turning onto Crossed Pine Road. It bisected High Moon, east to west, and led toward Morganberg.

The question had been directed at me, as if I had a clue what to do next. I loved Riva even more than a sister, but I could have clocked her right then as all eyes in the car – Mitch's included – seemingly turned my way.

Goddamnit!

Tempted as it was to tell her to head toward my home,

I wasn't sure what that would buy us. The house had once been warded against werewolves, but werewolves weren't the issue now. I wasn't aware of any anti-Draíodóir measures that had been taken.

That didn't mean there weren't any, but I wasn't sure where to look or what form such measures might even take. So far as I knew, we didn't even own a gun.

But I knew someone who did: Riva's Dad.

"Head to your place."

"*My* place?" Riva asked. "You do realize we have a naked guy in the backseat, right? My parents are pretty open-minded but..."

"We're not staying. We're going to drop you and Chris off there. Then I'm going to borrow your keys so the rest of us..."

"You're leaving me?" Chris cried, sounding much younger than his age for just a second.

"Listen to me," I replied, turning toward him. "They're not after you. You're just an innocent bystander in this. I have no reason to think they'll come looking for you. And if they do, Riva's dad has a gun."

Truth of the matter was, I was pinning my hopes on the fact that Carly didn't seem interested in hurting him. I hated putting Riva's family in danger, but I wasn't sure there was anyone else I trusted.

The only other person who came close was Ralph Johnson, the chief of police. He'd kept a ridiculous amount of cool in the face of last summer's werewolf attack. That was the type of person I wanted protecting my brother.

Problem was, so far as I was aware, he'd been mind-wiped along with the rest of the town. Trustworthy as he might be, showing up at the station on Christmas night with a crazy story about witches didn't seem a smart strategy. Even if the two werewolves with us proved to them that monsters were real, that could work against us. And that was assuming he was even on duty. If not, it would be a snipe hunt that would likely end with all of us in a holding cell.

If that happened, I had little doubt the Draíodóir – assuming they were still hunting us – had both the means to get to us and ability to ensure that none of the witnesses remembered anything about it.

That was quite possibly even scarier than dying – dying in a way that no-one remembered. It would be like we simply disappeared from the face of the earth.

I shook those thoughts from my head and turned to Riva. "Are you okay with this?"

Despite Chris's continued protests, she nodded.

"Good, then once we get there we need to..."

I was making things up on the spot, not sure where I was going with it. So perhaps I shouldn't have been too upset when a bolt of lightning slammed into the road immediately in front of us, exploding the asphalt beneath Riva's car, and sending us tumbling end over end.

Guess they were still hunting us after all.

32

In an instant, what had already been a desperate situation turned into a world of fear and pain.

Time itself seemed to slow down as the sturdy little station wagon violently flipped over and skidded toward the side of the road.

Though my seatbelt kept me mostly in place as the car crumpled around us, my head still slammed into the dashboard hard enough to make me see stars – a split second before the airbags deployed, nailing me in the face a second time.

The world greyed out and for a time everything felt detached. I could hear screams and cries of pain, but they seemed to be coming from far away. There was a sensation of movement, but as if it were happening to someone else. Wetness dripped down my face and the taste of copper filled my mouth.

On the upside, at least the car didn't explode.

As the movement around me seemed to ebb, I wanted nothing more than to retreat into that grey void, let it surround me in nothingness. I was safe there. There were no nightmares in that place. No missing parents, psychotic warlocks, or terrifying beasts waiting to…

There came a snarl from somewhere close by, followed by a squeal of metal. Focusing on it, I found myself unwillingly rising toward consciousness. I coughed, tasted blood, then licked my lips and tasted more.

I probably had a broken nose, maybe a gash on my forehead. Not great, but hopefully that was the worst of it.

Sadly, it wasn't.

I opened my eyes only to discover the greyness refused to retreat back to the shadowy recesses of my unconscious mind. My entire world was a blank slate.

I was blind!

~

Scratch that. It was just the goddamned airbag enshrouding my face. *Phew!* I pulled back a bit and, sure enough, saw a smear of blood – mine – against the rapidly deflating fabric.

Shaking my head to clear it a bit, and sending more droplets of blood flying, I realized I was lying at an odd angle. Judging by the trajectory of my dripping nose, the car had landed on its side with my end at the bottom.

Weak groans came from all around me, but they were drowned out by deep snarls from somewhere outside. *What's going on?*

I tried to raise my hands, panicking for a moment when they refused to move, until the realization hit that they were pinned to my side. The crash had jammed me up against the dash and I was stuck tight. I tried to push myself free, but to no avail. Whatever was going on outside, I was a sitting duck. Worst of all, I hadn't been the only passenger.

"Chris, Riva," I croaked, spitting out more blood and

trying to turn my head enough to free it from the deflated airbag and see how bad things were.

"How very disappointing."

Riva?

I finally managed to free my head, giving me a moment to look around. It was dark in the car. We'd definitely gone off the road.

But, as I craned my neck to look up toward my friend, things got a little weird.

Riva was still sitting behind the wheel of the car, but that's where the world took a left turn as apparently gravity no longer held any sway.

She appeared unharmed, her hair falling around her shoulders as if she were sitting upright. Gone was her seatbelt, meaning she was floating where she should have been falling.

How?

"Does it really matter?" she asked as if plucking the question from my mind.

Outside, the snarls continued, while inside I heard pained groans. I managed to turn my head and shoulders enough to see Cass and Chris. My brother was bleeding from a cut on his forehead, while the side of Cass's face was all bruised up. Both appeared semi-conscious at best, but they were alive.

"For now," Riva said, smiling down at me.

"How do you know what I'm..."

"Take a moment to remember, child."

Remember? What, the crash? A moment later, though, it all came back to me with crystal clarity.

Last summer, during my battle with Craig, there'd come a point when I was certain I'd lost. In those few seconds, I'd had a vision – more of a hallucination really – of my best friend. She'd stood there untouched among a sea of werewolves and then proceeded to admonish me for being a loser.

All in all, it had been kind of trippy.

Anyway, I'd managed to convince myself it was nothing but my subconscious giving me one final kick in the ass. Now, though, I wasn't so sure.

"You have already learned once that what you thought to be the sum of your reality was nothing of the sort," Riva said in a calm voice, as if we were discussing our classes for the coming semester. "Why should it surprise you now to learn that was nothing more than the uppermost layer of an infinite abyss of existence?"

I didn't really have an answer to that. Besides, it seemed a poor time to discuss philosophy.

"You have only yourself to blame for your current predicament," creepy possessed Riva said, again seeming to know my thoughts. Of course, that made sense if she was merely a figment of my imagination. "Such a shame," she continued, "letting yourself, a unique being – something that has existed only once before – be cowed against your wishes."

"Cowed?" I slurred. Was she talking about my pills? "I was trying to do the right thing."

"Right and wrong are but fleeting mortal constructs. Such concepts are not our concern."

"But ... hold on a second. You said that the last time."

She stared at me as if she had all the time in the world.

"Not that lack of concern stuff. The part about existing once before. What did you mean by that?"

"Exactly what we meant." Possessed Riva inclined her head as if considering something. Hopefully it had to do with what a bitch she was being with her answers. "Very well. We offer again the boon of knowledge. The blood sacrifice that was provided us has not been forgotten."

That was another thing freaky Riva had said last time.

I'd been too woozy to make much sense of it, but now I had to wonder. Did she mean...

"The window of worlds? Of course. It is where all of this began. Seek out that sacred place again. There you may find succor, or perhaps a less fortunate fate. It is not for us to say more. Our boon shall extend no further. You must stand or fall by your own strength."

"My own strength?" I asked, spitting out blood. "Hah! In case you hadn't noticed, I'm currently neutered. I still have another four hours until..."

"Do you? Or do you simply believe that to be the case?"

What?!

"The rest we leave to you. Twice now we have offered this boon. If we are forced to do so again, we may need to reconsider your part in the coming."

Huh? "The coming what?" A flap of airbag fluttered in front of my face, blocking my view for a moment. When I managed to shake it free, I saw ... Riva, but not as she'd been. She was still strapped into her seat, the driver's side airbag deflated in front of her. She had a black eye, and I could see a goose egg forming on her forehead.

More importantly, gravity seemed to be working again. She was slumped toward me, her black hair hanging down around her.

"Riva?"

She groaned once, fluttered her eyes, and then reached a hand toward her head.

"Ugh, Bent?" Cass's voice called weakly from the backseat. She was waking up as well – not surprising considering her werewolf physiology.

"Help Chris," I said, struggling to free my arms.

"Where's ... Mitch?"

The car lurched suddenly, as if something had struck it. I saw sparks fly past the window above Riva. Not good.

A few moments later, there came another snarl, further away this time. "I think he's out there fighting whatever did this to us." *Or running away.*

Whatever the case, the violent shuddering of the car told me it wouldn't offer much protection if whoever was out there decided to finish us off.

There was little doubt our foe was one or more of the Draíodóir. Either that or we'd run into a hell of a freak storm. The question now was who and how many, something none of us were going to answer in our current predicament.

I looked up to where Riva continued to stir, then glanced back around to find Cass working to free herself. It was too tight of a squeeze for her to change, at least without crushing me, so it was slow going. As for Chris, he was still unconscious.

We needed to get out of here. I wouldn't let him, any of them, die ... not like this.

I redoubled my efforts to free myself, unwilling to sit back and let Cass do all the work. We didn't have the luxury of time. We both needed to do our parts, even if I was still...

Come on!

I heard the groan of crumpling plastic and suddenly my arms could move a bit.

Possessed Riva's voice floated in my ear, as if whispered on the wind. "*Or do you simply believe that?*"

I flexed again, putting everything I had into it, certain I would rupture something, until I finally did. But it wasn't me. The seatbelt holding me in place snapped. *Yes!* I pushed against the dashboard and the plastic façade began to deform against my efforts. I continued to struggle against it until the frame of the car itself halted my progress. It wasn't much, but it was enough.

But how? I still had more than a few hours left. My

meds were usually like clockwork. Yeah, it had been months since last I'd taken them, but that shouldn't have...

But what if it did matter?

My powers had continued to evolve since the end of summer. What if super hearing and an overly sensitive nose weren't the only things that had changed?

A memory flitted through my head, something my father had said after learning the *withdrawal* from my pills had lasted mere hours instead of days.

We don't know a lot about how Tamara's metabolism works, but I think it has something to do with adrenaline.

There was little denying that I'd been running on nothing but that for the last couple of hours. I wasn't nearly back to full strength, but what if my body was fighting off the effects of my meds faster than normal?

But that usually brought with it a feeling of...

Almost as if on cue, my stomach lurched. *Ugh!*

Maybe it was a good thing dinner had been interrupted when it had. Otherwise I'd probably be lying there taking a shower in my own spew.

My stomach seemingly agreed, giving another unpleasant gurgle. I so fucking hated my goddamned pills.

Doing my best to keep my bile on the inside, I began working to right myself.

It was time to get out of this tomb and bring the fight to the enemy.

33

My gut was definitely not happy with me, but it was considerably more subdued than the last time I'd been on my meds.

Maybe it was adrenaline, or maybe I was developing a tolerance for it.

The car shuddered again as something exploded nearby.

Or maybe I should worry less about an upset stomach and more about saving our asses.

Another snarl sounded from outside. It would seem Mitch hadn't abandoned us after all. That counted for a lot in my book. But any compliments toward him would have to wait.

Cass managed to free my brother. Fortunately, the back door next to him had been sheared off in the crash, meaning all she had to do was shimmy out with him. "I'll come back and help you."

"Don't worry about us," I told her. "Get Chris to safety."

I managed to find my footing, stood up, and pushed past Riva's stirring form.

"Bent? Wha ... happened?" she groaned.

"Your parents' insurance premiums just went through the roof, that's what. Sit tight, I'll have us free in a sec." *Hopefully.*

I grabbed the handle of her door and gave it a shove ... nothing. It was stuck. Of course it was. If creepy possessed Riva were to be believed, the forces of the universe weren't interested in lobbing me softballs. Talk about weird. I no longer believed she was merely a delusion of my mind, but that didn't mean I couldn't hope she was.

That was a crisis of faith for later, though. For now, I needed to get us free. Whatever was going on out there, I didn't think Mitch could handle it alone for long.

"Don't move," I ordered my friend – not that she was going anywhere, still belted in like she was.

I threw a punch past her at the car door.

Thud.

Ow! That proved it. I wasn't anywhere close to full strength. But hadn't I felt the door give just a little? Maybe it was my imagination. Nevertheless, ignoring my bruised knuckles, I did it again.

Damnit! Oh, yeah. My hand was going to need a hot date with a cold ice pack, but there was no doubt this time. The door had definitely moved with a groan of tortured metal.

Third time's the charm. Crappy positioning or not, I put my shoulder into it this time. There came the crunch of plastic, a crack from one of my fingers – *ouch* – and then finally the squeal of metal.

I'd love to claim the door flew off like in the movies, but it merely popped open as the lock gave way. Fine, maybe it didn't look cool, but it had worked. We were free.

Now to make good on it.

~

"Watch it!"

"Sorry." I climbed past Riva, using her as a human ladder. Couldn't really be helped with the tight fit.

The upside, though, was that if she was awake enough to complain, then I had to consider that a good sign.

We'd gotten lucky in a way, lucky being a relative concept. The car had rolled off the side of the road, down a small ditch, before finally stopping just inside the tree line, affording us a bit of cover.

Good thing, too, because the Draíodóir weren't playing. I spied three as my feet hit the ground. Two were standing on the far side of the road. The third, however, floated above it. Not Aunt Carly, unless she'd changed into a Grinch costume at some point. It must've been another of those air wizards, whatever they were called. My brain was still too fuzzy to remember big words.

The two on the ground had their backs to each other, while the one in the air was slowly circling. That told me a lot about what was going on. Mitch was playing hit and run with them. Trees lined both sides of the road at this edge of High Moon, and he was likely using that to his advantage.

Almost as if in response, I saw a tree limb come flying out, missing the wizards by a wide margin. The Draíodóir, in turn, fired a volley of spells back toward the forest. Much as I didn't like their target, I found myself hoping they came up empty.

I helped Riva out and lowered her to her feet just as a shadow loomed over us. I quickly looked up, but thankfully it was just Cass in her wolf form, having shed the wizard robe at some point.

"Chris?"

She hooked a clawed thumb over her shoulder, toward

the trees, then turned to face the sounds of battle. I couldn't blame her. Mitch was both her uncle and pack beta. Her instincts must've been screaming to run to his aid.

"Hold on. We'll hit them together." My stomach gurgled again, which didn't exactly help my threat to sound legit. Whatever. I could always take some Pepto later.

I looked at Riva. She was a mess, but a living mess. "Can you walk?"

She nodded. "I might even be able to run."

"Good. Get to Chris and keep him safe. Don't come out unless you hear us give the all clear."

"And if you don't?"

"Call the police and make it a point to say nice things at my funeral."

~

At best, I was at maybe a quarter of my power, but hopefully that would be enough. "Wait for his next attack, then we rush these assholes together."

As far as plans went, this one sucked. We had open ground between us and our attackers, so our only chance was charging them while they were distracted and then hoping we got lucky. Much as I didn't care to think about it, I had a feeling the odds were not in favor of us all making it out of this.

Still, our chances were probably far worse if we didn't take the fight to the enemy. Running was a game of attrition and they likely knew it.

Besides, beneath my fear was a whole lot of anger just waiting to be unleashed. I wanted my pound of flesh from everything I'd been through. I *deserved* it.

Scoping out the wreckage of Riva's car, I found a loose

hubcap. That had promise. I picked it up just as a bowling ball-sized rock came flying out of the opposite tree line toward the Draíodóir.

"Now!"

I needn't have bothered. Cass was on the move before the word even left my throat. No one could claim she wasn't properly motivated.

I followed several steps behind her and with no chance of catching up, but I was still moving faster than I had been earlier. I'd take it.

Cass growled deep in her throat, causing the wizards to forget about their current target and turn to find her rapidly closing the distance. Not good, because they still had spells at the ready. We'd jumped the gun.

Fortunately, I had my souvenir from the crash. "Hey, assholes! Incoming!" I wound up and threw the hubcap, hoping my game of Frisbee golf had improved since last I'd played.

It hadn't. The projectile flew at them fast but wild. It hit the asphalt, sparked, then went tumbling off the other side of the road.

It was a shitty throw, but it had done the job – distracting the wizards just as they were about to turn Cass into fricasseed wolf. Two of them shot their spells wide of the mark, hitting every spot in the road except where she was. One was truer to his intended target but had aimed low, no doubt hoping to cut her off at the knees. However, she leapt over it at the last second.

Way to go, Cass!

Before they could launch another volley of hot, magical death our way, there came a roar of rage from behind them, followed by a werewolf charging out from the trees and headed their way.

What the fuck?

It wasn't Mitch, though. I'd been expecting one of

those massive mega-wolves to pop out and send wizard guts flying every which way. But this was a normal werewolf, relatively speaking – only slightly larger than Cass and with brown fur.

It seemed Mitch had run off after all. Of course, that begged the question: who the hell was this and why were they here? Mind you, regular werewolves were still scary as shit, so maybe I shouldn't complain.

The beast tackled one of the wizards before he could compensate, taking him down in a crackle of shattered bone.

Disturbing a sound as it was, it was still music to my ears.

Sadly, the one flying above us recovered quickly. With apparently no concern for his downed, but still screaming, buddy, he shouted, "*Sèididhteine!*" A ball of flame formed in front of him and blasted downward, engulfing both the werewolf and his prey in a fiery inferno.

Damnit! So much for these guys being a band of brothers.

In his haste, though, he seemingly didn't realize he'd lowered himself to within ten feet of the ground. Either way, it left him well within Cass's reach. Her vertical game, powered by heavily muscled lupine legs, was enough to make any NBA superstar weep. She plowed into the wizard with a snarl and dragged him to the ground.

That left one for me – a doofus dressed like the nutcracker, of all things. That was fine and dandy. I couldn't think of anything else I'd sooner crack right at that moment.

He saw me coming, closing fast, and I could see the indecision on his face. He could either save his friend and leave me at his flank, or blast me and have an angry Cass knocking on his backdoor.

Faced with a lose-lose proposition, he chose to do ... nothing. His eyes opened wide in panic and he hesitated.

Too bad for him I didn't. He was bigger but I had momentum on my side, as well as a moderate level of extra-normal strength. I hit him shoulder-first and he went tumbling end over end, landing in a pile of slush at the side of the road.

Before I could reach him again and properly introduce him to my fist, though, he scrambled away from me, crying, "No! Stay back!" Then, before I could *gently* explain that the chances of me doing so were effectively zero, a gout of flame erupted beneath him and he disappeared in a flash of fire, smoke, and light.

It hadn't exactly been the epic beat down I'd been hoping for, but it had felt good nevertheless. Running toward the bad guys was so much more gratifying than fleeing for my life.

As way of *celebration*, my stomach lurched and I promptly dropped to my knees and began to retch. Oh, I so fucking hated my pills!

Not helping was the sound of rending flesh from where Cass absolutely laid into the wizard she'd taken down. He'd likely been out of the fight the moment he'd landed with a couple hundred pounds of her on top, but she was making sure he was permanently grounded and then some.

Sucked to be him but, as the day wore on, I was finding it harder and harder to have much pity for our attackers. They could all...

The stench of burnt flesh hit my sinuses like a jackhammer, sending me into a fit of dry heaves again. *Gross!* Guess my other senses were starting to recover, too, although their timing could've been a bit better. Why couldn't they have waited until I was walking past a bakery?

Then I remembered where it had come from. I stepped past Cass, her teeth still buried in ... no, best not to look. My stomach was queasy enough as it was.

The third wizard was quite dead. He'd likely suffered mortal injuries from the werewolf's initial impact. However, being set on fire definitely hadn't helped. He wasn't going anywhere.

Sadly, our new ally wasn't either. The wolf was lying face down, having taken the brunt of the blast on its backside. It was trying feebly to get back up, but I saw that was a losing proposition. In addition to third-degree burns, a massive chunk of flesh had been gouged out of its shoulder, the wound completely cauterized. Werewolves could heal from a lot, but they weren't invincible.

There was also one other caveat. Creatures such as they were vulnerable to the attacks of other supernatural beings. I had no idea how that worked, but it did. A wound caused by another mythical creature was far more likely to be fatal than anything mundane.

It was likely only a matter of minutes before this wolf succumbed to its injuries. But whoever it was, they'd saved our bacon. They needed to at least know that.

I knelt by its side and put my hand on its arm. "Thank you."

The creature turned its head toward me and pulled its lips back in a snarl. Yeah, guess I still wasn't high on their popularity list. But then why was this one even here?

Far as I knew, Cass was the only other wolf, aside from my father, who I could count as a friend. The only other member of the pack who'd been even remotely civil to me had been...

Oh no! Not David.

But how ... why?

Cass finally disengaged from the wizard she'd turned into a Gaelic frappe. I heard her step up behind me, followed by the crackle of flesh and bone rearranging themselves.

I glanced back to find her fully human again, but absolutely drenched in blood. A look of horror lay upon her face.

I met her eyes. "I think it's..."

"Uncle Mitch?" she cried.

What?!

34

Mitch? But how? This was a regular werewolf, if such a term applied. Mitch was, well, *more* than normal – bigger, badder, all the above. Tough as the regular variety were, these mega-wolf guys were on a whole other level. Hell, I'd only beaten him by virtue of strategy and maybe a bit of luck.

Cass had to be wrong.

But she didn't seem to think so. She knelt down, cradling the werewolf's head in her arms. It must have been too weak to change back, burnt up as it was. It began to make low snuffling noises at her.

"It's okay. I'm here," she said. "Wait, what was that? No. I can't. That isn't..."

The wolf continued to huff at her, obviously talking in some canine dialect I didn't speak, which, interestingly enough, was all of them.

Finally after several seconds of this, each snuffle it made sounding more labored, the werewolf took a shuddering breath and became still.

Whoever he'd been, he was gone.

Cass stayed where she was for a few more minutes,

stroking his fur, misery etched onto her face. When she finally looked up at me, there were tears in her eyes. "We have to get to the hollows."

"Why?"

She stood up wiping her eyes, still covered in gore. Carnage lay all around us. I felt for whatever poor soul came this way next. Road kill was common in rural Pennsylvania, but this was nuts. "I'll tell you on the way. There's no time. They're obviously tracking us. Goddamned Draíodóir."

I didn't fully understand how scrying worked. Mom had never really explained it to me in depth except to mention she was constantly checking on me. The only thing I really knew was that salt blocked it. However, I doubted Riva kept any in her...

Riva and Chris ... shit!

"We need to go check on..."

Unfortunately, whatever words I had to say on the matter were drowned out by the sound of a police siren. It was distant, but after a second or two, it became obvious it was headed in our direction. Yet another unwanted surprise on a day full of them.

Merry fucking Christmas indeed.

Why couldn't Santa have just left coal in my stocking instead?

We probably should've made a run for the tree line, but I'm not sure that would have helped us much. With the snow still covering the ground, we'd be easier to track than if we were wearing neon lights. And there was still my brother and Riva to think about.

Mind you, all of this was kind of elementary anyway. Crossed Pine Road was mostly a straight run in this part of town. The cop car in question – a lone cruiser – appeared on the horizon within moments. If we could see him, he could see us.

"What do we do?" Cass asked.

I glanced at her, naked and covered in blood. "Fucked if I know."

"We could ... say we were abducted and fought our way free."

"Yeah," I replied, a chuckle rising in my throat. "We were abducted by two men and their really big dog ... one of whom blew himself up while the other threw himself into a giant blender."

"Nobody likes a pessimist."

I let out a laugh before the seriousness of the situation hit home. We were royally screwed. I didn't even begin to know how to explain this. And, no, cop killing was not an option. I voiced as much to Cass.

But there was one upside. Even as they arrested us – which they surely would – they could call an ambulance for Chris and Riva. If they could be spared anymore of this nightmare, I'd be all in for an extended stay in the town jail.

Speaking of which...

"Hey. Over here!"

I turned at the sound of Riva's voice to find both she and my brother standing at the far side of the road. Riva was waving at us. She still looked like hell, but she was awake and alert. Chris was upright, but that was about it. He had a glazed look in his eyes, barely seeming to register that Cass was standing next to me in all her gore-splattered glory. Poor kid probably had a concussion.

It was stupid of them to have come looking for us to begin with, as I'd given no sign that all was clear. I had little doubt that was Riva's doing. She was the best friend anyone could ever hope for, but she didn't listen for shit.

Oh well, there wasn't much I could do about that now, except maybe keep us from getting shot. "Follow my lead." I raised my hands over my head as the cop car began to slow down in its approach toward us.

Cass let out a long sigh. "That's your plan?"

"Feel free to run off into the woods on all fours. At this point, I doubt it'll be any weirder than what's already waiting for them."

"Tempting, but we need to stick together. Mitch said it's important."

I glanced at her. "Why?"

Sadly, any answers would have to wait. The police cruiser parked and the driver's side door opened. I expected an officer to step out behind the door, weapon pointed at us, and bark orders that we should kiss the ground.

Instead, the stout form of Ralph Johnson, chief of police for High Moon township, emerged. He casually sauntered over, taking the time to shut the door behind him, and then stopped in front of the cruiser with his thumbs hooked in his pockets.

"Well, goddamn. If this doesn't beat all. And on Christmas, of all days."

≈

Instead of drawing his weapon and telling us to get on our knees, he walked over to us as if this were the most normal thing in the world.

"Huh," Chief Johnson grunted, looking at the charred remains of Mitch and the wizard he'd taken down. "You sure as hell don't see this shit every day."

I'd known he was cool under pressure. That much had been evident from his handling of the werewolf attack this past summer. He'd shown no panic whatsoever that day, just doing what he could to contain the situation. But this? This went beyond calm and collected. There was no way even the most disaffected of people could stare at this and not freak the fuck out.

Johnson lifted his head to look at us. He sighed as he made eye contact with me but then, finally, a look of near surprise crossed his face as he took in Cass. Not sure if it was the fact that she was naked or drenched in blood ... maybe both. For all I knew, the guy had a fetish which, quite frankly, didn't make me feel any better.

"For God's sake, girl," he said to her. "You can't be out like that. There should be a small creek about a hundred yards that way." He pointed toward the tree line nearest where we stood. "With all this snow, it should be running a bit higher than normal. Go and wash yourself off. I have a spare jacket in my trunk. I'll go get it while you're doing that."

Cass glanced at me, but all I could do was shrug confusedly.

"I said get going!" Chief Johnson barked, before turning to me. "And you, put your hands down. You look like you're praying to the good Lord for salvation. Well, you can stop. Because, fortunately for you, salvation is already here."

35

"You might as well get your butts over here, too. I already saw you," Johnson called to the far side of the road where Riva had ducked down with Chris.

They walked over, her guiding my still dazed brother.

The chief looked them up and down, his expression softening. "Both of you, head over to my cruiser. The heat's on." He gestured at Riva. "You keep an eye on that boy. I'm going to call an ambulance for you both just as soon as I sort a few things out. Back door's unlocked."

Riva glanced my way, but I nodded. Right at that moment, jail was a secondary concern to making sure they were all right. I wasn't quite ready to face my losses for the day yet, but I'd be damned if I let anyone else be taken from me.

She led Chris to the cruiser, but not before my brother noticed the scene around us. He still had a look on his face that suggested he wasn't fully there, but his eyes opened wide for a moment. "Holy shit."

"Holy shit is right," Johnson replied before pointing toward the car. "Now do as you're told. It's cold as a witch's ti ... err, it's cold, that is. Get in the car before you catch your death."

I wasn't convinced that was the best way to phrase things, but it got Chris moving again. A minute or two later, when they were settled in, Chief Johnson turned back toward me.

By this point, I wasn't sure what to expect, so I let him take the lead. No way did I want to accidentally end up volunteering too much toward what was already a weird ass situation.

"Walk with me," he said, starting toward the patrol car. "Your friend will be back soon, but even with her abilities, I doubt she's gonna be toasty warm."

I fell in step behind him, but before I could say anything, he continued. "I saw the debris trail back there. Is it safe to say your car's in the ditch over that way?"

"Uh, Riva's car actually, but yeah."

"That'll work. Yeah, I think that will work well."

"For what?"

"You're that Bentley girl, aren't you? Tamara, ain't it?"

"Yes, sir."

"I remember seeing you at the state finals a few years back. Don't go thinking I'm getting mushy here, but I was proud as all hell to see one of ours make it that far."

"I lost."

"Yeah, but it wasn't your fault. Anyone with eyes could see that."

I didn't know how to answer that one. He was right. It wasn't entirely my fault. I'd been given a double dose of my meds that day, leaving me feeling decisively off my game. And no, I still wasn't entirely over it.

He led me to the back of his car, popped the trunk, and grabbed a jacket from it. But that wasn't all. "Here, hold this gas can for me."

"Um, why?"

"Because not everyone in this town is as open-minded as I am. Now, do you want to argue, or do you want to make sure that when the ambulance gets here they don't freak the hell out and run screaming their fool heads off?"

~

The chief instructed me to douse the charred bodies with gasoline. When I was done, he handed me a pair of rubber gloves and had me drag the remains of the shredded wizard to the side of the road. When I tried to ask why, he simply repeated his point about the ambulance.

That final part was messy business, requiring three trips and leaving a highly conspicuous blood smear leading to the side of the road.

"Perfect," Johnson said just as Cass stepped from the tree line.

Despite her werewolf physiology, she was shivering. Guess a dunk in a freezing cold brook will do that to even the best of us. On the upside, she didn't look like a reject from the Texas Chainsaw Massacre anymore.

"Put this on, girl. It's not much, but it's all I got. Can't have you walking around like that. We got laws in this town." Johnson tossed her the jacket. He was a big man with an ample stomach, so it covered her pretty well.

Once that was finished, he walked back over to the cruiser, checked on Chris and Riva, and then called for an ambulance. Then he sauntered our way again. "It'll take them a little while to get here. Long enough for us to take care of this."

"Take care of this? How?"

"Watch and learn."

He stepped over to the charred bodies of Mitch and the wizard, but then turned to face Cass. "This needs to be done, but if you want to say a few words first, now's the time."

She opened her mouth, then closed it and shook her head once.

"Don't be sad, child." Johnson clapped her on the shoulder with one meaty hand. "He stalks the great woods by Valdemar's side now."

My eyes almost bugged out of my head at his words. We were now well beyond the mere coincidence of him being cool as a cucumber.

"How much do you know?" I asked.

He merely chuckled as he reached into his pocket and pulled out a flask. Rather than offer it around, though, he uncorked it and poured the contents out onto the bodies.

"One for the road?"

"Nope. Unlike what you see in the movies, gasoline doesn't burn all that easily. And it definitely doesn't burn as hot as we need it to. So I'm adding a little something to help it along." He produced a book of matches from his jacket and lit one. "You might want to stand back, Ninja Girl. It's gonna get a little hot here."

~

Ninja Girl?!

The night the pack attacked High Moon, I'd worn a black t-shirt around my head as a crude mask, hoping to keep my identity safe. The chief had referred to me as Ninja Girl while I'd helped defend Main Street with him.

But the Draíodóir mind-wiped the whole town afterwards, with the exception of Riva. I could understand her slipping through the cracks, but the chief of police? That seemed a stretch.

Mind you, it was likewise a stretch that he'd be here now about to burn some bodies —one of which was obviously not human – rather than cuffing us and calling for backup.

"Ninja Girl?" Cass asked.

"Inside joke," the chief replied, throwing me a wink. "But same rule applies. Stand back."

He dropped the match, but it might as well have been a flamethrower. The bodies ignited, but far faster and hotter than they should have. White-hot fire rose from the corpses, consuming them in a brilliant blaze that I couldn't help but think was beyond any normal accelerant's capabilities.

"Damn near singed my eyebrows off," the chief said with a hoarse laugh before heading to the side of the road. "That's one. Now we need to take care of that other fella."

A few moments later and the deed was done. The first blaze was already dying down even as the second consumed the dead wizard. Though it was still smoldering, I could tell there was nothing left but ashes ... yet somehow the asphalt beneath hadn't been liquefied. That settled it. Whatever was in that flask was not normal.

There came the sound of a siren in the distance, a different warble than had come from the chief's car.

"It's about time," he said, turning to us. "You, Blondie, head into the trees and wait for us. Your lack of skivvies is going to give them more questions than we want to answer. As for you, Ninja Girl, walk with me. We're going to prep your friends on their story and make sure you all have it right."

"Our story?"

"Yep. You were coming back from Christmas dinner when a deer ran out into the road, a big ole buck. You hit it, which sent you into that ditch over there. Then, while you were helping your friends out of the wreckage, the deer crawled off to die. Ain't the first time it's happened."

I didn't doubt him, having lived here all my life. Roadkill wasn't exactly uncommon. What I had to wonder, though, was whether this was the first time it had been used as an excuse for something like this.

Considering the stuff in that flask, I had to assume it probably wasn't.

36

I watched the ambulance drive away, thankful that my brother and Riva were both safe. The chief promised that he'd keep an eye on them and I chose to believe him – not that I really had much choice.

The medics had looked me over, too, despite my protests to the contrary. Fortunately, some of my advanced healing must have returned along with a portion of my strength. I was still tender, but the worst I had to show for the ordeal were some minor cuts and bruises, and those simply served to back up our story.

The EMTs had, luckily, been far more interested in making sure everyone was okay than in questioning our story. It didn't hurt that High Moon was a relatively insular community. People knew each other here. I'd seen both of the technicians around town, and though I didn't know their names, I recognized their faces, and pretty sure the same was likewise true.

They'd wanted to take me in for observation, but I declined. Chris was none too happy about that, but I told him Riva would stay by his side while I followed with the chief.

It was a lie, but I needed him to get somewhere safe where his injuries could be tended to. And if they just so happened to give him a sedative to help him sleep through the night, all the better. Hopefully come the morning we could have a proper reunion.

For now, though, I had a feeling it wasn't wise for me to be at the hospital with him, at least not until I figured out a way to ensure our tormenters wouldn't follow me there.

There was also Cass to consider. I couldn't just leave her to her own devices while I returned home and put my head under the covers. After all she'd done, she deserved better.

"You can come on out now," Chief Johnson hollered after the ambulance had left.

For a moment I feared she might have already left, deciding to make her way back to Morganberg on her own, but then she stepped from the trees and walked toward us.

I grabbed her in a big hug the moment she was back. I couldn't help it. This day, Christmas of all days, had been a nightmare. And it wasn't over. I'd always thought I was tough, but in truth I was a scared twenty year old girl. Much as I wanted to believe I could shoulder this burden alone, I realized – forcing down the tears that wanted to come – it was too much. I needed help. Hybrid or not, this was all too much for one person.

"If you two are done, we should get moving."

I opened my mouth, meaning to express my thanks to the chief, and instead found a desperate plea for help pouring out of me. Maybe it was the fact that he was an authority figure or simply a *real* adult, but once the words started, they wouldn't stop, and I found myself telling him all that had happened in Crescentwood.

Johnson, no-nonsense he might be, wasn't entirely

unsympathetic. However, as Cass and I got into the back of his cruiser, he said, "I understand. And believe me, I'll be on the horn to my colleagues over in Crescentwood soon as I can, asking if they'll launch an investigation. I know they're out and about. Been chatter on the horn all morning. Something about a streaker jumping in front of cars over on Gossamer Lane."

Cass and I shared a glance at that, but neither of us said anything.

"But before I do that, I have a drop-off to make."

"What do you mean by that?" I asked, wiping my eyes.

He put the cruiser into drive, turned around, and started heading east. "You live here, Ninja Girl. So do your folks. And there are likewise provisions in the treaty that allow for either side to venture in under certain prescribed circumstances. But aside from that, there's an expectation that the Draíodóir will stay on their side of the fence while the Lycanthropes stay on the other. That applies to you, too, Blondie."

"My name is Cass."

"Whatever. The bottom line here is that High Moon's neutral territory and you're not a neutral party. Now, I realize there were extenuating circumstances, which is why we're driving and you're not ash like those folks back there. But that bottom line remains, you belong in Morganberg, so that's where I'm taking you."

"But Crescentwood..."

"Is Crescentwood," he replied to me. "And Morganberg is Morganberg and never the twain shall meet. But you have to understand, High Moon is under my watch. This town and its people are my concern. Now, if you want, I can turn around and take you back there after we drop your friend off. But right over the border is as far as I go."

I had a strange feeling he wasn't just talking about jurisdiction, but before I could ask, Cass said, "No. We need to stick together." She looked me in the eye. "We have to, Bent. You've gotta trust me on this."

I wanted to, but Morganberg wasn't friendly territory as far as I was concerned. In a way, maybe Chief Johnson and me were kindred spirits of a sort. High Moon was where we both belonged. "I need to make sure Chris is..."

"Your brother will be fine," the chief said, peering at us in the rearview mirror. "You have my word. Especially now that I'm aware there's some folks out there who are more inclined to wipe their backsides with the treaty than respect it. I'll make sure your brother is kept watch over."

"How do you know so much? Did my mom..."

"I know both of your parents, and they know me. We had ourselves a little sit down way back when the new truce was signed and they set about playing house. Tried to fool me then that it was all on paper, but neither's as good an actor as they think."

"That was twenty years ago. How long have you been..."

"Far longer than you know, girl," he replied. "And that's about as much as I care to say on the subject. You two are young and I can see you haven't sown all your wild oats yet, you especially, Ninja Girl. Maybe one day we'll have a sit down of our own and talk things through. For now, all you need to know is I'm first and foremost the chief of police. Step out of line and I'll throw your ass in jail if you so much as jaywalk. Got it?"

I didn't entirely get it, but for now it was enough to know my brother would be safe. "Got it," I replied. "But if you're wrong and my family gets hurt on your watch, we'll have that sit down a lot sooner than you might think."

He let out a laugh. "I would expect nothing less."

~

Despite his harsh words about the border, the chief wasn't entirely heartless. He veered off Crossed Pine Road at one point, eventually stopping at a neat Tudor house where he told us to stay put while he ran inside. When he came back, he was holding a bundle of clothes for Cass and a coat for me.

"Can't promise any of it will fit all that well, but never let it be said I sent anyone off to catch their death from the elements."

There were certainly plenty of other ways for death to catch us, but I was grateful nevertheless. Cass, despite her overclocked metabolism, was likewise happy to have more than a jacket covering her.

After we finished getting dressed, he tossed a few protein bars into the back with us. "Ain't much of a Christmas dinner, I know, but I have a feeling you both have some miles to go before you can get a proper rest. The Draíodóir are big on ceremony, even more so than your people," he said to Cass. "If they were willing to ignore the treaty for something as petty as hunting down a couple of kids, then I don't doubt they've still got their knickers in a knot."

It was a polite way of warning us this wasn't over.

A few more minutes found us crossing the town line. The chief continued for a ways, then took the same cutoff my dad had when we'd come here earlier in the week – though it felt like a whole other lifetime. Unlike my father, however, he stopped the car after only a few yards.

"This is as far as I can go. I believe you know the rest of the way, Blon ... Cass."

I was tempted to ask if he had a spare gun I could borrow, but that felt like an odd thing to ask a cop, even if he was likely much more.

Regardless, we'd been given a small break to rest and recover. With my powers partially back and Chris safe, I was far less afraid than I had been earlier. Anger began to fill the void it left behind. Taking the fight back to Crescentwood was what I really wanted, but there was still something Cass was insistent we do here first.

Mind you, Morganberg wasn't exactly a walk in the park for me. I needed to keep that in mind. If any other werewolves were running around, pretending to be some feral version of Santa who preferred eating his eight tiny reindeer, then I might find myself biting off much more than I could chew.

The Chief looked us over before turning around and pulling away. "It might not mean much, but may the council of the Elder Fae and the Great Huntsman both watch over you."

He was right. It didn't mean much to me, but I was willing to take all the help I could get.

37

The sun was almost all the way down. The shadows, already long in the hollows, began to take on a sense of foreboding.

After Chief Johnson dropped us off, we'd walked in silence for a bit. I think both of us were trying to digest the day best as we could. She'd lost an uncle. As for me ... I wasn't sure yet, and not knowing was killing me inside. Chris and Riva were safe, though. That's what I tried to hang on to as we continued walking.

For now, that and survival had to be at the top of my list. I couldn't leave Chris all alone in this world, but in order to find out what happened to my parents, I needed to do more than survive. I needed to win.

Mind you, I probably also needed to get my bearings and not get lost in the hollows first.

Fortunately, I had Cass with me.

"Come on. I think this is the right way."

Or not. "What do you mean you *think* this is the right way?"

She chuckled. "Kind of embarrassing, but the truth of

the matter is I don't spend a lot of time here. I ... actually don't like the woods much."

"Now you tell me?"

"I know where our meeting place is relative to here, and a few other hangouts, but usually there's others to follow. Right now, we're pretty much on our own out here."

I took a sniff of the air. The scents were definitely crisper and clearer than they were earlier. Cass was right, though. I couldn't smell any other werewolves in the area. Not that my sense of smell was back to...

Almost as if reminding me of the fact, my stomach lurched unpleasantly. Oh, I would be so glad when these pills were finally out of my system. Planning strategy while trying not to puke my guts out was probably not a winning gambit. "Where exactly are we going?" I asked, trying to take my mind off my intestinal distress ... not as easy as it sounds because I also had to pee. I swear, when it rains, it pours.

"We're trying to find Mitch's cabin."

Ah. Jerry had told me that the pack maintained some cabins deep in the hollows. Had our marriage not gotten permanently derailed, one of them was going to be gifted to us as our personal love shack. *Ugh!* There was a thought not destined to calm my stomach. "Okay, so what's the plan? Are we going to hole up and..."

"No," she said. "But there should be some supplies, stuff that can help us."

"He told you all that with a few growls?"

"Yeah. It's hard to explain, but communicating in our other form is a lot more concise. You may find this hard to believe, but it's actually a lot more efficient than English."

"Maybe I should take a few lessons."

"It's also a lot more complex. Part of it is ... instinctual, I guess. You either got it or you don't."

"Okay, guess I won't ask my guidance counselor if I can take that as an elective."

She laughed. "Sorry. Anyway, he told me to stop there first. After that, we need to..."

"We?"

"Yeah. He specifically mentioned you."

"Really? What for?"

She opened her mouth, then shook her head. "It's ... probably best if I show you."

Well, that was mysterious. Thing was, I wasn't sure I wanted any more surprises. "Spill."

"It's nothing bad. It's just ... you won't like it."

"If I won't like it, then how is it not bad?"

Cass threw up her hands. "I don't know. I only kind of half get it myself. Look, you're gonna have to trust me on this."

I glared at the back of her head for several long seconds but then let out a sigh. She'd definitely earned my trust. It was time to stop being a baby about it. "Okay. Fine." I lowered my voice and adopted a spooky tone. "All shall be revealed."

"Something like that."

"Speaking of which..."

"Like I said..."

"Not that. It's more about Mitch himself. Is there any reason he..."

"He what?"

I hated asking since he'd pretty much died in her arms. Sure, I hadn't liked the guy much, especially after this past week. Even so, I didn't consider myself a complete asshole. Nevertheless, I'd already cracked this can of worms. There was little to be gained by leaving it hanging. "Why did he hold back? With those wizards, I mean. Back in High Moon he looked like, well, a werewolf, but a regular one.

But last time I saw him he was closer in size to a grizzly bear."

She turned back toward me, sadness in her eyes, and shrugged. "That's part of the stuff I only half understand."

Ah. Okay then. Guess I needed to be patient and hope she was right about the surprise being of the beneficial variety.

∾

At least the walk wasn't too bad, especially now that I had a coat on. The forest was quiet all around us. Visibility wasn't great, but it was better than it would've been during the summer months, with the vegetation growing wild. Mind you, I should have thought to ask Chief Johnson for a flashlight while he was in a generous mood.

Oh well, there was no use crying over spilt milk. I could save that for when I tripped over something and bashed in my face.

"Come on. It's this way, I think," Cass said, veering off the trail.

I followed, the way forward a bit more difficult but not impassable. With my powers slowly returning, I also felt much better than I had earlier when we'd made our mad dash for freedom from my aunt's impossibly large basement. With any luck it wouldn't be much longer before...

What the?

I caught movement out of the corner of my eye and spun toward it, catching the barest glimpse of something low to the ground just as it disappeared behind some trees.

I shook my head. *Probably just a squirrel or ... another fucking raccoon.*

It was likely nothing. We were in the woods, after all. Even so, I stopped walking. "Hold on."

"What is it?" Cass asked over her shoulder.

This had been happening too much lately. Yes, it was still possibly nothing more than a coincidence, but this didn't seem like the day to dismiss anything lightly. "I saw something."

Cass stopped and sniffed the air. "I don't sense anything."

"Not a person or wolf. I mean something small, like an animal."

She took a long breath, then tilted her head to the side. "I think there's some squirrels hibernating above us, but that's about it."

"It was at ground level."

"Sorry, but I don't smell anything. Look, your eyes are probably playing tricks on you. Hell, I've been coming to these woods for years and still occasionally jump at the shadows. This place does that to you."

I couldn't deny that. There was something creepy about the hollows that went beyond the fact that it was infested with werewolves. Even so, my gut – still gurgling, by the way – didn't buy it. "Hold on a sec."

"Come on, Bent. We should get going. I ... really don't want to be out here like this."

I almost laughed. A werewolf afraid of the dark woods? It was worthy of a chuckle, or would have been any other day. I mean, technically we should have been safe from the Draíodóir here. This was enemy territory for them. At the same time, I couldn't help but think we'd done nothing more than give Belzar a bloody nose by taking out his assassins. He'd already crossed one boundary to find us. Would another really matter?

I doubted it. If anything, it seemed wise to indulge my paranoia for a moment or two.

Veering away, I stepped over to where I'd seen movement. There was nothing there. No burrows, no broken branches, no footprin ... hold on.

I dropped to my knees for a closer look, pulling out my phone and using the last of the battery to light up the area. The packed snow wasn't ideal for catching tracks, at least for small animals. They were too light to break through the top crust. Or at least most of them were. "Come over here. I want you to see this."

Cass did as I asked, apparently realizing that if she wanted to get where we were going anytime soon, she'd need to humor me first.

I pointed. "Does that look like nothing to you?"

The tracks were faint, easily missed. But once I saw one, I spotted more. The thing was, I hoped I was reading them wrong. Because if not, there was something weird about them.

I was no tracker, so it was possible that Cass would simply tell me I was being stupid. But instead she replied, "What the hell?"

"I'm not crazy, am I?"

She shook her head. "No. But ... there's nothing around us. No sound, no scents. These have got to be old."

With the snow packed as it was, there was no way for someone like me to tell. Except for the fact that I'd seen something. "I'm telling you, it was right here."

"I'm not doubting you," she replied in a tone that suggested she actually was.

"Okay, let's pretend for a moment that maybe your nose isn't working right. What made these?"

"Do I look like Bear Grylls to you?"

"No, but you do look like someone who's chased the occasional rabbit during a full moon."

Cass narrowed her eyes at me, but then sighed. "You got me there, but I still don't know. They're not raccoon tracks. Look here." She pointed toward one of the faint, nearly invisible depressions. "I only see two toes."

"What the hell has feet like that?"

"That's only half the question."

"Do I want to know the other half?"

"I'm not entirely sure. There's a lot of guys in the pack who would know this crap better than me, but if I had to guess, whatever made these was walking on two feet."

"So ... I don't suppose lemurs are native to the hollows."

"Lemurs have more than two toes."

"Um, crippled lemurs?" I offered. Her look told me what she thought of that theory. "Well, whatever it is, I think it's following us."

"Now you're being paranoid."

"Am I?" I explained to her all the near sightings I'd had since returning home, reminding her of the footsteps she'd picked up in my aunt's basement, then later the twig she'd heard snap.

"I really want to tell you you're overreacting," she said after I'd finished.

"But...?"

"But all the hair on the back of my neck is standing up." Quite the statement for a werewolf. "So, assuming neither of us is crazy, what now?"

"Isn't it obvious? We try to catch it."

38

That turned out to be easier said than done. It was dark and neither of us had any idea how to catch something I'd only seen from the corner of my eye. With only a few vague footprints in the snow and no scent to track, it was the very definition of a snipe hunt.

We soon realized we had a choice. We could stake out the woods and hope we got lucky – a dubious prospect at best – or we could hightail it to Mitch's cabin and find whatever was waiting for us there. Much as I wanted to figure out what was stalking me, the cabin was at least a tangible goal.

However, that didn't stop us from discussing the matter as we walked.

"You've been doing this longer than me," I said. "Is there any kind of creature that maybe fits the bill?"

"A ghost?"

"Great, so you're saying I'm being haunted by a phantom squirrel? Just what I need."

"Sorry, but I don't have a lot to go on. This isn't really my specialty. I mean, I know about the Draíodóir and that other types of shifters are out there, but I mostly just come here for the big get-togethers. I have a life and most of it doesn't revolve around this spooky shit."

Ah, just my luck to make friends with the one werewolf who wasn't into *spooky shit*. Talk about...

There! I spun, certain I'd seen movement off to my right. This time when I turned to face it, Cass joined me. Sadly, I was rewarded for my efforts with a big, fat case of nothing. *Damnit!*

"Now you've got me jumping at shadows, too."

I glanced at her. "Please tell me you saw something."

"I don't know, but the split second you turned your head, I thought ... maybe."

"Okay, at least I know I'm not going nuts."

"Or maybe we both are."

"Well, misery does love company."

It happened twice more in the next half hour. Cass was actually the first to make a move for the final one, her reaction time impressive even in her human form. Regardless, we still came up empty.

"We're being followed, aren't we?" I asked.

"I don't want to believe that, but I do."

"It's tracking us, trying to find out where we're going."

She turned and pointed. "If it is, then it already knows."

"Huh?"

"We're here."

I followed her outstretched hand and saw it. Tucked far back in a stand of trees was a small log cabin. If she hadn't pointed it out, I'd have walked right past it. I couldn't help but think that was purposeful. The front was covered in what looked to be moss, making it seem like just another piece of forest until you looked right at it.

"So this is where Mitch called home?"

She chuckled, but it was short lived. "No. He has ... *had* an apartment in Morganberg. I think this was nothing more than a hunting cabin."

"Or love shack?"

"I know you're joking, but you might not be too far off. Let's just say some of the pack bitches, and I mean that in both the wolf sense and the other way, aren't too shy about cozying up to our leadership."

Couldn't say I found that surprising. Power, whether social or financial, had been used by guys since time immemorial to get what they wanted. I'd seen it in high school and in college. Why should I assume a werewolf pack would be any different?

Of course, that once again brought to mind the alpha female. Was she simply another *pack bitch* – one who had eyes for my father?

It seemed a petty thing to worry about right then, but I couldn't help it.

No. It wasn't even remotely important compared to everything else. There I was, worrying about who my father *ran* with in the woods, when he might even now be...

"Are you ready?' Cass asked, pulling me from those unpleasant thoughts.

"Yeah. Let's see what's in there," I replied, taking a step forward.

The door wasn't locked, thank goodness. Way out here, there probably wasn't a need to. I mean, the chances of Goldilocks accidentally wandering by to try his porridge were probably slim ... unless that was some kinky role play he'd been into. *Gross.* Not a thought I really wanted bouncing around in my head.

As for other werewolves, well, who among them was

brave enough to snoop through the beta's stuff? Especially not big and bad as he'd been.

But there was still that, too. Why had he held back against those wizards? It wasn't like the Draíodóir would've been fooled into thinking he was just a friendly doggy looking for a game of catch.

I pushed those thoughts away as we stepped inside. Cass found an old oil lamp hanging near the door, as well as some matches. A few moments later, we – meaning I – had enough light to see by.

I'd been expecting something quaint – a cot and a wood stove. Maybe a deer head on the wall to add some atmosphere. Instead, we'd walked into what looked like a war room. A large map took up nearly one full wall. There were pins at several places, as well as writing all over it, one note clearly pointing toward a spot labeled High Moon.

Several military-grade storage crates were stacked off on one side. I had a feeling these weren't purchased from the local Target to store Mitch's summer clothes.

A gun rack dominated a third wall, but if those were hunting rifles, then I hated to see what he was hunting.

"What the fuck?"

"That was kind of my thought, too," Cass said, taking it all in.

"What exactly did he tell you about this place?"

"Not much more than I told you. There wasn't time."

"Did you know..."

"I had no idea this place existed before today. Nor have I heard anyone else mention anything like this."

"It looks like he was planning for a war."

"Maybe."

I turned toward her. "What about this says *maybe*?"

She stepped in further and I saw her nose working. Oh yeah. There was that. Although, I had to admit, after my love shack crack, I'd been kind of afraid to take too deep of a breath.

Pushing my stupidity to the side, I joined her. One quick noseful was enough to sense myriad odors, but they were all beneath a musty coating hanging over everything. "This place hasn't been used in a while, has it?"

Cass ran a finger over one of the crates, drawing a line in a layer of dust. "A couple of months I'd say."

"Do you think my dad knew about it?"

"No idea," she replied, turning back toward me. "And I'm not sure it matters right now. But, if I had to guess, I'd say this place is from back when Craig was running things."

She had a point. Debating who was in the know was probably a luxury for another time.

"Also, and I'm just speculating here," she continued, "but I think this was more for defense than offense."

"How so?"

"Look at this map." She pointed out several spots that were marked up. "There isn't much here about Crescent-wood. Most of these markings seem to be entry points to Morganberg and the hollows in particular. It looks to me like they were trying to predict the most probable points for an invasion." She chuckled. "Mind you, it's not like I studied much military strategy in high school. I'm just playing armchair general here."

She folded her arms and continued to study the map. "Not to speak ill of the dead, but Craig liked to talk tough. The thing is, I never got the sense that he actually wanted to start shit with the Draíodóir. Not like his dad anyway."

"Oh?" I didn't have any memories of my paternal grandfather. He'd died right before I was born. In fact, growing up, my father hadn't talked much about either of his parents.

"Caleb was a bit before my time," Cass said. "Just relaying what I've heard, but it sounded like he was more fire and brimstone. Before the new truce, the one that saw Curtis marry that ... err, your mother, I heard there'd been a lot of static between us and the Draíodóir. Apparently Caleb and their queen had a bit of a mad-on about each other."

She must have meant Grammy Nessa.

Those must've been tense times. I remembered my grandmother. Though I'd been nothing more than a kid, she'd been a force to be reckoned with. It wasn't hard to imagine two pig-headed leaders who didn't get along. Explains why Mom and Dad's first inclination upon meeting had been to kill each other.

Imagine how differently things would have worked out if either had succeeded. Hah. For starters, I wouldn't be around. But who knows what else might've happened?

It's amazing. I didn't consider myself a student of history, but I'd paid marginal attention in my classes. It was sometimes the smallest events that either pushed two societies away from the brink of war, or ended up lighting the fuse.

I shook those thoughts away. History could be inter-esting at times, but I doubted it was relevant to our needs at the moment. If Belzar came knocking again, chances were he wouldn't be dissuaded by a term paper chronicling supernatural conflicts throughout the ages.

Cass was apparently thinking the same thing. "It's interesting stuff but nothing that will help us."

I hefted one of the assault rifles from the gun rack. "The history might not, but the hardware could be useful."

"You know how to use that?"

I laughed, putting it back. "No. I was kind of hoping you did."

She shook her head. "I went hunting once or twice

with my dad, but he wasn't the type to go full automatic on a buck."

"Fair enough. Why don't we open some of these other boxes and see if there's maybe something else here that's more our speed?"

39

"You're serious?" I asked, holding up a boxy device that looked more like a losing entry at a sixth grade science fair.

"It might actually work."

"Really?"

"At least I think my uncle believed it could."

I raised a skeptical eyebrow. "How so?"

"He was babysitting me this one time, years ago, back when I was a kid. One of those ghost hunting shows was playing on the TV. My mom didn't like me watching them because they gave me nightmares, but she was out." She smiled wistfully, no doubt remembering the good times. "I remember him laughing his head off while I sat there next to him all wide-eyed."

"Not sure I blame him," I said playing with the knobs on the device, uncertain they actually did anything.

"Anyway, I also remember him telling me something about it. He said ghost hunting equipment wasn't worth jack shit when it came to finding actual spirits, but – as it turned out – it might not be entirely useless for other purposes."

"So you're saying we, what, should record voices over white noise to hear if any witches are..."

"No," she replied, taking the device from me. "This is a mel meter and this one is a spirit box."

"Um, okay. And?"

"You're talking about EVPs. You know, electronic voice phenomenon?"

"No, I don't know. I'm more of a *House Hunters* person."

She laughed. "Not sure that's any more realistic."

"Hey, it gives me hope that when I finally graduate with a degree in environmental science I, too, can magically have a budget of seven hundred grand for my first home."

Cass raised an eyebrow. "Maybe we should stick to the ghost hunting stuff. Anyway, if I recall correctly, Mitch told me that gald was simply another form of energy. And energy can be detected, either directly or when it interferes with something else."

"So you're saying these things will function as witch radar?"

She shrugged. "Maybe. I didn't realize he was being serious at the time, but why else would this stuff be here?"

"Maybe he fanboyed *Ghost Adventures*." I held up a hand before she could reply. "Relax, you've sold me. Truth is, I have nothing better to go on. Worst case is we look like dorks using them."

"But best case is they give us a heads up before an attack."

"And we still look like dorks."

"Yes, but living dorks."

I couldn't argue with that. Though I'd learned to rely on my strength these last few months, I wasn't above taking whatever help was at my disposal.

I also couldn't deny feeling a bit better armed with the

semi-automatic pistol currently strapped to my side. I hadn't gone to the range often. It hadn't been my thing but, growing up in rural Pennsylvania, it was something that almost everyone did from time to time. Now I was glad I had. Though one of the heavier pieces might've been the better pick, at least I knew how to work the handgun.

Being able to shoot back at fuckers who could pick us off at range would go a long way toward evening the odds.

Now, if Cass was to be believed, these silly looking devices might do just as much to keep us alive. Considering the displays of power I'd seen today, we needed every advantage we could get. The only downside, according to her, was they were extremely short range. So if they went off – assuming they worked at all – we'd need to hustle our butts without asking questions. Still, short notice was better than none.

We took maybe a half hour at most readying ourselves. Cass emphasized that we not dawdle, and I guess I couldn't blame her. If horror movies had taught me one thing, it was that cabins in the woods weren't exactly an oasis against evil.

"All set?" she asked after checking the crates one last time, just in case Mitch had left any spare hand grenades behind.

"Ready to go," I replied, glancing down at the mel meter, "and hunt down Civil War ghosts I guess, or maybe guys named Mel."

"That's the spirit," she replied with a laugh.

"Speaking of which, you never did tell me what's next on our agenda."

She looked away. "Mitch insisted that..."

"I know that part already. But why?"

"I don't know the why. Just the where." I stared at her for several seconds, until she finally said, "It's time for you to meet the alpha female."

~

I was both curious and a bit furious at the prospect. That latter was less directed toward Cass and more from what my imagination had been insisting all week. Sadly, my friend was mum as to the whys for this meeting, claiming she didn't quite get it herself.

All I knew was this had better not be a meet and greet with the *other woman*, some werewolf tramp asking me to think of her as a second mother. If so, she'd be lucky if she didn't end up beaten unconscious with a mel meter.

But, rather than argue, I decided to trust my friend. She seemed to believe this was both urgent and had bearing on our current conundrum. Rather than waste more time, I stepped aside and let her lead the way back into the dark woods.

And they were dark. Goddamn it, but of all the stuff Mitch had squirreled away in his personal weapons cache, night vision goggles hadn't been part of the equation. And why would they be? Werewolves didn't need them, and I sincerely doubted they gave a solitary shit for any non-lycanthropes who decided to ransack the place. I'd debated bringing one of the oil lamps with me, but had a feeling that could be risky in the woods should things go south for us.

Besides, I already had one hand full with ghost-hunting gear. That left the other free to draw my gun if I needed to. The meter gave off a dull red glow, but it was useless as a light source. The only upside was the snow on the ground offered enough contrast to keep me from walking into any trees.

Cass had undressed before we left, stowing her clothes in a backpack she'd found. That meant she was expecting to wolf out. It also meant I was following a naked woman through the woods, something that was rapidly becoming a common occurrence in my life.

"Where are we heading?" I asked in a low voice. For some reason, it seemed fitting in the quiet woods.

"She has a hut to the south, away from where the pack meets."

"Why there?"

"She's in charge of our spiritual well-being, our connection to the past. According to the rumor mill, there's a sacred glade somewhere close to where she lives. Allows her to commune with the old gods, if you believe that sort of thing."

I opened my mouth to make a crack, but then immediately shut it, memories of the past summer coming back to haunt my thoughts.

It couldn't be the same spot.

At least I hoped it wasn't. My late fiancé Jerry had told me it was his special place – one which had become his grave. But if it wasn't as secret as he, dim bulb that he'd been, thought, then that meant this alpha chick perhaps knew more about me than I wanted her to.

I mulled it over as we walked. Was this all nothing more than a ploy for petty revenge? Maybe she'd kept it from the others, waiting for a time when she could off me herself. And now, considering what was going on, Mitch had wanted her to get a shot before the Draíodóir could finish the job first.

Yeah, sounded a bit sketchy to me, too, but that was what my life had apparently become.

We continued walking, putting distance between us and the cabin. Hopefully Cass knew where we were going, because I sure as shit didn't have much chance of helping out in that matter.

What a way to spend Christmas night. I should've been home, trying on the new outfits I'd gotten and yelling at Chris to stop hogging the TV. Instead I was out here, wondering which monster would take me out first in this sick game of...

It was apparently a question that was about to be answered, because my mel meter picked that moment to start beeping.

~

I remembered what Cass had told me about the limited range of these things. Without thinking too much, lest that slow me down, I threw myself to the side in a dive roll. I could hear Cass doing the same in the opposite direction, but the heavy crunch of snow that followed suggested she'd changed, too. Probably not a bad idea.

I'd been expecting an explosion, or implosion maybe, in the spot where I'd been standing a moment earlier, but nothing happened.

Yet the stupid meter kept chirping like an angry goldfinch. Maybe the batteries were dying.

I gave the device a shake just as something moved in the darkness ahead of me, almost causing me to jump out of my skin. It was visible for less than a second at the far edge of my vision, and then it disappeared behind a tree.

Son of a...

Whatever it had been, it was small – just a tiny dark shape against the snow. Nevertheless, I had no doubt my little *friend* was back.

This time there was no hesitation. I bolted toward the opposite end of the tree, making it a point to keep an eye on both sides in case it doubled back. There came no more movement as I stepped around the trunk and ... found nothing.

Fuck!

No, that wasn't entirely true. I leaned down, using

what little light the mel meter offered, and spied more of those tiny indents in the snow. Footprints. But that's where things got weirder. They seemed to stop right in the spot where I assumed it, whatever the fuck it was, would be hiding. But it was empty space, nothing mor...

What in the name of...?!

Something slapped the meter out of my hand, knocking it to the ground with a dull clatter of cheap plastic.

Okay, that's not normal.

I let out a shriek as something brushed up against my leg, like it was trying to rush past me. So much for staying brave in the face of the unknown.

What the hell is going on?

I spun and, for just a second, saw it scampering away from me, and then – as I focused my eyes on the spot where it was – it simply vanished.

Seriously! What the fuck?

Was I actually chasing a ghost or simply losing my mind?

If so, at least I wasn't alone. There came a snarl, and Cass – now fully in her wolf form – leapt out from behind a bush and pounced on the spot I'd been tracking.

Judging from the confused whimper she made, she'd missed whatever it was – assuming it had been there at all.

"Let me guess, it just vanished?"

She threw me a single nod of her head.

I picked up the mel meter, undamaged fortunately, and walked over to where she continued searching the...

Movement caught the corner of my eye, something circling around us. But, once again, I turned just in time to see it move beneath a bush and then it was gone. There was nothing there.

Except the device in my hand said otherwise, continuing to chirp as if telling me, "Hey, stupid, you're wrong."

Either way, this was quickly growing tiresome.

I approached the bush, leafless due to the winter cold. It was sparse enough that I should've been able to see anything taking cover beneath it, but it was empty. There was nothing to be...

Hold on.

One of the branches swayed ever so slightly – except there was no breeze, at least not one strong enough to do that. It was almost as if something were pushing past it.

More and more, I began to consider whether we were dealing with an invisible foe. But that didn't make sense either. Both Cass and I had seen it, but it had always been quick and ... and out of the *corner* of my eye.

Was it even possible that something could only be visible in one's periphery? Well, not for something normal. However, normal and the hollows didn't always go hand in hand.

I heard Cass come up behind me, but I pointed off to my right. "I think I saw it go that way."

She moved off and I once more turned toward the branch I'd seen moving. There was still nothing there, at least nothing I could see. I began to turn my head toward where Cass had trotted off to, forcing my focus to change with it but being mindful of that spot where ...

Holy shit!

Where a moment before there'd been nothing, now I could make out a dark shape hidden beneath the branches of the bush. It was hard to make out details both due to the angle and the darkness, but I could tell at least two things: whatever was there was small, and it was standing upright on two legs.

All right, you little prick. My turn.

I started to move forward, mindful of keeping my focus elsewhere. "Cass," I called out. "I think it moved behind that tree over there." I had no way of knowing if this thing understood English or not, but in a world of monsters and magic, it seemed wise to not tip my hand.

Inching ever closer, I saw the creature move. It began to slide along the bottom of the bush in the opposite direction, no doubt hoping to avoid me. I turned my head slightly, still focused elsewhere, and tracked its direction as it moved too far for my peripheral vision to follow.

But that was okay. If I was judging its movement correctly, it was stepping out of cover behind me right ... about ... now!

I spun, dropping the mel meter, and took a leap of faith, hoping that I, for once this day, landed on solid footing.

40

I landed on something, all right, and it definitely wasn't happy about it.

Sharp claws scraped against my midsection as I fought to keep whatever I'd caught from escaping.

"I got it!"

Sorta, anyway. Whatever it was, it was a slippery little beast. I kept trying to grab hold of it, only for my hands to come away with tiny furrows clawed into them. It was like trying to wrestle down an angry bobcat.

Whatever the hell it was, it most certainly wasn't a raccoon. There was no fur on its body, just bumpy skin ... oh, and claws. Can't forget about those.

Heavy footsteps came up from behind just as I managed to wrap my hands around the form struggling beneath me. I must've pinned its arms to its sides because, although it continued to struggle, it had stopped scratching the shit out of me.

Gotcha, you little fucker.

I turned around and held it up for Cass. "See?"

She glanced down, tilted her head to the side, and

then shifted back to her human form. "See what? There's nothing there."

"That's the point ... I think. Turn away and look at it from the corner of your eye. Come on, this thing is squirming like crazy."

The look on her face suggested she thought I'd gone round the bend, but then she turned her head slightly. All at once, she backed up a couple steps, her eyes wide. "What the fuck is that?!"

Truth of the matter was, I'd been so busy trying to hold it, that I hadn't bothered to look myself. I shifted my gaze and the struggling mass in my hands became visible.

What the fuck is right!

It was almost enough to cause me to drop it. Vaguely humanoid in shape, with grey, wrinkly skin, it kind of resembled the creatures from that old movie *Gremlins*. From the neck down, anyway.

Where a head should have sat, however, there was only a fleshy bulb with a single massive eyeball staring out from the center of it.

The creature squirmed in my grasp, turning that eyeball to glare at me. Even in my periphery, I could feel its malevolent gaze, as if it were staring into my very soul. The hairs on the back of my neck – hell, everywhere on my body – stood up as if this thing was line dancing across my grave.

It was too much to take.

That feeling of revulsion combined with the creature's grotesque alien nature caused my fight or flight instinct to kick in. Before I barely realized what I was doing, I spun and slammed it *face*-first into the nearest tree trunk. The gigantic eyeball atop its neck splattered in a disgusting spray of goo and the creature fell limp in my hands.

The moment it did, I inadvertently glanced directly at it and realized I could now see it normally.

"Is it dead?" Cass asked, sounding just as freaked out as me.

"I think so. Ewww, and it's leaking eyeball guts all over my hands! Here, you take it."

She backed up. "No way."

"Scaredy cat."

"I'm a wolf, not a cat, and still not taking it."

"Well, get me a napkin or something."

"From where?!" She finally stepped forward to take a better look. "What the hell is it?"

I shook my head, trying to keep from puking. "I was really hoping you knew."

"Are there more of them?"

"God, I hope not."

"Why was it following us?"

I took a deep breath to steady myself. The fucking hollows! Why was everything here so goddamned weird? Other forests had squirrels and chipmunks. This one had creepy little cyclopes with freaky-ass camouflage abilities. Christ, that sounded more like a shitty movie my brother would watch than anything that should actually exist.

Finally, I forced myself to calm down a bit. "Do me a favor. Pick up my mel meter. I dropped it over there." As she did so, I continued to stare at the body in my hands. "I don't think it was following us so much as me. I've been seeing this or something like it out of the corner of my eye ever since the solstice. Thought it was just my imagination. Now ... I really wish it had been."

"Tell me about it. What the hell is this thing?"

"*That, child, is what we call a puck,*" a deep, gravelly voice replied from somewhere disturbingly close by. I looked up to find the source, but didn't see anything in the surrounding darkness.

"*We used to joke as kids that if you saw a puck you were royally fucked. Sadly, that's not too far from the truth.*"

~

I reared back, prepared to use the ... puck, I guess, as a projectile, when Cass's hand fell on my shoulder.

"It's okay."

"But..."

"Sorry to sneak up on you like this," the voice said, sounding far more human this time, "but I wasn't expecting visitors, especially not you."

An elderly woman stepped out from behind a tree. She had stringy grey hair, a stooped body, and was naked as a wrinkly jaybird. Apparently the hollows attracted nudists as much as it did monsters.

I realized her face was vaguely familiar. I'd seen her somewhere ... and that's when it hit me. She'd been at the Winter Solstice gathering. But that wasn't all. She was also the sour old lady who'd confronted me at the grocery store the day I'd gone to see Jerry ... the same day he'd died.

Somehow she'd approached us completely unnoticed. That made sense for me. My powers still weren't back to full. But Cass's were working fine. Either the thing in my hands had freaked us out more than we cared to admit or nature nanny here was one stealthy customer.

"Grandma Nelly," Cass said, nodding at the old woman.

"Grandma?"

The newcomer, Nelly I presumed, turned toward me. "A figure of speech. Everyone here calls me that, mostly because I'm old."

"You're not that old," Cass said with a smile.

"Flattery will get you everywhere, dear, but let's not bullshit ourselves. I'm old, maybe not quite as old as the dirt of this forest, but I go back a ways, longer than I'll admit to."

"Um, nice to meet you," I said, curious as to why

she was running around in the woods stark naked on Christmas. That struck me as strange even for a werewolf.

"We've met before."

"I know."

"My mind's not as sharp as it used to be, but it was at the Shop Haven, wasn't it? My apologies for playing dumb at the time, but I was curious to see how things would play out between you and that Sandwich boy."

"Play out?"

"Yes. Can't say I was too surprised when you finally killed him."

Oh crap. "It was an acc..."

She placed a withered hand on my arm, well away from the dead puck. "Relax. The boy was a dullard, nobody who'll be missed in the long run. Besides, if you ask me, it was stupid for Craig to force you to marry him. I tried to tell him as much, but he wasn't one to listen. Nope. That one, always with his head up his ass ... until you replaced it with your foot anyway."

This was starting to get uncomfortable. It was like she was rattling off a list of my most notorious werewolf hits.

"Mind you," she continued, as if discussing the weather, "that was nothing compared to dumping Jerry's body in the Grove of the Valkyries on the night of a blood moon. I swear, child, you couldn't have made a worse choice if you'd drawn a pentagram and sacrificed a virgin to Old Scratch himself."

That didn't sound particularly promising.

"But that is neither here nor there. You'll have to deal with the consequences of those actions, but on another night." She glanced down at the dead thing still in my hands. "I think you have enough problems right now, but maybe I can help with that."

"Listen, I'm sure a ... cup of tea would be lovely, but

we're kind of looking for someone, the alpha female. She and I need to have a few words."

"Um, Bent..." Cass started, but Nelly held up a hand.

"Is that a fact? Well, then you've come to the right place."

"Wait, *you*?"

She threw Cass a wink. "Maybe not as bad of a match with that Sandwich boy as I thought." Then she turned back toward me. "Tell me, do you think I'm out here in my birthday suit on a night like this because it does my bones good?"

"Um..."

She sighed and turned away. "Come with me. My place isn't far."

"You're the alpha female?"

"I believe we've already established that."

"Well, y-yeah," I sputtered. "It's just that, my dad ... I sort of figured, he..."

"Ah, yes Curtis. Such a fine boy. So much better suited for the job than his brother." She stopped and made eye contact with me over her shoulder. "You know, now that I think of it, my nickname is actually more apt for you than most."

I'd started to follow, but that comment caused me to stop dead in my tracks. "Hold on. Are you saying you're my..."

She laughed, seemingly pleased with my discomfort. "Relax. I'm Curtis's stepmother, so I guess that makes me your step-grandmother, if there is such a thing."

That threw me for a loop ... albeit probably not quite as much as the dead puck I was still inexplicably carrying. Apparently I wasn't alone in thinking this.

"Why don't you throw that nasty thing away, dear?" Nelly suggested.

"Um..."

"It's quite obviously dead. Sadly, whatever mischief it was up to has already been dealt. There isn't much time. Its master will no doubt be quite angry."

The weirdness factor had just been ratcheted up again. I'd figured between what I'd learned this year and the things that had happened at school there wasn't much left in the world that could surprise me. Now, here I was in the woods with a dead eyeball demon and two naked women, one of whom was apparently my grandmother.

I tossed the puck away, glad to be rid of it, then continued following Nelly. I had a ton of questions and no real idea where to start, but the beginning sounded as good a place as any. "So, if you're my grandmother ... step-grandmother, how come Dad's never mentioned you?"

"A fair question, but first..." She turned to Cass and fixed her with a stare. All at once, Nelly's head seemingly split in two, causing me to step back with a squeak of fright. However, I was wrong. She'd merely enlarged her fangs in her still human mouth.

Mind you, that didn't quite do it justice. It was as if her teeth had turned into railroad spikes for a moment before receding back to their normal size. Maybe some sort of reminder of her rank in the pack. Either way, it was disturbing as fuck to watch.

"I shouldn't need to remind you, dear," she said to Cass, once she'd dialed her teeth back to the point where she could talk again, "that what is said here stays between us."

Even Cass was left wide-eyed by the display. "I ... understand, Grandma Nelly."

"I thought you would. Good to know at least one of you respects our rules." Then she addressed me again. "To answer your question, Curtis and I had a falling out some years back."

That was odd. Dad had always struck me as an easygoing type of guy. Of course, that was the persona I'd grown up with. I'd since learned he had more of an edge to him. But still, Nelly seemed nice enough, if a bit blunt and to the point. "Any reason why?"

She shrugged, raising one bare shoulder. "It probably had something to do with the fact that I killed his father."

41

"Come again?"

"It was regrettable," Nelly continued, walking along as if the cold didn't bother her in the least, "but necessary. You see, your Grandpa Caleb was, to put it succinctly, a mean old bastard. His first wife, your real grandmother, died under mysterious circumstances some years before you were born. None of the pack would confront him about it, of course, but the rumors persisted. By then I'd already taken over as the pack's oracle."

"Oracle?"

"High priestess, if you will. I maintain our connection to the old ways, confer the blessings of Valdemar, that sort of thing. I wasn't too hard on the eyes back then either, if I do say so myself. I tried to curb your grandfather, keep him in check, but he could be a real son of a bitch when he wanted to be."

"So why…"

"I'm getting to that. Patience isn't really one of your virtues, is it?"

"Can't say that it is."

"What a surprise. I would say you got it from your grandfather, but then I don't think it's in heavy supply on either side of your family. Now where was I? Ah, yes. It was right around the time your parents began putting forth the idea of a new treaty, a marriage of convenience to unite our two warring people." She shook her head and sighed. "Sadly, Caleb might have been a bastard but he was no idiot. Your father's so-called treaty didn't fool him for a second."

"It didn't?"

"Of course not. When you've been around the block a few times, young love – especially in a close family member – is as easy to spot as a sunny day."

Cass perked up at that. "If he knew, then why didn't he tell the rest of the pack?"

"As I said, Caleb wasn't a fool. Telling the others would have potentially incited them to war which – if we're being honest here – wouldn't have bothered him in the slightest. What did bother him, though, was how it would look. If it was made known that his own son had turned traitor by falling in love with a witch, it could have undermined his position." She must have seen the look on Cass's face, because she added, "I never said he wasn't petty. That's what really tweaked his balls, the possibility of losing face in front of his pack. So he told no one, aside from me of course, that he planned to kill them both."

"Mom and Dad?"

"Who else? Not only would it save him the embarrassment, but it would eliminate the potential rival your father was rapidly becoming."

"Sounds like he was a real asshole."

"Now do you understand why I killed him?" she asked over her shoulder.

"Beginning to."

"Don't get me wrong, girl. I didn't give a flying fig

what happened to your mother. But murdering Curtis was a step too far even for me. Oh, wipe that grimace off your face. I was simply being honest."

Grimace? Her back was to me. How did she know I'd made a...

"I can smell it on you, in case you're wondering."

Oh, yeah, this was definitely weird.

"Sadly, despite my having his best intentions at heart, your father never forgave me. So I've kept my distance, lived by myself in the woods ever since."

"But I saw you at that supermarket."

"I'm the keeper of the old ways, child, not a crazed hermit. I didn't exile myself from all of humanity. I merely enjoy the solitude."

"Oh."

"Keep up. We're almost back to my cabin. I've already prepared the offering."

"What offering?" I asked. Cass glanced back at me and shrugged, her meaning clear. This was one of those parts she didn't entirely understand.

"The one to Valdemar, of course. A tithe must be paid to the Great Huntsman so that he might confer his blessing."

"Why do you need Valdemar's blessing? I thought you were already his..."

"Not me," she replied with a huff. "You. You have to be properly anointed, touched by his power."

"Why?"

"Because you're the pack's new beta."

∼

Before I could reply, she continued. "Oh come now. You should have realized that."

"Why would I?"

317

"Because you defeated Mitchell in combat. Kicked his ass, as a matter of fact. What did you think would happen?"

Actually, I thought I'd be yelled at. I figured Dad owed me a good tongue-lashing but had refrained because of the scheduled peace talks. "But how? I didn't challenge him. I simply defended myself."

"He initiated the challenge by attacking you. That was no mere scuffle. He had intent to harm. It was a full-fledged battle. Our ways are very clear about those and what the outcome means."

"But I don't want..."

"You don't get a choice, neither does Curtis. No matter how much he's been hemming and hawing about it this week, our ways are quite clear about that, too. Although, I will admit, it's odd."

"Because of what I am?"

"Female? Yes."

"That's not what I meant."

"I know exactly what you meant, but your mixed blood is irrelevant. It became so the moment your father inducted you. But normally, the duties of alpha and beta are split between the sexes. Yes, it's a bit outdated, but as I said, I'm our connection to the old ways. Some traditions don't die simply because women are free to wear their so-called skinny jeans wherever they please."

"So, I'm the beta female then?"

"No. That position is already filled. You are the full pack beta. You defeated Mitchell. Soundly at that. His position and power are now yours."

"Hold on a second. Didn't you say you killed Caleb? Then why didn't you take his place?"

"Because mine wasn't a fair fight. It was premeditated murder. There's a difference." She turned and grinned at me, making me wish I hadn't asked.

Great! I'd somehow gone from reluctant pack mutt to ranking member, all because that idiot couldn't keep his paws to himself. I could only imagine what that entailed. Maybe I was now in charge of refreshments for all future meetings and...

Wait. Position *and* power?

I thought back to Mitch's death some hours earlier. He'd attacked those Draíodóir as a normal werewolf. I couldn't figure out why. But what if it was because that was all he could do? The truth was, I hadn't seen him since he'd attacked me. I had no way of knowing if anything had changed with him.

Cass was apparently thinking the same thing. "Was that why Uncle Mitch was, err..."

"Less terrifying?" I offered.

"Of course," Nelly replied. We stepped into a small clearing and suddenly I could see again. It wasn't because of any magic, though. A path lay ahead, lined with those solar powered walkway lights that could be purchased at any Home Depot. How disappointingly mundane. "I was forced to withdraw Valdemar's blessing from him after his defeat. Can't say I was too upset. He struck me as a poor choice for beta from the start, but I guess your father was trying to smooth things over with the contingent still loyal to his brother. And it's not like anyone listens to me anyway. Why would they? I'm only the chief mystic of these woods."

"If you removed the blessing from him, and that's what you're preparing now..."

"I see you're beginning to catch on, dear. We should hurry. I need to transfer it to you and, judging by that puck you killed, we don't have much time."

∾

I was busy contemplating this as we approached Nelly's cabin. Unlike Mitch's hunting shack, this was larger, harder to miss. That said, we were still deep in the hollows, meaning trespassers were unlikely. And, if what I'd seen earlier was any indication of what Nelly could do, she didn't have much to worry about even if someone did try to break in.

The place had a mixed feel about it. The cabin itself looked old, but some of the accoutrements, such as those lights, were far more modern.

Perhaps sensing my confusion, she turned toward me as we reached the front stoop. "I may be the guardian of the old ways, girl, but that doesn't mean I care to suffer for the cause. When you reach my age, you don't turn down whatever creature comforts you can get."

She held the door for us, and we stepped in. Nelly followed, locking up behind her. For a moment, we were bathed in darkness, the only illumination the glow of cooling embers in the fireplace. But then I heard a click and a couple of overhead light fixtures turned on. "Generator?"

"Yes, but only for backup purposes," she replied, moving past me. "I had the pack run power lines out here years ago. One of the benefits of my station. Why, I've even got cable TV."

I looked around. Inside there was that same disparity between old and new, almost as if the cabin were divided: one half in the present, the other in the deep past. I saw a TV on one wall and relatively modern looking appliances in the small kitchen near the back.

Closer to the fireplace, though, things took a more rustic turn. There was an old table, with multiple bowls atop it. Incense burned in one. Strung above the fireplace was what appeared to be a string of ... teeth – no, fangs – amongst other creepy things.

It was as if one could wake up here, watch some daytime television, then stroll over and make sacrifices to ancient deities, all without leaving the comfort of one's home.

"Sit at the table," she directed. "We'll begin in a moment."

I wasn't entirely sure I wanted to begin, but then I remembered those black mega-wolves. Powerful as a regular werewolf was, they put them to shame. Under normal circumstances I was pretty content being me, not to mention my complete lack of interest in howling at the moon. But the circumstances of the day gave me pause. I still wasn't back to full, albeit only a few more hours were left until my meds fully wore off. Even so, I probably needed every edge I could get, both to survive and take the fight back to Crescentwood.

Or maybe not... "Right before we got here, you said we didn't have much time. Why is that? Does it have to do with the..."

"The puck? Indeed," Nelly replied, stepping to the fire where – of course – a cauldron hung. She scooped some dark muck out of it into a large mixing bowl and took a seat at the table.

Cass sat next to me. "I think what Bent means is, well, what the hell was that thing?"

"Bent?" Nelly raised an eyebrow then, just as quickly, waved off her question. "The Draíodóir call them the fachan, but those are just names. The truth of the matter is they're nasty beasts conjured from Outside."

"Outside?" I asked, hooking a thumb behind me.

"Not outside the door, child. I mean outside this world."

"Oh."

"Think of them like single purpose imps. They're summoned for specific jobs, usually by vile assholes who don't mind screwing with the natural order. Pardon my editorial."

That fits Belzar to a tee. "No problem at all."

"I thought not." She pointed to a nearby shelf. "Be a dear and get that packet on the mantle for me. The one at the top."

I stood up and grabbed a small zippered case, handing it over as asked. Nelly opened it and pulled out a thinly rolled cylinder of paper. She held it over the fire, lit one end, then popped the other end into her mouth.

"Is that for the blessing?"

"No," she replied, taking a deep pull. "This is from my personal stash. It's so much easier to perform this ritual if I'm mellowed out first."

"I don't suppose you want to share," Cass said.

"Back off, girl," Nelly replied with a puff of acrid smoke. "This shit ain't cheap, you know."

Okay, then. This was getting odder by the moment. I decided to steer us back on track. "So these pucks, they're pretty nasty?"

"Not physically, but they're rarely conjured with the best of intentions. There's often a blood ritual involved and the caster has to be willing to offer a piece of themselves, one associated with the task at hand, to seal the pact."

I considered this. "The one we captured had a giant eyeball for a face."

"I see you're catching on."

"You were right, Bent," Cass said. "It was sent to spy on you."

Nelly nodded. "Yes. And even if it was alone, whoever conjured it is going to be mighty pissed that you popped its skull like a pimple."

"Fucking Belzar," I growled.

"What's a Belzar?" Nelly asked. "No. Don't tell me.

Some of those idiots are still picking coven names they think sound cool, aren't they? I thought that went out with the seventies."

"He's from New York."

"I guess that figures." She stared at me as she smoked, continuing to mix things into the bowl. "So what's his beef with you, aside from the obvious?"

"You mean my unique ancestry."

"Semi-unique, but yeah."

"Semi..."

"Don't worry about that now. Focus. We haven't got all night."

I gave her the abridged rundown of my aunt's fiancé and what had happened, including how Craig had purposely screwed us over.

When I was done, she nodded. "Yep. That sounds like Craig, all right. He wasn't half the leader his father was, but he sure as hell inherited all of his spite."

She took another puff, held it, then blew it out. "Almost done here. Do me a favor and hand me that other box on the shelf."

"More ingredients for the offering?"

"No. It's full of Saltines. This shit makes me powerful hungry."

42

Nelly finished her joint, tossed the stub into the fireplace, then stretched, affording me a better look at her liver-spotted body than I really needed. She picked up the bowl and directed me to a torch sconce in the wall close to the fireplace.

"Light that – preferably without burning my house down – then follow me."

"Where are we going?" I asked once we were outside the cabin again.

"To confer the blessing, of course."

"But I thought we were doing that here."

"You thought wrong. Come on. I want to get home and put my nightgown on. These old bones can't handle the chill like they used to."

I was sorely tempted to point out that she could have gotten dressed back in her hut rather than traipsing about with all her wrinkles dangling in the wind, but decided there were more pressing concerns. "Where exactly are we headed?"

She glanced back at me, a twinkle in her eyes. "I think you already know the answer to that."

"I do...?" *Oh crap!* "You're kidding me, right?"

"What are you two talking about?" Cass asked.

"It was ... Jerry's secret place."

"It's much more than that," Nelly explained. "Have you ever wondered why the Draíodóir choose to live in such close quarters to us when they could have easily moved anytime in the last two centuries? Us, too. It's not like these are the only woods around."

I shrugged at her backside. "I figured it was stubbornness, each side refusing to budge."

"You're not entirely wrong. However, much as I might dislike those gald-slinging sons of whores, I'm old enough to realize a good deal of that is simply how I was raised. How we've all been raised. Hell, half the pack would gladly eat a silver bullet if they thought it would spite someone over in Crescentwood. Good old fashioned racism at its finest."

Cass leaned toward me. "Just for the record, I'm not one of them."

"Save the sucking up for another day, Ester," Nelly snapped. "Because your gal pal there is just as wrong as she is right. And, again, I'm pretty certain she has half a clue as to why."

"Does it have to do with where we're headed?" I asked.

"Give that girl a cupie doll!" she cried. "You see, there are *soft spots* in this world, if you will, places where the walls are thin. Whereas most of what we call reality is solid plaster and two by fours, there are some spots where the creator put up cheap drywall and called it a day. Know where to knock and you'll see just how hollow it is."

"Way to go with the carpentry metaphors."

"Your grandmother Vanessa – Queen V, Caleb used to call her – she had a mouth on her, too. And you have both their blood running through your veins. I swear, you must've been a hit at the debutante ball." The words left her mouth in a wisp of white mist, reminding me just how cold it was. "Now what was I saying? Oh yes. On certain days, special days, that drywall becomes thin as paper."

"Like during a blood moon?"

She nodded from up ahead. "Exactly. And the hollows just happens to be home to one such soft spot, as I'm sure you're already aware."

My silence was apparently answer enough as she pushed through some thick brambles. "There's one or two thin spots over in Crescentwood, or so I've heard, but nothing like the one here."

"So how did..."

She was ready for me, though. "Depending on which side is telling the story, either we settled here first and refused to move, or the Draíodóir were here and we drove them out. Regardless, the end result is the same. Neither side is willing to budge, which is kind of hilarious, if you think about it."

"How is that funny?" Cass asked, echoing my thoughts.

"Because most of our people wouldn't know what to do with it if you handed them an instruction manual. It's like a group of hippies squatting over a uranium mine. All they know is this is our land and that's that."

I stepped up my pace to walk next to Nelly. "And what would happen if the Draí ... you know who I mean, if they got it?"

Nelly laughed. "Oh, I'm sure they'd give you a mouthful involving their ancestors and the fae court, that sort of shit. But the truth is, aside from making them feel smug about themselves, not much. Even though everyone wants to talk about the past and the old gods, people these days are mostly smart enough to not turn those soft spots into open doorways." She turned her head and fixed me with a glare. "At least purposefully."

∽

We walked the rest of the way in silence, Nelly apparently content to let me chew on that one for a while. The memory wasn't a pleasant one – killing Jerry, then watching in horror as the very ground itself seemed to drink his blood. Murdering him was bad enough, but what if that had been the least of my crimes?

Finally, we pushed through some brush and stepped into a glade. Though it looked like any other clearing in the forest – basically a circle of land devoid of trees – the hairs on the back of my neck stood up. This was the place.

We'd come from a different direction than the last time I'd been here, so my bearings were off, but it wasn't like the glade was huge. It was easy to make out the opposite end, even with the meager light of the torch. I walked to the center, almost heedless that my feet were carrying me, and turned in a circle. Almost immediately, I could hear faint whispers in my mind, calling to me as if from far away ... hopefully just my imagination, but I couldn't be sure.

A part of me expected to see Jerry's remains lying where I'd left him, a monument to the crime I'd committed, but there was nothing to be seen. His body had either been moved, eaten by scavengers or ... devoured by this place.

"You okay, Bent?" Cass asked. "You look like you've seen a ghost."

That set Nelly to cackling again. I could kinda understand why she lived alone.

I ignored her and closed my eyes for a moment, listening. Those voices fell silent, assuming they were ever there to begin with. Maybe it was all in my head after all.

"Good, you're already in place. Stay there," Nelly commanded, stepping in to join me. She pointed a finger at Cass. "You, wait at the edge. Trust me, it's for your own good."

Cass nodded then backed up to the tree line, becoming little more than a shadow at the edge of the glade.

Nelly stopped about ten feet away and began to pour out the contents of the bowl – a thin dribble, nothing more – as she walked in a wide circle around me.

Realizing that weirdness was afoot, a part of me wanted to call it off and back the fuck away. I had better things to do: a brother to check on, parents to – *mourn* – rescue. But Cass had insisted on this. And, truth of the matter was, I'd take whatever help I could get. Hell, as the beta of the pack, I'd be the acting alpha in my father's place. Even if they all despised me, they'd still have to get with the program if I said so. Or challenge me to a duel, but hopefully most were content with falling in line. Guess we'd see soon enough. For now, though...

Nelly stepped into the wide circle with me, bowl still in hand. "Now light it on fire."

"Light what on fire? The snow?"

She sighed. "The gunk I just poured onto it. Don't ask stupid questions. Just do it."

Okay, so maybe they wouldn't *all* fall in line.

"With this flame, we seal the pact," Nelly cried out. "Oh mighty Huntsman, hear our plea!" She glanced at me and whispered, "That was your cue, in case you were wondering."

"Oh." I bent down and touched the lit torch to the ground, really hoping the end result wouldn't be burning down the hollows around us. The mixture immediately caught fire and spread, racing around us in a perfect circle.

The flames appeared normal at first but then began to change color as they rose up higher: first blue, then white, and finally black.

Oh yeah, nothing strange about that.

"Return to me, child, and prepare to receive his holy blessing."

I stepped back toward the center, forcing my eyes away from the freaky black fire encircling us. As I did, though, I felt a hum deep in my bones. Next came a tingling in my hair as if the air became full of static electricity. The power within this place, it was waking up. I couldn't help but feel that wasn't entirely a good thing.

"Don't worry about that, worry about me," Nelly said, no doubt noticing I was beginning to get a little doe-eyed. "Back up a few steps please. Give me room."

I was about to ask what for but, a moment later, it became obvious why she'd made this circle so wide.

Earlier, I'd seen her *smile* at Cass, showing off ridiculously large fangs in her little grandma mouth. Now it was time to see the rest of her.

Nelly's body began to enlarge. Coarse grey fur sprouted from everywhere, covering her as she filled out from frail old woman to werewolf-sized and then kept going.

Holy fuck!

My eyes grew wider as she grew larger, hitting mega-wolf stature and still not stopping.

She'd been shorter than me when she started and I topped out at five three – maybe a bit more in heels, which I certainly wasn't wearing at the moment. The beast which stood in front of me now, though, had to be nearly twelve feet tall with arms and legs as thick as tree trunks, ending in wicked six inch claws. They were connected to a body as thick as a truck and twice as durable. And that wasn't even counting the nightmare head that topped it all – as if someone took the face of a mastiff, crossed it with a gorilla, and then ordered it in extra extra-large.

Perhaps the worst were her eyes. All other werewolves

I'd seen had yellow eyes that seemed to glow in the night as if lit from within, but not this thing. Soulless orbs of pure, angry red stared down at me from its face and I suddenly understood what it was to be small and helpless.

What the hell could I, even at full power, hope to do against this ... uber-wolf? She made my father look like a mere pup in comparison. Earlier, when she'd confessed to killing my grandfather, I'd assumed poison or maybe shooting him in the back. But now I was forced to rethink that.

The monster that had been Nelly bent down toward me, almost to the point where it had to put its front paws on the ground. Hilariously enough, she was still holding the bowl. It had been large in her human hands but was now a mere teacup to her.

She bared her teeth and growled, the sound of it finally snapping me out of my fugue. Those whispers in my head cried out again and with it came clarity. This was no ritual, and definitely not a blessing. This was an ambush, plain and simple. She knew what I'd done to Jerry, Craig, and so many others, and this was her way of paying back blood for blood. I didn't know whether it was this glade or if she was normally this terrifying, but it didn't matter.

What did was that I needed to act first before she fell upon me. I might not have been at my best, but I was far from powerless. I balled a fist and swung for the fences, looking to send this creature a clear message that I wasn't going to lie down and make it easy.

Or at least that was the plan.

Faster than I could imagine, she lifted an arm to block my swing, expending seemingly no effort to stop me. *Oh shit.*

I'd been wondering about the limits of my power. What a lousy time to discover them.

43

I'd given it my best shot and come up short. Now the ball was in Nelly's court.

I had little doubt she could've taken off my head with one swipe of her claws, or bitten me clean in half with the shark's maw she called a mouth.

But instead a curious thing happened. Her face contorted and collapsed in on itself, shrinking in the time it took me to blink – becoming fully human again.

It was almost comical, her tiny little head on that massive body. It was like she was wearing a giant mechanical wolf suit, except I knew better.

She looked me in the eye and those whispers in my head fell silent. "What the hell are you doing, girl?"

"Me?"

"Yes, you."

"Um, defending myself?"

"Really?" she asked, the strange sight of her head on that body coming close to unhinging my already tenuous grasp on sanity. "Because from where I'm standing, it looks like you were trying to nail me with a sucker punch."

"You ... growled at me."

"Of course I did. I was trying to tell you..." She stopped and took a deep breath, terrifyingly long as the lungs in this new body were no doubt several times larger than they had been. "You don't speak our tongue, do you?"

"Sorry," Cass called from the edge of the clearing. "I should have mentioned that."

I turned and fixed her with my best withering gaze before focusing on Nelly again. "Um, what she said."

"Oh, very well. Water under the bridge and all that bullshit, I suppose." Nelly turned her head skyward and muttered, "Ah, the stupidity of youth." Then she addressed me once more. "Here's what's going to happen. I'm going to mutter an incantation. You won't under-stand it, but that's okay so long as *he* does." I was tempted to ask who *he* was, but figured it was best to keep my mouth shut. "When I'm finished, you are to hold your hand out, palm up. I'm going to cut you. You're to let it dribble into this bowl. I cannot emphasize this enough, *into the bowl*. Do not let any spill onto the ground. Is that clear?"

I nodded. "Crystal. And then what?"

"Then you leave the rest to me. Trust me, child, you'll know when the ceremony is complete."

I hated cryptic statements like that, but before I could voice that opinion, Nelly's head enlarged again, filling out to match her mammoth body.

Again, she bent over and growled at me, baring teeth I could have used to saw lumber in half. As much as my instincts screamed to knock them out, I held myself in check. Besides, there was little point in embarrassing myself again.

Nelly huffed, chuffed then, instead of blowing my house down, raised her head to the sky and let out a howl.

It was loud and so low-pitched that I was fairly certain the trees around us shook from the intensity.

A second howl rose up to join hers, too close for comfort until I realized it was just Cass. She'd transformed as well. Considering her professed lack of knowledge with regards to all of this, I assumed it to be a dog thing. When one started barking, they all had to.

Nelly's howl continued, growing lower in pitch the longer it went on, until it was as if someone were blowing the horn on a passing cruise ship.

Eventually Cass stopped. At first I thought maybe it was because Nelly's had reached a cadence she couldn't match, but then I realized it was more likely due to what was happening inside the glade.

A thick ground fog had sprung up from seemingly nowhere, spreading across the floor of the clearing. It was knee deep to me, meaning it was maybe up to Nelly's ankles. Weirder yet, lights of various colors began to dance just below the surface of the mist, as if tiny little garden gnome ravers were running around with glow sticks.

Talk about a thought that didn't bring me any comfort.

Regardless, something was happening – the blessing of Valdemar, I presumed. Considering my father's status as a mega-wolf, it was almost certain he'd participated in this ritual at some point. That caused me to wonder how it would affect me. Despite having lycanthrope blood running through my veins, I didn't change like they did. Or at least that *had* been the case. Who was to say what this blessing would do to me?

I briefly thought about getting undressed. Seemed to be all the rage these days in the hollows. It would also spare me from trying to sneak back home bare-assed if I did somehow change into an eight-foot monster.

Sadly, I got the sense it was too late for that. Nelly

stopped howling and looked down at me. She held out the bowl, tiny in her massive paw.

This was the part she'd told me about. I rolled up the sleeve on my borrowed coat and held out my left hand over the bowl.

Nelly chuffed once then gave a nod of her head. Guess I wasn't screwing this up too badly after all. Go me!

She lifted her other hand, extending one finger and the wicked saber at the end of it. *Whoa.* Talk about a steak knife. One wrong move and she could have lopped off my hand with the barest of motions. A part of me was glad that Uncle Craig had *only* been a mega-wolf. Had he looked like Nelly, I'd have probably noped the fuck right outta that fight. I didn't consider myself a coward, but werewolves the size of dinosaurs seemed a reasonable line in the sand.

Nelly raked her claw across my palm in one quick move, yet I didn't feel a thing. For a moment I wondered if she'd missed, but then I saw blood begin to well up in a line.

Her claws were so sharp that it was like being cut with a surgical scalpel. Yeah, definitely not a wolf I wanted to fight. She could probably drop someone's guts to the ground before they were even aware they'd been disemboweled.

Speaking of being cut, I needed to let the blood drip into the bowl so she could...

"lann a mharbhadh!"

The cry came from out of nowhere, in that strange triple-voiced effect the Draíodóir favored.

No! Not now!

I jerked my hand back and turned to see if I could find the source before...

Nelly let out a growl, more a warning than one of anger. I glanced back to find her holding the bowl out toward me when she was cut off mid-snarl by a black scythe of energy that slammed down into her shoulder from above.

"Nelly!" Cass cried out, but we were both too late.

The spell, powerful killing magic, cut about halfway through the uber-wolf before it winked out of existence. Sadly, it was more than enough. Nearly bisected, the edges of the wounds red hot and cauterized, Nelly stood where she was a second longer before crumpling to the ground with a heavy thud.

I clenched my fists and tried to spot whoever had so casually murdered her. "Show yourself!"

So angry was I in that moment that I didn't notice the blood seeping through my fingers and onto the ground below.

~

All at once, the ring of black flame winked out of existence. Simultaneously, it was as if those tiny ravers decided to switch to red spotlights. The glade pulsed with crimson color as the ground fog began to swirl around my legs.

I wasn't interested in a special effects show, however, although perhaps I should have been more mindful. Voices, unintelligible yet persistent, began to once more gibber inside my head. I couldn't understand what they were saying but their meaning, their anger, seemed clear enough.

They wanted me to make sure Nelly's corpse wasn't the only body left to rot in this place tonight.

As I stood there, remembering everything that bastard Belzar had done to my family and friends, I couldn't think of any good reason not to heed the bloodlust building up inside of me, egged on by the whispers in my mind. The concept of running seemed little more than a joke at that moment.

A hand fell upon my shoulder and I spun, fist raised. But it was only Cass, still in her wolf form. That she'd been able to sneak up on me unheard reminded me that there was still time left before I was back to full, but somehow that seemed an unimportant detail.

More telling was the frantic look on her face. Were-wolf or not, she was terrified. She pointed back toward the trees, her meaning obvious, but I held my ground. The voices in my head were starting to win out over reason and I was happy to let them.

"No more running," I said.

"*P...puh-lease*," she growled, forcing her canine mouth to form the words. "*L-et's go!*"

"*Mhéara ar tintreach!*"

Before she could break through the cloud of rage engulfing me, an actual cloud of crackling energy surrounded us both – bolts of miniature lightning striking us multiple times.

It was like a massive static shock – unpleasant as all hell for me, but far worse for my friend. She dropped to the ground, stunned into submission by the spell.

"Much better," a smooth voice said from just outside the glade. "Gotta love the sound of silence."

Belzar stepped to the edge of the tree line, looking smug as ever. Three other wizards were right behind him. Between their clothes and the red haze lighting up the glade, they appeared to be decked out for the world's most ridiculous Christmas pageant.

"Quite the place you've got here," Belzar said, letting out a whistle of appreciation.

More movement caught my eye and I spotted a fifth member of their war party – my cousin Mindy, the expression on her face every bit as intent as the rest of them.

For a split second, my head cleared and I remembered what had been taken from her. But then the whispers grew more insistent again, erasing all doubt.

Kill them all.

I barely noticed the fog beginning to snake its way up my legs, my thoughts rapidly becoming just as cloudy. Deep down, I knew I should be protecting Cass and doing what I could to free Mindy. But all of that seemed insignificant compared to spilling more blood, and what better place to do so than here?

The sound of swirling wind from above caught my attention and I looked up to see something buzz past through the trees, catching a glimpse of a white winter coat. So my aunt was here, too. Fitting. Whatever happened next, we could at least ensure we settled matters once and for all.

With any luck, I could break through Belzar's magic and save – *kill* – her along with Mindy. Break her – *neck* – free from the spell and...

I glanced down and saw that strange fog had wrapped itself around me all the way up to my chest. As it inched higher, rational thought faded, replaced with something far more primal.

Perhaps my attackers saw my hesitation, or maybe the bloodlust of this place was getting to them, too. Regardless, before I could do anything else, six voices all shouted out simultaneously, calling killing magic down upon me.

44

"*orn an bháis!*"

A sextet of lethal energy was unleashed my way. Resistant as I was to magic, I knew that would be too much, weakened as I was.

I'd been hit with this spell earlier and almost gotten pulped by it, and that had been a mere third of what was headed toward me now.

The only upside was that my impending death cleared my head for a moment, giving me a chance to say a silent apology to my family, wherever they were. I'd failed them and, worst of all, if I fell in this accursed glade, I had a feeling they'd never know what had befallen me.

In that same instant, the fog enveloped my being, cocooning me in mist, but I paid it no heed as the torrent of magic converged on me from all sides.

Bracing myself for what was to come, I cried out as the spells struck ... and seemingly flowed around the mists covering my body, leaving me untouched.

What the hell?

Mouth agape in shock, the fog began to force its way down my throat as if it were a tangible thing. The elation of not being vaporized was quickly lost as I found myself unable to breathe. The magic of this place had seemingly spared me so that it could kill me itself. Talk about crazy.

The Draíodóir magic continued to swirl around me, blocking my view of anything outside my little mist prison. I briefly wondered if the spell casters trying to kill me would be irked, but I doubted it. Dead was dead. And with me finished off, Cass would be next. After all, it wouldn't do to leave witnesses to the fact that they'd broken the treaty in spades.

The pack, all of Morganberg, would be left vulnerable with no leadership, but somehow that seemed of minor importance compared to the power choking the life out of me from within – misty tendrils invading my body and violating every fiber of my being in these last few seconds before unconsciousness claimed me.

It was as if this place knew the secret that only my parents did: I could resist magic from the outside, but not nearly as well from inside. The infernal power of this glade could do whatever it pleased so long as it kept hold of me like this.

Darkness collected at the edge of my vision, and it had nothing to do with the magic swirling just outside my mist prison.

I was on the verge of passing out but then, all at once, the power pulled back from my extremities and seemingly coalesced in the pit of my stomach in one sickening lump. Images of being forcibly impregnated with the bastard offspring of this strange and terrible place raced through my mind – the proverbial fate worse than death.

Just as quickly, however, all of that was replaced with nausea as my digestive tract did a flip flop in protest at whatever was going on inside me. In the space of a second, I realized I was about to hurl despite my airway being blocked. Great. Suffocate or drown in my own puke – quite the choice of obituaries.

My innards heaved and suddenly my airway was open, the power of this place becoming little more than mist again just as the energy from those spells dissipated around me.

Sadly, there was no time to rejoice in the fact that I could breathe. I doubled over and prepared to make a deposit at the bile bank. My stomach forcibly expelled its contents, but what came out was like nothing I'd ever had the displeasure of puking up. I could only watch teary-eyed as I retched up a stomachful of... *Yellow dust?!*

The yellowish cloud floated before my eyes for a moment, then began to dissipate into the air around me.

I was afraid of what else I might puke up, but then realized I felt better – *a lot* better. It was as if someone flipped a switch in my body from first to high gear. Not only did I feel light on my feet, but the sounds and smells of the forest all became crystal clear around me. Even without looking, I could sense the others in this place – Cass's hitched breaths from the floor of the clearing, the crackle of leaves as the Draíodóir closed in, the whoosh of air from above that said my aunt was still flitting around in the treetops.

How?

The last remnants of what I'd coughed out faded away before my eyes and it all became clear. That yellow dust – the same color as my pills! That had to be it. This place hadn't been trying to kill me. It had purged the last of the meds from my system, giving me a fighting chance.

But why?

Kill!

And with that final whisper in my head, I knew what I had to do.

≈

I stood up, whole and renewed. I may not have received whatever blessing Nelly had been trying to convey, but maybe now I didn't need it.

"How the fuck are you still standing?"

I glanced Belzar's way. Shock stood out on his face along with two of his soon to be much less merry elves. That was fine. My ears had already told me Mindy and the other Christmas minion were moving in from my flank.

Good. Let them try.

As for my aunt, I kept my senses open. If she tried to swoop in, I'd clip her wings real quick.

Cass was starting to stir, but I paid her no heed. The buzzing in my head, the voices of this place, told me she was inconsequential so long as she stayed out of the way. It was cold advice, inhuman, but I didn't fight it.

Instead, I stepped to where Nelly's corpse lay, grabbed hold of one of her support pillar sized legs, and gave a heave.

She was heavy, not to mention a mess of charred flesh. For a moment, I doubted whether what I had in mind would work, but I should've had faith in myself. I spun and let go, sending her massive body flying into one of Belzar's men. I had a moment to recognize him as my *buddy* from earlier, Rudolph, and then he was gone, crushed against a tree by roughly eight hundred pounds of werewolf.

Guess he should have stayed in that Jell-O mold after all.

"That's Rudolph the dead-nosed reindeer," I said with a grin. "Who's next?"

≈

Rudolph's death shook the Draíodóir from their shock at seeing me still alive.

A moment later, the air was rent with the screams of multiple different spells and curses.

I didn't bother to catalog who said what. They were all fired with reckless abandon. Too bad for them I was already on the move.

The weirdness of the glade provided me with enough light to see by, but also left me an easy target. Counting on the mists still flowing along the ground to save me a second time seemed an unwise strategy.

I feinted to the right, then spun and charged toward the *elf* who'd been doing a piss poor job of trying to flank me quietly. If he wanted to be next, that was cool in my book. I wanted to save the asshole in charge for last anyway, make him watch as I picked off his minions one by one.

Twinkles, the not-so-happy Christmas elf, unleashed a spell as I closed the distance, an energy blast of some sort. It zapped me point blank but barely slowed me down. Oh yeah. This was more like it.

His eyes opened wide in panic as I reached him and wrapped my arms around his body. Tempting as it was to simply crush him like a bug, that would take too long. I'd shrugged off his attack, but that didn't mean the others wouldn't hit back with something harder. Instead, I fought against the whispers in my head just enough to maintain a smidgeon of control. With four other enemies ready to take pot shots at me, it was best to play to my strengths.

I reared back and suplexed the bastard over my head, putting some extra oomph into it. *That's one elf driven straight through the shelf.* There came the crunch of bone as his skull impacted with the ground. The mists around us pulsed a bright crimson in response, as if we were adrift in a swirling sea of blood.

I let go of the wizard's limp form and kipped up to my feet. I didn't need to look to guess the ground here was already cleaning up anything that had spilled out of him.

Drink up. Hopefully this place had a healthy appetite, because I wasn't done feeding it assholes yet.

The voices whispered to me their appreciation of that plan, right before they were drowned out by a much louder voice.

"*Dust of devils!*"

In the chaos of dealing with those at ground level, I'd almost forgotten about my aunt. Sadly, she hadn't forgotten me. On the upside, unlike the other Draíodóir, at least I understood what she was sending my way.

I'd seen this spell earlier, but that was small comfort. My aunt wasn't stupid by any stretch. I could take their energy blasts all night if need be, but an indirect spell was potentially a whole other ball of wax.

As if in response to my thoughts, a miniature tornado touched down mere feet away from me, sucking up both mists and snow into its funnel – turning it into a thing of pure white menace, dotted with infernal eyes that seemed to gaze out from its core.

More cries came from the periphery of the glade, their meaning lost to my ears amid the ruckus already going on. But I understood nevertheless. My remaining foes were getting smarter about what they threw at me.

The earth beneath my feet erupted as multiple bolts of magic struck the ground around me before I could leap out of the way. I was catapulted into the air just as the dust devil surged forward and sucked me into its hungry maw.

It was about as unpleasant as you can imagine. I went from standing still to eighty miles an hour in the space of a second. It was a good thing my stomach was empty because otherwise I would have coated the funnel cloud with my insides.

I was forced to close my eyes against the wind and debris being swept along, but I could feel ... *things* grasping for me, like talons of ice as I swirled uncontrollably in the maelstrom.

It was a minor miracle my aunt hadn't used this spell against me earlier. Depowered as I had been, it would have surely killed me from the stress alone, not even including whatever evil gremlins called this swirling hell home.

Around and around I flew, completely blind. I could have been ten feet off the ground or a thousand, for all I knew. Hell, I wouldn't have been surprised to open my eyes and find myself in Oz surrounded by Munchkins. Of course, that would've been a lot sweeter had I a house to drop on my enemies.

The only upside to my pummeling was the roar of the wind drowned out the whispers, clearing my head for the time being. Mind you, it wasn't exactly an ideal time to enjoy clarity of thought.

Still, it allowed me to remember, even if momentarily, that not all the participants trying to kill me here were doing so of their own free... "URK!"

That train of thought ground to a screeching halt along with the rest of my body as I slammed into the thick trunk of a tree.

Blood sprayed from my shattered nose and I was certain I'd snapped at least a few ribs. On the upside, I was free from the swirling winds – free to fall to the cold ground, landing in a heap with a heavy thud.

As I lay there dazed, taking a moment to catalog all of my life's poor choices, I heard soft footfalls heading my way. Maybe Cass had...

"*Sèididhteine!*"

Or probably not. I pushed off with my arms, my torso

screaming in protest, and rolled to the side just as a tongue of flame lashed out at where I'd been, sizzling as it lanced against the packed snow.

At least being cold wasn't an issue anymore, although staying alive might soon be. The magic itself might not hurt me much, but I sincerely doubted I'd enjoy my skin instantaneously heating up to eight hundred degrees.

I sat up and spied a lithe form stepping nimbly through the trees, backlit by the crimson glow emanating from the glade – Mindy.

The mini-tornado had deposited me somewhere just inside the tree line. That afforded me a bit of camouflage as well as gave my mind a chance to recover from the red haze of murderous rage that had gripped it.

Every instinct within me begged to not step foot in the glade again, but I didn't think that was possible, especially not with Cass...

There came a buzz of energy from within that accursed place, followed by a yip of pain. I was already too late. They had her.

Damnit!

"Come on out, little girl," Belzar cried. "Care to guess how much for that doggy in the window? The one with the electrocuted tail."

Oh yeah. That guy was definitely being force fed his own teeth.

Douchebag was in the clearing and I knew Mindy was out here somewhere with me. That left my aunt and the last of Santa's little helpers unaccounted for.

I backpedaled, staying low and keeping my ears peeled for my cousin. It didn't leave a lot of room for stealth, but I thought it was better than turning my back on her.

"*Dhó Slabhrai!*"

Which was apparently what the rest were counting on.

I tried to dive to the side, but my injuries rendered me a bit too slow for my body to cash that check.

Cords of laser-like energy wrapped around my legs mid-leap, cutting my escape short and dropping me to the ground like a trussed up Christmas turkey.

45

Yeah, these guys were definitely playing it smart now. It had taken the loss of two of their number to make them wise up to the fact that I was no longer helpless. Sadly, they'd brought enough spares to make up for it.

"I got her!" Belzar's remaining minion cried out, his red and green outfit visible as he pushed past some bushes to get to me.

Too bad for him he'd only gotten my legs, otherwise he might've been on to something.

Mind you, it wasn't ideal for me. I could hear Mindy heading this way, too. It stood to reason my aunt wouldn't be too far behind to rain death on my parade.

I wiped the blood from my face, wincing as the pain of my injured torso reminded me I wasn't invincible. There was no time to lick my wounds, though. I needed to trust in my enhanced healing to keep me going. But if I wanted it to have a chance in hell, I needed to free my feet first.

Lying there was a death sentence against enemies like these. I reached down to snap the magical bonds ... but then hesitated as my hand brushed against the holster still strapped to my side. I'd forgotten my foes weren't the only ones capable of dealing out punishment from a distance.

What an idiot I was.

The whispers in my head – that haze of rage – had also been a haze of stupid. I'd completely forgotten that Cass and I had come prepared for this.

"You've been a naughty girl," Asshole the elf said, standing over me with a triumphant grin on his face. "It's nothing but coal for you."

Pity for him I had the perfect response. "Ho ho ho, I don't have a machine gun."

"What?"

"But this will have to do."

I drew the gun I'd taken from Mitch's cabin and pulled the trigger.

≈

What I lacked in a proper shooter's stance, I made up for by being at point blank range.

My first shot barely clipped his bicep but almost stunned me in the process. Holy crap! I hadn't realized how loud that would be with my super hearing. I'd be lucky to not need a truckload of aspirin after this.

However, much as it had surprised me, that was nothing compared to the other guy. The schmucky sorcerer stood there, one hand on his bleeding arm and a look of utter shock on his face. He opened his mouth, no doubt to lay into me with another spell, but that was the beauty of a semi-automatic – it had a ready-made response.

I fired twice more.

Maybe a gun couldn't teleport or conjure demons

from beyond, but in a pinch it could ruin someone's day every bit as well as magic.

Jerkface went down screaming with two slugs planted in his side. A part of me was tempted to empty the magazine into him as he tried to crawl away, but I was neither foolish enough to waste the ammo nor – with my head clear – so callous as to shoot a retreating foe in the back.

Taking him out of the fight was good enough. And, judging by the gout of flame that erupted from the ground a few moments later, teleporting him away, he'd had more than enough. Fucker should've thanked me for plugging him out here instead of in the glade.

"*Sèidi…*"

Oh no you don't. I hadn't forgotten about my cousin. Before Mindy could complete the spell, I rolled over and fired twice in her direction, purposely aiming high.

I had no beef with her. If anything, I liked her and her late sister. There was little doubt she was going to be utterly crushed the second I could free her from whatever mind control she was under. And that had to be my goal for her and my aunt: take them out of the fight and free them.

As for Belzar, I'd cross that bridge when I came to it … and saw how many bullets I had left.

Mindy, proving that whatever hex she was under wasn't strong enough to override basic survival instinct, screeched in panic and dove out of sight behind a downed tree trunk.

Good, but not good enough. I didn't want to shoot her, but trying to scare her off was a poor strategy when your opponent wasn't lobbing warning shots.

"*Wind blade!*"

Make that two opponents.

I couldn't see my aunt, but her voice floated down from above in that strange trebled cadence.

Sadly, the spell binding my feet hadn't dissipated when the *elf* had zapped away as I'd hoped it would. Now, with two more Draíodóir closing on me, neither of whom I wanted to hurt, it didn't take a genius to realize I'd taken one step forward only to end up two steps back.

I looked up, ready to roll out of the way when... "Oh fuck."

My aunt, once again proving what a formidable witch she was, hadn't been aiming at me. No, her strategy was way smarter.

The whoosh of air from her incoming spell was far less daunting than the sound of splintered wood. A moment later, it was as if half the forest had been blown apart – all of it falling toward where I lay.

Even had my legs been free, I'm not sure I'd have been able to dodge it all. It wasn't hard to guess that was her ploy. Limbs, branches, and what looked to be whole tree tops rained down with wild abandon. Most missed me, but most wasn't all. I raised my arms and blocked a four inch wide branch from colliding with my face, only to have a heavier limb land on my already injured midsection, driving the air from my lungs so thoroughly I couldn't even scream. More debris rained down, knocking the gun from my grasp and blotting out my view as it piled up atop me.

I needed to take Carly out of the equation, no question about it. Concentrating on the ground level guys had made sense at first. There'd been too many of them. But now it seemed I needed eyes on the top of my head, and since I wasn't one of those freaky puck things, there was little chance of that.

First, though, I needed to not die. With Cass down

and Nelly out of the equation, I couldn't count on a last minute save.

The weight atop me wasn't exactly a walk in the park but, aside from my injuries, which were nothing to sneeze at, I wasn't in any danger of being crushed to death.

However, a moment later, I realized that wasn't the plan so much as my foes throwing themselves a good old-fashioned pig roast.

"*Sèididhteine!*"

Mindy had come out of hiding and was burning to get back into the action, literally. A lance of flame struck the branches lying atop me, setting them ablaze. The upside was it gave me light to see by, but the obvious downside was the only things in sight were branches, leaves, and the fact I was lying inside a makeshift crematorium.

46

Sucking in a deep breath before the air became too superheated, I rolled over onto my side and reached down until I was able to grab hold of the whips of tangible light still wrapped around my legs.

Kudos to the wizard I'd shot that they were still there. That spoke of dedication to the cause, or being so mind-fucked as to not care that he was bleeding from multiple gunshot wounds.

Regardless, now was not the time to appreciate good craftsmanship. I pulled – gritting my teeth against the pain in my midsection – and finally felt the spell give way against my strength.

I was free, but had wasted precious seconds I didn't have.

My cousin screamed out her fire spell again, and the blaze above me doubled in size. Sweat poured off my face and steam began to rise from where the flames touched the snow lying upon the branches.

"*Wind Blade!*"

Mindy wasn't alone, though. I saw now what they were trying to do – keep piling on the weight and the fire.

Eventually I'd either be crushed, burned, or suffocate from the smoke rapidly building up around me.

Too bad I had no interest in any of that.

I forced myself over onto my hands and knees, the branches atop me settling like a canopy over my body – a burning canopy. Doing my best to ignore the heat and pain, I began to crawl, inching my way forward – not sure where I was going, but not caring so long as I got out from beneath this inferno.

Direct strikes with their magic might not affect me much, but they'd definitely wised up to the fact that they didn't need to hit me to kill me. The only advantage I had was that the unnatural fire blazing above my back was hopefully obscuring their view of me.

The way forward became slick with mud as the snow around me melted from the heat above. Several times I burned myself trying to push past a heavy limb that obscured my way. At last, however, I saw a way out up ahead.

The downside, though, was the unearthly red glow coming from it.

~

The smell of burning fabric assaulted my nose and I realized time was up. My coat was on fire. It was either move my ass or be burnt alive.

Talk about an easy decision.

I braced my legs beneath me, tasting copper as my nose continued to drip blood – not fun, but nothing I could waste time worrying about.

Lifting my arms so as to shield my face, I pushed off, knocking burning branches aside as I leapt out of the conflagration and back into the cursed glade, shedding my coat in the process.

Unfortunately for me, they were ready for that.

I had a moment in which I caught sight of Belzar standing over Cass's downed form. And then all hell was unleashed upon me.

"*Adh iongantach!*"

"*Lasadh biast!*"

"*Lightning Hammer!*"

It was as if a chorus of voices cried out from every direction, but I didn't let that fool me. Three different spells, none of which I was familiar with, had just been cast. Sadly, there was no time to stick around and catalog them.

I sucked up the pain and launched myself toward the opposite tree line about thirty feet away.

Amazingly enough, their strategy of aiming for everything around me worked in my favor this time. There came a tremendous racket as the ground quite literally exploded right behind me. Heat, static discharge, and a hell of a shockwave slammed into my backside, propelling me forward.

I doubted I looked all too graceful flying through the air and pinwheeling my arms, but the end result was worth it as I caught hold of an evergreen limb maybe ten feet off the ground and pulled myself up.

Every move hurt like hell, but I didn't allow myself the luxury of pain right then. I needed to lose myself in the surrounding foliage before they could launch another volley my way.

I jumped onto the branches of another tree and continued scrambling up, using my strength and speed to the best of my ability.

"Do you really think that will help you, Tamara?" my aunt called out. "The air is my domain."

I was tempted to tell her where she could shove her domain but realized she was likely baiting me. Continuing to move undercover, trying to avoid any trees with bare branches, I dared a glance back.

That red haze continued to dominate the glade, made all the thicker by the smoke rising from where they'd tried to fry me a few minutes earlier. On the upside, the fire on the far side of the clearing seemed to be dying down, no doubt helped by the cold, damp surroundings. That was good. The werewolves of Morganberg disliked me enough as it was without also blaming me for burning down their precious woods.

I paused for one more moment as something caught my eye – a mountain lion made of pure flame sniffing around the crater where I'd stood a few moments earlier.

Guess Mindy had more than just fireballs up her sleeve. Good to know for later. For now, though, I was too busy playing Sheena queen of the jungle, minus the leopard skin bikini, as I struggled to climb ever higher while staying hidden.

I needed to give my aunt top priority. Her ability to fly was leaving me a sitting duck. Here in the trees, though, she was hopefully as blind as me. That and I doubted she could maneuver too quickly through this mess without clonking herself.

Sadly, my options were limited. Winter had left a good deal of the forest bare and uncovered and they likely understood that. Whatever time I'd bought myself was limited at best.

Even so, if I could take my aunt out of the equation, then I could focus on Belzar. Hell, I might not even mind the voices in the clearing whispering nasty things in my ear. Who knows? Maybe they had some good suggestions as to what to do to him.

Yeah. Much as I didn't want to think of myself as a monster, there were some atrocities I was more than happy to...

For a moment, it became hard to think, and I realized that – even outside the glade – I could still hear this place whispering to me. It was low, but still there. *Damnit!* Between Nelly's spell and the fact that I'd spilled a lot of blood here, I'd not only woken this place up – blood moon be damned – but its influence was growing stronger.

I neither knew what that meant nor was given the time to speculate, though.

"*Winds of winter!*"

For a split second I was confused, my muddled brain wondering why my aunt was screaming out George RR Martin titles, but that was quickly put to rest as the temperature around me – already unpleasantly low – seemingly dropped a good thirty degrees, and me without a coat again.

Snow and sleet began to rain down from the sky, propelled by what felt like gale-force winds. We didn't exactly suffer from a lack of snowfall in northern Pennsylvania, but what came down made our last storm look like a sunny day by comparison. Within the space of seconds, both me and the tree I was hiding in became coated in a thin layer of ice.

My feet almost slipped out from beneath me, but I managed to compensate by digging my fingers into the bark of the tree. I'd probably be pulling splinters out from beneath my fingernails for the next week, but if Carly was hoping to dislodge me so easily, she had another thing coming.

Sadly, it was naïve of me to think such a simple ploy was the extent of her plan. I was dealing with a seasoned witch, one who – like my mother – had been groomed from birth to deal with her peoples' ancient foes. Conversely, for all of my training on the mat, I was the one thinking two dimensionally here.

I should have realized that, not only was she making things slippery, but in coating everything in a sheen of pure white frost – frost which would melt rapidly against my body – she'd made it nearly impossible for me to hide among the treetops.

"Ah, there you are, Tamara," Carly said from somewhere close behind me.

"You've led us on quite the merry chase, freak," Belzar cried from far below. "I'll raise a toast to you later, but for now, it's time to end this farce."

～

They had me dead to rights, I knew as much. Stuck as I was, holding on for dear life, my aunt had a clear shot at my back.

But maybe therein lay my salvation.

Digging my fingers in even harder, I lifted my legs and braced them against the slippery trunk. There was almost no purchase to be had, but I wasn't trying to find any. All I needed was a solid surface to push off from.

"*Wind...*"

Now!

"*Blade!*"

My aunt seemed to favor that spell and I could understand why. Every time she'd unleashed it, she'd done a ton of damage, slicing through the thickest branches as if she were swinging the Grim Reaper's scythe.

However, there was one thing I was hoping it couldn't cut through: me!

Even as my aunt shouted out her incantation, I kicked off blindly, propelling myself backward through the air toward where I heard her voice, keeping my fingers crossed for two things: that my aim was true and that I had enough momentum to overcome the spell once it...

There came a flare of pain, like being whipped with a riding crop – not that I'd had much occasion lately to indulge in that kink. I felt my sweater flay open from the force of the spell ... and then I was through it, my natural resistance overcoming the force of the magic unleashed my way.

However, if that was a small taste of victory, what came next was icing on the cake. I blindly crashed into something – no, make that *someone* – a lot more malleable than the tree I'd been hiding in.

It was only a glancing blow, but that was fine. I wasn't trying to kill my aunt, just knock her down a peg. She cried out from the impact and I caught a quick glance of her flailing limbs as whatever spell held her aloft was cancelled out. Then we were both in freefall, headed for the forest floor.

Fate was apparently in a kind mood at that moment, as we both hit a cluster of small branches on the way down, slowing our descent a bit. Then we were through and I lost sight of Carly as I came down atop a conveniently placed shrub. It wasn't exactly a soft landing, but my aunt's unnatural snowstorm had laid down enough cover to cushion things a bit.

That was good for me. As for her, hopefully she wasn't much worse than stunned, but I couldn't spare the time to check. I needed to get to Belzar and end this before he could reclaim his hold upon her.

I pushed myself to my feet then, just as quickly, fell to one knee, the impact having added to the damage I'd been steadily accumulating. *I swear, I'm pre-taping my ribs next time I go into battle.*

Willing my body to hold it together for a bit longer, I tried again, putting extra effort into staying upright as I stepped forward into the clearing again.

Fortunately, Mindy's flaming cat was gone, probably

snuffed out by my aunt's snowstorm. One less distraction to keep me from my prize – Belzar, standing where he'd been, with the glade lit up like ... well, Christmas, all around him. Guess the spirits of this place had a sense of irony.

Pity for him, the only gift I planned on delivering was pain.

The fucker was staring at where Cass still lay when he looked up and saw me coming. His eyes opened wide with delicious fear at the sight of me advancing upon him. If only my phone wasn't dead. I'd have loved to take a picture to remember this moment by.

Belzar threw his hands up, all attitude gone. "No. Wait!"

"No wait necessary. The doctor will see you now!" I cried out, feeling the voice of this place take hold, demanding I tear this fucker to pieces.

He backpedaled out of my reach as I threw a sloppy swing his way. But then the dumbass tripped over his own two feet – perhaps the glade's doing – and fell onto his ass.

It was time to end this.

I loomed over him, any quips dying on my tongue. The only thing I wanted now was to pay him back for everything he'd done to me and my family.

"P-please."

"Shh," I replied, my voice devoid of all emotion. "Don't you know this is supposed to be a silent night?" Okay, maybe there was time for one more quip.

"You have to listen," he cried, trying to scoot away. "I'm free now."

"Oh, you're definitely not free."

"I mean up here!" He pointed to his head. "You stopped her. I can't hear her in my mind anymore. You have to believe me! I never wanted to do any of this. She made me. She made all of us."

I cracked my knuckles, preparing to end his lies once and for all, but then a voice called out to me from the edge of the glade.

"He's telling the truth, Tamara." I turned to find Mindy standing just inside the tree line, but not as she'd been. Shock, fear, and grief shone plainly on her face, as if she were waking from a nightmare. "It was Carly. It was her this whole time."

"What?"

47

The voices of the glade were practically screaming at me, making it hard to think. They demanded blood, that I make sacrifices of both the traitor Belzar and my impudent cousin.

They told me to ignore their lies, to spill their life's fluid upon these sacred grounds and empower those within, kept from stepping foot into this world by the thinnest of veneers.

B-but, that's ... not what I'm h-here to do.

I just wanted to find my parents, to put an end to this craziness.

This place wanted me to become a murderer, a butcher, a *monster* ... and that wasn't who I was.

"Stop it," I whispered. Then, much louder, "STOP IT!"

Belzar must've thought I was screaming it at him because he cried out, "Please! I surrender! You have to believe me."

The voices quieted down in my head, enough for me to think again. I forced myself to back up a step. "Talk fast," I told him. "And pray that I like what you have to say."

"Carly," he replied. "This was all her doing."

"Bullshit. She's an air witch. You're the psycho ... mind guy."

"I was teaching her. We were engaged, after all, and she seemed interested. I thought it was, y'know ... a couple's activity."

"Enslaving others is a couple's activity?"

"No. It wasn't meant to be that. That's not what I do. It was simply meant to expand our mutual skills." He got to his feet, no doubt sensing I was going to let him say his piece before deciding whether to rip his arms off. "But after what happened this summer, she changed."

"Go on."

"Carly showed me that video, the one the lycanthrope made. At first I thought she was just upset, but she became obsessed with it. I told her to let it go, that he was obviously unhinged, but she refused. What your mother did, what you are, it began to consume her."

I glanced over at Mindy. Tears streamed freely down her face. "Please. Hear him out."

Taking a deep breath and doing my best to ignore the ceaseless whispers of this place, I nodded.

"I tried," Belzar said. "I talked to her, listened, even suggested counseling. But as the months wore on she became more and more withdrawn. She started going through her family's old library – their history, spell books, stuff that had been locked away for years."

Though the voices told me he was lying, his cadence suggested something else – *fear*, and not of me.

"It wasn't until later that I realized why."

"And that would be?" I prodded.

"Dark magic. We're talking stuff most of us know not

to mess with. She started trying to commune with outsiders, summoning things to do her bidding ... using them as spies. I thought it was to check up on her sister, maybe see if that wolf had been lying after all, but it went beyond that. Far beyond." He ran a hand through his hair. "That's when I knew I needed to get out. I broke things off between us, told her she needed help. Please, you have to believe me."

I'd been doing my best to listen, only realizing at that moment my fists had been clenched so tightly I was digging furrows into my own palms. "So then how ... did this," I growled, holding it together by the thinnest of threads. "How did all this happen?"

He must've seen the barely contained violence on my face because he began to talk faster. "It was right before the solstice. She showed up at my coven. I thought maybe she was ready to talk. All I wanted to do was help. But it was nothing but a ruse, to force us all here."

"Here? What do you mean by that?"

"She caught me, my people, off guard. She murdered half my circle and ensnared the rest, using the same magic I'd taught her."

"I thought you were supposed to be some kind of mind master."

He chuckled, although it held little humor. "So did I. But it was like she was supercharged, amped up on something. I remembered the things she'd been trying to contact and realized she'd been successful." Tears began to drip down his face. "The rest is like a bad dream, trapped in our bodies like we were nothing more than puppets while she forced us to do things, terrible things."

"I..."

"Listen to me. So far you're the only person who's managed to stand up to her. I don't know exactly what you are and I don't really care, but I'm telling you we need to stop her before..." Belzar's words trailed off and his eyes opened wide.

"Focus here, Belzy. Before what?"

"Look out!" Mindy cried, a moment too late as something knocked me to the side with the power of a small freight train.

I was sent tumbling away, my insides screaming in agony, as a snarl rose up from disturbingly close by.

Sadly, there was no time to convalesce. I forced myself to a sitting position as a high-pitched scream rose up – Belzar – one which quickly turned into a choked gurgle.

Cass was back on her feet, her claws latched onto Belzar's arms and her teeth locked around his throat. She gave her head a shake, like she was a dog playing with a chew toy, and there came the snap of bone. Belzar fell limp in her grasp, his blood pouring out from between her teeth.

Shit! "What have you...?"

She turned toward me and the words caught in my throat as I saw her eyes. They'd turned a malevolent red, like how Nelly's had looked.

Unlike the former alpha female, however, there was no hint of anything other than rage in hers. *The voices!* I'd assumed they only affected me, but now I had to wonder whether they'd wormed their way into her unconscious mind and taken hold.

She snarled at me, then ripped a chunk of flesh from Belzar's shoulder and swallowed it whole.

Oh, yeah. This was definitely not normal behavior for her.

"Oh my God!"

Both of us turned toward where Mindy still stood at the far edge of the glade, her face a mask of horror and revulsion.

It took me all of a second to realize she was likely next on the menu. No way was I about to let that happen. "Run!" I shouted. "Get out of here!"

Cass spun back toward me, snarling and... *What the hell?* Was it me, or did she look bigger?

Regardless, my distraction worked. Mindy was no fool. Much as I wouldn't have minded having her on my side for whatever came next, I was equally relieved to see a gout of flame sprout from the ground beneath her. A moment later, she was gone.

I could only pray that, whatever happened to her next, it was kinder than the waking nightmare she'd been forced to live the last several hours ... a nightmare that wasn't finished with me yet.

The illumination within the glade turned an even deeper shade of red, no doubt thanks to Belzar bleeding out like a stuck pig. A moment later, those whispers in my head became a hideous grating chuckle, filling my brain with the unhinged cackling of the deepest abyss of Hell.

That couldn't be a good omen.

I envisioned some grotesque gas tank buried beneath this clearing, rapidly filling up as more blood was spilled. Once it was all gassed up and ready to go, then what? Truth be told, I really didn't want to know.

However, I likely had bigger things to worry about first. Cass stood up tall and this time there was no mistaking it. She'd put on at least a foot in height, maybe more. She wasn't far off from my father's size but, call me cynical, I had a sinking feeling her growth spurt wasn't finished yet.

I had no way of knowing if this was how things had started for Nelly, but there was little doubt in my mind that Cass's next move would have nothing to do with blessings ... outside of maybe saying grace before making me her next meal.

"You wouldn't like me. I taste terrible." Okay, that probably wasn't the most upbeat thing I could've said, so I tried again. "Come on, Cass. You're my friend. You don't want to do this."

"She's no longer your friend. She's the avatar of Valdemar, the false god, now."

Carly was awake and back on her feet. She walked to the edge of the glade and turned to face me, revealing a ruined socket of raw flesh where her right eye had been.

"In fact, my dear Tamara, I think it's safe to say you're all out of friends here."

A strange thing happened ... even stranger than what had been going on so far. Where my aunt stepped foot into the glade, the crimson color that permeated this place seemed to part and a multi-hued glow began to swirl around her feet.

Cass, for her part, seemed split on which of us to kill first. At least that was one plus. Whatever bloodlust had taken hold of her didn't seem inclined to play favorites.

"*Away from me, brute,*" my aunt commanded, her voice tripling in cadence. "*I call upon the gatekeepers of this glade to accept my challenge. For too long this sacred circle has been the domain of beasts. I consecrate it in the name of Brigid and her most holy court of the Seelie.*"

To my surprise, Cass backed up several steps as the color of the ground beneath my aunt's feet began to change, turning from blood red to a glowing green. It truly was like Christmas in Hell.

Carly glanced at me again and I noticed something odd. The laceration on her face. It should have been gushing blood but was already scabbed over. That, and she appeared way too smug for someone who'd just gotten their eye punctured. I got the sinking feeling this particular wound hadn't been caused by the fall she'd taken.

"The puck," I said, as the greenish color continued to spread from her. "It was yours."

"A crude name for such an elegant creature," she replied. "But yes, I summoned it to do my bidding. It carried my sight far indeed, until you severed the link we shared."

From the look of her face, it seemed safe to assume what that link entailed. *Gross.* "So Belzar was right."

She laughed. "Belzar. Oh goddess, what a stupid name. But yes, Roger was telling the truth. Pity you didn't figure it out sooner."

"I've got to hand it to you, you forced him to play a convincing asshole."

"Not that, you silly girl. Did you not once stop to ask yourself how someone with ill-intent got past the threshold of my home? I know you were aware of my wards. I caught you looking when that mongrel father of yours sullied my doorstep."

"Um…" Oh yeah. Guess she had a point. Nancy Drew I was most certainly not. But now that I thought back on it, there had been other signs, too.

Most of us weren't happy when your mother married Curtis… And then you were born soon after…

Hell, my aunt had pretty much spilled the beans in front of my face that she knew my secret, and it had gone right over my head. God, I was such a freaking moron!

"As for this," she continued, gesturing at her face, "a small sacrifice for having my suspicions confirmed."

"And that would be?"

"This place and your connection to it. After learning what you were, I began to dig deeper, calling upon *others* so that I might peer through the mists of time and learn the truth. This is where it all began for you, Tamara. You're connected to this place, its champion, its catalyst. With you here now as its witness so, too, shall the balance finally change."

I had no fucking idea what she was talking about and doubted there was much time left for Q&A. A low growl turned my attention back to Cass. She'd backed up even as her body continued to swell – ten feet tall and still going.

Holy guacamole.

She wasn't the only thing that seemed to be growing, though. At her size it should have taken her a few steps at most to reach the far side of the clearing, but she kept going until at least fifty feet separated her from my aunt. Whether an optical illusion or some weird space time thing best explained by *Star Trek*, the glade now appeared to be roughly three times its original size. Oh yeah, this was getting weirder by the minute.

The greenish hue around my aunt flared and then expanded until it took up a full half of the clearing. A straight line dividing red and green could be seen, bisecting the whole area and running – *you have got to be kidding me* – directly beneath my feet as if I'd been chosen as the defacto referee in this grudge match. Great. Just what I needed.

"What the hell is going on here?"

"This?" Carly replied, her body now aglow with power. "It is destiny, a chance to reclaim that which was lost to my people so long ago. Cheer up, my darling niece, for you're about to witness history. Hopefully it'll be enough to ease your transition to the next world.

"The next..."

"Don't worry. Your parents are already waiting there for you."

What?! Before now, I'd held out hope, but this bitch

had just confirmed my worst fears. I felt tears begin to gather in my eyes but shook them away. Grief could wait until later.

Someone was definitely going to be joining my parents, but it wouldn't be me.

48

I launched myself toward my aunt, ignoring the pain still wracking my body.

But if she was worried about the pummeling I was about to deliver, she didn't show it. She merely turned my way as I closed the distance and blew me a kiss.

And a hell of a kiss it was. It was like walking into a hurricane force wind, one which swept me off my feet and tossed me back to where I'd started, as if I were little more than a piece of garbage blowing in the breeze

That had been no mere spell. I had a feeling it ran much deeper. It was this glade empowering her. No, empowering them *both* ... preparing them for battle in this place where the walls between worlds were thinnest.

"Do not interfere, child," my aunt said, turning to face Cass, who was rapidly reaching Nelly size. All trace of my friend appeared to be gone and in her place was a nightmare creature from a forgotten epoch. "Your time will come soon enough. For now, this is between me and the chosen guardian of this place."

Guardian? Cass? But then I realized she was likely right. This wasn't so much a fight between my aunt and my friend as it was between differing ideologies given form. I remembered what Nelly had told me about soft spots and why both sides had laid down roots here so long ago.

Carly was challenging the current keeper of this place, and that power – the will of Valdemar supposedly – had chosen a new champion, Cass, to fight for the status quo, whether or not she was a willing participant.

Mind you, interesting as that might be, I couldn't have given less of a shit. "Fuck you," I spat. "You fucking murderer. My mother loved you. And my father, he never wanted..."

"Don't speak to me of that mongrel. He corrupted my sister and she let him. Lissa is the one to blame here. She turned her back on me and our ways because of her so-called love."

"Doesn't make up for the fact that you killed them in cold blood."

She laughed. "I didn't kill them, you foolish girl. I meant what I said. They were both sent to the court of our most holy queen, the realm beyond this one, as an offering. Even now the mistress of the fae waits to see what shall transpire here. This place has already accepted multiple sacrifices in the false god's name. Your parents serve to merely balance the scales, but not yet. Their blood will be my gift to Queen Brigid upon my victory."

"That won't happen."

"It isn't for you to say." She turned to Cass. "Isn't that right?"

Cass glanced my way. For a single moment, I held out hope she was still in there somewhere – that she'd throw me a wink letting me know it was time to team up and beat the ever-living fuck out of this bitch masquerading as my aunt.

Sadly, that wasn't to be.

She let loose with a roar so loud and deep that I could feel it in my bones.

I didn't speak werewolf, but the meaning seemed clear: my friend was gone and in her place stood a beast who would gladly gut anyone who got in its way, me included.

"I thought so," Carly said once the echo had died away. "Now, stand there and bear witness to what will transpire. This won't take long."

She and Cass turned to face each other, each bathed in the unholy power of this place. Cass let out a low growl as my aunt began to gather power, the mists at her feet starting to swirl in a clockwise direction.

I was tempted to rush her again but realized that might be suicidal. Even if I got past her defenses, Cass would be waiting to tear into me from behind. With my current injuries, I wasn't sure I could stop her.

Standing there, one foot on each side of the proverbial fence and unsure of what to do, the voices of the glade began to speak to me again ... low at first, but growing louder in my head until I began to make out the meaning behind their urgent plea.

This need not be their fight alone. Kill them both. Kill them so that we might be free.

～

Unlike football, amateur wrestling and professional wrestling are related in name only. For instance, on the amateur side of things we wear a one piece singlet, whereas the pros wear anything from glorified underwear on up. From there, the differences keep going.

The most relevant disparity right at that moment, though, was that there's no such thing as a handicap match on the mat. A three-way dance was the sort of spectacle you mostly saw on pay-per-view. However, considering the lighting, fog, and the fact that one of my opponents was a monstrous werewolf, I had little doubt the WWE could've sold the shit out of this.

Much as I rued that one of the combatants was a friend, the voices in my head demanded I be the sole victor. And the more they whispered in my ear, the more sense they made, and the more they drowned out the concept of rationality.

I had the perfect opportunity, too. Both opponents were focused on each other. They were aware of my presence but were acting like I was going to do nothing but watch. Even if not, I had little doubt they both thought they knew who I'd go after first.

It was time to fuck with their expectations.

There was one upside to the incessant whispers inciting me to action. What had seemed impossible only minutes earlier – tackling an uber-wolf like Cass had become – now felt more than doable. Fear and doubt receded to the back of my mind and I began to envision the possibilities. Eyes could be gouged, necks broken, and throats slit. Everything living had soft spots, no matter how big or terrifying they might be

Yes. I was a hybrid of these two races, something that had existed only – *once before* – in their fairy tales. I was neither, yet at the same time more than their sum. It was time to prove that to them and to myself.

A part of me didn't envy what I needed to do to Cass, but I could make it quick, ensure she didn't suffer.

As for my dear aunt, with my friend out of the way, I had every intention of enjoying myself.

The standoff between the two ancient foes ended as Cass let out a roar of rage followed by my aunt unleashing the stored magic she'd been gathering.

"*Binding flames!*" she shouted, but I was only paying the basest attention to her.

They weren't the only ones to break the impasse.

I sensed movement in my periphery, Cass diving out of the way with far more agility than a creature her size should possess, but I was too focused on something else in the glade to pay it much heed.

Even as they both fired their opening volleys in this battle to the death, I was on the move. *There!* Belzar's corpse was still where Cass had dropped it. I picked him up, marveling at how light he felt even with my enhanced strength.

But, considering this – *holy* – accursed place and its hunger for blood, perhaps I shouldn't have been surprised to find his remains a bit lighter than expected. Even empty husks had their uses, though. I flung my aunt's former fiancé at her even as I pushed off again, intent on flanking my friend.

There came a shout of surprise followed by a hollow *thunk*, telling me my aim had been true, but I couldn't stop to admire my handiwork. Cass was already moving to capitalize on the distraction I'd provided.

Now fully on her side of the glade, its angry red haze lighting up the dark forest, the whispers in my head abruptly ceased – giving way to an animalistic snarl that filled the void left in my mind with a primal need to hunt and feed.

It was as if the red glow, the side Cass represented, was pure predatory instinct – instinct which was now trying to guide my actions. It commanded me to leap atop my friend, to slash at her with my nails and sink my teeth into her neck, but it wasn't nearly as overpowering as the whispers. Perhaps that was a result of my half-breed heritage, but either way, I was able to partially resist it. Good, because what I had in mind required a bit more strategy than pretending to be some sort of half-assed vampire.

Suck it, Valdemar!

Before Cass could reach my aunt, still tangled up beneath Belzar's corpse, I kicked out at the back of her knee. Big she might be, but she still adhered to the basic rules of human-like anatomy. Cass stumbled, bringing her massive frame down to my level. One on one, I didn't doubt she'd be more than a match for me, but that assumed a fair fight. Too bad for her there were no referees to call me out for a cheap shot.

Before she could recover, I reached over her head, and – *gross* – grabbed hold of one of her nostrils. Disgusting as it was, it was still smarter than putting my hand in her mouth. I sucked it up as a necessary evil and yanked her head back.

She let loose with a yelp that was half surprise and half pain, but before she could do anything to counter my grip, I slammed a thunderous left hook into the side of her head.

It was the proverbial irresistible force meeting the immoveable object. It was kinda like punching solid rock, but I wasn't exactly chopped liver. Though I was pretty sure I broke at least two fingers, the blow echoed through the glade like a baseball bat against a tree trunk.

Cass's eyes rolled back into her head and she slumped forward as I let go of her nose. In the space of an instant I envisioned a dozen different ways to end her. The primal snarl of this side was demanding a kill, and she was ripe for the picking.

Before I even realized what I was doing, my hand clenched in the shape of a claw and I lifted it, preparing to ram it through her eye socket and into her brain stem.

Kill her!

Another voice – my own this time – cried out in protest. Cass wasn't a monster. She was my friend. None of this was her fault.

My own free will seemed a tiny, insignificant thing compared to the power of this place, but it was enough to remind me of everything I'd already lost.

Yet still, this damnable glade demanded a victor.

Fine. I'll give you one, but in my own way.

I stepped around my friend, amazed to see she was already starting to shake off my blow. I'd been right to fear her. Her ability to recover was even greater than a normal lycanthrope's.

Thus, I felt relatively safe in assuming she'd recover from what I did next.

I backed up to give myself some room, then kicked out with everything I had.

The top of my shoe connected with the bottom of her jaw. Teeth shattered and she was sent flying. Massive as she was, it had been a hell of a blow – enough to score a field goal in the next town over.

More important was her trajectory. She tumbled out of the glade, rolling end over end before disappearing into the darkness beyond the tree line.

With any luck, removing her from this place would also protect her from its influence. But that was all the worry I could spare her right then.

There came a whoosh of ice-cold wind from my flank, telling me that my aunt was on the move again.

49

"**D**ust of Devils!"

Sure enough, Aunt Carly was hovering about fifteen feet above the floor of the clearing, giving her a *slight* advantage when it came to taking pot shots at me.

But she didn't appear to have any interest in prolonging this. She cried out the spell three times in an echoey voice, creating a trio of demon-infused tornadoes at the far edges of the glade.

It was impressive magic – not to mention terrifying as all hell – and a small part of me was amazed she was able to do so much yet remain aloft. But then I remembered what Roger had said about her being supercharged when she'd attacked him. Something from *outside* was empowering her just as an opposing force had empowered Cass to new heights.

Pity it couldn't do the same for me.

We have granted you boons aplenty, a voice whispered in my ear – Riva's. *How you choose to use them is up to you.* It was so clear and convincing that I actually wasted half a second to check to see if she was there.

She wasn't, of course, but a big-ass wall of wind was, one that was going to suck me up and tear me to pieces if I didn't move quickly.

Sadly, the concept of quick wasn't what it used to be, not with the beating I'd taken so far. But fortunately grace and athleticism weren't required so much as getting the fuck out of the way.

I launched myself to the side just as two of the demonic whirlwinds converged on the spot where I'd been. For a moment the combined force of the swirling funnel clouds threatened to suck me back in, but then the competing vortexes cancelled each other out as they slammed together in a burst of low pressure that caused my ears to pop.

Ow.

A cry, like a thousand raccoons being shoved in a blender, rang out and then they were gone.

I had a moment to register that the light in the glade was changing, the greenish glow of my aunt's side was spreading, but then my spare second was up as the remaining dust devil screamed my way.

Sadly, this one seemed more ... *persistent* than the first two. I zigged out of its path and it course corrected, buffeting me with winds strong enough to almost knock me on my ass.

"Go ahead and run, Tamara," my aunt cried out from above, her voice magically amplified to be heard above the maelstrom. "This should be fun to watch."

Have I mentioned how much I was rapidly coming to despise my extended family? Talk about being born under a bad sign, even if it was more the bad weather I needed to watch out for.

Unfortunately, as much as the tornado wasn't exactly capable of turning on a dime, it was still fast. Every time I dove out of the way, my reaction speed barely enough due to the high winds at its periphery, it turned and came back at me. I had little doubt my aunt was controlling its course. Not good, because it was only a matter of time before she figured out my moves and compensated enough to suck me in.

The damned thing came at me again but this time, rather than leap out of the way like some half-assed matador, I ran. Screw this! If she wanted me, she'd have to knock down half the forest first.

"I think not, Tamara."

My plan was abruptly cut short as Carly cried something out from above, too distorted by the wind for me to fully understand. However, a moment later her intent became crystal clear as a shimmering wall of prismatic light appeared at the edges of the clearing. It was the same spell my mother had used earlier, except this time I had a feeling it wasn't meant to protect so much as corral.

I was tempted to charge it and see if I could break through. It was defensive magic, which I didn't seem to be quite as good at brushing off, but my odds had to be at least fifty-fifty. Problem was, with a monster storm chasing after me, I couldn't quite afford to play those odds. If I lost, so too would die any chance I had of saving my parents.

It wasn't a bet I was willing to take.

I veered hard at the last second, stepping over onto the rapidly spreading green side of the glade.

The snarling in my head instantly ceased, replaced with another voice – female, a melodic singsong quality to it. I couldn't understand her whispers, but it was a stark contrast to the other side: regality as opposed to rage.

Mind you, though the words eluded me, the emotions it conveyed didn't. I sensed arrogance and a longing greed for this place. Go figure. No matter who held the mic, there were no good guys standing on stage.

"Wind blade!"

Shit!

As my aunt cried out her attack, the voice in my head turned into a staticky hiss, but I couldn't waste time worrying about that. I'd already survived a direct hit by that particular spell, but that didn't mean it couldn't trip me up at the worst possible time. So I did something I hadn't done since grade school – I cartwheeled to the side just as the ground beneath me ruptured from the force of impact.

"Bravo, Tamara," my aunt called down. "I give it a seven point five."

Bitch. We'll see how you like it when I give you five across the eyes.

I kept that opinion to myself, though. With the roar of the wind, there was no way she'd have heard me throwing shade. Besides, the fatigue of battle, along with my growing list of injuries, was starting to add up. Wasting time with a war of words was taking away energy best spent elsewhere.

The voice of the glade, this side anyway, resumed whispering in its alien tongue. The arrogance behind it was annoying but preferable to the feral snarling. At least it wasn't weaseling its way into my subconscious, trying to fill me with uncontrollable rage.

"Let's see you dodge this, child. *Lightning hammer!*"

Almost simultaneously, the voice in my head lost its shit again, hissing like a snake. *The hell?*

Sadly, it was a particularly poor moment to dwell upon anything other than survival as I risked a glance up, only to see a wall of pure electricity descending my way.

Oh fuck!

～

There was no way to avoid the spell. My aunt was apparently through playing games. I lowered my head and raised my arms as if it were a solid thing to fend off.

I almost wished it had been. Every hair on my body stood up on end as what felt like a full body taser rippled through me. It was like licking a nine-volt battery with every pore of my body – not exactly lethal, but it hurt like hell. More importantly, it slowed me down.

Just as the worst of it passed, my legs left the ground as the mini-tornado dragged me in. Dozens of icy-clawed fingers grasped at me from within the storm, but they were a secondary concern compared to crashing into something solid at a hundred miles per hour.

Apparently my aunt was thinking the same thing. Unable to see, I didn't realize I'd been carried to the very edge of the glade until I was slammed up against a flat surface. Dazed from the impact, I cracked my eyes open and saw a shimmer of light. It was the force field she'd erected around the clearing, and I'd just been thrown into it at a speed that was akin to skydiving onto concrete.

The tornado wasn't finished with me yet. It held me off the ground, the force of its winds keeping me plastered face-first against the magical construct. My insides groaned in protest from the pressure and the sickly taste of copper filled the back of my throat.

It only got worse from there. I was stuck fast, the pressure of the demonic storm buffeting every inch of my body. Even with my strength, I could barely move my arms much less free myself.

Was this my aunt's plan – to crush me like a bug against a windshield?

"*Rain of razors!*"

Apparently not. Needless to say, that didn't sound particularly promising.

Seemed the voice in my head agreed as it once again hissed angrily.

All at once, the wind let up ever so slightly. At the same time, the force field became slightly malleable – deforming a little to fit the shape of my body.

What the?

Sadly, that question became moot as what felt like a million needles stabbed me in the back, shredding my clothes. I screamed from the pain, feeling as if I'd just been dragged across a giant cheese grater.

Anyone else would have likely been turned into confetti by such a spell. As it was, it still hurt ... a lot, like a session with Hell's acupuncturist.

"How'd you like that, Tamara?" my aunt asked, her voice amplified against the storm. "It's a new spell I've been working on for just such an occasion."

I had no magic with which to be heard over the roaring winds, but that was fine. I doubted I could add much to the conversation beyond inarticulate blubbering.

I was tempted to flash a middle finger her way but doubted she'd see it. Besides, I was too busy being flattened like a pancake as the winds resumed their full force at the same time the shimmering field solidified again.

Whatever caused them to momentarily weaken had passed.

"You're tough, I'll give you that," Carly continued, "but even you have limits. What do you say we try to find out what they are? *Rain of razors!*"

In the moment she screamed it out, that strange hiss reverberated in my head again, followed by the two spells holding me in place weakening ever so slightly.

Was the effort of throwing out three spells at once too much for her?

But if so, why the strange hissing, as if whatever was on the other side ... didn't like it?

Was that even possible?

~

Call me a moron, although I think it was more a symptom of being busy fighting for my life, but I finally began to put two and two together. That hissing in my mind, the weird way my aunt's magic seemed to weaken momentarily, they all seemed to coincide with her screaming out new spells.

But why? Didn't Carly represent the green side of things, her high and mighty Queen Brigid who – for all I knew – was the one calling the play by play on my mental microphone? If so, why get pissed whenever my aunt came one step closer to winning this fight?

Sadly, such speculation would have to wait as my aunt's attack found its mark. All rational thought was lost to a haze of pain as the teeth of a thousand magical piranhas locked onto my scent for a taste testing.

Carly was right. There were limits to my power. I'd been smashed, burned, and blasted by multiple magic users. Full strength or not, my body was one big bruise of lacerated flesh and cracked ribs. I could feel tiny wounds being torn open up and down my back. None were serious by themselves, but magnified by the dozens and I had a feeling I was about to find out what those limits were.

At least I'd make a good meal for the glade.

No! That was quitter talk. And I was no quitter, especially now. I couldn't afford to be. More than just my life was at stake here.

Biting my tongue against the pain, I struggled to recall what I'd been thinking before being subjected to death by a thousand cuts.

This place, it was powering my aunt, yet somehow also angry with her. Why?

I racked my brain, trying to think of something. This clearing was special, a sacred glade, a place where the walls between worlds was thin. But its ownership was apparently up for grabs. That's how both sides were able to call upon their respective deities – one side feral and bloodthirsty, the other full of conceit and avarice. And through it all, there were other voices calling for both sides to die.

Problem was, none of it really helped me.

"That one looked like it hurt, Tamara. Pity I'm just getting started. This place, it feeds me, beckons me to lay claim to it. Even now, Queen Brigid sits in her court eagerly awaiting the outcome, an outcome which you helped me achieve."

Oh great. Now she has to gloat, too.

"The old Celtic gods shall rejoice in my victory, perhaps even name me their Earthly avatar."

From the sound of things she was floating right behind me ... just out of reach of her damned devil tornado. Too bad I couldn't do much to reach...

Hold on. Celtic gods! Every other Draíodóir I'd met, my mother included, screamed out their spells in Gaelic ... which was a language of the Celtic people. I'd assumed that's how their spells were empowered, but my aunt had proven that wrong. She yelled out hers in plain English, proving linguistics didn't play into the equation.

Unless it actually did.

I didn't pretend to understand the finer nuances of their culture, but what if that was it? Brigid was a Celtic faerie queen, an arrogant one if the whispers in my head were to be believed. What if, much as she wanted this place, she wasn't overly fond of the way my aunt was calling upon her power? I mean, with all the other witches and wizards using the old language, the one their ancestors would've spoken, might my aunt's use of contemporary English be akin to a slap in the face?

It wasn't much to go on, but it was all I had.

"*Rain of razors!*"

And I had a feeling I was only going to get one chance to test that theory.

~

I had a second or two, maybe less, to make good on this. If it didn't work, then I was finished.

But then, almost as if on cue, the voice whispering in my mind screeched an angry hiss, as if they were a cat whose tail had just gotten stomped on. At the same moment, the buffeting winds pinning my tortured body slackened ever so slightly and the shimmering force field I was pressed against became semi-pliable.

Knowing that I was about to be torn apart by another of my aunt's spells, I pressed my foot into the force field, feeling it give just enough to gain a tentative foothold.

It's now or never.

I pushed off with everything I had left in me.

For one terrifying moment, I was certain the winds were too strong for me to overcome, but then momentum took over and I found myself flying up and back ... not exactly in a graceful arc, don't get me wrong, but I'd take it.

My foot tingled painfully as one of those magic ice picks lanced through the sole of my shoe, but that was all. I caught a quick glimpse of grasping fingers and malevolent red eyes and then I was through the storm.

"It's not possible!"

Carly's amplified voice seemed to come from right next to me. By sheer luck, I turned my head just as I was sailing past her, barely a foot away.

I'd love to say this next part was planned, but that would be pure bullshit. I reached out, more on instinct than anything else, and somehow managed to hook two fingers in her ruined eye socket. They sank knuckle deep into grizzle and raw flesh.

Gross!

Mind you, if I thought that was bad, my aunt's opinion on it was far less generous.

She let loose with a scream that echoed throughout the glade, her voice still magically boosted. Even as we tumbled through the air, I could see her dust devil spell begin to dissipate, her concentration somewhat preempted by my fingers probing her optic nerve.

Whatever magic held her aloft faltered, along with her other spells and we began to fall.

I had no way of knowing if I'd been right in my theory or not, but it seemed a safe guess. Even if not, I realized it couldn't hurt to stack the deck in my favor as the one bit of Gaelic I'd remembered from my research popped into my head. Somehow, it was fitting.

"Póg mo thóin!" I shouted, flexing my arm and whipping her body past mine.

She slammed into the ground within the red zone and lay there stunned as I landed, somewhat less than gracefully, a few feet away. I stood up and almost immediately toppled over again from both pain and fatigue. The truth was, I wanted nothing more than to curl up into a little ball and forget all of this, but it wasn't over yet.

Instead, ignoring it all, I stumbled over to where my aunt lay, straddled her body and raised my fists over my head.

"Dear gods, Tamara, please!"

I hesitated for the barest of moments, but then the angry snarls from this side of the battlefield began to permeate my consciousness, demanding I end this once and for all.

And this time I decided to let them.

386

EPILOGUE

I only stopped once the entire glade lit up around me,
as if I were standing dead center atop a spotlight.

One moment I was bathed in red, a combination
of the glow from this place and the blood splatter rising
from each fall of my fists. The next, it was as if someone
had turned on a million watt lightbulb.

I stood up, covering my eyes, and staggered back from
my aunt's body. Maybe it was a good thing I couldn't see
much of anything, because I had a feeling I didn't want to
know what I'd done to her. She wouldn't be leaving this
place ever again, that much was evident, but the rest was
lost to a haze of numbing anger.

After several seconds, the light – near blinding even
with my hands over my face – subsided and I was able to
open my eyes again without fear of my retinas melting.
The glade was still aglow with power and the ground fog
seemed to be rising – now at knee level, high enough to
obscure my view of the bodies still littering this unholy
place.

However, my focus wasn't on any of that.

Riva, or possessed Riva anyway, was standing in the

center of the clearing as if she'd been there all along. She wore a simple frock of pure white, which told me that, whatever she was, she definitely wasn't my friend. Riva was the type to wear a sweater once the temperature hit the seventies. No way was she traipsing around like that in a freezing forest.

"You've done well," she said, her voice conveying little emotion. "We had our doubts, but you have proven yourself worthy of your heritage. Indeed, you truly are more than the sum of your parts.

A million questions ran through my mind, but somehow the one that opted to come out of my mouth was, "Why do you look like my friend?"

"We appear as we always have, one Outsider to another."

"That doesn't make any sense."

She shrugged as if she couldn't have cared less. "Impressive as you are, you are but a child. We take no offense at your failure to grasp the nuances of the eternal."

Okay, this was getting me nowhere fast. It was like reading a mystery, only to discover the final page was garbled nonsense. I decided to switch gears. "What happens now?"

"Now?" She raised one side of her mouth in a lopsided grin. "Now you may leave in peace. As shall we."

"So you're going back..."

"Free to once more tread upon this world, so long glimpsed but forever denied."

"Wait, what do you mean by that?"

"Go," she replied, her tone implying it wasn't a suggestion. "Return to your own and enjoy their company ... while you may."

Before I could question possessed Riva about what the fuck she meant, the mist around her feet ignited into flame and began to spread.

Judging by the heat being put off, I got the impression this was neither illusion nor bluff.

I didn't need to be told twice. I bolted for the tree line, turning back once I reached it to see smoke rising from the fire – smoke that began to gather around Riva and coalesce into shapes with glowing eyes.

Sadly, before they could fully form and give me a clue as to what I'd done, the entire glade erupted into a sea of flame.

~

Thank goodness whatever was happening in the clearing seemed to end at its borders. The flames, the heat, even the smoke spread no further than the edge of the glade.

Hell, standing just a few feet back in the tree line, I couldn't even hear the crackle of the fire. It was as if the entire thing was some elaborate hologram. Mind you, I wasn't quite brave enough to stick my hand in and test that theory.

As I stood there gawking, there came a groan of pain from somewhere off to my left, loud in the oppressive still-ness of the forest.

Fortunately, the raging inferno only a few yards away cast more than enough light for me to see by. Within the space of a minute I found Cass, alive – thank goodness – and back in her human form. She was lying on the cold ground, massaging her bruised jaw as I approached. I bent down and placed a hand on her shoulder. Her eyes jerked open and panic flared in them for a second or two, but then she focused on my face and calmed down.

"Ugh. What happened?" she croaked.

"What do you remember?"

"Those Draíodóir ... poor Nelly. It's all ... fuzzy after that."

Maybe that was for the best. She deserved to know, but it could wait. "You don't have to worry about them anymore. They're..."

All at once, the firelight illuminating the forest around us winked out, leaving us in darkness. I dared a glance back and saw nothing but the barest outline of the glade's edge. It appeared to be nothing more than a normal clearing in the woods, back to its original size and all.

Regardless, I didn't care to find out if that was actually the case or not. I'd had enough for one night.

I turned back toward Cass and helped her to her feet. "It was all my aunt's doing. Belzar was nothing but a puppet."

"Is she..."

"Like I said. It's over."

She nodded, still looking a bit dazed. "Your parents? Curtis?"

I hesitated before answering. The truth was, I had no way of knowing whether Carly had been blowing smoke up my ass or not. For all I knew, she could have murdered both of them and merely offered false hope as a way of messing with me.

But why? And, if so, why not just tell me they were being held captive. Why make up a story about sending them elsewhere ... *outside*?

There was also the fact that the Draíodóir seemed to love their ceremony. Disposing of one's enemies outright seemed more a werewolf thing to do. What better way to further distance themselves from their hated foes than by doing something elaborate and over-complicated, like some wizardly James Bond villain?

I didn't know either way. Worse, if she had been telling the truth, I had no idea how to save my parents.

Much as I wanted to wallow in my misery, though, I felt a small pool of hope blooming in the pit of my stomach regardless. Though my rational mind insisted on the worst, my instincts were saying my aunt had spoken true. As a wrestler I'd always gone with my gut. Also, half of me was lycanthrope – a creature of instinct. Perhaps it was time I explored embracing that half.

Besides, it was still Christmas. Late as it was, didn't I deserve to hold out hope for a miracle?

A tear slipped down my cheek. I wiped it away and smiled at Cass. "Alive, but in danger."

"Where are they?"

I shook my head. "I'm not..." My voice trailed off as I thought of everything I'd done and learned since returning home.

Blessing of Valdemar be damned, I'd beaten Mitch in fair combat. That made me the beta of the pack. With Dad missing, I was in charge.

Then there was the Draíodóir. If Mindy was any indication, the others who'd been snagged by my aunt were now awake and in control again. I didn't officially have any standing among them, but their queen needed saving and I was my mother's daughter – whether they liked it or not.

"I don't know," I continued, finding my voice again, "but we're going to find them, no matter where they are. We're going to find them and bring them back home again."

"How are you doing, baby brother?"

The hospital staff had sedated Chris to calm him down and help him sleep. But he was finally beginning to stir just as the light of the morning sun was starting to peek through the windows.

Chief Johnson had been good to his word and then some. Not only had he assigned an officer to keep watch on my brother, but he'd gotten him a private room and left word that I was to be let in regardless of the time.

After leaving the glade, we'd made our way back to Nelly's where we'd helped ourselves to some of her clothes. Cass wasn't happy about it, but I dropped a not-so-subtle hint that the hut and all the belongings within were likely hers now.

She hadn't been sure what to say about that, but at the same time seemed to make it a point not to change into her other form as we'd hiked out of the hollows and back to civilization. I had a feeling neither of us was ready to see what she turned into.

From there, it was a minor issue to get back to Mitch's apartment where her car was parked and then over to High Moon General Hospital ... the irony being that the worst of my injuries had healed by then.

Neither of us wanted to say goodbye, but we were both mindful of the chief's warning from earlier. Besides, I think we both needed some time alone to lick our respective wounds.

We'd hugged each other long and hard and then I made my way inside, alone, exhausted, but alive.

There was no sign of Riva when I'd finally reached Chris's room, but that wasn't too surprising. Visiting hours were long past and, much as I considered her a sister, she didn't qualify as family as per hospital rules. That was fine. I figured I'd catch up with her later as I sat down and kept watch over my brother until eventually dozing off myself.

I'd only woken when he'd started to stir, my acute hearing being more than enough to rouse me.

In the light of day, the whole ordeal seemed almost like a bad dream, but I knew better. And Chris, once he'd opened his eyes and looked around – seeing only me – seemed to realize it, too.

He tried to sit up, but I put a hand on his shoulder

and guided him back down. "Relax, you little turd muncher. The doctor says you clonked your head pretty good. Move around too much and it's liable to fall right off."

"I'm not five," he groggily protested, lying back down.

"Could've fooled me."

He took a deep breath, for a moment looking much older than his age, then said, "Yesterday. All of that was real, wasn't it?"

I nodded.

"Mom and..." His voice cracked and his eyes grew glassy, "Dad?"

I was tempted to lie, tell him they were waiting at home for us, but that was unfair. He deserved more credit than that.

Remembering the hope I'd felt earlier and my desire to hold onto it, I told him, "It's hard to explain. They're alive, but they need help."

"Is Aunt Carly..."

"Don't worry about her. Trust me. I took care of it."

"Do I want to know?"

"Depends how many nightmares you're in the mood for."

He shook his head weakly. "I think I have enough."

"Same here."

"What do you mean by they need help?"

"They're ... stuck somewhere, far away."

"How far?"

"I'm not sure. But I'm going to find out. And when I do, I'll bring them home."

"You will?"

"I promise."

He looked thoughtful for a moment, a rare expression for my brother, then said, "You can do *things*, can't you?"

After a moment, I nodded. "Yeah. I can. And those things are going to make sure we get the help we need."

"Are you sure?"

I cracked my knuckles for emphasis. "One hundred percent positive."

"What about me?" he asked after a pause.

"You rest up for now. I'll talk to the doctor and see when I can get you out of here."

He looked at me skeptically.

"Relax. Chief Johnson talked to the staff about it. Not to mention I'm technically an adult. As your loving sister, I get to take responsibility for your irresponsible butt." He smiled at that, to which I said, "But for now, get some rest."

I stood up, but he grabbed my hand, looking once again like a small scared child. "Tamara?"

"Yeah, kiddo?"

"Don't leave me."

I realized with sad certainty that he wasn't just talking about me going to grab some coffee. For all the crap we gave each other, my heart went out to him. "I promise." After a moment of thought, I added, "Actually, I can do one better. Scoot your ugly butt over and make some room. I don't know about you, but I'm dog-tired."

He smiled at me then shifted over. "Really, dog jokes? After everything we went through?"

I laughed and put my arm around him. "Oh, they're not so bad once you get to know them. Trust me on this."

THE END

~

Tamara Bentley will return in
Bent On Destruction

BONUS CHAPTER

BENT ON DESTRUCTION

THE HYBRID OF HIGH MOON - 3

"My fellow aberrants, though I know our respective peoples haven't often seen eye to eye, the time has come for us to put our differences aside. I stand before you as living proof that our two species can not only work together, but flourish as one. But now, a grave injustice has been wrought, one that requires us to work side by side to retrieve our leaders – my parents, your queen and your alpha – so as to bring them home safely."

I locked eyes with each member of my audience, daring them to challenge my words.

Finally, after several long seconds, Chris broke the impasse. "My money's on them kicking your ass."

I narrowed my eyes at my dweeb of a little brother, but then realized Cass wore the exact same expression. "The aberrant line was too much, wasn't it?"

She held up a hand, her thumb and index finger an inch apart. "Just a bit."

"Sorry. I figured it was better than me calling them monsters or butchering Draíodóir in front of everyone."

"Maybe just skip that line altogether," she said. "I have a feeling you're gonna be dealing with a hostile enough room as it is, so it might be best to get right down to business rather than let anyone argue semantics."

She probably had a point. The fact that I'd managed to make it this far was a near miracle in itself, not that the werewolf side of the delegation was being given much choice in the matter.

I was currently the acting alpha, with Cass as the newly chosen female alpha – even though we were both girls. Go figure, in the space of a single evening we'd somehow managed to drag lycanthrope gender politics into the twenty-first century. Even so, I knew we were barely hanging on by a thread. The majority of the Morganberg pack was less than pleased to suddenly find themselves under the command of two *kids*, and that wasn't even counting the fact some were still looking for an excuse to gut me over what I'd done to their previous alpha, my late uncle Craig.

At least I had rank and tradition on my side with them, along with the dangled bone of retrieving their true leader – my father. Over in Crescentwood, the only pluses in my favor were the confusion and betrayal they'd suffered on Christmas day – that, and a cousin who, in her grief, had been willing to speak on my behalf to their remaining elders.

Mind you, it was still risky as all hell. I remembered Mom's warning of what her people would do if they discovered the truth of my existence. Much as I didn't like being in charge of the Morganberg pack, I had a feeling it was the only thing staying their hand. Resistant to magic I might be, but alone there wasn't much I could do if they decided to bombard High Moon with a magical meteor shower.

But with the pack in my back pocket – in theory

anyway – the equation changed significantly. Between that and the bloody nose my aunt had recently given them via way of her betrayal, they'd been receptive to the proverbial olive branch my cousin Mindy offered them on my behalf. At the very least, they seemed to be taking a wait and see approach, for now anyway.

Either way, my entreaty for parlay was accepted. Somehow, I'd managed to cajole both sides to the negotiating table. That was good, because I wasn't prepared to take no for an answer. If saving my parents meant busting some heads, then so be it.

But perhaps it was best to at least try refining my carrot before reaching for the stick

"Okay, Maybe I'll work on that opening speech a bit." I shrugged. "At least I still have homefield advantage."

"Yeah, about that..."

I cut my brother off at the pass. "We already talked about this. Not happening. You're staying home."

"C'mon, Tamara. Can't I just sit in the back and watch?"

"This isn't some pep rally. It's not open to the public."

"They're my parents, too."

His reply stopped me in my tracks, but fortunately Cass was there to pick up the dropped ball.

"I know, but if we want to help them then this is for the best. Both sides are already going to be on edge as it is. No offense, Chris, but having a human there is only going to distract them. We need everyone to stay focused on the task at hand."

I wasn't sure whether it was her logic or being a pretty blonde but, rather than protest, Chris simply nodded ... for now. I didn't doubt he'd try again, though.

Good thing I didn't plan on telling him where it was being held. Mind you, it probably didn't hurt that I didn't know yet either.

The Draíodóir elders had initially insisted we hold the talks in Crescentwood. Big surprise there. After some back and forth, though, with Mindy arguing on my behalf, a compromise was reached. Any ceremonies, spells, or whatever was needed to retrieve my parents, would be conducted there. After all, it stood to reason they were best equipped to contact the *outside,* as they called it. However, the talks regarding our plan of action would take place in neutral territory, and that meant High Moon.

Thankfully, according to Chief Johnson anyway, my request was within the provisions set forth in the current treaty. That was good. Less good was his insistence on finding a proper venue to host our supernatural summit. Obviously, this wasn't something we could simply host down at borough hall. He wanted to find a place that was a bit more off the beaten path, a spot where any shenanigans from either side could be quickly contained and neutralized – his words, not mine.

Nevertheless, the pieces were slowly falling into place, albeit not all of them.

I took advantage of the lull in conversation to step into the kitchen and check my phone. Still no word from Riva. I'd planned on asking her to keep an eye on Chris while this all happened, to make sure he didn't try anything stupid. But I hadn't heard from her since Christmas, back when she'd accompanied my brother to the hospital.

I'd figured maybe she needed a few days to collect herself or was simply just busy, but it wasn't like her to not even acknowledge my texts. Being best friends for well over a decade meant you kind of knew what to expect from each other. This wasn't like her.

Screw it. I need a break anyway.

I walked over to the closet and grabbed my coat. "I'm heading out for a bit."

"Where to?" Cass asked.

"I'm gonna pop by Riva's. Hey, do you mind keeping an eye on..."

My voice trailed off as I saw the look on her face.

I'd informed Chief Johnson in advance that, as my fellow "alpha", I needed Cass's help to set up this meeting, thus ensuring he didn't take steps to forcibly eject her from High Moon, as he'd threatened back on Christmas. Regardless, I could tell she'd been nervous when I'd invited her over, although perhaps he wasn't the only reason why.

My house was the home of the true alpha of the Morganberg pack, which probably precluded her from making herself too comfortable. However, if thoughts of my father made her nervous by way of his rank, my mother – the so-called Queen of the Monarchs – terrified her because of her power. She held an almost boogeyman-like status among the rank and file of Morganberg, one which was well deserved.

I guess I could understand how sneaking a bag of chips in a house potentially warded to blow up werewolf intruders could be a bit daunting.

And, well, it's not like I minded her company.

"On second thought, you up for a quick ride?"

The three of us piled into my mother's car and pulled out of the driveway. Normally I wouldn't think twice about leaving Chris home by himself for a short while, but he'd been a bit squirrelly ever since Christmas, and with good reason. In the space of a day, his entire world had been upended. Not only were our parents both missing, but he'd learned that there really were monsters in the prover-bial closet. So, I wasn't about to argue when he grabbed his coat to join us.

The day was overcast and cold, but otherwise unremarkable – a typical winter day for rural Pennsylvania. For now, all was quiet and peaceful, even if nearly everything about our town and the surrounding area itself were as atypical as it got. Turning down the side streets – and making it a point to take them extra slow being that I was technically sans license – it was easy to lose myself in the fantasy that the last several days had been nothing but a bad dream and that we'd return home to find our parents waiting for us.

It was a dream that I had every intention of making a reality for me and my brother, but I didn't dare fool myself into thinking it would be smooth sailing. Hell, I wasn't even sure the rescue mission I planned to propose was even possible – locating and plucking my parents from the court of the fairy queen. Tell me that wasn't the plot of a bad teen fantasy novel.

Still, my aunt had somehow sent them there, so I had to hold onto the hope that a round trip was possible. Without that lifeline to grasp onto, I would surely be lost.

"Nice neighborhood," Cass remarked from the passenger seat of the mid-sized sedan as we turned onto Riva's cul-de-sac. She pointed out the window. "Except for that place. Bet they're a real hit with the local homeowner association."

I followed her gaze, noting the broken mailbox post at the curb of Riva's house. "When did that happen?"

An older Volvo sat in the driveway – Mr. Kale's work car, but there was something off about it. It wasn't until I parked at the curb that I realized it was sitting on four flats, the body covered in scratches and rust marks.

"What the hell?"

I'd been here only a couple of days earlier, picking Riva up for a sleepover. It had been late at the time, but not so dark that I wouldn't have been able to tell what a mess his car was. Hell, now that I took a better look around, I saw the entire property had a neglected feel to it that hadn't been evident when last I'd been here, culminating in... "Oh my god."

The picture window that looked in on her family's living room was completely shattered. Only a few jagged shards of glass around its periphery remained.

"Are you sure this is the right place, Bent?" Cass asked.

I shut off the engine and opened the driver's side door. "Wait here."

"But...," my brother started.

"Don't argue with me."

The tone of my voice must've been harsher than I realized because he zipped his lip. Oh well, I could always apologize later.

For now, I stepped out of the car and started walking up the driveway.

"Wait up," Cass cried from behind me, the sound of her door slamming shut catching my ear.

"Stay with..."

"Take a look around. It's broad daylight. Nothing's going to happen to him."

Normally, I would've concurred. Hell, everything else here seemed right as rain except for Riva's place. Still, she was probably right. Rather than protest and waste time, I shrugged and continued forward.

It was only as I approached the house that I realized the storm door was the only thing standing between us and the interior. The actual front door was missing, the foyer visible beyond.

What in the name of...

I quickened my pace, panic starting to set in. "Riva?"

Bursting inside with Cass hot on my heels, I stopped as I stepped foot into their living room.

The place was a mess, the furniture bloated and discolored. Mold could be seen on the walls, and water stains marred the floor – a far cry from the obsessive neatness Riva's mom usually insisted on.

"Is your friend squatting in this dump or something?" Cass asked from behind me, but I paid her no heed.

My eyes were instead focused on the massive hole in the drywall next to their staircase.

I remembered it well because I'd been the one who made it.

It had happened this past summer, the night the Morganberg pack attacked High Moon.

Two werewolves had come here, under orders from my uncle, to take out Riva and her family. They'd found me waiting for them instead.

The battle played out in my mind as I surveyed the scene before me. One of the wolves had gotten a fist through the stomach, followed by a one-way ticket out the front window. The other I'd slammed through the wall, right before breaking its jaw in half.

The damage we were seeing now was the same I'd caused back then … only appearing much older, as if the house had sat neglected ever since.

"What the fuck?"

~

To be continued in...

Bent On Destruction
Available in ebook, paperback, and audiobook

AUTHOR'S NOTE

I wrote this story in parallel with Strange Days – Bill of the Dead 1. A lot of people asked me during that time whether I found it confusing to be working on two stories of paranormal mayhem at once.

The answer is not really. If anything, I found the disparity between Bent's world and Bill's to be refreshing. Bill Ryder is all about his friends – dumbasses though some of them may be. However, Tamara Bentley's life is much more family focused, and I personally find the dynamics between her, her friends, and her parents to be fascinating.

I mean, it's one thing to be confronted with an ultra-powerful being from beyond our world. It's quite another when that being is your mom or dad. Tamara is just coming into her own, both as an adult and in terms of her powers, so their interplay is something I really enjoy. After all, you can be the baddest mofo on the block, but that won't get you very far if you still have to ask permission to borrow the car.

And then there's High Moon itself – a self-contained demilitarized zone, sitting between two supernatural powder kegs. I have a feeling we've just barely scratched the surface of this sleepy little town's secrets. As for what we'll discover next, that remains to be seen.

Personally, I can't wait to dive into Tamara's next adventure and see where it takes me. I sincerely hope you're enjoying her story and plan on joining me for the ride, wherever dark places it may take us.

Rick G.

ABOUT THE AUTHOR

Rick Gualtieri lives alone in central New Jersey with only his wife, three kids, and countless pets to both keep him company and constantly plot against him. When he's not busy monkey-clicking words, he can typically be found jealously guarding his collection of vintage Transformers from all who would seek to defile them.

Defilers beware!

Also by Rick Gualtieri
THE HYBRID OF HIGH MOON
Get Bent!
Hell Bent
Bent Outta Shape
Bent On Destruction
Bent, Not Broken

TALES OF THE CRYPTO-HUNTER
Bigfoot Hunters
Devil Hunters
Kraken Hunters

THE TOME OF BILL UNIVERSE
THE TOME OF BILL
Bill the Vampire
Scary Dead Things
The Mourning Woods

Holier Than Thou
Sunset Strip
Goddamned Freaky Monsters
Half A Prayer
The Wicked Dead
Shining Fury
The Last Coven

BILL OF THE DEAD
Strange Days
Everyday Horrors
Carnage A Trois

Made in the USA
Monee, IL
03 January 2023

24262362R00240